PACIFIC TAILS

MOST FAIRY TALES ARE STORIES.
SOME ARE REAL.

MICHELLE SAUER

Sweet and Sauer Books, LLC.
First published in the United States of America by:
Sweet and Sauer Books, LLC.

Visit Sweet and Sauer Books online at:
www.sweetandsauerbooks.com

Cover and internal design © by Books and Moods
ISBN:
979-8-9887613-2-7

For Hobbes.

And to those who have ever wanted to be merfolk.

Author's Note

This is a New Adult urban fantasy adventure. Although I personally find the following warnings to be mild and minimal, you may not, which is why I'm including this list of content trigger warnings. Mental health matters; take care of you.

Murder, assault, harsh language, depression, PTSD, bullying, demons and possession, reincarnation, sexual situations.

Also note, the maps are hand drawn by me, which means there are imperfections. But I love maps, especially ones depicting new kingdoms and realms and hope you enjoy perusing over them as much as I enjoyed making them.

Lastly, I have tried to make the real locations, history, events, pop-culture Easter eggs, and mythology, as accurate as possible, however, this is a source of fiction and some things may have been altered to fit the story.

Now, time to check out of reality and enter my altered reality where magic, creatures, ancient beings, and the paranormal co-exist with us, mere mortals.

N
Sundry Southeast
Seven Realms of the Pacific
Lively North to East
Severn South
Near North West
Ancient Northwest
Far West
Deep Southwest

Fierce
Varied North
Fiery West
Rebellious West
Tropics
Powerful
Pacific
Vital Southwest
Luscious
Southeast
Six Realms of the Atlantic
Industrial Indian
N

PROLOGUE

Amid all the enchanting locations in her underwater king-dom, the queen's favorite spot was on the railing of the open-air veranda at the Cliff House, an entertainment venue for the elite. The Victorian chateau, complete with turrets, spires, and an eight-story observation tower, teetered on the edge of a cliff and overlooked the sea.

The queen often crept up to the veranda at night when the crowds of people retreated for the evening. Her long tail draped over the railing and fluttered in the wind, finding her inner peace as she listened to the rhythmic waves. The light from the new moon shimmered across her scales, highlighting a myriad of purple hues.

Tonight, however, a dense fog rolled inland and cloaked the area in darkness. The wind whipped across her bare torso; her hair danced around her. The restless sea lashed out across the rocks. Angry at her, perhaps.

Relinquishing a realm wasn't a common gesture for royalty.

She fiddled with the heart locket on her gold bracelet, a gift from her fiancé. Her decision hadn't been rash. She never imagined leaving her world for any man, but after centuries of ruling, she found someone to settle down with and experience a new way of life.

A life away from magic.

She hadn't been a saint, but she felt her adventures had given her the ability to offer a lot of good to the human world, especially with all the promising innovations and growth with the turn-of-the-century.

She swallowed the lump in her throat. No matter how much someone prepared for change, it didn't make the process easier. The queen had no reason to delay any longer. She weaved her fingers through the delicate silver chain dangling from her neck and gripped its colorful stone pendant that resembled the petals of a hibiscus flower. She snapped the chain. As she opened her palm, a tear trailed down her cheek and splashed across the stone; a kaleidoscope of colors surged across the rock, as if reacting to her inner turmoil. She ran the pad of her thumb over the smooth surface and wiped away her tear.

She lifted the necklace, hanging the stone at eye-level, and flicked it. A single, high-pitched tone rang out across the night.

The wind shifted.

The fog swelled.

Heavy storm clouds churned and rumbled.

Lightning flashed.

She drew in a long breath.

> *"Gods, hear the call to release my ties.*
> *Walking on land, I'm keen—"*

The wooden planks on the viewing deck creaked. She looked over her shoulder, annoyed at the interruption, but there was nothing there except the imposing structure. She flicked the stone again.

"Gods, hear the calls to release my ties.
Walking on land, I'm keen.
With this last request, I will advise.
A new king to replace your old queen.
This realm will thrive and rise.
With the leadership of—"

The deck creaked again.

The hair at the base of her neck stood on end. A mysterious presence loomed behind her. She whirled around, her eyes narrowed and focused.

Who would dare interrupt me?

Again, she saw nobody.

She snapped her fingers above her head. Purple flickering lights rained down on her, transforming her tail into legs and dressing her in a white-fitted blouse, a purple flowing skirt, and black-laced ankle boots. She hopped off the ledge. "I know you're there."

The intruder ran away from her, its boots striking against the wooden planks. A flash of lightning revealed a row of electric lampposts along the perimeter of the viewing deck. The queen puckered her lips and blew a beam of sparkling white light into each lamp, illuminating the veranda.

She hiked up the front of her skirt and headed forward. As she rounded the corner, she saw the fast-moving figure at the far end of the balcony disappearing behind the structure. She raced down the wooden platform. The heels of her boots hammered in rhythm with her unwanted guest.

She kept up the chase until she returned to where she started, unable to catch the intruder. She leaned against the railing and stretched her hands out in front of her, sending a parade of fluttering black sparks out from her fingertips.

"Oh, come on. Don't fail me now." She flicked her fingers until a steady wave of energy floated over the grounds, snuffing out all the lampposts and leaving her in darkness once again.

She clenched her jaw and leaned over the railing. "You shall not stop me! Whoever is out there, hear me—I no longer wish for this life. Let me be!"

She lifted the necklace once more and flicked the pendant. But as the spell played on the tip of her tongue, a rush of agonizing pain wrenched through her.

She staggered.

A blaze of white lightning ripped across the sky. She spotted a metallic glint too late. Another stab into her flesh, and she dropped to the ground; she clenched her side and twisted in agony. Large drops of rain pelted her face. The rumble of thunder shook the Cliff House's regal structure.

She clawed at the collar of the blouse, her bloody fingers staining the silk. The tips of her fingers trailed along the backside of her bare shoulder, gliding over a tattoo of a trident jutting out of turbulent water. The black ink glowed with a halo of white. She reeled her hand away as a real trident appeared in her hand. She forced her eyes open, and through her blurred vision, she aimed it. An electric purple energy field fired out of the three prongs, hit her attacker, who sailed across the deck and slammed into the building's exterior wall.

Using the staff of the trident to stand, she labored to her feet, then hobbled off, splashing through a puddle of rain stained by her blood. Her palm covered her wound, trying to staunch the bleeding. She stumbled and fell against the railing. The trident slipped from her hand and toppled over the ledge.

She reached for it, screaming. As it disappeared into the water, the ground trembled, and the waves surged. Sea foam spewed high and crashed on the rocks.

She tried to stand again, but collapsed to her knees. Reeling from the unexpected shift of her plans, she knew she couldn't die there. Her kingdom would suffer if she did. She needed the last bit of her energy to carry on.

She had to protect her friends.

The words of an ancient, and rare, spell came to her mind. Still gripping the necklace, she lifted her blood-covered hand and double-flicked the stone. A warm, golden light haloed around it. She drew in a ragged breath and sang out,

> *"Magic stone: break into five and hide.*
> *One-hundred-year season.*
> *A reincarnation to arrive,*
> *My loyal guardian a beacon.*
> *Restore my realm and thrive,*
> *To end those who commit such treason."*

She fell forward.

The side of her face thudded onto the wooden planks. Her hand fell opened and released the necklace. The stone pendant clattered to the deck, shattering into five fragments. Each piece glowed and vibrated as if charging with energy. One by one, the broken stones zoomed away like shooting stars, ensuring her kingdom's protection.

But as the last stone jetted off to safety, a white-gloved and bloodied hand snatched it mid-air. Stealing it. With utter dismay, the woman strained to look at the figure hovering over her, desperate for one glimpse of the person who stole her life—of the person who stole her future. As the last bit of her life faded away, she drew in a ragged breath and whispered her killer's name.

CHAPTER 1

ZOE

ZOE VAUGHN'S BACKPACK SLAPPED against her lower back as she zipped across the red-herringbone pathway, threading her way through the crowds of students walking on the University of Southern California campus. She entered the glass doors of a boxy relic from the fifties and wiped the beads of sweat from her brow. In one fell swoop, she gathered her black trusses and secured the strands in a high ponytail. She adjusted her tank top and nonchalantly sniffed her armpits. She was running late, as usual, and drew in a calming breath before turning the corner, ready to enter the lecture auditorium and take her last exam.

A wall of students blocked the three large entrance doors. For a split second, she thought Baxter, her mythology professor and mentor, who liked to be referred to by his last name, also ran late.

She snorted. Baxter was like an atomic clock.

She slinked past a few people, pushing her way further into the crowd, hearing bits of conversations speculating about the delay. A tall auburn-haired woman with a nasty scowl stepped in Zoe's path.

Tanya.

Zoe cursed under her breath as a few more women encircled her. She tried to push past them, but like the children's game of Red Rover, they wouldn't let her break through their wall.

Tanya, still scowling, said, "Can't you see we're all waiting to enter? Typical. Always needing to be first."

Jessie, a woman dripping in pink from her eye shadow to her sundress and Doc Martens, leaned in closer to Zoe. "Need some PEDs to help with your impatience, cheater?"

The small group of women snickered.

Zoe rolled her eyes. The relentless bullying from her former teammates had been going on for over a year. Being accused of taking Performance Enhancing Drugs simply because she always broke records, out-swam her team and competitors, and was on her way to the Olympics, had been the perfect breeding ground for petty jealously amongst privileged youths. Tanya and Jessie ran with it, successfully accomplishing Zoe's dismissal from the team. The anger of dealing with a witch-hunt style persecution for more than a year still boiled within her.

"Cheater?" Zoe snapped. "At least my parents didn't have to use a back door to get me into USC." She cut her eyes to Tanya. "Your false accusations need to stop before I actually go through with getting a restraining order against you."

Tanya shrugged her shoulder. "Why bother? You're running away to the East Coast, aren't you?"

Zoe's face warmed. She hated that her ex-teammate was right. In just a few hours, she would catch the red-eye flight to New York and move in with her recently retired parents, just to get far away from the night-mare Tanya and the others spurred on during the past year.

So sure, she was running away. But it didn't matter. She had plans. Plans that included attending Yale, becoming a shark of a lawyer, and representing athletes who had their careers crushed by petty a-holes. She elbowed past Tanya, breaking through the circle of tormentors, and snaked her way to the closest lecture hall door and took a breath. She had a hard time focusing on positivity over sinking into the dark-ness plaguing her mind. She knew if she didn't escape those thoughts, she wouldn't pass her test.

And if she didn't pass her test, she wouldn't be able to move the hell away from California.

Inhale. Exhale.

"Hey-yo!" A muscular guy wearing a USC Trojans football shirt looked over the sea of people behind him. He ripped off a piece of paper hanging on the door and waved it high. "Baxter canceled the exam 'til tomorrow at one. He's attending an emergency meeting at the moment and offers his sincere apologies."

A collective cheer erupted in the hall, but the blood drained from Zoe's face. She couldn't take her final exam the next day. To enter Yale in the fall, she had to commit to a mandatory orientation and testing session at nine o'clock the next morning. Missing the meeting would mean waiting until spring to start, and she couldn't handle that kind of setback. For her mental well-being, she required the immediate change in her life.

She needed to act fast.

If she could catch Baxter before his meeting, he would understand. He would help make things right. She was his teacher's assistant and that had to count for something.

As the crowd shuffled out, she hurried passed them and ran across the walkway toward the Social Sciences building, where Baxter's office was located. She raced down the steps to the sunken courtyard and entered the structure.

Lacy, a student worker, sat behind a receptionist's desk. She looked up from painting her nails. "Can I help you?"

"I need to speak with Baxter. It's urgent."

Lacy smacked her gum, dipped her brush in the polish, and continued to paint her fingernails. "He's in an emergency meeting with the entire History Department and, like, I can't pull him outta' that."

"Listen," Zoe said through gritted teeth, "Baxter postponed the final exam until tomorrow, but I have a plane to catch tonight—"

"Like, this is finals week for a reason. You shouldn't have planned on leaving town 'til Friday night, like the rest of us. Not much I can do."

Sure, anything could happen on finals week, but she had no control over the meeting at Yale. She slammed her hand down on the counter ledge.

Startled, Lacy knocked her nail polish bottle over. She squealed and grabbed some tissue to soak up the puddle of paint. "What the hell?" Lacy whined.

"When do you think he will be finished with the meeting?"

Lacy raised her pencil-thin brow and tightened her jaw. "Probably in an hour or so."

"I need to leave him a message."

Lacy trashed the tissues, plopped into the chair, and examined her nails. "My nails are a mess because of your rudeness, so, like, call his office and leave one yourself."

"Baxter rarely checks his voicemail. Here, I'll write a note," Zoe said, reaching for a pen next to a sign-in sheet. "Just, please, tape it on his door. Besides, it's your job to help me communicate with my professor."

Lacy smirked. "Of course. I'll be sure to give him the message before the end of his office hours."

Zoe dropped the pen, forgoing writing a note that Lacy would never deliver. She drummed her fingers on the desk. She'd have to try something else.

But what?

As she reached for the shoulder strap of her backpack to readjust it, a figure moved across the hallway behind Lacy.

"Baxter!" Zoe ran around the desk faster than Lacy could react.

The man in his early thirties held a stack of papers in his arms. He lifted his head, squinting through rectangular black-rimmed glasses.

"Zoe?"

He repositioned the stack and pushed his glasses up on his head, burying them in his messier-than-usual chocolate-brown hair. A sleeve of his rumpled button-up shirt slid down past his elbow.

Zoe's brow knitted at his appearance. Whatever situation he was dealing with, had him rattled. Her stomach knotted, now asking him to deal with her troubles...

"I'm sorry to bust in on you like this, but—"

"The exam. Your flight." His green eyes squeezed shut as he expelled a sigh of frustration. "I completely forgot." He stepped toward her. "This meeting was unexpected and caught me off guard."

Zoe drank in his appearance. "I can see that."

Baxter's loose tie swayed against his chest. He made a failed attempt at straightening it.

"Look, I hate asking this, but is there any way for me to take the test now? I can't miss that orientation." Needing strings to be pulled for her, like other people she knew, was not her idea of a good foundation for a friendship.

Desperate times...

Baxter shook his head. "I cannot miss this meeting."

Zoe's fist curled into a ball. Her fingernails dug into her skin.

"But because of it, I had to move the exam to the other course section. That one will take place at six tonight. If you can take the exam then, you should be on time for your flight."

The tension in her body released. She sighed. "Thank you, Baxter. Yes, I'll be there."

He smiled, a warmth spreading into his eyes. He escorted her toward Lacy. "All will work out in the end." He patted his free hand on her shoulder; his fingers brushed against her bare skin.

She hissed. Recoiled as a static shock pierced her skin.

Baxter dropped his papers.

She rubbed her shoulder. "You got me good," she said. "You, okay?"

Baxter rubbed his eyes.

"Baxter," Lacy called from her desk, holding the phone in her hand. "Why are you looking all dazed and confused?" She waved her hand, dismissing her own question. "Never mind; I don't care. Professor Raznor wanted me to tell you they're waiting for you to, like, hurry."

"Yes... ah, of course." Baxter squatted to gather his papers.

Lacy pointed at Zoe. "As for you? Time to go."

"Sorry for keeping you. See you at six." Zoe shuffled away, feeling his eyes on her. She glanced over her shoulder.

He stood in the hall, rooted to the floor, looking like he saw a ghost.

CHAPTER 2
BAXTER

BAXTER ENTERED THE CONFERENCE room and slid into a seat sandwiched between two tenured professors. He stared at his notepad and could hear the gravelly voice of Dr. Raznor, the department chair, but for the life of him, he couldn't focus on the situation at hand. He mulled over the brief physical encounter with Zoe.

Anger radiated through him as he allowed himself to lose sight of his actual profession. So much so that after several semesters of mentoring and befriending Zoe, he didn't realize her true identity. He waited his entire life for that electric spark to mark the person he needed to find, only to succeed hours before she'd step out of his life forever.

Baxter scrubbed at his face, trying to ground himself and regain his composure. He reached across the table, grabbed a silver pitcher, and poured himself a glass of water. He clasped both his hands around the goblet, numbing the warmth of his pulsating hands against the chilled glass. After a moment, he touched the rim to his lips and sipped the refreshing water.

"Bennett." The man next to him tapped him on the arm. "Bennett? Did you hear what Carmen asked you?"

Baxter put the glass down. "Apologies, Carmen. I was lost in thought for a moment. Will you repeat that?"

Carmen tucked the single gray streak in her dark hair behind her ear. "No worries, darling," she said and pointed to the stack of papers he retrieved moments earlier. "Are those the exams from Rutherford's office?"

Baxter shifted in his seat and straightened. "Yes." He separated the pile in two and handed them to the people on either side of him.

Dr. Raznor settled into the chair at the head of the table. "Each of you look over these exams and try to determine if there is plagiarism or any other abnormalities that could identify the cheating scandal."

"Alleged plagiarism or cheating. The anonymous letter could be a hoax," Carmen said. "It wouldn't be the first time the school received fake letters."

Everyone mumbled in agreement. The situation was urgent and needed their attention, but Baxter could only concentrate on plotting a way out of the room. He scanned the exam.

What am I looking for again?

He glanced at the clock. Time slowed to a crawl. Only four minutes passed. His leg jumped, willing the second hand to tick faster. He read and re-read the same questions and answers, never fully comprehending the words. He loosened his tie, reached beneath the collar of his shirt, and fiddled with the delicate chain of his necklace.

The older man next to him leaned over and whispered, "Bennett, you seem distracted. What's going on?"

Baxter forced a smile and drummed his fingers against the wooden table. "Battling a headache. Also, slightly overwhelmed and disturbed by the situation. Thank you for asking, though, Jonathan."

Jonathan.

The name sparked a memory from another time that rocked Baxter's world. He propped his elbow on the table and rested his head in his hand, giving him the appearance of concentrating on the information in front of him. But his mind was nowhere in the present. He thought about the Jonathan from his past. The one who helped usher Baxter into the dire situation he faced with Zoe.

Baxter opened the heavy front door and found an elderly man with a straggly beard standing on his porch. Like Baxter, he wore a black suit. "Jonathan," Baxter said.

"I know it's been a long day, dear boy, but I need a moment of your time." He handed Baxter a small package wrapped in parchment, and a letter stamped with the red wax seal of the Baxter family crest. "These were Sophia's last possessions."

Confused and slightly befuddled, Baxter retrieved the items and looked them over with narrowed eyes. "I thought they had distributed everything to my mother's beneficiaries. What is this about?"

"I'm only doing as ordered. She wanted you to have this after her funeral and was quite insistent about you reading and following her strict instructions before opening it."

"Mother always had that insistent way about her. She could convince anyone to do what she wanted."

Jonathan stroked his white beard. "Her habits were often unique, but it was what made her special and why she was a dear friend."

Baxter scoffed, "Unique habits? Her dabbling in the mystics went well beyond unique. You are aiding her in another secretive deal, even after her death. This is most unsettling, Jonathan."

The elder man shrugged a bony shoulder. "It was never my place to judge, especially as her lawyer. I'll let you be, but remember to read her letter of instructions first and follow them explicitly."

Baxter nodded and closed the door as Jonathan sauntered away.

Baxter entered the parlor and sat at an oversized writing desk. In usual fashion, he ignored his mother's words and went straight for the rectangular package. He untied the twine, discarded the parchment, and revealed a gold box no bigger than his palm. He lifted the lid. Displayed on a cushion of black velvet was an irregularly shaped stone pendant attached to a fine silver chain. The colors of the stone imitated crystal quartz with purple hues ranging from rich darks to soft pastels. An aqua-and-silver vein snaked across the stone with three black letters etched in the center.

B.I.B.

His initials. Bennett Irving Baxter.

He lifted the necklace from the box for closer inspection. He flicked the stone and watched it spin, twirl, and catch light from the nearby window.

As if bewitched, he had a sudden urge to wear it. Strike that. He needed to wear it. He needed to wear it like he needed oxygen to breathe. He straightened his back and slid the chain over his head; immediate relief washed over him. As the pendant came to rest upon his chest, a gust of wind blew through the room like a tornado. It threw him from his chair and slammed him against the built-in shelves; knickknacks and books hit the floor.

He shielded his eyes as bright purple lights jetted out of the stone, coiled around him, and stabbed his skin like tens of thousands of pins and needles. His body writhed, trying to escape the pain. A guttural scream sprang from his mouth. He clawed at the necklace, but it refused to leave his person. Foam bubbled over his lips; he convulsed. The end approached and death would finally take him.

Yet, it didn't, and the horror of the moment disappeared; the sound of his ragged breath echoed across the room. With a shaky hand, he lifted the stone from his chest and re-examined it.

His initials vanished.

His eyes drifted to the skewed Baxter family portrait hanging next to the door. He glared at his mother. Her piercing eyes bore into his. A smirked played upon her rosy lips.

"I know, I know. No need to gloat, mother: I should have read your instructions first."

"Found them!" Johnathan startled Baxter back to reality.

"Carmen and I will take this to the dean," Dr. Raznor said. "Carry on with your exams and I'll let you know our next steps soon. Meeting's adjourned."

Baxter slumped, relieved he could properly think about Zoe. He eyed the clock above the door. Time sped up. He had less than two hours before he saw her again.

He stuffed his belongings in his briefcase and bolted out of the conference room. As he flew past Lacy, who was brushing her hair instead of working, he called out directions over his shoulder. "I need to head home for a moment. Take any messages and put three packs of Scantron sheets on my desk for my evening class."

Thirty minutes later, Baxter entered his mid-century modern home in the Hollywood Hills. He hurried up the stairs, swung open the door to his office, and padded to the opposite wall. A realistic oil painting of a Queen Anne Victorian mansion hung in the center, flanked by floor-to-ceiling shelves stuffed with books and oddities. He pulled against the bottom left corner of the canvas and revealed the black door of a wall safe.

With trembling hands, he twisted the dial clockwise, careful to stop at nine. One full rotation counterclockwise, stopping at three, then back clockwise until he reached ninety-nine. He pressed the dial inward and opened the door. He reached inside, bypassing the stacked bars of gold, porcelain figurines, and a glass jewelry case. He retrieved a worn, leather-bound journal and closed the safe. He sat it on his desk and as he opened it, a familiar musky smell wafted across his nose. An aged letter with a broken red seal rested just inside. Beneath it was a hand-colored monochrome photograph with frayed edges.

The young woman in the portrait had her black hair pinned up. She wore a lavender silk dress adorned with white lace; a colorful stone pendant hung from her neck.

Baxter stared into the woman's uniquely violet-blue eyes.

Just like Zoe's.

Excitement rushed through him like electricity. The young woman in the photo was Zoe. There was no denying it. He simply had to convince her. And sooner rather than later.

Baxter glanced at the desk calendar. He blinked.

The world tilted.

He had exactly thirty-one days to make her believe.

Because in thirty-two days, they both would be dead.

CHAPTER 3
ZOE

ZOE ENTERED THE THREE hundred-seat lecture hall and waltzed to the fifth row, settling into the seat next to the center aisle. Baxter stood at the podium shuffling through papers and adjusting the tiny microphone clipped on his tie, looking nothing like the disheveled mess from earlier. She rubbed her shoulder where her skin still tingled and wondered if he had lingering effects as well.

A rising warmth spread to her cheeks. She shifted in her seat.

Why do I feel like some ridiculous tween caught spying on her crush?

She twirled her pencil between her fingers like a baton. She tapped her foot in rhythm to the ticking analog clock hung above the podium. The lights dimmed. An image of a book cover projected on the large white screen at the front of the lecture hall. The book title, *The History of Mythology 2*, in an aqua-colored sans serif font, had an ink-drawn mermaid twisting around the words.

"Quick announcement and shameful promotion," Baxter's voice boomed into the microphone. "If you plan on taking the second half of this course in the fall, my newest book is available in the campus bookstore for you to order and get ahead on your reading. The course will continue to explain myths and legends from around the world. It will have a more in-depth look at mermaid lore, magical creatures, and ancient gods. We will even delve into the darker aspects found in different cultures."

Baxter pointed to someone in the middle of the auditorium. "Yes?"

Zoe twisted around. A thin guy with spiked bleach-blond hair and his feet propped on the seat in front of him spoke. "What kind of dark things?"

Baxter stepped away from the podium and ascended several stairs; he stopped directly next to Zoe. She inched closer to him. Leather and coffee waft passed her nose.

"Since the second half of this class is an advanced course, it will be much smaller," he said, slipping off a thick silver ring from his right hand, "meaning I can bring in more objects like this." He held the ring between his thumb and forefinger to show the captivated audience. "And tell you how I retrieved this from a—"

Baxter froze. Zoe followed his stone gaze to a man sitting in the back row. He wore a fitted suit, not the usual attire for a college class.

Clearing his throat, Baxter honed his attention back to the student. "—from a demon."

Several people snickered. Others murmured among themselves.

"Demons? Sure, Baxter," the student said.

"Before you start to doubt and debate me, Mr. Jones, I suggest you take the class to hear my evidence."

"I'm sure the ring will be just like the time you brought in the horn of a unicorn, which ended up being the tusk of a narwhal."

Baxter chuckled, but Zoe knew him well enough to know that it was more of a nervous laughter. As he slid the ring back on his finger, she leaned in closer, eyeing the black etchings inlaid in silver. As she fell back in her chair, she wondered what the actual story was behind the ring.

"What can I say? You sure see right through me, Mr. Jones. I must hook you somehow so that you, and others, take my courses."

Mr. Jones beamed. "Already signed up."

"Excellent." Baxter surveyed the audience. "Now, to convince the rest of you." He pushed a few buttons on his remote. A series of images, from mythical gods to mystical objects, flashed across the screen like a movie trailer. It was a preview of his next class, but Zoe couldn't take her eyes off Baxter. She noticed the sweat glistening on his brow. The last few hours of his day seemed to be one nuisance after another. Having a whole slew of those the last several months herself, Zoe empathized.

Baxter squatted next to her. She leaned into him, drawing in another whiff of him. Her mouth curved into a smile and looked up at him from below her lashes. He switched a button on the black box clipped on his belt, turning off his microphone. "I know it will cut it close to the time you need to leave for the airport, but come by my office after class so I can give you a copy of my new book as a going away gift. In my haste to get here, I forgot to bring it."

"Sure thing. I'd like that."

A group of young women giggled. Zoe grimaced.

Baxter stood; his brows lifted. "Ladies?" he said.

One girl, who looked like a fresh-faced freshman, leaned forward. "We were just sayin' how you're kinda like Indiana Jones."

A smirk crossed Baxter's lips. "Minus the fedora, of course." He winked and sauntered away as the girls giggled.

As Zoe faced forward, she rolled her eyes, the same betraying ones which just batted at the man. It annoyed her to admit it, but they were right. Baxter *was* like the rugged archaeologist: full of adventure, knowledge, and based on his reaction to the creepy guy in the top row, probably the keeper of a few secrets.

In a pathetic way, Zoe felt a twinge of jealousy toward Baxter. She would love to have adventures. Moving to Connecticut with her retired parents didn't fit the bill. Besides Yale, what did Connecticut offer her? Sure, New York was a train trip away, but she was a California girl who enjoyed sprawling cities, swimming pools, and sunshine, not buildings that blocked the rays of the sun because they were too close together and too tall.

She nibbled on her pencil.

You gettin' cold feet? Or is it because you don't want to leave Baxter?

Being near him gave her a thrill. Besides, she didn't *really* want to move across the country. But the decision was a necessity to get away from the shitshow of the past year.

At the sound of catcalling and whistling, she looked up at the screen and saw an image of the classic Disney princess mermaid sexualized by the juveniles in the room.

"All right, all right," Baxter lectured. "Before your exam, I want to reiterate one detail: Disney's Ariel is not a strong reference to use in your answer for today's essay."

The image changed to a portrait of a thin, dainty gentleman with a hooked nose and broad forehead. "Remember: Hans Christian Anderson wrote *The Little Mermaid* in 1837, which, in all reality, is quite recent. And her name was not Ariel. Mermaid lore is ancient. Although summer classes are shorter than regular terms, we still have gone over a semester's worth of information regarding this. Since I have so kindly reminded you of these facts, if anyone references Disney's Ariel in their essay, expect a large deduction. You may begin the test once you receive it."

Baxter pressed a button on the remote once more. The lights brightened, and the screens went blank. As the test and Scantron sheets traveled down the aisle, Zoe glanced behind her. The man in the suit had left the room.

Zoe surveyed Baxter. He, too, noticed the creepy guy gone. He glanced at the clock and fidgeted with the screen remote. Adjusted his tie and took off the clip-on microphone. Glanced back at the clock, and fanned himself with the extra copies of the test.

Zoe shook her head. That was one way Baxter was *not* like Indiana Jones. Even when faced with booby-traps, henchmen, and Nazis, Indy never revealed his genuine fear of a situation.

Unless it involved snakes.

Chapter 4

BAXTER

As an educator at USC, a post Baxter did not take lightly, there was a responsibility to uphold the policies the university placed on him when he began teaching several years ago. Therefore, dismissing three hundred students before a final exam began, only because his *actual* profession unexpectedly and urgently demanded every bit of his attention, was not a strong enough reason to disregard those policies.

But, oh, how he wished he could. The unnerving silence of the room and the slow *tick, tick, tick* of the minute hand on the clock hung above him, taunted him. Tested his patience.

His nervousness didn't come from the moment his skin grazed Zoe's, catapulting him into a life-and-death situation. It certainly didn't come from the boring task of proctoring an exam or not being able to react in the proper manner the situation called for.

No, it came from the man lurking in the top row of his lecture hall.

Lucas had a notorious habit of showing up at the most inopportune times and disrupting Baxter's life. After the encounter with Zoe, he expected to see him, just not as fast as he had.

How did Lucas even know about the situation so quickly?

As discreetly as possible, Baxter glanced across the lecture hall to battle Lucas in another round of intense glaring, but he no longer occupied the chair. Light-headed, he gripped the edge of the podium. It was one thing to see Lucas at his place of business, but it was something completely different to know he was there, out of sight, waiting to ambush him. All Baxter had was hope. Hope he could speak to Zoe before the impending chaos ensued.

Over an hour later, the lecture hall cleared, leaving Baxter and Zoe alone. He gathered his belongings and escorted Zoe out of the building. He walked close to her, but was careful not to graze her shoulder. His eyes darted in all directions as they made their way across the campus. He clutched the handle of his briefcase should he need to use it as a weapon.

As they entered the History Department, Lacy was packing her mini salon into her purse to leave for the night. Ignoring her, Baxter ushered Zoe into his office and closed the door behind her. He dropped his briefcase on top of an L-shaped oak desk.

Baxter shifted a small stack of his new textbooks into a perfectly straight tower, gathered a few loose-leaf papers from his desk, and piled them next to the books. "Pardon the mess."

"What mess?"

Zoe. Always impervious to the clutter. In fact, she usually added to it.

Ignoring the hooks next to the doorframe, she tossed her purse and backpack on the ground and gravitated to the large aquarium against the wall. She peered into the tank, enchanted by the seahorses hovering around some coral. She touched the glass, careful not to tap it. The seahorses swam over to her fingers as if they were magnets. "I'm gonna miss these little guys."

"They will miss you, as well. They never come to the glass for me, or anyone else." Baxter slinked around from behind his desk and inched closer to her.

She slid the tips of her fingers across the glass and watched the seahorses follow it. "'Cause no one has my special touch."

"You are right. You *have* a special touch." Her violet-blue eyes glowed in the dark aquarium. He wiped his palm on his trousers. He snatched her wrist. The searing electric pain zipped through his veins once again. Purple lights sparked around their hands. Zoe's agonizing wails harmonized with his own as she twisted out of his grip.

"What the hell?" She rubbed her reddened wrist and blinked away the tears swelling in her eyes.

Baxter yanked at his tie and unbuttoned the top buttons of his shirt. "We do not have a lot of time," he said. "Remember when I taught about the legend of the Pacific Ocean's mermaid queen?" His words rushed together as he noticed her eyeing the door, ready to bolt.

Her brows perched low. "Yeah. What about it?"

"Well, I did not tell the class the entire story." He reached beneath his collar, lifting the silver chain up, and revealing a purple and silver stone pendant. "This is a piece from her necklace. I am the queen's guardian and keeper of this stone. I have been searching for the queen, you, for nearly one hundred years."

She threw her hands up in the air. "That's absurd!"

"Zoe, please. Look at the stone. When I grabbed you, you saw the lights and felt the same force as I did, right?"

It took her a moment, but she ripped her befuddled gaze from him and stared at the swaying stone. It mesmerized her. The color of her eyes shone brighter. Twinkled. She blinked and took a few steps backward, shrinking away from the calming trance. "You mean this stuff is... real? That's not possible."

She pivoted and headed toward the exit. Baxter pushed past her, slammed the door shut and barricaded it with his six-foot frame. She shoved against him. "Move!"

"How can you run from this? The Zoe I know would be curious."

Zoe backed away, her hands trembling. "Curious?" Her voice an octave higher than usual. "No. No, Baxter, I'm not curious. I'm freaking out! Have you lost your damn mind?" She swayed on her feet. "You've just stated that you've been searching for me, the reincarnated mermaid queen, for a hundred years! That's practically impossible, especially when you look like you're what? Thirty? You certainly look great for your age, old man."

Baxter sighed. He stepped aside and put his arm over the top of a metal filing cabinet and strummed his fingers against it. "Very well, then. Leave."

Zoe tensed.

"Go on."

Zoe swept past him and reached down to pick up her purse and backpack, but as she did, Baxter gripped *both* her wrists and drew her into his chest. He couldn't—wouldn't—let her squirm away.

The familiar electric force surged through them once again. She screamed and thrashed against him, but he held tight, overpowering her, while doing his best to suppress his own distress. Purple twinkle lights buzzed around them, and tickled Baxter's skin like a feather. A tornado of wind howled through the room and upturned books and trinkets from their shelves. The water from the aquarium sloshed over the sides of the tank. Loose papers swirled around, some slapping Baxter in the face. The ground trembled. Zoe's backpack and purse skidded across the floor.

Just as Baxter couldn't stand the pain searing beneath his skin anymore, the spell dissipated. The room calmed and fell silent. Unbalanced and weak, Baxter collapsed, releasing his hold. Zoe stumbled backwards and fell, smacking the back of her head on his desk.

Alarmed, Baxter steadied himself and clambered to her side. He looked her over, careful not to touch her, though. "Zoe? Can you hear me?"

She moaned and forced her eyes open. Baxter helped her sit up and lean against the desk. She rubbed the back of her head. "What the hell was that about?"

"We should get you to an emergency room."

"No," Zoe said. "I didn't hit my head that hard. Besides, I have a plane to catch."

The office door swung open and startled them both. Lacy leaned against the doorframe, sipping on an iced Starbucks drink. "Heard weird noises. Do I, like, need to call an ambulance?"

"No," Baxter and Zoe said in unison.

Baxter eyed the mermaid logo on the cup Lacy held. It was a not-so-subtle reminder that no matter the risk, he could not let Zoe, a *real* mermaid, out of his sight.

"But before you leave, please get her some ice," he said.

Lacy took a long drag on the straw. "Fine, but I'm not filling out any reports. My boyfriend's waiting for me." As she walked away, she kicked Zoe's purse.

Baxter's eye twitched. If only he had the power to fire her.

He offered his hand to Zoe to help her up, but she stood on her own, using the table for support. He picked up his leather chair and rolled it to her. She plopped into it and rested her elbows on the desk, planting her head in her hands.

Lacy peeked inside and tossed an icepack at Baxter. "Don't forget to lock up."

Zoe brushed the hair away from her eyes and tucked the strands behind her ears. Baxter handed her the icepack, and she covered the back of her head. "All right, Baxter, I can't argue that something is happening between us. You've never lied to me before. You're a highly respected professor, and you've become a good friend. I will listen to you until this ice helps with swelling. Then, I'm walking outta here and pretending this never happened."

He could work within those parameters. He took a breath.

"As I said in my lectures, the mermaid folklore is intriguing because the world's oceans are ninety-five percent unexplored. Even with the advances in technology, nobody really knows what is out there. That's true only to those who know nothing of the magical world as I do. The myths and legends I teach about *do* exist. You and I are a part of them. You are the reincarnated queen from the northeast Pacific Ocean."

Zoe eyed him. "You're sayin' I'm the queen from those old myths who was murdered and left her kingdom in ruins?"

Baxter nodded. He rubbed the pad of his thumb over the stone's glossy surface. "Let me start over. The murdered mermaid queen was from the Pacific northeast realm. Her stone came into my possession when I was eighteen and life as I knew it changed forever."

He glanced at her. She looked skeptical, but she was listening. "The stone has four brothers; each contains a piece of the queen's magic. She placed a curse on the completed pendant right before she was killed; it broke into five pieces. As her guardian, it's my duty to find the reincarnated queen and help her acquire the other pieces so she can return to her kingdom. Her realm is in danger of losing all its magic and has been under constant threats from other realms."

"Who killed her?"

Good, she's still asking questions.

Baxter shrugged his shoulders. "Sadly, it is still unsolved." He searched his briefcase for the leather journal. "There are some theories who may have done it, but none that seemed plausible."

He flipped open the journal and retrieved the painted photograph and showed it to Zoe. "That was her. It is you. Your eyes are the same."

She glanced at it but didn't take it from his hand. "People resemble each other all the time. It's called having a doppelgänger. Remember that lesson?"

She had a point. Doppelgängers were popular in myths, and he always touched on them during his classes. He tucked the portrait in the journal and carefully picked up the folded parchment. "Your eye color makes up about one percent of the world's population. There is no denying she is you. But if you truly don't believe me, read this letter. It explains a lot."

She refused to look at the delicate paper. She glanced at the door.

Baxter tucked the journal and letter into his briefcase, worried their presence made Zoe even more uncomfortable with the conversation.

Zoe slapped the icepack on his desk. "So, you're telling me you've been searching for a murdered mermaid queen for the past hundred years, and you have no idea how to find the pieces that will restore her magic? Oh, and you wholeheartedly believe this queen is me, simply based on a small painting?"

Baxter held his finger up, ready to make his point. "I may not have all the answers—"

"You have *no* answers, Baxter. And time's up." She rose to her feet.

"Please. Stay and—"

"And what? You know this past year has been hell for me. And now you want me to stay? For some fantastic illusion you've created? No way. I have a *real* meeting to get to tomorrow. I—I need some air." She stomped past him and gathered her spilled belongings, stuffing everything inside her backpack.

"How can you deny the magic that surrounded us?"

Zoe ripped open the door and rushed out of the office.

Baxter went to follow her, but something on the ground next to the base of the aquarium caught his eye. He scooped up the rectangular piece of paper.

Zoe's plane ticket.

CHAPTER 5
ZOE

THE HALLWAY FROM BAXTER'S office to the lobby narrowed on Zoe. Two worlds trapped her; one with a madman spewing nonsense about a damn fairytale, and another, the reality of an unknown future.

At that moment, she didn't want either. Not like that, anyway.

From behind her, Baxter said, "Hard to travel without this."

Zoe came to a stop. She pivoted, intent on demanding him to leave her alone.

Baxter waved her plane ticket at her.

Her eyes widened at the possible disaster of a situation she would've suffered if she left without it. To have Baxter bring it to her, after he begged her to stay, felt even worse. With a tight-lipped smile, she marched over to him, plucked the ticket from his grip, and stuffed it into her backpack.

"Please do not leave," he pleaded.

Zoe's brows furrowed and in a low voice, she said, "Don't contact me." She turned on her heel, determined more than ever to put California behind her.

Beyond Lacy's desk, in the dimly lit lobby, stood three figures. Zoe stopped dead in her tracks as the sudden warmth of anxiety ignited within her. Something negative and thick hung in the air. Zoe took a hesitant step back.

The strange man in the suit stood between a tall blond with sharp features like a spider, and a bald man with a thick beard and a gnarly scar dragging over his right eye.

Baxter sidestepped past her, shielding her from view. "Gentlemen."

Zoe peered around Baxter, understanding what it felt like to be in the wrong place at the wrong time. She shifted her eyes from the door they blocked to the fire escape door behind her.

"Bennett," the man in the middle said as he advanced into the light. He shed his suit jacket and tossed it on a chair behind him. He rolled the sleeves of his dress shirt over his elbows. From the light above Lacy's desk, Zoe could see he had a tattoo on his left forearm of a sword with a raven perched on the hilt. It stabbed into vibrant reddish-orange flames, highlighting the engraved Celtic markings down the blade. Another tattoo, tribal with curved lines and rune symbols, curled around his right wrist.

The man oozed danger. But even more strange, the two other men also had the same tribal tattoo around their right wrists.

Baxter stepped behind Lacy's chair and rested his hands on the back rest. The receptionist's desk stood between Baxter and Zoe and the trio, an invisible line. Would the tension in the room keep itself at bay long enough for her to leave before she saw one of them cross that line?

"Lucas, always a pleasure. I see you brought some new friends. Is William still laid up from the last encounter he had with me?"

Lucas sneered. "Now, now. Is that how you should talk to an old mate?" Lucas's English accent was strong and unexpected.

Zoe stood next to Baxter and held her chin high. She wanted out of the situation, but the men wanted to waste her time. She folded her arms over her chest. "Who are you?"

"A constant menace in my life," Baxter mumbled.

Lucas puffed out his chest. "Someone in search of a valuable treasure, dearie." His eyes cut to Baxter. "And considering how we felt the immense charge of magical energy through the air, I should offer my congratulations on your find."

Magical energy? Zoe didn't like the sound of that.

The spider-looking guy stepped forward. "She even looks like Melantha," he said in an accent Zoe didn't recognize, but thought he might be from a Nordic country.

"Good eye, Sebastian," Lucas stated, gawking at Zoe.

Zoe clenched a fist. "The only person someone has ever accused me of looking like is Elizabeth Taylor. I don't have time for this. Especially from a boy's club where you get matching tattoos." She made a move to leave, but the scar-faced man slammed his hand on the receptionist's countertop, much like she did hours earlier.

He blocked her path. He rolled a toothpick between his teeth. "Dmitry will hear no more useless small talk. You come with us."

Zoe arched a brow at him. Never mind the odd collection of men in her way, there was no way in hell she'd be addressed like that, especially by someone who referred to himself in third person. The Russian held out his hand as if he thought she would be naïve enough to take it. As she looked at Baxter for his reaction, she noticed an opened box cutter on Lacy's desk. Studying at a prominent football university had its perks, and she knew all too well the best defense was a strong offense. In one swift movement, she seized the box cutter and swiped the razor-sharp blade across Dmitry's forearm.

He cursed and clutched his bleeding arm to his chest. Zoe wrenched Baxter's wrist, urging him to unfetter his feet from the ground and move. She had every intention of running to the door, but Lucas lunged across Lacy's desk and tackled Baxter, throwing him to the ground.

"Run!" Baxter yelled while wrestling Lucas.

Zoe, wide-eyed and panicked, pirouetted, and darted for the door. Before she reached it, a wooden chair flew at her and knocked her off her feet. A high-pitch ringing blared in her ears. She rolled over. Her breath came in great heaves. Hands clamped around Zoe's wrist and dragged her across the carpet and up to her feet.

"I got her!" Sebastian shouted.

Zoe blinked away her tears and tried to focus. She twisted her neck toward the receptionist's desk. Lucas, disheveled and bloodied, popped up from behind it. Baxter, also a mess, crawled around from the right side.

A wave a nausea swept through Zoe. No matter the drive to fight, these men outnumbered her and Baxter.

"Take her to the car." Lucas wiped the blood from his mouth. "Dmitry and I will follow behind with Baxter."

Zoe met Baxter's eyes.

Sebastian nudged her to move. "Walk," he demanded.

Zoe clenched her jaw and took a few steps. How had she found herself in this situation? She should be on her way to the airport, brooding about unimportant things like not getting her favorite spot next to the window.

"I have the pendant," Baxter said.

Zoe stopped. Baxter rose to his feet. He held up the stone from beneath his collar. "You need this. Not her. Let her go, and I will come on my own accord."

Zoe and Baxter's eyes met. A silent communication passed between them. Zoe knew he was buying her time.

But can I really leave him here in danger?

"I could've taken that necklace from you years ago," Lucas said. "*She's* a better find."

Baxter extended his arm and pointed at the door. "Go!"

With no other choice, Zoe reared her leg back, and kicked Sebastian square in his groin. He doubled over, released his grip, and howled.

Zoe's legs were heavy, but somehow, she ran across the room and opened the door.

"Watch out!" Baxter yelled.

She skidded to a stop and firmly planted her feet, ready for a rear impact. But an orb of flames rushed past her and through the doorway, hitting the wall across the hall.

With a morbid curiosity, Zoe looked back at Lucas. He touched the tattoo on his forearm, glowed red, and a split second later, a fiery orb danced in his palm. Like a baseball pitcher, he cocked his arm backward. Zoe dove through the threshold as it streaked over her, adding to the smoke and fire filling the hallway.

"Get her!"

Zoe scrambled to her feet and raced down the hall. Her eyes on the red metal box bolted on the wall next to the stairwell. She reached inside and pulled the alarm. Lucas stood at the opposite end of the hallway, his newly formed fireball dissolving as the water from the sprinklers rained down.

Zoe raced down the stairs and exited the building. She ran across the campus without another look back. Sirens wailed, coming closer and closer. Before she knew it, she reached her car. Her erratic breaths deafening as she slid inside and repeatedly locked the door. With a trembling hand, she started her car and drove off, trying to process what in the hell just happened.

Chapter 6
Baxter

The unexpected screaming of a campus fire alarm usually caused confusion and panic; for Baxter, it was a much-needed signal of relief. Lucas and his goons always avoided conflict with authority. They immediately fled as soon as Zoe pulled the alarm. For a moment, he was safe. Wet from the overhead sprinklers, which put out Lucas' handy-dandy magical flamethrowers, but safe.

Baxter flicked the water from his face and raced to his office, careful not to slip on the tile. He would never admit it out loud, but Lucas had the right idea to leave before the fire department showed up.

How awkward, time consuming, and full of lies would my explanation need to be if I'm caught here?

He wasn't keen on dealing with that scenario. Besides, in his hundred-year-long quest as the queen's guardian, fleeing a scene had been something of the norm.

He found his keys beneath his briefcase, opened the bottom drawer of his filing cabinet, combed through the folders, and found a file labeled "Teaching Assistants." He unlocked his briefcase, stuffed the manila folder inside, and made his way out of the building.

As he exited to the busy major thoroughfare on USC's campus, he heard the sirens of a fire truck. He hustled to blend in with the evening students. He scanned his surroundings.

Where had Lucas and his goons gone?

With an added sense of urgency, he dipped his chin and powered on across the main quad toward the parking structure. Just as Baxter reached the opposite end, he skidded to a stop.

William, the other goon he expected to see earlier, waited near the pathway to the parking structure. Unlike Lucas with his fashionable suit, William blended in well with the college crowd, in a Trojan's V-neck T-shirt, dark denim, and short, bleach-blond spikes. In fact, it was only William's intricate tattoo tracing along the left side of his neck that caught Baxter's attention. It was a three-quarter view of a screaming skull that had vines weaving in and out of its orifices and different hues of orange, like molten lava, spilling out of the top of its head.

Baxter cursed, U-turned, and tucked behind a nearby tree. He didn't have time for another showdown. He peeked around the tree to plot his escape route, when he noticed a female walking up to William and planting a kiss on his cheek. Baxter narrowed his eyes. Even in the near darkness, he couldn't mistake the young lady.

Lacy.

"That girl seriously needs to be fired," he growled. No wonder Lucas and William knew exactly where to find him.

She's a traitor. No better than Benedict Arnold. No, too harsh. Probably an unsuspecting victim.

Baxter looked for the other goons. Dmitry clutched his wounded arm and leaned against the stone wall of the library. Sebastian was on the opposite end, hovering by the crowd of people. Lucas lurked in the dark shadows near William. Baxter's sixth sense about them sticking around had been spot on.

At least Zoe is safely out of their grasp.

He hurried his way to the closest emergency blue light phone, something all university campuses had, and reported them as suspicious characters in order to buy him enough time to get to his car. By the time he returned to the tree, the campus police were questioning them.

Baxter raked his hands through his hair, adjusted his clothes, and sauntered down the pathway. He beamed as he strutted past the detained group. William noticed Baxter first, and his face twisted in anger.

Baxter gave a small nod to the officers and a tiny wink at William, who spouted out several obscenities as Sebastian and Dmitry lunged at him. Fortunately, the campus police were quick to restrain them. Lucas, though, was the only one who sat calmly on the edge of the fountain, and not face down on the ground like his compadres. He eyed Baxter.

"Game, set, match," Baxter mouthed as he strolled past him.

Lucas smirked, and somehow, with an air of respect, gave Baxter the middle finger.

Baxter rushed to his black Toyota 4Runner. When he entered, he retrieved the damp folder from his briefcase and flipped through the pages, finding Zoe's home address in her emergency contact information. He had a small window of opportunity to keep her from getting on the plane and keep her in his sights. With Lucas aware of the reincarnated queen, it wouldn't be long before he figured out her modern-day identity.

Zoe lived in Los Feliz on Vermont Street—the same road that the campus of USC was on, making her less than ten miles away, and at least, a thirty-minute drive in Hollywood's traffic. He tossed the file aside and started his SUV. If he hurried, he could make it to her house before she left for the airport. If all else failed, he knew what airline she would take from LAX and had no problem booking an impromptu seat on the same flight.

As he pulled out of the parking structure and turned onto Vermont Street, the realization that she lived down a few blocks from the Greek Theater, a place Baxter visited on numerous occasions, hit him hard. He wondered how many times he passed by her home. He groaned; she had been at the tip of his fingertips for so long.

CHAPTER 7

ZOE

ADRENALINE FUELED ZOE AS she ran on autopilot. She gripped the steering wheel with her clammy palms and drove a twenty-minute backtracking detour through Hollywood, wanting to lose anyone possibly following her. Only when her keys fell from her hand and thudded onto the concrete floor of her garage, did she realize she was home.

But am I safe?

She scooped up her keys, struggled to unlock the door, and entered the oversized kitchen of her 1920s Mediterranean mansion. The kitchen, newly expanded and renovated, boasted espresso-colored cabinets that reached the ceiling. A copper stove hood hung over a gas range. Zoe tossed her backpack along the sleek marble countertop on the island. She leaned over the porcelain sink and splashed cool water on her face. She kneaded her neck muscles, dipped her head, and drank straight from the tap.

After she dried her hands on a towel, she rummaged through her backpack. She couldn't lose her plane ticket for a second time. Relieved to find it crumbled at the bottom, she removed it and sank onto a leather barstool at the kitchen island. Her shoulders slumped. Drew in a calming breath.

Zoe wondered if she had a fairy godmother who heard her innermost desire to want an adventure like Baxter and decided it would be fun to turn her world upside down. If Zoe *had* a fairy godmother, the fairy had a sick sense of humor. What she experienced was not adventure—it was a nightmare.

She rubbed her temples. She already had a tarnished reputation because of the PED accusations; she could add assaulting people with a weapon, running from a crime scene, and leaving her friend alone to fend for himself to her rap sheet.

What type of person have I become?

"A survivor, that's who." She straightened.

Now what? Will someone come after me? Those men? The cops?

She knew Baxter sure would; he was relentless.

The lights in the backyard flicked on. She gasped and clutched her hand to her chest. After a minute, maybe more, she relaxed. Years ago, her parents set the lights on an automatic timer to signal ten o'clock when it was time for her to stop swimming and come inside. Ten o'clock. She had two hours until her flight took off. Her leg bounced as she stared at the airline ticket. Her escape.

She nibbled her bottom lip, a bad habit when contemplating decisions. She dropped the ticket on the table and meandered over to the French doors leading to the backyard. She stepped across the threshold, padded across the flagstone patio, and stalked down the hundred and thirty-four steps that welcomed her to the lagoon-style pool. The warm glow of the lights hidden in the gardens illuminated the perimeter of the pool. Up-lights placed around the rock waterfall dramatically spotlighted a life-size bronze mermaid statue on top of the boulder.

The mermaid was poised on a rock, tanning, and soaking up the sun's rays. Her head tilted to face the sky and exposed a slender neck. Her hair puddled on the rock behind her. Her tail dangled off the edge with the tips of her fluke lifted at the ends as if flicking water from it.

Her parents gifted her the statue for her sweet sixteen; it represented her love for swimming and childhood desire of wanting to be a mermaid.

Hello, irony.

Am I crazy for wanting to believe Baxter about mermaids? Could I possibly be one?

The men who attacked her and Baxter were real. That ball of fire thrown at her sure as hell was real.

Being a mermaid would explain her far superior swimming abilities.

Zoe swayed on her feet. She couldn't live with herself if she disregarded the past few hours. The titter of her laughter echoed in the still night. She had a reason to stay, even if it was to clear her conscience and satisfy her own curiosity.

She hurried away from the pool and up the steps, locked the French doors behind her, and tossed the plane ticket into the trash. She seized her backpack, grabbed her day planner, and flipped it open to her contacts. Her finger traced down the page, stopping on Baxter's home phone number. As she lifted the cordless phone off the charging base, the doorbell rang.

Zoe jumped; the phone clattered onto the marble tile.

The bell rang again, but not just a single ring. It was a rapid-fire, heart pounding, *ring, ring, ring*, as if she didn't hear it the first time.

Her mouth ran dry. The cops. Here to ruin her adventure before she even started.

She returned the phone and looked around her kitchen. She jetted over to the light switch and switched them off, thankful the kitchen was at the back of the home. She plastered her back against the cabinets. Another set of insistent ringing echoed through the house, followed by a hard pounding at the door.

She tiptoed across the dark hardwood, careful to step around the known squeaky areas, and down the hallway to the circular foyer. She peered around the corner, expecting to see red and blue lights streaming in through the ornate iron and glass entrance doors. Instead, a man peeped through the glass.

"Baxter!" She tore across the floor and swung open the heavy door.

Baxter slumped against the stucco. "Thank goodness you're home."

"Thank goodness you're okay! I was about to call your house. I thought maybe you'd be... I don't know. Come in, come in." She ushered him through the threshold and locked the door behind him. "Do you think they followed you? Who were those guys? Are you hurt? Are you in trouble?"

Baxter shook his head and lifted his hands to slow her down. "Take a breath, Zoe."

She nodded and exhaled.

"I left before anyone arrived," Baxter continued. "I assume the campus police will investigate, and they will question me, but that is not our immediate danger." Baxter's eyes bore into hers. "Those men also believe you are the mermaid queen, and they *will* find you."

Zoe shifted from one foot to the other. She wanted to ask him if they were going to kill her, but she couldn't gather her strength to say the words aloud.

"I need you to believe me. To trust me," he said.

Zoe raised her chin. "After what I just saw? Yeah, I trust you."

Baxter's brow arched as if her statement surprised him.

She took a breath before continuing, "I'll admit: I'm curious. This whole idea will take me time to truly wrap my head around, but I'm starting to buy what you're selling. I still have a ton of—"

Baxter winced and pulled at the necklace.

"What's wrong?"

His brows furrowed together. "The stone is burning against my chest." He lifted the silver chain and dangled the pendant away from his skin.

Zoe bounced on her toes. "So, take it off. Don't just hold it up!"

Baxter stiffened and held a finger to his lips, quieting her. He cocked his ear, listening. Zoe set her mouth in a hard line. Rushing water echoed through the foyer.

"We're too far from the beach to hear that," she whispered. Salty sea air wafted past her nose. "Or to smell that."

"Indeed." Baxter peered down the dark hallway.

Zoe rubbed her eyes as a thick fog trickled out from under a door, hovering over the hardwood floors.

Baxter tested the temperature of the stone with his fingertips. Satisfied, he dropped it and let the pendant hang over his shirt. He pointed to the first door in the hallway. "What is in that room?"

"My father's study. We prepped the house for the season since my parents planned on returning during spring to get out of the cold weather back east. There shouldn't be any windows open in there."

They crept down the hall. Zoe imagined Lucas and his men breaking inside, and she scolded herself for not setting the alarm. Baxter reached for the handle and pushed the door open. She reached into the room, slid her hand against the wall, and switched on the lights.

The room looked like an old-fashioned gentleman's club with wooden panels and leather club chairs. Displayed on a shelf of the built-in cabinetry, were an assortment of seashells, sand dollars, and starfish. Like a waterfall, the fog trickled from the collection.

Baxter headed straight for the shelves.

Zoe trailed behind him. "How is this even happening?"

"Magic. It makes everything possible." He reached beyond the large conch shell and grabbed the nautilus. As soon as he touched it, the misty clouds and the sound of waves vanished.

Baxter retracted his hand. Zoe tilted her head in surprise.

He pointed to a framed photo sitting next to the shell collection. "When and where was this taken?"

"Oh. I was eight and just discovered this exact collection of shells. It was a rare find, which is why my father treasured them. It was on a beach in San Francisco. Why?"

Baxter staggered away from Zoe as if she had slapped him. "San Francisco?"

"Yeah. Why?"

Baxter slumped into the chair nearest the fireplace. He rubbed his forehead. "I am originally from San Francisco and have not been back in some time." His eyes locked onto hers. "San Francisco is where all of this mermaid business stems from."

Zoe raised her brows and raked her fingers through her hair.

"Your shells came to life because of the queen's pendant. As soon as you admitted you believed, the magic must have activated. Magic attracts magic. It's one of the reasons why Lucas and his cohort arrived so quickly this evening. The shells are a clue and want us to go to San Francisco."

Zoe perched on the edge of the chair across from him. "A clue for what?"

"To the location of the next stone. Once the reincarnated queen is identified, my role is to help her find the rest of her stones so she can restore her power."

Zoe rose to her feet. "Magic, murder, mermaids. And now a scavenger hunt?"

"And we do not have a lot of time."

"Because of what's his name and his goons?"

"Lucas and the others may be a nuisance, but they are not the threat. When Melantha cast her spell to be reincarnated, there was a hundred-year time limit."

Zoe scoffed. "Of course."

"September third will be exactly one hundred years since her death. If she has not returned by then, she never will. The effects can be catastrophic."

Zoe wrapped her arms around herself. "But wouldn't there be a new queen or king after that? Maybe it wouldn't be that bad."

Baxter stood; his jaw clenched. "From what I learned, if another takes the realm, it could cause substantial shifts in the environment—especially if the new leader makes adjustments, causing weather or climate changes. It is also rumored that the mermaids in your realm are losing their magic, since much of their energy source stems from the pendant and their leader. Without either, the community will either be forced to live on land, take the risk and be ruled by someone who may or may not have the same ideals as them, or simply die off."

He took a step closer to her. Leather, coffee, and musk infiltrated her nose. "But *most importantly*, our lives, yours, and mine, are tied to those stones. If we fail to collect them in time, we will die."

Zoe swayed. She plopped down into the leather chair and took a sharp breath. "Death? Seems a little harsh."

"It is."

The lives of so many, including Baxter's, counted on her to take a leap of faith and do everything in her power to help them. An insurmountable pressure rested on her shoulders, but there was no way in hell she couldn't at least try.

"You realize we only have a month to do all this, right? It would've been nice to have a little more time."

Baxter dropped to his knees in front of her. "That is my fault. A regret I would like to atone for. However, it may be that everything is happening right when it needs to."

No matter what choices she made in her life, her path was destined. If that was the case, it was out of her control. However, fate would never control her attitude and beliefs. "I won't have others suffer because denying reality is the easy thing to do, or because I failed to act on their behalf."

Baxter exhaled; a light glinted in his eye. He bowed his head as if a weight lifted from his shoulders.

Always wanting to do her absolute best in everything she did, Zoe silently vowed to treat this situation the same, even if they died trying. "Do ya think we can exchange my first-class ticket for two coach seats to San Francisco?"

Chapter 8
Baxter

Two days later, Baxter and Zoe arrived in San Francisco. They stepped out of the rental car and surveyed the ominous Queen Anne Mansion poised in front of them. A white structure with a massive turret capped with a coned roof resembled a witch's hat. A wrap-around porch with gingerbread-style trim welcomed them.

It represented an era Baxter tried to keep buried for a century.

Zoe stepped around the vehicle. "Is this where we're staying?"

"No." He sauntered up the cement steps leading to the porch. "This used to be my family home. In 1951, I sold it to a family who wanted to make it into a museum and a site for private events."

Zoe let out a low, long whistle. "I can't imagine having to do that, especially with it being something so connected to your family."

They reached the mahogany entry door. Baxter stopped and faced her. "It was difficult, but it was a necessity. As the queen's guardian, I knew I would have to have a healthy sum of money to find you and be the financial backer to complete our journey. Traveling around the world does not come cheap, even considering the inheritance my family left me. I planned my finances early, took some risks and made investments in companies like

Coca-Cola, radio, and eventually broadcast networks like ABC television. Money is of no object to me. To us. You will want, or need, for nothing."

She pushed her sunglasses into her hair. "You certainly have quite the story, don't you? I may not understand all the things you've been through to get to this point, but I feel like I already owe you so much."

Baxter smirked. He often felt like somebody owed *him* something for the life he'd been cursed with. But since the reincarnated queen was his favorite apprentice, nay, his friend, his attitude shifted. "You only owe me your best." He opened the door for her.

Zoe grinned. "Well, one day, you'll have to tell me your experiences seeing all the changes the world went through. I'm sure it was absolutely fascinating."

"Indeed."

They stepped into the foyer. Zoe stopped at the sight of the entrance. A grand staircase with ornate wooden posts and a hand-carved railing extended to the second floor. A gold-plated two-tiered crystal chandelier, holding at least two-dozen candle lights under a drapery of crystal beads, hang high above them.

Baxter leaned into her. "My father had that chandelier imported from France."

She ran her hand over the polished wooden chair rail. "Beautiful."

Baxter rested against the stair railing and reveled in the stained-glass window on the second-floor landing. The ache of loneliness stabbed his heart as he remembered the hundreds of times his family ran up and down these stairs.

"Welcome to the Baxter House Museum."

A mature woman wearing pleated slacks and a cashmere cardigan shuffled into the foyer. "Our first tour doesn't start until ten." She refilled the museum brochures on a stand on a receptionist's podium next to the stairs. "But you are more than welcome to wait in the café gift shop."

"Good morning, ma'am. We are not exactly interested in a tour." Baxter reached for his wallet in his back pocket, pulled out a California identification card from behind his driver's license, and handed it to her. "I'm Travis Baxter. Is the owner available?"

Baxter felt Zoe's eyes on him. He strummed his fingers on his wallet as the woman looked at the card.

The woman beamed and handed it back. "Of course. One moment, please." She hurried into the café and gift shop, which had been the parlor at one time.

Zoe raised a challenging brow. "Travis?"

"Just go with it," he said through a tight-lipped smile.

The woman returned with a man who ran his hand over his graying hair. "Sir, my name is Howard. My father purchased your grandfather's home almost fifty years ago." He smoothed the lapels of his blue suit before extending his hand. "It is such a pleasure to meet you."

Baxter gripped his hand; pleased, Howard gave a firm shake. "Pleasure is mine. I'm Travis, and this is my sister, Mary. Our father never brought us to his father's home when we were children, but we were told our family could always visit if we were ever in the area. We probably should have made an appointment, but we were too excited to get here."

"You never need an appointment. You are always welcome here. If you are hungry, our café serves some of the famous baked goods just like your family once did, still using their recipes, of course."

Baxter nodded. "That would be great. Perhaps a to-go bag? We recently ate."

"I'll pack you one," the woman said from behind Howard.

"My father always spoke of a mural my grandmother painted. Is it still here?" Baxter asked.

"Absolutely!" Howard ushered them up the stairs, his hands as active as his mouth. "I was pretty young, but I actually remember going to Los Angeles with my father when he purchased the property from Bennett, your grandfather."

"That is some memory." He also remembered that moment. Young Howard had been a charming, but chatty, little boy—not much changed.

Zoe suppressed a chuckle. Baxter elbowed her arm.

"Everything in the second story has stayed the same since we acquired the property. We added a ballroom to the back to accommodate events such as weddings. With that addition, the home is close to ten-thousand square feet."

"Damn," Zoe said.

Howard stopped in front of a wooden door. A door Baxter used to charge in and out of as a child. It even had the same crystal door knob that he used to believe was made of real diamonds.

"Oh, yes. She is quite impressive. We have photographs of what she looked like in her heyday displayed in the library. I hate to leave you, but I have a few meetings to attend. Feel free to take your time and roam around the property. This is still very much your family's home, as it is ours. There are baskets of white cotton gloves in every room if you would like to touch anything. Come by the café before you leave. Annette, my wife, will have your goodies ready. I will be sure to duck out of the meeting to say my goodbyes. Enjoy."

"We appreciate it."

Howard trotted down the hallway as Baxter opened the door.

"Explain," Zoe said, refusing to enter.

"You saw how he behaved when he thought we were the grandchildren of Bennett Baxter. Can you imagine how he would react if he knew I was *the* Bennett Baxter? In order to survive the past hundred years, I've had to become a master of deceit."

Zoe pursed her lips. "You could have let me in on that little tidbit before we entered, so I didn't nearly blow your cover."

Baxter lowered his head. "Apologies. I am used to handling situations on my own."

"Well, not anymore. We're partners."

Baxter nodded. "Agreed."

She waltzed into the room. "Now, what's in here you wanted to see?"

Baxter took several steps past the doorway and inhaled the familiar scent of wood and mothballs. As he walked over to the double bed, he ran the pads of his fingers across the redwood wainscoting. The floral wallpaper above the chair rail had faded over time, but it was still as classy as it was when his mother picked it out. He sat on the edge of the lumpy bed and was thankful for modern advances in comfort. His eyes swelled with tears as he stared at the trunk in the corner. It was open and displayed some of his old childhood toys.

The bed dipped when Zoe sat next to him and placed her hand on his shoulder. "You, okay?"

Baxter cleared his throat. "There is nothing like nostalgia."

Zoe's eyes searched his. He appreciated her doing her best to sympathize, but it was a burden Baxter carried for a hundred years. Nobody could understand how truly alone he felt.

Zoe pointed to a framed black-and-white family photograph on the bedside table.

"You had an older brother?"

Baxter sighed. "Technically, no. That's my uncle. My father had two older sisters and a much younger brother. Months after he was born, however, my grandparents, my father's two sisters, and their husbands, all perished in a terrible train accident in Ohio. My parents had just married, but not wanting to lose any more family members, they adopted him. He was six years older than me."

Baxter hadn't spoken of his uncle in so long that the heartache over his loss somehow felt fresh. He cleared his throat. "When I was sixteen, my uncle became engaged, but unfortunately, they both disappeared shortly after that. I refused to believe they eloped and ran off like many people claimed. That wasn't something my uncle would've done. Something terrible must have happened to them."

"I'm sorry you endured such a tragedy in your life."

Baxter shrugged his shoulders. He didn't want to linger on the subject anymore, not right now, at least. There were more important things to be done. He straightened, and in his best light-hearted tone, said, "No matter. That was long ago."

"I can see where you get your charming, good looks," Zoe said. "Your mother was stunning."

Baxter cheeks flushed. "Yes, indeed. She was a beauty, from the 'old country' in Syria. I may not have always agreed with some of her beliefs and practices, but I was fiercely protective of her when others called her ways odd and unnatural. She even claimed to foresee the future. I had my doubts, but I should have known better. It's actually why we are here."

Zoe tilted her head. "What do you mean?"

Baxter looked past Zoe to the wall across the room. "That mural."

She twisted around, the bed creaking and straining from their weight. "You were serious about seeing this mural?"

Baxter nodded and led her to the opposite side of the room. Side by side, they stood in front of the fading scene. "My mother painted this in 1894, when I was twelve, shortly after my father passed away. She said it was of a vision of something important in my future, but she could offer no other details."

The painting was of a beach. A young girl with black hair sat by herself in the sand. She had a pile of beautiful seashells in front of her. To her left, walking alongside the water, was a blonde woman watching the little girl from beneath her oversized sunhat. To her right, a plain, square building loomed high on the cliff. "I always thought the painting might be of my wife and child, but after I left San Francisco and traveled the world in search of you, I knew that dream would never become a reality. Truthfully, I forgot about the mural until I saw the childhood photograph of you with your shells. My mother's vision was of you and your mother. Yet more proof you are the queen. I never appreciated her gift when she was alive. I wanted to show it to you because there must be a clue or—"

"Baxter."

"Something of importance about—"

"Baxter!"

He stopped. She took a step back, her head shaking ever so slightly.

"What?"

She pointed to the woman in the scene. Her face paled. "That isn't my mother."

Baxter frowned. "Then who?"

"A stranger. It was a totally weird moment, and I will never forget it. I remember playing in the sand as my parents walked along the shore. I dug up this massive pile of shells and wanted to get my parents' attention. When I looked up, that woman was there instead. She had such a profound look on her face I thought I'd done something wrong. I thought the shells had been hers and I'd disrupted them or something, but she told me I was the rightful owner. Not talking to strangers had been pounded into my head, so I scooped them up in my arms and was about to run away, but when I looked up, she was gone. Like gone, gone. Nowhere on the beach or in the water, as if she had disappeared. Totally freaked me out. Thought I'd imagined it until now."

"Whoever she was, she must be important or my mother wouldn't have painted her. Do you remember which beach you were at?"

Zoe's brow knitted together. "Uh, obviously. Even your mother knew it was Ocean Beach." She pointed to the building on the cliff. "That's the famous Cliff House in the background."

Slightly miffed, Baxter said, "You are mistaken. That is *not* the Cliff House. The Cliff House was majestic. Grandiose. Modeled after a French Chateau." He thrust a finger at the mural. "*That* is a box. An atrocity and scar on prime real estate."

Zoe tried to suppress her smile. "Yes, you're right. But remember: your mother painted the future when the Cliff House looks like that, not the Victorian estate you're used to. The one you remember survived the 1906 earthquake, but burned down shortly after and was rebuilt to look like that."

"Well, no wonder I never understood this mural." Baxter sank his hands into his pockets. He didn't like missing clues, especially since he allowed his clouded perception to dictate his rational thoughts.

"When's the last time you were in San Francisco?"

"Nineteen hundred. I left shortly after my mother passed. I was incredibly bitter, angry, and confused about my new life. With no family and an unwanted quest to find a mythical creature, I traveled the world, looking for answers. Local news was not easily accessed in those days. San Francisco and its memories are something I've kept locked away and had no interest in."

"I can certainly understand that."

Baxter let out a swoosh of air. "It was foolish. The queen died here, making San Francisco important. I could have saved so much time." The truth was, he could have saved even more time if he'd done his damn job and not given up on his quest all those years ago. A shameful scar on his self-respect.

"No use dwelling on it. Like you said to me, we can do this. Together."

To pacify her, Baxter nodded, but he was still angry at himself. His pride nearly cost them their lives. He had a feeling it would not be the last of his past mistakes affecting the present.

"You know," Zoe said with a quizzical grin, "you've never said *how* you've been alive for so long without aging."

Baxter took a breath as he dug himself out of his private hellhole of self-berating. "Well, with magic, of course. The necklace is enchanted and has kept me alive. Even during my darkest moments when I repeatedly tried to take my life, in many different ways, the magic infused in the stone pendant kept me safe. I have not suffered a simple scratch, bruise, or broken bone. If I should have died from an act upon myself or from another force, I would simply fall asleep, like being unconscious, and would awaken in the current place I called home."

Zoe considered this for a moment. "So, you would what? Physically disappear from your place of death and reappear in your home, completely fine?"

Baxter nodded. "Pretty much."

"Creepy." Her eyes widened. "Wonder what would've happened if you were decapitated?"

"How about we not find out?" he stated.

She blushed. "Not that I want that to happen, but I'm just sayin'. What if? Be kinda weird seeing you headless one minute then—"

"Indeed, it would." He cleared his throat and walked away from the mural. "I have aged, though I didn't notice it for about twenty or thirty years. It seems for every decade, I age one year, which makes me nearly twenty-eight. Technically, though, almost a hundred and eighteen."

Zoe swept by him, tossing her hair behind her shoulders; cucumber and melon lingered in the air. "Well, you're quite handsome for such an old man. Come on, *Travis*, let's grab some pastries, say our goodbyes to Howard and Annette, and head to Ocean Beach."

Chapter 9

Zoe

Zoe examined a local guide and map as Baxter piloted their rental car through traffic. She suppressed a yawn and glanced at him. "We should probably find a hotel."

"See anything close to Ocean Beach or the Cliff House?"

Zoe scanned a list of bed-and-breakfast inns near the area. "How 'bout Seal Rock Inn? It has a small restaurant attached to it, and the Cliff House is within walking distance."

"Let us hope they have a vacancy. Tell me how to get there."

Twenty minutes later, Baxter drove past the front of Seal Rock Inn's three-story, brown, square building at the top of a hill. Each level had a white, horizontal roofline reminiscent of fifties' modern architecture. The hotel itself was nothing fancy, but the view of the ocean was killer.

Baxter found a parking space at the back of the building. They gathered their belongings and headed inside.

"We only have a family suite available," the thin woman at the front desk explained. "There is a queen bed in one room and two twin size beds in another. It's on the third floor and has a small living space with a gas fireplace."

Baxter shifted and looked at Zoe. "Are you comfortable sharing a room with me?"

A room? Hell, I'd share a bed if I had to.

Zoe untucked her hair from behind her ears, letting it fall to the sides of her face, covering her betraying cheeks.

"It has an accordion-style partition wall that can separate the bedrooms for privacy," the woman added.

"Sure, that's fine."

"Excellent." Her fingers made the familiar *clickity-clack* on her computer keyboard. She handed them a room key and directed them to the elevator.

As the woman described, there were two bedrooms with a small living room between them. The furnishings were a light-colored oak with mauve-and-white fabrics. Zoe placed their bags on the luggage rack inside the small closet in the room with the twin beds. Only fitting, Baxter took the queen bed since he was the one paying. She stretched back on the bed, her head burrowing into the soft pillow.

She heard the queen-sized bed squeak as Baxter fell onto it. "The stress of traveling exhausts me. I need a nap. We can head down to Ocean Beach around four or five."

Zoe yawned. "M'kay."

Around four o'clock, Zoe woke and made her way to the living room. She curled up on the overstuffed chair and watched the early evening traffic drive by. At a quarter 'til five, the alarm from Baxter's room blared. She chuckled as Baxter slammed his hand on the bedside table, looking for the clock to shut it off.

A few moments later, he entered the room and ran his fingers through his wild hair. Zoe motioned to the open box of pastries. "You need to eat something before we go." She took a bite of a cinnamon roll. "These are divine, by the way. I can see why your father's business was so successful. I'm glad Howard and Annette honor your family and still use the same recipe."

Baxter stuffed an apple fritter into his mouth. "My father was an amazing baker, and I am happy to say he taught me well. Perhaps, one day, I can teach you to make these."

Zoe licked the icing off her finger. "I would love that."

"We should change into clothes that are more suitable for a coastal hike along sand dunes and rocky cliffs. The evenings can be brisk." He grabbed a second fritter.

Zoe reached for her sneakers and slipped them on. "I'm ready," she said as she tied her shoes. "I even put on my bathing suit; in case we get in the water. Just waiting for you, sleepy head."

Baxter marched off, stuffing his mouth with another bite, grumbling something about needing his beauty rest.

Thirty minutes later, they walked the half-mile down the road toward the Cliff House. They reached a wooden fence along the cliff's edge overlooking the ocean's dark blue waters and beach, which was eerily free of people. To their immediate right, a hill peppered with trees and dirt pathways, led down to the rocky inlet and the concrete ruins of the Sutro Baths.

For a moment, she found it hard to believe she stood there—that her and Baxter's little adventure was real. Somewhere below those waters was a world of magic and mermaids; a world where she was queen. It pained her to think, at any moment, she could wake up from a dream.

"When the tide is low enough, you can see an old shipwreck near that area." Baxter pointed to the right, at a cliff jutting out the furthest.

"Wicked."

"But this beach is not like the ones found in L.A. There are no lifeguards because the waters here are too dangerous to swim in. The rip currents are strong and there are too many rocks."

"No wonder there aren't any people around."

"It was one of the many reasons Adolph Sutro built the indoor swimming pools, or baths, as they were known. They were glorious structures with iron columns and beams encased by large glass panels and an arched roof. If I remember correctly, there was one freshwater pool, and the rest were saltwater, filtered in from the sea using giant turbines. At the time, it was a technological marvel."

He puffed out his chest. "I remember going down the slides at top speed, then racing back around to jump off the springboards. And when you were tired of swimming, you could visit the museum that featured Sutro's art and historical artifacts or listen to bands in the amphitheater."

Baxter's eyes longed for a time and place that no longer existed. Zoe couldn't imagine what it might be like to have Baxter's memory of the grandiose building that once was the Cliff House and the playground of the baths that sat next to it. She thought about how strange it would be to stand somewhere that you had outlasted.

"And now look at it," he said, referring to the ruins. "It is nothing more than vandalized concrete rubble. Fitting, I guess, since they're near the square abomination they call the Cliff House. It truly is a travesty how the city has allowed this entire area, which was once riddled with life and luxury, to become a ghost of its former glory."

"I'm sure, in time, it will be respected for its beauty and history," Zoe said, not knowing what to say to make him feel better. She wanted to reach out to him. To comfort him.

He caught her eye and gave her a hint of a smile. "No matter. Dwelling on it won't help our situation. Let us go down to the beach."

Missing her moment, Zoe matched his pace along the pathway. They passed the entrance of the Cliff House, and followed the windy road down to sea-level. Before trekking across the shore, Zoe kicked off her sneakers and socks and buried her toes in the cool sand. She tipped her chin up and released a heavy sigh. It had been way too long since her last visit to a beach. She stuffed her socks inside her shoes and carried them.

"This is right about the area I found my shells." She stepped next to Baxter, who ran his fingers through the fine grains of sand.

"Not much here now, though." He stood and brushed his hands together. "Since magic has been here once before, there could be some kind of residual energy."

Baxter walked the shoreline, away from the Cliff House, but Zoe couldn't stop staring at the jagged rocks supporting the restaurant. She nibbled her bottom lip. She took a step to follow him, but something from the cliffs called her attention.

"We should search the base of those rocks," she called over her shoulder.

She waited for him, not tearing her eyes away from the cliffs and rocky terrain, looking for the best place to search.

Baxter placed his hand over her shoulder. "Something calling you there?"

She nodded. "Down at the base of the cliff, by the water and rocks."

"I suggest you put your shoes back on," he said. "The rocks can be sharp."

Zoe nodded and did as she was told. "Hey, how come when you touched me just now, that weird electric thing didn't happen between us?"

Baxter scratched at his stubble along his jaw, mulling over her question. "The energy between us must have been an identifier of who you were. Since I have identified you as the mermaid queen, and you've acknowledged that as truth, there's no reason for it anymore. We are free to touch each other." Baxter's eyes widened. "That sounded wildly inappropriate. I meant…"

Zoe chuckled. "I know what you meant. But why didn't it happen before that? We've known each other for a while."

Baxter stuffed his hands insides the pockets of his shorts. "The only explanation I have is that I was a fool and ignored the signs. And only when you were moments from slipping from my grasp, the magical energy presented itself, shocking both of us into the truth, so to speak."

"Makes sense, I guess."

The silence between them was heavy. They were down to thirty days before their death. She wanted to keep probing him for more information, but didn't want to annoy him and waste more time.

Baxter nudged her shoulder. "Go on, out with it."

Zoe brushed her hair behind her ears. "How come I don't wear the necklace? Are you supposed to safeguard it until we find the other pieces?"

Baxter stopped; his forehead creased. "Hmm."

Zoe held her breath.

Did I probe too much?

"You must understand that the necklace and I have been one and the same since the day I put it on. It simply refuses to leave my person." Baxter lifted the necklace to remove it from around his neck, but he could never slip it over his head, as if an invisible shield stopped him. "We are bonded together, you could say."

Zoe took a step closer and narrowed her eyes at the silver chain. Each time he tried, a purple pulse of light shimmered through the links, refusing to leave him. "Literally chained to it. How dreadful."

He nodded and dropped the chain against him once again. His eyes caught hers. His brows rose. "But if you tried..."

"As its rightful owner..."

Baxter dropped to his knees, like he was about to be knighted.

Zoe's limbs tingled. If the necklace stopped her, it probably meant Baxter would be in control of it until all the pieces were found. If she could remove it, it would make her destiny, and their little adventure, that much more real.

Zoe's hand trembled as she reached out and gripped the silver chain with both hands. It warmed against her fingers. Like removing a bandage, she thought a quick movement to take it off would be best. A bright flash of purple light blinded her. She stumbled backward and plopped down in the sand. She rubbed her eyes and blinked away the momentary stars. She held the necklace in her open palm. The silver veins of the stone gleamed in the sunlight. Excited, she looked at Baxter.

He had collapsed.

Kicking up sand, Zoe scampered over to him. She traced her hands down his body, giving him a gentle shake to try and wake him. "Baxter! No, no, no. Please..."

He moaned. His eyes fluttered open.

"Thank goodness," she sighed. "What happened?"

"That was intense," he said, as she offered him a hand to help him sit up. "Like waking from a nightmare that felt very real." He noticed the necklace clutched in Zoe's other hand. "Put it on."

Zoe, once again, nibbled her bottom lip. She half expected she wouldn't be able to take the necklace off of him, and now, he wanted her to wear it. It was dizzying how fast their lives changed from moment to moment.

She locked eyes with him.

"Go on," he said. "It is yours to wear."

She squared her shoulders, dipped her head, and slipped the chain over it. A painful jolt surged through her, stabbing into her chest like a knife. She screamed. The grains of sand scratched against her skin as she collapsed into a full body spasm. Death attacked her, drawing her soul from her body. No, not death. The necklace.

She grappled with it, trying to wrench it off her.

The pain stopped.

Sweat dripped down her neck as a sense of calming peace engulfed her. Baxter hovered over her, touching her forehead with the inside of his wrist.

She lifted the stone off her chest and studied how it glistened and glittered as if alive. "You weren't kidding. That *was* intense."

"Zoe, I had no idea that would happen to you, or I would have warned you."

He offered his hand to help pull her to her feet.

"Why does it hurt like that?" She brushed the sand from her clothes.

Baxter looked around the beach. "I assume it has something to do with the magical energy entering the body."

Zoe eyed Baxter, not loving the concern look plastered on his face. "What's wrong?"

"Checking to see if anyone noticed us. Even though Lucas and his goons are nowhere near, I am sure someone in the magical community felt that surge of energy. We need to hurry and find whatever it is we're looking for."

She nearly forgot about Lucas and his goons. They didn't need an additional concern about someone else in the magical community.

What else is out there?

She shook away that thought, since she didn't have time to think about all the other happenings in the magical world. She continued walking with Baxter, but their pace increased. As soon as they reached the base of the cliff, she pointed to a small alcove just around the bend. "Can we make our way in front of the cliff?"

"Only one way to find out." He waded into the rising tide.

Zoe moved carefully across the rocks. The water reached their knees. The foamy white cap surf crashed into them, knocking them this way and that.

"The waves are too rough to make our way around the cliff and reach the other side. We have to go the long way around if you want to search over there," Baxter shouted over crashing swells.

Damn. It would take even more time to walk back up the hill by the building, just to hike down the other side.

She led the way out of the water. They traipsed across the beach and up the stairs that led them to the main walkway next to the road and then marched up the inclined path.

Half an hour later, they stopped at the entrance of the Cliff House. Even though Zoe was fit, the walk winded her. She completed a few legs stretches as Baxter leaned against the wooden fence and caught his breath.

She led the way to a dirt pathway nestled between trees. The downhill hike passed quickly despite the wind's best efforts to push them off the trail; the pebbles had more success in making Zoe stumble. When they reached the end, they looked around the vicinity. To their left was the beach, with the Cliff House looming over it. To their right were the concrete footings, outlining the structure of the former Sutro Baths. Beyond the ruins, there was an opening of a cave.

"There's a lot to search on this side of the cliff," Zoe said. "Maybe we should split up? If we don't find anything, we can regroup, have dinner, and make another plan."

"Good idea. Use all your senses to search. I will look for something more concrete. Plan to meet back here in an hour."

Zoe jogged down to the small beach area and left Baxter to search the graffiti-covered ruins. Like the other side of the cliff, the sand was fine and had nothing of interest hidden in it. But the tugging sensation in her chest felt stronger than ever. Just offshore, three major rock formations peaked out of the water, the tops of an underwater mountain. A flock of seagulls sat on the furthest, and largest, rock. The birds scattered and squawked as if something spooked them and headed her way. She dropped to her knee and shielded her head, expecting something disgusting to fall on her. Once the ear-splitting squawks died away, she peeked out from under one arm and got up. A sparkling light beamed from the top of the largest rock. She stepped to the side. Moving her head about, waiting for the sun's rays to catch the light again.

Bingo!

CHAPTER 10

ZOE

ZOE SPRINTED INTO THE water and dived into an oncoming wave. The roar deafened her. Even though she was an accomplished swimmer, she struggled against the powerful tide, but made it to the base of the boulder.

She clawed at the algae-covered rock, until she found a good ridge to scale the massive boulder up to the plateau. She wrapped her arms around herself as the wind whipped around her. In the distance, she could see the Golden Gate Bridge; on the shore, she noticed Baxter near the cave opening. The Cliff House teetered over the terrain like a king looming over his nation. She shook her head, not realizing how far away, and dangerous, her swim had been.

Wanting to make her time on the boulder quick, she reeled around, searching for the shimmering object. Her heart hammered as she spotted a pink conch shell nestled in a crevice; it gleamed in the setting sun. She raced across the plateau, lunged forward, and grabbed the shell.

As she lifted it out of the fissure, the rock below her feet fell away.

Like Alice falling through the rabbit hole, Zoe plummeted straight down into a hollow cavern. She splashed into a narrow pool of cool water which shocked her body like electricity. Her lungs constricted. She thrashed against the watery grave and fought to reach the surface. She gasped for the cool air, wiping water from her face.

Her swimmer instincts kicked in, a little too late for her liking, and she floated on her back. She concentrated on her breathing. In for one count, out for two.

Once under control, she examined herself for physical damage. Except for some scrapes, she was fine. She kicked off her shoes and socks and discarded her heavy street clothes, leaving her in her swim suit. She stretched out her legs, reaching to touch the bottom with a toe, but found that a futile effort.

She looked up at the hole where she broke through. It was only a few feet wide and jagged around the edges. She ran her hand over the cavern wall. Smooth and wet, crushing any plans of exiting back through the entrance.

A rumble echoed around her. The ground stirred. Tremors were something that was expected as a Californian, but trapped in an underwater cavern during a quake, no matter its size, was something *nobody* would ever prepare for.

Water sloshed, spitting in her face. Rock fragments rained on her. Panic bubbled inside her, sitting in the back of her throat like acid reflux.

She paddled next to the wall to support herself from being thrust around. And then she saw it: a faint light beneath the water illuminated the conch shell at the bottom of the cavern. Air bubbles floated to the top.

Did the quake open a way out of the cavern?

She counted to five, drew in a deep breath, and dove. She forced her eyes open even though the salt burned them.

She propelled forward, her arms outstretched to reach the shell.

But what do I really expect to happen once I get hold of it? Sprout a tail and be able to conjure magic? Or worse, get pulled into an alternate universe, forever leaving this world?

Her hand hesitated over the shell. Her fingers over its glossy exterior.

Nothing.

The shell no longer called to her; its job done since it led her into the cavern.

But then what keeps tugging at me, wanting my attention?

To the right, the light source pulsed. She paddled closer to an opening large enough for her to fit inside. She needed to swim through it. Something on the other side called to her.

She pushed off the wall to resurface and catch her breath. She wiped the salty water from her eyes and leaned against the rocky wall.

Am I a good enough swimmer to fight against the current and *hold my breath long enough to make it through the tunnel?*

She looked up at the small opening again and wrapped her arms around her chilled body. It wouldn't be long before the sun disappeared, and the temperature of the water plummeted, becoming colder than it already was. The surf crashed against the boulders, muffled, but still loud enough to know there'd be no way anyone could hear her cries for help.

Who knows how long it'll be before Baxter realizes I'm missing and alerts search and rescue?

She'd have to try swimming through the tunnel to reach the open sea and rely on her training to keep her safe.

Wait!

She wasn't just an accomplished swimmer; she was supposed to be a damn mermaid, right?

So why haven't I transformed yet?

She squared her shoulders. Seized the pendant and ran the pad of her thumb across the smooth stone. "Why aren't you working? Come on. Show me who I am."

She dropped the stone against her chest, closed her eyes and floated on to her back. The waves hit the rocks like a metronome. She inhaled the salty air on one beat and exhaled any negativity on the next. Images of her swimming and competing flashed through her mind. Of winning championships. Of breaking records. Of being so good, the local press nicknamed her 'The Chlorine Mermaid.'

Funny how they were right.

She'd always been a mermaid.

Her lips parted. "I believe," she whispered.

A pleasing tingle surged from the stone and trickled across her body, warming her from head to toe.

Her eyelids blinked open.

The corner of her mouth quirked up.

She was no longer a part of the human world.

Chapter 11

BAXTER

BAXTER WATCHED ZOE DARTING across the top of the largest rock formation just offshore. "What the hell?" He waved his arms at her. She needed to notice him and stop whatever reckless thing she was doing. Instead, she picked something up.

Then dropped out of sight.

Baxter took off in a sprint, leaping over the remains of where the longest wall of the Sutro Baths once stood. He reached the sandy beach in less than a minute. Ignoring the constriction in his chest, and the high-pitched ringing in his ears, he splashed into the water, intent on reaching her.

But the current was too strong and the water too cold. Muscle fatigue left his body trembling. He gulped the air and tried to avoid the salty spray from the crashing waves. The unattainable rock loomed in front of him, gloating at his failure.

He cried out her name again, but his voice lost to the echoes of the surf. Cursing, he allowed the waves to push him back to shore, and abandoned his efforts. He crawled across the wet sand and collapsed. The adrenaline spike faded and left him shivering. His head spun, as if he could feel the rotation of the earth. Trying not to vomit, he pinched his eyes closed.

A massive cramp ripped through his calf. He hollered and shot up, flexing his foot, and massaging it until it stopped. He fell back on the sand, wiping away the involuntary tears that drained from his eyes.

What is happening to my body?

He had done some careless things before, but never felt this way. He reached for the stone pendant, like he always did in times when he needed to calm his mind. His stomach knotted at the dark realization that Zoe possessed it. But worse, the magic of the stone no longer protected him.

How many times did I wish away my role as guardian in trade for some sort of normalcy?

Now that he had it, it made him sick. He never imagined that he didn't want his role as a guardian to end. It pained him to admit that even with all the years of research, dead-end leads, and failed attempts to seek out the mermaid queen, he truly loved the adventure.

Without the necklace giving him added strength and immortality, he felt rejected and unworthy from the world he came to love. Just as his journey came to its end, alone and cold on a beach in a city he pushed out of his life for far too long, Zoe's journey just began.

"Get up, dear. Nothing is ending."

Baxter's body stiffened. That voice. He hadn't heard it in decades.

He jolted upright. Rays of golden light beamed from behind his mother like a halo. "Nice of you to finally pay me a visit."

"You haven't needed me."

Baxter scowled. She would only visit him during his lowest times.

"Habibi, did you hear me? Stop sulking. Nothing is ending."

Baxter raked his hands through his hair. "But without the necklace—"

"You are still valuable. Besides, the magic of the stone is with you, perhaps not as strong as when you wore it, but it still protects you. Your guardianship lasts until she is fully restored as the queen, and beyond that, if she desires. Which, by the way she looks at you—"

Baxter's eyes widened. "Mother, please." He averted his attention by plucking off the flecks of sand from his hands.

His mother giggled. "My dear, go after what you want."

Baxter puffed out his chest. Yes, he would do that.

She gave him an adoring gaze as her surrounding light faded. "Go on, now, get up."

Baxter blinked his heavy eyes. "Mother. Do not leave yet—"

"Get up!" she demanded, her voice harsh and cold.

Baxter forced his eyes open.

When did they close?

A figure leaned over him. "Sir, you need to get up."

Baxter was shocked back to reality like a bucket of ice water poured over him. A police officer stood over him, commanding him to get up; not the ghost of his mother.

Clearly, he passed out from exhaustion, but even worse, Zoe hadn't reappeared. "Yes, sir," he mumbled and pushed himself up from the cold sand. His eyes panned the landscape. Swirls of sapphire blue and fuchsia clouds peppered the evening sky. The golden rays of the sun kissed the horizon.

"One of the patrons at the restaurant reported a body on the beach. They thought you were dead."

Baxter folded his arms tightly over his chest, trying to keep the onshore breeze from chilling him to the bone. He noticed the flashing lights at the top of the cliff. Baxter strummed his fingers against his biceps. "Not dead. Merely exhausted from searching for my necklace, an heirloom that I obviously should have not worn while hiking."

The officer—a thick, bald, Latino man—studied Baxter. "You're not from around here, are you?"

Baxter shook his head. "It feels like a lifetime since I was here last."

A woman officer with two male paramedics came over to them. One of the paramedics wrapped a wool blanket around Baxter's shoulders while the other fussed over him.

The woman officer snapped her hands to her hips. "Did you get his license, Dominguez?"

"We were just getting to that," Dominguez said.

The woman turned to Baxter and jutted her hand out. "License."

Baxter clenched his jaw and reached for his wallet. He slapped the wet plastic in her palm. She immediately handed it off to officer Dominguez. "Run it."

Officer Dominguez's eyes flashed at Baxter before he took off hiking back up the hill toward the Cliff House. Baxter wanted to comment on her rudeness, but bit his tongue, knowing he would only make his situation worse.

"We need to get him up to the ambulance for some fluids," the paramedic said to the officer.

Baxter was grateful for the interruption. The officer complied and let the paramedics help him to the top of the cliff. They had him sit inside the ambulance while they cared for him.

Baxter watched Officer Dominguez and the woman bicker before Dominguez padded over to him and handed his license back.

"Here on vacation, professor?"

Baxter grinned. "Research, actually. For my lectures. With some minimal down time. But after tonight, I think I am ready to get back home."

A paramedic peeked around the opened ambulance door. "Would you like us to take you to the hospital?"

Baxter declined, signed some waivers, and exited the ambulance.

The woman officer marched over to them. "Beach closes at sundown, Mr. Baxter. There's a pay phone outside the restaurant to call you a cab. Next time you go hiking, I suggest you come bettered prepared, even bring along a friend."

Dominguez glanced sideways at his partner. "He is staying at Seal Rock Inn, which is less than a mile from here, and on our way back to the station. We can drop him off just to make sure he doesn't stick around here."

His partner gave him an icy stare. "Fine."

Fifteen minutes later, they arrived at the inn. Dominguez opened the back door to the police cruiser and allowed Baxter to exit.

Dominguez leaned into the opened passenger window. "I'm going to escort him inside."

The woman officer groaned. "Just hurry up."

Baxter walked beside Officer Dominguez. "Subtlety is not her strong suit."

"Being demoted to working with a rookie cop tends to make a person that way. Good thing it's only temporary," Dominguez said as they entered the dim-lit lobby.

Baxter eyed the stairs, ready to drag himself to bed, but Dominguez clasped his hand around Baxter's arm. "Before you go," he asked as he ushered Baxter to a quiet corner and flicked off his radio. "Can I ask what you're really up to?"

Baxter cocked his head. "What do you—"

"I can feel the magical energy around you."

Baxter's brows rose. This was most unexpected. He cleared the dryness from his throat and countered. "Who are you?"

Dominguez smirked. "Just your normal Lycan. The question is, who, or what, are you? A faint part of your energy is something I've only ever encountered once before."

Baxter edged closer to him. This was not the first Lycan he met, but it always caught him off guard when someone could place him as a magical entity, while he himself couldn't sense the magic in others. From his experience, the truth was always best in situations like this.

"I am nothing more than a guardian. I truly was searching for a priceless necklace. It belongs to the one I watch over."

Dominguez brows drew together. "A guardian? I thought guardians were myths."

Baxter shook his head. "Well, there is at least one in our modern day."

Dominguez's eyes widened as he stepped back. "Wait. Baxter? The ocean. The Cliff House. ¡Ay, Dios mío! You're *the guardian*, aren't you? The one who must protect the new mermaid queen!"

Baxter nodded, but held his finger up to his mouth, reminding him not to be so loud.

Dominguez drew nearer. "You're a legend around here, man. A story passed down to all magical creatures. We thought it wasn't real, though. But here you are, standing right here in front of me. You have mermaid magic intertwined with your energy. It's not strong, but that's what I felt before."

"Take a breath, Dominguez." Baxter held up his hand to stop the man from babbling.

The officer took a sharp breath and put his hands on his hips.

"There you go," Baxter coached as Dominguez continued breathing and found a chair to slump down into.

Baxter knew there were other types of guardians, and they were rare, but he never encountered a reaction like this.

"I'm sorry for being so surprised," Dominguez said. "Beings who've grown up around here are passionate about the legend of the Pacific Ocean's mermaid queen. Did you know this year marks the hundredth year of her being murdered? Of course, you know that. And she's still gone. What will happen to the magical community if a new king or queen comes in? It could be disastrous. But wait. Is that why you're here? Is she... back?"

Baxter smirked and squatted down next to the officer. "I have only just found her. She is out there, tonight, in the waters. Safe, I hope. She wears her necklace, which made me weak from not having it after all this time. I was trying to reach her, but did not have the strength to swim. But, please, be careful with whom you speak to about this. She has enemies."

Dominguez placed his hand on Baxter's shoulder. "I promise you, friend, she has nothing but support from this community. Is there anything I can do to help you?"

Baxter rose to his feet and considered this for a moment. "Do you know of any mermaids who might be landside?"

Dominguez shook his head and stood. "Sadly, there haven't been any in this region since her death. From what I've heard, they stay away from here like it has the plague. Probably scared of being murdered too. The only reason I could sense the mermaid magic on you is because I met a few near my grandparents' home in Puerto Vallarta when I was a child."

Baxter sighed. "Then, at this moment, no, there is not much you can do for me. What is the earliest I can be at the beach tomorrow?"

"Sunrise. The tide should be low and usually the waters aren't as rough at that time. But if you are going back in, let me send my pack to watch over you, just in case."

"I would appreciate that," Baxter said.

Dominguez flipped opened his notepad and jotted down some information before he handed Baxter the piece of paper.

"This is my personal contact information. Call me if you decide to go out there."

Baxter extended his hand. "Thank you. If, when, she is fully restored as the queen, I am sure she would love to meet you."

A spark flashed across Dominguez's eyes. "That would be an honor, sir. And might I say, it was such a pleasure meeting you."

Baxter dipped his head. "You as well." He made his way back to his room.

He stood in the quiet room, not sure what to do with himself. The rush of emotions over the past several hours exhausted him. But a new light of hope reignited inside him. The magical community, and his mother, both confirmed he still had magic within him, and he needed to tap into it. He would be able to guide Zoe through her journey just as he was destined. But the question was how.

He staggered into the bathroom. The person starting back from the mirror horrified him. He leaned against the counter, getting a closer look at his face. His five o'clock shadow did little to hide his sallow skin or the dark circles under his eyes. He tried to comb through his hair with his fingers, but the ratted knots won that battle.

He peeled the damp and torn clothes off his body, turned the shower on as hot as he could get it, and jumped in; he let the jet streams pound against his sore back. But the guilt of enjoying his blissful peace and knowing Zoe was missing rattled him. Even though he was beyond exhaustion, he had to go back and search for her, screw the police warning. Well, not completely. He liked Dominguez. In his gut, he knew he could trust him and would at least give him a heads up of his plan.

Moments later, he was out of the shower, dried off, and dressed. He sat at the small desk in the living area and picked up the phone. He glanced at the piece of paper on the desk and dialed the number Dominguez had given him.

"Dominguez," the man said on the other end of the phone line.

"This is Baxter. I can't sit around here while Zoe's possibly lost. There are others searching for her. It is my duty to protect her. I just wanted to let you know I'm headed back to the beach, despite the warning of it being closed."

Dominguez chuckled. "I was wondering how long it was going to take you to head back there. I don't blame you. But you're drained. And only one person. Like I said, I have a pack. Let me send them out to search and keep an eye out for anyone who might cause harm. You, meanwhile, need to get some rest. You can return to the beach tomorrow morning at sunrise, as planned."

Baxter sighed. In his heart, he knew she was strong and would be okay, even in an unknown world. But it made him feel even better knowing there was a team of people watching out for her while he rested. "There are no words to express how appreciative I am of that offer. If anything happens, specifically, if anyone with British accents should show up, promise your pack will alert me immediately."

"You have my word."

Chapter 12

ZOE

ZOE'S DESIRE TO CELEBRATE her eighteenth birthday by bungee jumping one-hundred feet off of California's famous Bridge to Nowhere, a 1936 arch-style bridge in the San Gabriel Mountains, had been the most heart-racing and adrenaline-inducing moment of her life.

But giving up all control and plunging toward a rushing river was *nothing* compared to the surge of an ancient, magical energy awakening throughout her body.

The cool pool of water now engulfed her like a warm, fuzzy blanket straight out of the dryer. The pungent earthy odor emitting from the algae plastered along the rocky enclosure, was a smell she recognized; peacefulness coursed through her. It may have been a long and arduous trip, but she knew she was home. But there was only one thing she wanted to see.

For stability, she leaned her back against the murky green rocks and lifted her lower body out of the water. Something between a snort and a laugh escaped her mouth as she drank in the sight of her true form. Water rained off her fluke as she lifted it out of the water. The U-shape scales of her elongated tail looked like a watercolor painting with lighter hues of lavender and periwinkle seamlessly blended with darker tones of amethyst and eggplant. Metallic silver peppered the various shades of purple and glimmered in the dark cavern.

She lowered her gorgeous tail and stretched, feeling the tips of her fluke scrape across the bottom of the cavern. She was a good three to four feet longer than her human form.

Zoe draped her hair over her bare chest. Before people identified her as the cheater who took PEDs, she was known as the swimmer with the larger-than-normal chest size. Being comfortable in her own skin was a luxury she never felt.

Until now.

Zoe's brow furrowed.

What am I doing? Embrace who you are now, not the person you were.

She flung her locks behind her shoulders and straightened her back. Confidence was not some magical power to gain. It was a state of mind.

She ran her elongated fingers across the line of scales wrapping around her torso; the skin smooth instead of ridged. The scales on her torso were like tattoos, an image stamped onto her skin. Like an S-shape, the tattoo scales traveled from her waist up her right side, over her chest like a tube top, and around her left bicep. A line of scales traced upon her shoulder blade up toward her neck. She swept her fingers behind her ears and found tiny slits for her gills, then felt her face, but nothing seemed different or out of place. She hooked a thick piece of her hair around her finger and examined the glistening hues of purple entwined amongst the black strands. Never in her life did she want to look into a mirror more than she did now.

Without any hesitation, she dove into the water and torpedoed herself through the small passageway, easily slicing through the canal of water and the undertow that batted against the rocky terrain. Breathing was simple, just as if she were on land; except, every once in a while, tiny bubbles trickled from the corner of her mouth, tickling her lips. Swimming came naturally and she inherently knew how to maneuver herself.

She pushed forward and entered the widespread ocean, not truly surprised that the underwater world looked and behaved differently than what her human eyes experienced. She perched herself onto a slate-blue rock, drinking in the sight in front of her. In her new world, visibility wasn't cloudy; she could see into the far-off distance. Everything was painted in soft, yet vibrant colors, as if the ocean world had been digitally edited with the latest software giving the underwater water a look of realism with a dash of an animated illustration.

Zoe watched a cluster of ruby-red crabs creep over their rocks and through the shimmering, golden sand. An array of orange Bat Stars gripped the reef as a shoal of yellow angelfish darted around her and ducked behind some pink-and-aqua-colored coral. In the distance, a forest of kelp danced in the current.

"Stunning view, yes?"

Zoe shrieked, not expecting to hear a voice, never mind a voice so clear that it sounded as if she had been on land. A vanilla-blonde mermaid with a bubble-gum-pink tail snaked out from behind the coral.

"Didn't mean to frighten you," the mermaid replied with what sounded like a hint of an Irish accent. She glided closer and toyed with the spikes of a reddish crown-of-thorns sea star who comfortably rested upon a bed of coral.

Zoe willed herself to say something, but her slack jaw and unblinking eyes would do nothing but scrutinize over every aspect of the creature in front of her.

The pink mermaid's fluke wasn't as wide as Zoe's. It was angular, unlike Zoe's flowing, crescent shape. She had thin, stringy-like dorsal fins jutting out from each side of her hips and sported diamond-shaped scales down the length of her tail.

Her face was heart-shaped, and she had bright blue doe-eyes with full rose-colored lips. Pink glittery highlights twisted through an elaborate braid on one side of her head with the rest of her locks floating freely behind her. On her shoulder, near her collarbone, was a small black tattoo of a raven with pink eyes perched upon a delicately drawn symbol of a double spiral. Unlike Zoe, she wore a strapless bathing suit top that had a random pattern of white hibiscus flowers upon a fuchsia-colored background.

Why does this mermaid get to wear a bikini top, and I don't?
Zoe shook her head.

Of all the things you ask in your first experience with a mermaid, how could fashion, something you've never cared about as a mortal being, be a priority?

A primitive, guttural sound escaped Zoe's mouth in an attempt to say something intelligent.

"Transforming into a mermaid and keeping your swimsuit top on is easy," the woman replied, as if she had heard Zoe's personal thoughts. "Mermaids like to enjoy the conveniences of modern times, just as Landwalkers."

"Landwalkers?" Tiny bubbles escaped Zoe's mouth. She found the sensation of talking underwater and not having water fill her mouth or sound distorted odd.

How will I ever get used to this?

The pink mermaid swam near her and ran her slender fingers through Zoe's hair. A strange tickling sensation swept across the back of her neck.

"You'll get used to speaking underwater, don't worry, lass."

Zoe's brows knitted together, and she narrowed her eyes. "How... how did you do that?"

The mermaid fluttered around Zoe. "The different colored mermaids each have their own specialty. Pink-Tails, like me, can read minds."

"Seems like an invasion of privacy."

"My apologies for listening, but your emotions are so charged that your thoughts are loud and clear, and I couldn't help it. We usually use our powers on enemies, since not everyone is an ally. Only highly skilled Tails can block us, which is something you will do in time. But don't worry, I'm the only pure-colored Pink-Tail in your kingdom, which means I am the only one with the power strong enough to invade your thoughts. Mixed-tails would need to use a hypnotic spell to read your mind."

Zoe leaned against a nearby cluster of rocks. Her mind reeled from the amount of information spewed at her.

Enemies? Mixed colors? Spells?

Not knowing where to start, she simply asked, "Tails?"

"You, Landwalkers—humans—call us all mermaids or sirens. But we refer to ourselves as Tails."

"Oh."

"We're considered Pacific-Tails," the mermaid continued, clearly not noticing the anxiety of information overload in Zoe's awkward response. "But that's a general term. There are several kingdoms within the Pacific, much like the fifty states which make up the United States of America. Specifically, our realm is the Northeast Pacific."

Zoe nodded, trying to follow along as the other mermaid began ticking off names.

"Then there are the Atlantic-Tails, who, for your understanding, would be equivalent to Europeans. The Arctic-Tails, or the out-of-touch Tails, as I like to call them. The Freshwater-Tails—"

"I get it, I get it," Zoe said, putting her hand up to cease the ramblings. She massaged her forehead, unsuccessfully rubbing out the overwhelming thoughts flooding into her mind.

How many kingdoms made up the Pacific Ocean and other locations? How many colors and variations of Tails are out there? Which type of specialty magic did each of them have? What enemies do you face?

A sharp pain seared the side of her temple, and she winced.

The beautiful creature paddled over to Zoe, disrupting her chaotic thoughts. She bowed her head and sat on the rock next to her. She rested her hands in her lap, fluttered the tip of her fluke in the water, and stared out across the ocean as if admiring a sunrise.

The silence of the moment gave Zoe a chance to breathe, releasing the tightness in her chest and jaw. But it wasn't exactly silent. Like the rumblings of a city, Zoe heard the underwater world come alive. Murmurings of the different species of animals, along with the roar of waves taking shape, and the far-off sound of boat engines, sounded like a beautifully composed symphony of everyday life beneath the sea. Taking a cue from the mermaid next to her, Zoe nestled herself on the rock and listened; she meditated into a calm and peaceful state.

Finally, although she had no idea how much time it took, Zoe was in the correct mindset to receive a bundle of new information. She pictured herself in the lecture hall with Baxter up front, presenting a new topic. She was always eager to learn more, and this situation wasn't all that different. "What does the color of my tail represent?"

The blonde woman cocked her head as she studied Zoe, like she was unsure what type of answer to give. "Royalty," she finally stated.

Zoe shifted her position; she didn't expect that answer. She lifted a brow and imagined herself waving like a fool during a royal mermaid parade and wondered if royalty in the mermaid world was as pompous as the ones found on land. "Please go on," she encouraged.

A ghost of a grin danced across the pink mermaid's lips as she perked up, excited to tell Zoe all she knew. "Purple-Tails are the rarest of our kind. Some are even the oldest Tails to roam the seas. But Purple-Tails don't have a singular specialty of magic like the other colors. We all can do basic magic like casting simple spells and curses, but our most powerful magical trait is color based. Purple-Tails inhibit all of them, naturally making them the worthy ones to rule the oceans."

Zoe's brows furrowed as she twirled a piece of her hair around her finger, absorbing the information.

What is the magic that each color-tail possessed? How will I remember all of this?

Another sharp pain pierced her temple.

"You're letting your thoughts run away again."

Zoe blinked, snapping her out of her trance.

"Sorry. You were saying I'll be able to perform the magic of all the colors, so that means I will read minds like you?"

"Eventually, yes. And control the light and darkness like White-Tails, and have amazing healing powers like Blue-Tails, and so-on."

Zoe chewed on her lower lip. That seemed like an awful lot of power for one being, which could be a dangerous line to walk. History proved that possessing too much power usually ended badly; something about having great powers and responsibility echoed through her mind.

Perhaps that's why the previous mermaid queen had been murdered.

What if this pink mermaid knows more than she's telling?

Zoe sure would love inside *her* mind.

The pink mermaid tossed her hair behind her shoulders. A preserved, light-pink water lily hung on a thin gold chain around her slender neck. The pink mermaid smirked. "And you can stop thinking of me as the 'pink mermaid,' lass. I should've introduced myself properly, but I was so excited to talk with you." The mermaid slipped off the rock and gave Zoe a slight bow. "I'm Aislinn. Your second-in-command."

"Pleasure to meet you, *Ash-lynn*," Zoe said, emphasizing the mermaid's name in order to pronounce it correctly.

Aislinn nodded. "Aislinn, yes. It's Irish and means vision. Once upon a time, you once knew me as Orla. Perhaps that name is more familiar to you?"

Zoe shook her head. Since the moment Baxter claimed she was a mermaid, nothing in her life felt familiar. "Your name *used* to be Orla? Do you change it often?"

Aislinn chuckled. "Not usually. We try to keep up with trends in the mortal world to blend in easier while on land. Our names often reflect our personality, or the magic we specialize in, or even a geographical region we are attached to. You were once known as Sirena, which meant sea goddess. In the modern era, though, we called you Melantha."

Zoe stiffened. Melantha. *That* was a familiar name. "What does Melantha mean?"

Aislinn paused and gave her a tight-lipped smile. "Dark Flower."

Zoe clutched the necklace, but before she could inquire anything more, Aislinn rushed to her side and eagerly gripped Zoe's hands in hers. "Never mind the past. What do we call you now?"

"Zoe." She cleared her throat and continued. "It means life."

Aislinn smiled. Her pearl white teeth glimmered in the blue waters. "How fitting! Well, Zoe, are you ready to meet your closest advisors before your time as a Tail expires?"

"Expires?"

Aislinn nodded and gently pulled her through the water, still holding her hand. "Whenever a piece of your pendant is found, your time, along with your magic, increases. I estimate that you have until sunrise before you must return to land."

What if I am deep underwater and suddenly my legs appear?

She pushed the thought out of her mind and concentrated on the other information Aislinn mentioned. "The pendants. Do you know where the others are? How do I find them?"

Aislinn shook her head. "No one knows where the other pieces are, but I know that the broken pieces will always try to be reunited with the king or queen. I'm sure you will be led to them somehow. Did Bennett not tell you this?"

Zoe stopped swimming; her muscles tightened. "You know Baxter?"

Aislinn giggled. "Everyone knows of the guardian, silly." Aislinn twirled in the water and faced Zoe. "As your second-in-command, I tried helping him locate you, desperate for your return. A long time ago, I buried enchanted seashells up and down the coastline of our realm, hoping they would act like a beacon for the reincarnated queen. And it worked. Don't you remember finding those shells on the beach when you were a child?"

If Zoe had legs, she would've collapsed. From the synchronicities of it all.

Aislinn crept forward. "As soon as you touched the first one, it activated, alerting me to your presence. I hurried inland to see you, but you were so young, and clearly not ready to be queen." Aislinn lowered her chin. "I could never tell him who you were. A magical energy always stopped me anytime I tried to contact or talk to him. Apparently, one of the many outdated mermaid laws is that Tails aren't allowed to give direct help to guardians."

Zoe chewed on this bit of new information. Something had always woven her life into the world of mermaids. She almost felt comforted knowing it was Aislinn watching her the day she found the shells and not some stranger who wanted to kidnap her, like she once believed. She briefly wondered about the pink conch shell she grabbed before dropping into the cavern.

Did Aislinn plant that, too?

"I did," Aislinn replied. "But a very long time ago. As soon as the shell felt your energy, the magic activated, which is why you were drawn to it. Its energy surged through to me, so I quickly swam to the location of the shell to greet you."

Aislinn reached for Zoe's hand again. "I think it's time for the others to meet you, too."

Zoe reached out, ready to enter her new world.

Chapter 13

Zoe

Zoe and Aislinn sailed through the water, weaving through kelp until they came upon an underwater mountain. At the base of the rocky terrain, a massive sunken ship, the kind associated with pirates, lay in its grave. The sharp aroma of algae floated through the water the way a scented candle filled a room. Wood splintered out from a substantial hole in the hull. Several broken masts pointed upward like deadly spears. Pockets of seaweed and coral climbed upon the smaller remains scattered about.

A merman with a green-colored tail swam up to them. He had short, dirty-blond hair and muscles that could challenge any linebacker in the NFL. Almost directly over his heart was a tattoo of an intricate-looking sword and shield. He swung a coral branch out to his side like a sword, stopping the stingray behind him like a well-trained pet. "Aislinn, we are ready for you."

"Thank you, Ewalt," Aislinn said.

Ewalt bowed his head and swam off, with the stingrays fast behind him. Zoe noticed the different hues of his tail weren't as vibrant as Aislinn's or hers.

Aislinn motioned for Zoe to follow her toward the hole in the hull, "Green-Tails enforce laws and can weaken other's magic, much like the police on land."

Guarding the entrance was another merman, just as fit as Ewalt. He sported a red tail and shaggy brown hair with a haven't-shaved-in-a-few-days scruffy beard. Like Ewalt, his tail seemed dull, and Zoe concluded that women probably had more vibrant tails than their male counterparts.

A shadow of contempt darkened Aislinn's visage. "Murdock," she growled.

Murdock didn't hide his icy contempt.

Every society suffered from drama and conflict, but the two shared a sordid past. That much was clear.

Curious.

"I'm Zoe," she said to break the awkward silence.

Murdock's gaze shifted to hers. "It's a pleasure to meet you," he said in a gravelly, baritone voice.

Aislinn leaned into Zoe. "Red-Tails are sea-warriors and can cause physical pain to any being. Come on."

Aislinn tried to tug Zoe past him, but Murdock reached out to shake Zoe's hand.

Zoe beamed and grasped his hand. "Pleasure is—" she froze as she noticed the tattoo on his forearm. It was a sword stabbing into reddish-orange flames and had a raven perched upon the hilt, with Celtic markings engraved along the blade.

The tattoo was exactly like the one Lucas had on his arm.

Murdock cocked his head. "Interested in tattoos?"

Zoe swallowed. A familiar rush of trepidation surged through her as she compared Murdock to the betrayal of her swim team. Did he really work for Lucas and his goons? How would she know who to trust? "No, sorry. I feel like I've seen it before, is all. I notice others have tattoos too. They are like what, exactly?"

"Well," Murdock began, "the tattoos—"

"She doesn't have time for that lesson, Murdock," Aislinn spat. She gripped Zoe's wrist and yanked her past the red-tail.

"Sorry," Aislinn said as they entered the wreckage. "But your time is valuable and small logistics like that can be explained later."

Zoe followed her through the dilapidated ship and entered an open area that used to be the deck. Against the dark wood and earthy tones of the algae was a rainbow of color. Mermaids and merman of all different hues milled about. Some of them tinkered with found treasures, or gossiped in a corner while others munched on something that looked like an underwater eggroll.

A ribbon of wonder twirled inside Zoe. This is what Dorothy probably felt the first time she saw the beautiful colors of Oz, or how Bilbo felt the first time he walked into the mines and encountered Smaug.

Next to her, Aislinn snapped. Pink magic rained upon the crowd like tiny fireflies. The group of mermaids immediately stopped their chatter and faced them, smiling perfect, beautiful smiles. They waited quietly, as if a spotlight illuminated a stage. Showtime.

"It is my pleasure to introduce Zoe, our reincarnated queen," Aislinn announced.

Emotion welled in Zoe's throat. She hated being put on the spot.

All at once, the group bowed, an unnecessary action that made Zoe even more uncomfortable.

Being captain of a small swim team and giving motivational speeches was one thing, but being in front of magical creatures in an unknown setting was entirely different. Not sure what a re-incarnated mermaid queen was to do next, Zoe lifted her right arm and waved. "Hey there."

The mermaids beamed, ready to explode from excitement. Thankfully, Aislinn held her hand up, a signal for them not to rush at her. She faced Zoe. "I will continue to reign until you are fully restored. I have some duties I must attend, so I will be leaving."

"What?" She didn't want Aislinn to go. She was her anchor, steadying her in the new reality.

As if Aislinn read her thoughts again, she placed one hand on Zoe's shoulder and said, "Don't worry, lass. Only a few of them will come talk to you today. They will see that you are comfortable and return you to shore safely. I know this is a lot to take in, but I believe you will do just fine without me. We will meet again soon."

"Thank you."

Aislinn zipped away as a charismatic mermaid somersaulted through the water and wrapped Zoe in a crushing hug.

"I'm Farah." She released Zoe from her grip. Without a pause, she continued. "Do you remember me? I know it's been so long, and you've only found your way back to us, but if you don't, that's okay."

Just like the yellow hues of her tail, this mermaid was a ray of happy sunshine and perhaps a little too chipper for Zoe's liking. "I teach the young Tails how to live in our world and maneuver among Landwalkers. I can also sense the magic other magical creatures have—"

"Slow down, Farah," a teenage-looking mermaid said, pushing Farah to the side with her stark white tail with red spiraling through it like a candy-cane. "Give her some room to breathe."

The teen winked her blue doe-eyes at Zoe, showcasing her sparkly red shadow painted on her lids. She swam forward and shoved a green sushi-like roll into Zoe's hand.

"I'm Callista. Kelp rolls are a fav' of the Tails and are de-lish. Especially with Campbell Cove's clam meat. The. Best. Ever."

Zoe examined it. Sniffed it. The bile in her stomach churned like it did when she passed the seafood counter at the grocery store. She would not be eating.

Callista picked it out of her hand. "Maybe another time." She gobbled it down in one bite.

An aquamarine mermaid with wild strawberry-red hair and emerald-green eyes swept behind Callista and placed her hand on the young mermaid's shoulder. "Zoe will fully immerse herself in our world in good time, Callista."

Callista shrugged a shoulder and retreated. She plopped on top of a wooden barrel and pulled out another kelp roll from a small satchel tied around her waist.

"Pardon our excitement," the aquamarine mermaid said. "Your presence is overdue. I'm Sefarina."

Sefarina reminded Zoe of her mother. She had an air of formality about her, but also radiated calmness and warmth.

"It's okay. I'm excited too, but I'm not a hoity-toity, fragile little princess either," Zoe said. "I can handle all of this."

"You are a queen, not a princess," Serafina stated.

Callista smacked Sefarina's tail with her hand. "Get a clue, 'Rina. She's saying she isn't all formal and stuffy."

Zoe chuckled, as a tight-lipped smile plastered across Sefarina's face. "Well, if that's the case, do you mind if we go somewhere and I show you something? We still have some time before you need to return."

Before Zoe could answer, Callista pushed off the barrel and clasped her hands together. "Sea-trip!" She flicked her candy-cane colored tail around. In her excitement, a jet of red energy whizzed out from the tip of her tail, hitting Zoe in the face.

Zoe shrieked, grabbed at her face, and fell backward into the wooden hull. Blood trailed from her nose, floating through the water. She blinked, trying to focus.

"Hita," Sefarina cried out, turning to look over her shoulder. "Help!"

Zoe strained to see past Sefarina. From the mass of mermaids, a mermaid with cinnamon-colored skin a beautiful hue of cerulean-blue on her tail paddled over to them. She sported a gold nose piercing, several dangling necklaces, and a delicate golden hip chain.

"I'm so sorry," Callista repeated several times as she looked over Sefarina's shoulder to check on Zoe.

Hita waved her hand in front of Zoe's face, jingling her gold bangles. Blue sparks of light trickled out from her palm, erasing any pain she felt. "Accidents happen with Callista," Hita explained. "Poor darling means no harm. Her magic is unstable because she's young and has a mixed-tail."

Zoe caught the teen's worried eye. "It's okay, Callista. I'm fine."

Hita and Sefarina let Callista squeeze by them to sit next to Zoe.

Zoe gently touched her face. No more pain. No swelling. "Magic is amazing."

"Indeed, it can be," Hita said.

"When it works." Callista wrapped her arms around herself.

Strange how I want to console the teen when I was the one hurt.

Zoe patted Callista on the shoulder.

Screams of terror echoed through the water. Zoe and Callista stiffened as Ewalt and Murdock swam into the deck area.

"Makos!" they both shouted, sending the rainbow of colorful mermaids scattering in all different directions.

"They smelled Zoe's blood," Callista shouted.

Zoe scowled. "Why are you panicking over sharks? If we don't provoke them—"

Sefarina latched her hand around Zoe's wrist and pulled her through the water. "Sharks and Tails don't mix well. It's like humans with bears, or moose, or any other animal they shouldn't be challenging."

"Our blood is richer than humans and they can smell it from miles away and are savage in trying to get a taste of it," Hita said as she swam next to Sefarina.

The pointy noses of two sharks rammed through a damaged wall and snapped their jaws at anything that moved. Zoe screamed and reactively shielded her eyes before someone tugged her away. "Snap out some magic and get rid of them!"

"We can't!" Sefarina exclaimed as she tried to help Hita through an old porthole.

"Get Zoe out of here first," Hita shouted at Sefarina as she struggled to fit through the small opening.

There was no way Zoe would leave her behind. She pulled at Hita's other arm, freeing her from the porthole, but not without damage. Blood trickled out of her side where the jagged wood dug into her. A shark charged at them.

"Go!" Hita screamed and darted away, seeking cover behind Murdock and a small army of red-tail warriors.

Sefarina laced hands with Zoe. Aquamarine colored magic danced around their connection, binding Zoe to Sefarina. A whirlpool of water whipped around them, spinning them upward into an underwater waterspout. Zoe couldn't breathe; the wind knocked out of her. But when she thought she would succumb to her death, the agonizing suffocation and wall of water were gone.

"What happened?" Zoe looked around, trying to find others. But they were alone, nestled on a sandy shoal. Above, Zoe could see the surface water. "Where are we? Why did we leave them?"

"It's my duty to keep you safe above anyone else," Sefarina explained. "Murdock and Ewalt will take care of everything. Trust me, Zoe. Hita, Callista, and the others will be okay."

Zoe's hands trembled as the rush of adrenaline faded.

Is Sefarina telling the truth, or is she just trying to make me feel better? How could something so terrible happen so fast?

"Those sharks were awful. What if they kill someone?"

Sefarina sighed. "It's possible, but we usually get away from them. Besides, there are worse creatures to worry about."

Zoe shuddered. The underwater world was much more dangerous than she imagined, and she didn't want to encounter anything worse than sharks anytime soon. She looked around at her new surroundings, still confused. "How did we get here without swimming?"

"Aquamarine-Tails can translocate across great distances in seconds."

Zoe grunted. "Sounds like teleportation."

"Similar, yes."

Zoe gave Sefarina a once-over. The beautiful aqua blues on her tail dulled as patches of gray appeared. Her skin seemed sallow, and she had dark, puffy circles forming beneath her eyes.

Zoe scooted next to her. "You feelin' okay?"

"Oh, that?" Sefarina gestured to the gray patches. "It's what happens when Tails lose their magic."

Zoe sighed. "So, it is true, then. Baxter said it was rumored that you all were losing your magic because you had no leader, and time was quickly running out. Is... is that why some Tails I met today seemed to have dull-looking colors?"

"Yes. And it's why the majority of the mixed-tail community has abandoned our realm and become permanent Landwalkers. Their magic was never as strong as pure-tails, and they couldn't survive anymore. It's why Callista's magic is unstable."

"What can I do to help?"

Sefarina shook her head. "Right now? Nothing. Eventually, 1 will rejuvenate with some rest, but we need to return you to shore before you transform back into your human form."

Before Zoe insisted Sefarina rest immediately, the mermaid pushed off the sand, motioned for Zoe to follow, and swam toward the surface. Cool air brushed Zoe's face as soon as she poked her head out of the water. Tiny pricks tickled the sides of her neck and before Zoe could question it, she noticed the small gills on Sefarina were gone. She inhaled and filled her lungs with the crisp air of the night sky.

The reflection of the moon illuminated the mirror-like water, mesmerizing Zoe as she could finally see her reflection. Her violet-blue eyes had always been striking, but now they were simply hypnotic. Shimmering lilac eye shadow brushed on her lid with a plum-colored winged liner. Purple hues of different-sized dots stippled across her lower lash line and feathered out from the corner, imitating tiny bubbles dancing across the side of her face. Her cheeks had a subtle rose color with tiny scales peppering her cheeks.

Sefarina nudged Zoe, and she pulled her eyes away from herself. "You know, there is a reason why humans usually portray mermaids as vain creatures who stare at themselves all day." Sefarina smirked and removed a teal flower pinning up the side of her red hair. Under the flower were the teeth of a comb. She ran the comb through a lock of her wet hair. Within seconds, the lock became dry and full of bounce. "But you must be careful; your beauty can be deadly to others."

Zoe wasn't sure what that warning meant. She didn't have the desire to ask, though. For the moment, she could not stop staring in awe as Sefarina continued combing her entire mane until it looked as if she stepped out of a salon.

Sefarina paddled behind Zoe and slid the comb through her tangled strands. "I always thought mermaids were myths," Zoe said. She closed her eyes and enjoyed the dreamy relaxation she felt anytime someone brushed her hair.

Sefarina placed her hands on Zoe's shoulders and leaned into her ear. "Myths grow from truth."

A thin smile traversed her lips as she thanked Sefarina.

As Sefarina replaced her flower in her hair, her eyes fell onto the purple-and-silver stone pendant around Zoe's neck. "You know," Sefarina purred, "old mer-tales say that there's writing on the stones that the kings and queens wear."

Sefarina shifted her eyes to Zoe's, which blazed with such ferocity that it made Zoe shudder. "But that's probably a myth," Sefarina mused and swam past Zoe.

Sefarina appeared to be a mermaid who followed all the rules, but really, Sefarina was a sneaky little redhead with an appetite for loopholes. She couldn't wait to return to Baxter and tell him all she found out.

"Swim back to the beach and allow the waves to wash you ashore," Sefarina said as they cut through the water. Imagine yourself in your human form, clothed of course, and you'll transform back. When you enter the ocean and want to be in your mermaid form, relax your thoughts, imagine yourself as one, and let the magic of your pendant engulf you. But don't forget about your limited time. The stone will vibrate when you have only a few minutes left and become more intense the less time you have."

Zoe nodded. She was relieved to know she had a warning system and wouldn't turn into a human hundreds of feet under the water. "Thanks. Get some rest. I'll see you soon."

Sefarina winked at her before dipping below the water and leaving Zoe to make her way back alone. As she washed onto the beach, she gripped the pendant and concentrated on changing back. Before long, the stone warmed in her palm and jets of purple lights swirled around her body. Within seconds, she was human again, wearing her swimsuit once more.

She stood on wobbly legs and hugged herself, protecting her not only from the early morning's cool air that chilled her body, but from the loneliness she felt. She noticed a cliff jutting out of the water. Perched on the edge was the immense structure of the Cliff House.

Her stomach grumbled. At least she was close to the inn and not somewhere lost along the Pacific coastline. As she marched across the beach toward the street, she held onto the thought that Baxter was patiently waiting for her return and hadn't called the cavalry in search of her.

CHAPTER 14
BAXTER

BAXTER GROANED. HIS HEAD throbbed as if he suffered from a hangover. He opened his eyes, slow, adjusting to the early morning light streaming in through the sheer curtains. *Bang, bang, bang.* Baxter propelled himself out of bed. His heart hammered in his chest. He padded over to the door, expecting Dominguez, or someone from his pack. He wrenched opened the door.

Zoe.

Without a thought, he wrapped her in his arms, crushing her to his chest.

She gripped onto him, matching his same intensity.

He looked over her shoulder. Dominguez gave him a subtle nod and left them alone.

"I'm starving," she said. "And freezing."

Baxter shuffled her inside and steered her toward the shower. Once she was done, she gobbled up the remaining goodies from Howard and Annette while recounting her adventure. Baxter let her talk with minimal interruption, imagining all that she saw and experienced. Once she finished, she curled up on the bed and fell asleep. Not wanting to leave her presence, Baxter laid down next to her, staying above the covers, and decided they would return to Los Angeles as soon as possible.

Forty-eight hours later, they arrived at Zoe's house. Without needing to be convinced, she gathered some belongings from her home in order to semi-move into Baxter's house. She said it was for convenience and safety, but Baxter had a feeling she didn't want to be away from him anymore than he wanted to be away from her.

Piles of leather-bound books and loose papers littered Baxter's kitchen as they spent another two days scouring through every journal, relic, and file that he collected over the decades. They hadn't found a clue to aid them in their quest. He sighed. There wasn't much left to search.

Zoe sat at the dining room table, practically hidden behind stacks of journals. "What's this?" She retrieved a worn, folded parchment from between a stack of journals.

Baxter eyed the object. "Incredible. I haven't seen that in decades. In fact, I completely forgot about it." With tender care, he took the parchment from her hands, unfolded it, careful of the frayed edges, and set it on the black granite countertop of the kitchen island.

Inked like an illustrated page out of a fantasy novel, the map was of the world, split into two parts: the Pacific Ocean and the Atlantic Ocean. Various drawings of ships, krakens, mermaids, and other sea creatures were depicted in the oceans, whereas other mystical beings, including unicorns, djinn, and witches, were drawn on the landmasses.

The bottom-left of the map, near New Zealand, featured a half circle cartouche. A mermaid with a pink tail and a crown made of kelp, coral, shells, and a starfish were pinned in her hair. She sat on a boulder overlooking the horizon. In the rays of the sun, dusted with gold leaf, were the words *Seven Realms of the Pacific.* The Atlantic-side of the map had a similar cartouche. A blue-tailed mermaid laid across a rock, trailing her hand through the waves. Behind her was the moon with the words *Six Realms of the Atlantic.*

Zoe's eyes scrutinized the intricate drawing. "This is *so* not your typical antique world map."

Baxter swayed on his feet, remembering why he had buried the map with his journals. It had been right before he dedicated his time as a tenured professor at USC. He felt shameful for taking a break on his quest and tucked away anything related to it.

"Where did you get this?" Zoe leaned over it and surveyed it carefully.

"A woman who had an unhealthy obsession with mermaids gave it to me. She never told me where she acquired it, though. I half suspect she made it herself."

Zoe let out a low whistle. "That's some hobby. I assume she was a magical being if she knew this much about mermaids."

"Incredibly so, yes."

Zoe looked up. "If she was that obsessed, why did she give it to you?"

"I asked for it, but I presume she gave it to me for her own selfish reasons."

"Sounds like there's a story there."

Baxter cursed under his breath and scowled. There was a story, all right. But not only did they not have the time for it, discussing *her* was not something he was keen on. "For another day, perhaps."

Zoe held her chin high and shrugged a shoulder. "So where is she? Do you think she can help?"

Baxter glanced away as he fidgeted with the silver ring on his right hand. They weren't desperate enough for *her* help.

Zoe smacked her forehead. "I'm such an idiot."

Baxter straightened. "What do you mean?"

"She's not alive anymore, is she?"

Baxter let out a bitter laugh and strummed his fingers on the granite countertop. "Even if she was, I wouldn't have anything to offer her in exchange for her help."

Baxter shifted his attention back to the map. Dashed lines divided the Pacific into the seven different realms, much like a spoke and wheel design, with Hawaii being the center hub. Zoe touched the trident jutting out of the water in the Lively North to East realm. Fixated on it. "Feel like I've seen this before... weird..."

Baxter eyed the rest of the map. The cartographer split the Atlantic Ocean down the middle with the Mid-Atlantic Ridge separating the east and west halves, creating six realms. He noticed major lakes and rivers labeled with F.T.

"Look at this," Zoe ran her finger along the dashed lines that spanned from the Aleutian Islands near Alaska, straight down to Hawaii, and east toward Panama. "Now I get what Aislinn meant when she said our realm was just a small section of the Pacific."

Baxter leaned in to read the tiny script written in the triangular shape of her realm.

Free-reign circa 633

Pallas 633-1220

Sirena 1220-1724 Melantha 1724-1899

"Aislinn said that Sirena had simply changed her name, so it makes sense that she and Melantha are on the same line. I wonder what happened to Pallas, though."

Baxter shrugged his shoulder.

"Melantha's much older than I thought." She tilted her head to the side. "So why, after all that time, was she killed? Do you think she was caught in the wrong place at the wrong time?"

Baxter straightened and ran his fingers through his hair. "No. She was purposely murdered. That much I am positive about."

Zoe crossed her arms over her chest. "What makes you so sure?"

Baxter sighed. Their journey as queen and guardian was much more weaved together than he originally admitted. Not wanting to overwhelm her with too much information, he had been selective in what he shared, but she was ready for the next piece of the puzzle.

He slid the barstool out from under the island countertop and motioned for Zoe to do the same. With a determined look, she sat and faced him, their knees brushing up against each other.

"There is one decree that most, if not all, magical communities and creatures adhere to. When someone from the magical world is blatantly murdered, there is a sliver of time, right before absolute death, where they can recite the guardian's spell. If all goes well, they will be reincarnated, and either lead a new life, avenge their death, or save their realm, depending on their need. But most do not enact the spell."

Baxter reached over to Zoe and hooked the silver chain of the dangling necklace around his finger, running the pad of his thumb over the stone. He had a love-hate relationship with the damn necklace, but the stone's smooth texture always comforted him.

Zoe locked eyes with him. "Why *wouldn't* anyone want to cast the spell if their life was being ripped away?"

Baxter studied her for a moment, then dropped his hands in his lap and sat back. "Because of the cost of it."

Her brow lifted. "What cost?"

"If the victim's totems are not fully restored in one hundred years—"

"They, and the guardian, die forever," Zoe said. "Yup, got that. What other cost is more expensive than that?"

"The guardian is chosen, not by the spell caster, but from the energy of the magic itself. It seeks the one individual that had the purest heart toward the dying ruler, cursing them to a life not of their free will."

Zoe shifted her gaze and nibbled her lower lip. "You're right, that is costly. It's like the poor guardians are punished because they don't have any ill intent toward the one being murdered. What kind of backward crap is that?"

Baxter scoffed. "I agree. It is backward. But it ensures the guardian will follow the righteous path in returning the magical being to its rightful role. Eventually."

Zoe rolled her eyes. "Man, I'd be so pissed off if my life was altered like that." She sat up. Horror flashed behind her eyes. "I'm so sorry for the things you have endured. For things I'm responsible for."

Baxter placed his hand over Zoe's, which was soft to his touch. Her pity was the last thing he wanted. "Melantha made that choice. Not you, Zoe. Although you once were her, she isn't who you are now. You are your own entity. Never lose sight of that. Besides, I do not blame Melantha. I truly believe she must have had a sound reason to have enacted the spell."

"Perhaps," Zoe said as she plopped her elbow on the bar counter and rested her chin in her palm. Her silence was confirmation that something bothered her. Baxter had a pretty good idea what it was, but would play the waiting game.

Letting her mull things over, he slid off the barstool, poured two glasses of lemonade, and sat one in front of her. She ignored it and instead cut her eyes at him.

"Tell me, Baxter. How *did* you know Melantha?"

There it was. The moment he waited for.

She straightened her back. Fixed her eyes on him.

It was simply astonishing how fast her attitude toward him could turn on a dime.

"Knowing her is the only way you could've been chosen as the guardian."

Baxter lifted his glass to his lips and sipped on the cool beverage. It calmed his nerves before he confessed a truth that he kept quiet for the past century.

"Indeed, I knew Melantha. Sterling, my uncle—"

"The one who disappeared with his fiancé?"

Baxter nodded. "Yes, him." He took a cleansing breath. "He was engaged to Melantha."

Zoe's unblinking eyes widened, and the color drained from her face. For a moment, it felt like all the air left the room as neither of them breathed.

Zoe slammed her hands on the counter and jumped up, knocking the barstool onto the hardwood floor. "You're more connected to this than you let on." She growled, stomped over to the window, and stared outside.

Baxter took a step forward, wanting to pick the stool up, but her icy gaze and flushed cheeks stopped him. "How could you not tell me Melantha and your uncle had a thing? You said he and his fiancé had disappeared, but *clearly* you knew they were murdered! How could you keep this from me?"

Baxter edged around the island. "You were already dealing with a lot of new information. First, it was learning about your true identity and fighting off Lucas and the others. Then, it was seeing the mural and connecting that to your past. Then it was experiencing your first transformation and trying to find the clue for the next pendant."

Zoe exhaled. Her nostrils flared.

Baxter lifted the stool into its upright position. "Zoe, I have had the time to digest this situation. For your sanity, I was trying to give you a few pieces of information at a time. Please understand that."

"So, what really happened?"

Baxter held his hand up, motioning for Zoe to stay. He scurried to the foyer and retrieved his briefcase from the console table near the front door. He returned to the kitchen, pushed aside the map, and dropped the leather case on the island.

Zoe sulked over to him. "And what else aren't you telling me?"

Baxter pressed the two fasteners with his thumbs and unlocked the latches.

"First," he strummed his fingers against the leather, "I am telling you all that I know." He swung open the briefcase. "And second, I did not know Melantha was murdered until *after* my mother passed. As for Sterling, it is only a theory he too was killed, as there is no proof of what happened to him. Furthermore, I do not know why or who murdered her, which I suspect are the reasons she enacted the spell to bring her back."

Baxter retrieved the delicate photograph of Melantha and the folded letter with the broken red seal. "You hardly looked at these the last time I attempted to show them to you." He handed her the two objects. "I want to share these with you."

Zoe studied the photograph, truly looking at her former self for the first time.

"I was young, and I adored Melantha. It excited me for Sterling to marry her so I could have a sister."

"And hence the reason it chose you as her guardian," Zoe stated.

Baxter dipped his head in acknowledgement. "On the night they announced their engagement, Melantha gifted me my first journal and two photos: this one of her and the other of Sterling, which I foolishly ripped up in anger when I thought he had abandoned his family. Thankfully, my mother interrupted my fit and stopped me from destroying Melantha's."

Zoe smirked as she handed Baxter the photo. She opened the letter, raising her brows "That's some fancy penmanship."

Baxter peered over the top of the parchment, adoring the sweeping lines of his mother's calligraphy.

Zoe held the parchment closer to her face. "Gotta be honest with you; I'm having a hard time reading this. Just tell me what it says." She handed the delicate paper back to him.

"The letter was given to me after my mother's funeral." He folded the letter once more and tucked it inside his briefcase. "It starts off with my mother trying to convince me of the magical world, outing Melantha as a mermaid. She explains the reincarnation spell and the role of the guardian.

And that my suspicions of their disappearance were legitimate. She feared Sterling met the same fate as Melantha. She recalls how the necklace and a set of instructions appeared on her dressing table one evening. The stone came to her for safekeeping until I was ready for the responsibility of the position, which would be at the age of majority or upon her death—whichever came first."

Zoe cocked her head. "Age of majority? You always use such strange terms."

"Get used to it. The magical community is filled with an all-new language."

Zoe chuckled. "All right, all right. Go on, then. Age of majority?"

"It was an old common law saying when you were considered an adult. Today, we recognize eighteen to be the legal age, but it was twenty-one back then. I was seventeen when Melantha was murdered. Eighteen when my mother died, forcing me to take upon my role a few years earlier than expected."

Zoe ran her fingers through her hair. "This is so twisted. Suppose you had to wait until you were twenty-one, that'd given you even less time to search for the queen."

Baxter nodded. "Technically, I've only been searching for you for ninety-nine years." His shoulders sagged. "Well, even that isn't correct. I actively, and regrettably, stopped looking for you about a decade ago."

Another truth he never admitted out loud.

Zoe shrugged her shoulder. "Don't stress about it. Everything seems to be working out. I feel bad for you, though."

"Why?"

"The spell basically robbed you of your life. It only chose you as her guardian because of your pure heart toward her when you considered her as your sister." She paused and lowered her eyes. "Is that how you see me? A sister-type?"

Baxter lifted her chin with his finger, forcing her to lock eyes with his. A bold move, but she didn't pull away. "No. You are not Melantha anymore. Physically, you may look similar, but you are not her twin. Even if you gain all her memories back, that was a different life and a different time." He took her hands in his. "Zoe, you are sassy and confident. I have seen you overcome some of the worst situations an athlete could endure, and you did it with grace and without compromising your education or your integrity. Since the first day you began as my teaching assistant, you have simply amazed me."

A rose-pink flush crept across her cheeks.

"From what I remember of Melantha, she was calm and even-tempered. Some would even say cold. You are not her."

"Thanks. I think I needed to hear that. But it doesn't take away from the fact that we have less than four weeks to find the rest of the stones. We've already wasted two days and still have nothing."

Baxter removed his hand and cast his eyes downward. "True. Even with our modern conveniences, we are struggling."

"It makes me wonder how many other guardians actually succeeded."

Baxter understood her concern. Throughout his life, he learned about a handful of guardians who fulfilled their destiny, but the success rate was low.

"Do you know about any other guardians and their quests?"

Baxter nodded and motioned for her to follow him. "Reynolds completed his mission in 1876."

Zoe groaned. "Because *that* was so recent."

Baxter strode over to the white-stone fireplace in his living room. From the sleek wooden beam serving as the mantel, he took two hardback books stacked next to a vignette of pillar candles. "I dare to imagine how different the world would be if he had failed."

"How so?"

Normally, beautifully bound books on mantels are simply decorations. But not for him. They were reminders of his quest. One book was bound in leather, embossed with patterned branches and thorns, and pewter lettering down the spine. The other was encased in nondescript brown leather and had worn gold lettering on the cover.

"It started in 1849 when a famous American writer had mysteriously been left for dead in the streets of Baltimore. He suffered for a week in a hospital. Because he had the blood of a sphinx in him, he invoked the guardian spell as he came out of his coma, moments before his death."

"A sphinx? What's so important about a sphinx?"

"They are known for their clever riddles, puzzles, and stories. They are often in the blood of those who exhibit exceptional strengths in those areas." He tossed the black book at her. She caught it, flipped it over, and glanced at the cover. Her eyes searched for the unbelievable truth of what he said.

"Poe?"

The corner of Baxter's mouth twitched. He loved revealing a good story. "It took Reynolds, his guardian, twenty-seven years to find the reincarnation of the writer."

Zoe took a step forward.

"You can imagine how difficult it must have been to search for his ward without our modern conveniences, but Reynolds never gave up. He found him at the University of Edinburgh's medical school and once the totem was restored, the magic of the sphinx flowed through the reincarnated man once more."

He handed Zoe the second book.

"And because of that, the man was able to craft clever detective stories."

Zoe ran her hand over the cover and let out a long breath. "That's some story, Baxter. Especially since you're claiming that Sir Arthur Conan Doyle is the reincarnation of Edgar Allan Poe."

Baxter tipped his head at her and took back the brown leather book, a collection of Sherlock Holmes' stories. "Indeed. But my point is this: do not lose hope. We are just as important as Reynolds and his writers. If they did it, we can do it."

"But twenty-seven *years* is nothing compared to the twenty-four *days* we have left."

"Because I foolishly gave up. Silently quit. Neither of us can make that mistake again. Besides, we have more support and resources than Reynolds ever could have had. Do you think he had the creature community helping him?"

"Probably not," she said and handed him the other book.

He placed them back on the mantel and took one last look at the spines. Poe and Doyle and the mysterious Reynolds. He couldn't imagine what the fiction community—nay, the world—would have been like without those two writers. Terrible. Just like a world without Zoe as the queen of her realm, he assumed.

"You're right." She sauntered back to the kitchen. "We have lots of support and we can do this." She slouched over the map again, searching for answers. The necklace dangled away from her chest and brushed against the delicate paper.

He stood across from her, the dangling stone caught his eye. He plucked the stone away from the map and inspected it. "I have scoured over this thing for years and know it better than the back of my hand. But this tiny black spec near the edge is new; as in the past few seconds new."

He held the stone up between them to show Zoe what he was referring to.

"I told you that Sefarina said there were old mer-tales that talk about the writing on the stones."

She lifted her chin, locking her eyes on his. Baxter's heart raced. Their lips were so close that Baxter could smell her strawberry ChapStick. His pulse throbbed in his groin.

An image of him kissing her flashed across his mind.

Never had he thought of her like that before, but the past few days, well, he couldn't help himself. She was the epitome of the type of partner he always wanted. Not only was she stunning, but she was fierce, sometimes maddening with her stubbornness. Curious about the world, witty, with firm beliefs, but also compassionate and soft when needed. Most of all, she made him feel like a schoolboy, giddy at the very thought of being near her. He hadn't felt that way in so long, he almost didn't know how to behave properly.

With a strong desire to taste that damn strawberry ChapStick across his own lips, he inched closer to her.

I should not be doing this.

His breathing deepened. Mouths parted. She leaned closer. Eyes drifted closed.

His fingertips singed as if he had been playing with the flame of a candle.

Zoe collapsed to the floor, screaming about something burning.

Baxter dropped over Zoe, fighting against her flaying body as she tried snapping the necklace off her neck. Baxter grabbed the chain and moved the stone away from her skin, which left it red and blistered.

"I have it, I have it," he shouted over her.

Zoe pushed her hair away from her face, strands sticking to her sweaty forehead. The pendant swayed over her. She rubbed at her chest where the stone had burned her.

"Are you okay?"

Zoe sat up on her elbows. "What the hell happened?"

He felt his cheeks flush. "It must be the stones' way of getting our attention."

How dare you even attempt to act on your desires instead of focusing on the problem at hand?

"There are nicer ways to get our attention."

"Perhaps. But would we have noticed?"

Zoe shrugged her shoulders, then narrowed her eyes at the glowing stone. "You have our attention. Reveal what you want."

Tiny ribbons of black script appeared across the stone.

Baxter had seen the script once before. When he received the stone, it had engraved his initials on it until he claimed it. He should have known the stone could do this.

Baxter scrambled to his feet and dashed across the room and snatched a pen and yellow legal pad from out of his briefcase.

"Read it," he commanded; the tip of the pen pressed against the paper.

Zoe peered even closer at the rock. "I can't. It's gibberish and looks like a cross between swirly Russian and Mandarin Chinese—wait! The script is morphing into letters I recognize."

Under a sudden spell, Zoe's back stiffened, and her face went blank. A haunting melody sailed past her lips.

> *"Clock is science. Mermaids are not myth.*
>
> *Shatter a friend's treasure.*
>
> *Healing, sensing, seeing you'll be with."*

Baxter finished scribbling down the message. Zoe groaned, rubbed her forehead, and rose to her feet. The necklace rested against her chest, and the stone no longer glowed. She blinked. "What do you think it means, and how did we activate it?"

"When you transformed into a mermaid, you unleashed the magic surrounding the stone. That much is obvious. As to how?" Baxter sank onto the barstool, his head in his hand. "The black spot showed up right after you started looking at the map again."

Zoe shoved Baxter's briefcase aside and re-opened the discarded map. "All because we put our hope into this old map?"

Baxter shook his head. "Not on the map, no. In each other."

Zoe beamed. "Of course. It revealed its secret when *we* were ready for it."

Baxter leaned his lower back against the granite countertop and folded his arms across his lap. "Now all we need to do is solve the riddle."

Zoe leaned against the counter next to him, her arm brushed against his. "Kinda like Sherlock, huh?"

Baxter chuckled. "We know mermaids are not myths," Baxter said, more to himself than to her, "and clocks keep track of time. The science of time has been a long-heated debate among scientists and philosophers. Perhaps there is a connection between time and mermaids."

"*Clock is science* isn't even grammatically correct," Zoe stated as she looked at the written riddle again. "And you're kinda reaching into science-fiction territory with talk about time."

Baxter smirked at her. "I believe all authors of the genre would agree that science fiction is simply ideas that haven't yet been proven. It does not differ from the fantasy world you and I know about, or the myths and lore that I teach. All these ideas are rooted in reality, and only a select few know the truth. Who is to say the magical world doesn't cross over into the science world?"

Zoe clicked her tongue. "Good point."

She stared across the kitchen, at nothing in particular. Her forehead creased.

"What are you thinking?"

"I have this really strong gut feeling I need to get back in the water. Like, now, if possible."

He studied her. Her demeanor changed. She was on edge and impatient. Something happened to her.

Her mermaid magic is calling to her.

"Think it's too late to rent a boat and head into the ocean?" she asked.

The corner of Baxter's mouth lifted. He waited for this very moment. "No need to rent one. I have a power cruiser docked at Marina Del Rey. We can be out to sea in less than two hours."

CHAPTER 15

ZOE

JUST AS BAXTER PROMISED, two hours later, they sped across the water in his boat, *The Guardian*. Everything on her was white as snow, gleaming brightly against the golden hue of the late afternoon sun. The boat had a swim-deck in the rear, with a ladder that dropped into the water. Two sets of steps led to the cockpit and a deck with cushioned benches to sunbathe on. A narrow set of stairs led down from the cockpit to a small kitchen, captain's quarters, and a tiny restroom. He spared no expense.

Baxter fiddled with the switches at the control deck and anchored the cruiser so far offshore that the hills of Malibu looked like mere bumps along the horizon. Zoe stood up from the bench and kicked off her flip-flops and unbuttoned her jean shorts. From the corner of her eye, she noticed Baxter lifted his head and absentmindedly eyed her over the top of his pilot shades. She turned her back to him, not because she didn't want him to watch her, but to hide the flush of her cheeks.

Back in San Francisco, Zoe succumbed to a hard truth; beneath a mound of insecurities, she had a growing desire for Baxter. At first, it irked her thinking she did not differ from the other students who fancied the professor, but she quickly stopped herself from comparing their simple crushes against their friendship. Their bond was strong. Something that started well before the truth of her identity brought them even closer. Baxter made her feel like she could trust again and that nothing was impossible with him. By the way he looked at her the past few days, she suspected he felt the same about her.

She lowered her jean shorts and pulled off her vintage Mickey Mouse T-shirt, revealing her purple-and-white pin-striped bikini. She stuffed her clothes, sunglasses, and ponytail holder inside her rattan beach bag, then tussled her hair. "Ready to see the reason for your extended life?"

Baxter removed his sunglasses. They slipped from his hand, he juggled to catch them, only to drop them on the deck. He swooped them up and cleared his throat, trying to recompose himself. "Indeed."

Zoe suppressed a giggle as she padded over to the stern, ready to dive off the swim platform.

"How will you know where to go, or what to do?" Baxter joined her at the rear of the boat.

"Instinct, I suppose. Hopefully, whatever made me want to come here will present itself. I plan on returning before the sun fully sets, though." Before Baxter could respond, she dove off the boat and splashed into the calm sea.

The cool water shocked her skin. She gripped the stone, willing herself to transform into her mermaid form, but with the bonus of wearing the bikini top. In an instant, the familiar warmth of being wrapped inside a cozy blanket engulfed her. She opened her eyes and reveled in the vivid and clear colors of the world.

She was glad to see a bikini cover her chest instead of the tattoo-like scales that revealed too much of her body. She wasn't sure if she was ready for her bare chest to be displayed. After spending most of her life in a swimsuit, she felt comforted by her covered top in this foreign world.

Zoe kicked her tail and leapt out of the ocean like a dolphin, splashing water over the boat's edge and drowning Baxter, who patiently waited for her appearance. She floated on her back, presenting her majestic tail. This was the first time she saw it in the direct sunlight and loved the glint of sparkle that shimmered along her scales. "Whatcha' think? Pretty awesome, right?"

Baxter wiped the water from his face. "Stunning." He knelt down as she paddled to the ladder and gripped it for stability. He reached over and slid his warm hand across her tail, which felt no different to her than somebody rubbing her thigh. "Your colors are dynamic, especially the way the luster gleams in the sunlight."

Zoe grinned, flapped her fluke, and smacked the water, dousing Baxter again. Without hesitation, he leaned over the edge and splashed her back.

Joy rippled through her. She laughed as she flicked the water away from her eyes. "You dare challenge a mermaid to a splash-off?"

Baxter backed from the edge of the platform and held his hands up in defeat. "How about a truce?" he said with a toothy grin.

Zoe smirked. "For now." She reached up with her hand.

He squatted down and shook her hand. "You are going to be trouble, little mermaid."

Their eyes locked. Her body tingled as a flame of desire ignited within her. He leaned closer. Her breath hitched as the warm breeze carried the sweet scent of his coconut sunblock. The boat teetered as the current sloshed against the hull, rocking them closer together. As Zoe lifted her chin, desperately wanting to capture his lips, a fluttery irritant tickled her eyes. She flittered her lashes.

Splash!

She jerked her head up.

Baxter dropped into the water, sinking like a stone.

She plunged beneath the surface, ready to grab him. But the faster she swam toward him, the faster he sank, as if an anchor wrapped around him and reeled him toward the sea floor. His sultry grin and lust-filled eyes called to her. She wanted to breathe a new life into him, so they could live together forever beneath the sea. If she didn't reach him fast, death would win. She stretched her arms out, their fingers mere inches apart. So close...

A force rammed into her ribs, propelling her sideways into a nearby boulder.

The agonizing pain of their connection breaking tore through her heart. Without a care of what hit her, she scurried to reorient herself, panicked she wouldn't reach him in time. She pushed her hair from her face and stopped.

Baxter was in the arms of another mermaid.

Anger boiled within her.

Who would dare?

She screamed like a teapot on the stove, and pushed off the rock, determined to stop the mermaid from taking Baxter toward the surface.

The tip of her fluke caught something. She reached around to free herself, but a second mermaid, a yellow one, gripped the tip, holding her back.

Zoe barred her teeth.

Why are they keeping Baxter from me?

The yellow mermaid tugged at her. "Zoe!"

Confused, Zoe pulled back. What was the yellow one's name again? Fauna? Fiona? No. "Farah?"

The yellow mermaid released her fluke but was quick to grip Zoe's shoulders, forcing her to look at her. "You must relax and concentrate on transforming back to your human form."

Fear burned a painful trail to her heart. Tears distorted her vision. "Baxter," she cried. "It hurts…"

Farah took Zoe's hand and made her grip her necklace. "Transform," she whispered, stroking Zoe's hair as she swam them upwards. "The pain will go away. Trust me."

Zoe took a shaky breath. The same fluttery irritant tickled her eyes once more. She rubbed away the nuisance, then willed herself to change back just as she and Farah broke the surface of the water.

"Baxter, can you hear me?" Zoe heard someone say.

She furiously scanned the horizon. There was another mermaid next to the boat, but Zoe wasn't sure who it was. All she could see was Baxter's lifeless body draped in her arms.

"Farah! Help me with him!" cried out the other mermaid.

"Stay in your human form," Farah demanded before lurching forward, leaving Zoe behind. Even with all her swimming strengths, being in the open water versus a pool was completely different, and it would take her time to fight against the current and reach him. She knew she needed to keep calm, but accomplishing that was another story.

As she inhaled and paddled forward, she realized the pain in her chest vanished as Farah promised. It was hard to admit the only way to help Baxter was to trust Farah, somebody she hardly knew.

Once she was calm, and her mind cleared, Zoe swam toward the boat, counting her strokes, to keep her at ease. She grabbed the small ladder on the swim platform. Waiting for her was Sefarina, who wore a linen sundress. Her red hair danced in the wind like a flame. She reached for Zoe's hand and helped her out of the water.

"Where's Baxter?" Zoe asked.

"He's okay. He's at the helm, relaxing on the seat."

Zoe clutched her chest and exhaled. "Thank goodness."

"It was only luck that Farah and I weren't too far away when we felt your energy entering our realm. No one else would have made it here in time to save him."

Save him. Those two words pierced Zoe's heart. Her stomach churned at the thought of unintentionally losing Baxter. She tightened her jaw, swallowed the thick lump in the back of her throat, and muttered a grateful thank you.

She rushed up the steps to the sunbathing deck. Farah's gold bangles and hooped earrings jangled as she adjusted the sunshade over the deck where Baxter rested.

Zoe squeezed by her. Baxter lounged on the long bench, sipping on a bottle of water. She plopped down next to him. She reached out for him, but pulled back. "What happened? Are you okay?"

Baxter drew in a long breath and ran his fingers through his wet hair. "Not sure. When our eyes met, I had this gut-wrenching desire to follow you into the water, so we could never be apart."

He capped the bottle and shifted to address Sefarina, who sat down across from him. "I knew mermaids lured humans to their watery graves, but I thought it was by casting a spell with their song, not their eyes," he said.

"That's mostly true," Farah answered before Sefarina. "But some Purple-Tails can enchant a human with just their icy stare."

Zoe smacked her thigh. "Damn. I should've remembered that you, Sefarina, even warned me to be careful of my beauty because it could be deadly to others. I'm such a fool."

Sefarina hung her head. "No, this is my fault. I should've explained it better. I'm so sorry."

"You both need to stop blaming yourselves. Everything worked out in the end." Baxter covered Zoe's hand and held tight. "You will not get rid of me that easily."

"I don't understand what happened. One minute I thought we were about to—" Zoe paused and glanced away.

Baxter squeezed her hand. "I thought we were too." The pad of his thumb ran across her skin. "But then you pulled back, and I fell into the water. I guess I will have to avoid looking directly into your eyes when you're in mermaid form."

Zoe clicked her tongue, *tsking* at his response. "That makes me sound like I'm Medusa or something. But instead of turning people to stone when they look into my eyes, I make them drown themselves."

Baxter chuckled. "At least you don't have snakes for hair." An eyebrow rose as he stiffened at his own thought. He shuddered. "I hate snakes."

Zoe's eyes rolled, and she let out a small giggle as he reminded her of the rugged, fictional archeologist. That was so like him, making jokes and comforting her when he had been the one in danger. She squeezed his hand tighter, knowing they both used humor as a defense mechanism to avoid reality.

She only hoped he didn't fear her the way she feared herself.

CHAPTER 16
BAXTER

ALTHOUGH HE TRIED TO brush off his near-death experience as nothing, Baxter was nervous. The vision of his mother said the magic of the stone still protected him, but he wasn't keen on finding out if that was the case or not—especially by being pulled into a watery grave.

What bothered him most was not knowing what truly happened. Why did he drop like a stone into the water when he only wanted to follow Zoe to the depths of the sea and have her rosy lips against his?

The only good thing that came from the event had been hearing Zoe confirm they were about to kiss before the incident. It was clear she wanted him as much as he wanted her.

"Well," Sefarina began, "Zoe's theory of turning people to stone isn't wrong. In fact, it's exactly what your eyes are cursed to do."

Zoe tilted her head to the side. "Cursed?"

"Why is she cursed?" Baxter asked.

"As Farah said, *some* Purple-Tails have a deadly, icy-stare. To understand why, you must know about the mermaid lineage of the Ancient Greeks."

"Oh, a history lesson," Baxter quipped and sat up straighter. "Please enlighten us." He gestured for her to continue and wondered how well his theories matched up with the actual history of mermaid lore.

Sefarina looked toward the sun. "I'm not sure we have the time for this."

Baxter released Zoe's hand, folded his arms over his chest, and focused on Sefarina. He wanted answers, and nothing would stop him from getting them. "Make time."

Sefarina arched her brow, but then settled back into the cushioned seat. "Farah, this is your realm of expertise. But please, give them the abridged version."

Farah completely abandoned her efforts to cover them in the sun shade. She adjusted her clothes, straightened her back, and cleared her throat. The epitome of an overachieving intellect.

Baxter grinned. He, too, often exhibited the same look right before one of his lectures.

"So, there are three lines in the Ancient Greek mermaid pantheon. The first line of Tails descends from the Greek's Primordial Gods: Gaia and Pontus, or Mother Earth and The Sea. Gaia and Pontus had a son, Nereus, who was known as the Old Man in the Sea. Nereus had fifty beautiful sea-goddess daughters known as Nereides, who were the first mermaids.

"The next lineage comes from the Titans, the gods that succeeded the Primordial Gods. Oceanus, the god of the rivers, and Tethys, the goddess of the ocean, were two of the twelve Titans who produced thousands of river gods called the Potamoi and Oceanides, goddess-nymph daughters. The Potamoi and the Oceanides are where the Titan mermaids descend from."

"The third lineage has gotta be from the Olympians," Zoe interjected. "They were the gods after the Titans, and you haven't mentioned Poseidon. He and his brothers Zeus and Hades are probably the most-well known gods of the Greek Mythology."

Baxter beamed. She had always been one of his best students.

"Yes," Farah stated. "The third line is from the Olympians. Poseidon married Amphitrite, who was Nereids. Their son Triton had sea-demon and sea-goddess children called Tritons and Tritonides, which is where the Olympian mermaids hail from."

"Which one of the three lineages has the cursed eyes?" Zoe leaned in as if Farah were telling a ghost story around a campfire.

"Well, the curse starts from Nereus' other siblings, Ceto and Phorcys, who birthed some fearsome creatures, including the Gorgons. The most famous one being—"

"Medusa," Zoe and Baxter stated in unison.

Farah nodded. "Medusa was cousin to Amphitrite. Before Medusa was infamous for the snakes in her hair, she had been a beautiful mortal woman, unlike her two monstrous sisters."

Baxter couldn't contain himself. "Oh, we are well aware of this myth. The story says that Medusa was a maiden to Athena, the most beautiful goddess in the land. Poseidon, who was Athena's rival, made claims that Medusa's beauty paralleled Athena's. He seduced Medusa inside a temple of Athena's, just to infuriate and slander Athena."

"There are many myths about Medusa, but yes, that is the correct one," Farah said. "When Athena found out about their coupling, she became furious with Medusa for allowing Poseidon to make such claims and take advantage of her inside her temple. Athena punished Medusa by transforming her into a monster."

Zoe's jaw tightened. She shot to her feet. "Coupling? Are you serious? Poseidon raped her."

Farah's eyes widened at Zoe's outburst. Sefarina scooted closer to Farah, almost protectively. Baxter stood up and positioned himself between Zoe and the other two; they weren't used to her rants.

"And Athena, her supposed friend," Zoe continued without noticing the reaction from the two mermaids, "victim-blamed Medusa instead of bringing Poseidon to justice!" Her cheeks flushed, and her voice level increased as she paced around the sundeck. "Athena cursed Medusa into an ugly, snake-headed, stone-casting creature, and even had the audacity to aid Perseus in slaying her. She displayed Medusa's head on her shield as a symbol of power after Perseus lopped it off!"

Zoe pinned her arms over her chest, pivoted, and glared out at the sea. From the corner of her mouth, she mumbled, "Athena was a jealous bitch."

Baxter placed a hand on Zoe's shoulder. He knew how it enraged her when innocents were targeted. Her wounds from the experience with the swim team allegations were still fresh. It was no wonder she wanted to study criminal law and had such a passion for justice and equality. She was like a ticking time bomb, ready to explode on anything that stood against those beliefs. Baxter knew she needed to save that energy for the right moment and the right person.

Zoe shook her head and exhaled the pent-up frustration. She gazed at Baxter with apologetic eyes. He patted her shoulder; glad she understood his supportive message.

Zoe looked past him at Farah and Sefarina. "Sorry, I can get heated."

Farah's eyes cast downward. Sefarina sighed, her shoulders sagged; yet her eyes were warm and there was a sweet grin on her face. "Melantha often felt the same way about injustices. I'm glad to see you have her fire."

Zoe tucked her hair behind her ear. "Thanks. But how do my cursed eyes fit into the Athena-Medusa-Poseidon triangle?"

"You're from the Tritonides lineage and are related to Poseidon," Farah said.

"Figures," Zoe grunted.

Farah stood and took a timid step forward. "Medusa thought her relationship with Amphitrite would prevent Poseidon from having relations with her, which, of course, it didn't work out. He said his wife supported him in defiling Medusa, so they could hurt Athena's reputation as the most beautiful woman. After Athena cursed Medusa into the monster, Medusa got revenge on both Amphitrite and Poseidon, blaming them for Athena's curse upon her. Medusa figured the one thing that would affect them both was their son, Triton, and his heirs. Medusa placed a curse similar to hers on any Purple-Tails born through his line."

Baxter scratched the scruff on his jaw. He knew a lot about the history of Medusa, but this was a new twist.

"So, the mermaids who descend from Triton really *do* lure people to their death by turning them to stone?" Zoe asked.

Farah nodded and shifted her feet. "Medusa wanted Triton and his heirs to suffer by taking away what—who, they desire. The same way Poseidon had taken her most precious attribute—her virginity. While in mermaid form, the eyes of Triton's descendants will enchant the object of their affection and turn them to stone. Meanwhile, the Purple-Tail becomes incapacitated, not being able to stop the curse or save the person, which will torment them with heartbreaking sorrow. It makes it difficult for Purple-Tails to find, and keep, romantic relationships."

Baxter wondered if Sterling ever saw Melantha in mermaid form. Hell, did he even know she was a mystical being? Or worse, had he suffered the ill-fated curse of being changed to stone? That surely would explain his sudden disappearance. But then why was Melantha murdered? Logically, Baxter knew it was beneficial to learn of this new information, but emotionally, it was yet another layer added to the mystery and almost felt like he took two steps backward.

Zoe raked her fingers through her hair and dropped onto a cushioned bench. "No wonder I had that weird fluttering in my eyes just before Baxter fell in the water. The curse had activated." She faced Farah. "That's why you made me transform back to a human, so he wouldn't turn to stone and that heart-aching pain I was suffering from would stop, right?"

The corner of Farah's lip lifted. "Yes. It's a good thing Sefarina got us to you in time."

Sefarina stood up next to Farah. "The sad thing is that Poseidon lied to Medusa. Amphitrite did not know about what he had done, and when she found out, they say her fury caused a volcanic eruption. Before Amphitrite could find Medusa and fix their relationship, Perseus killed her."

"That's so messed up. Medusa suffered and never knew the truth. And because of some terrible choices by some really awful gods, I almost killed my guardian, which could've prevented me from reclaiming my realm, and would've had dire consequences for our world."

Silence fell. The choppy waters rhythmically beat against the hull. Baxter looked out at the endless blue water. The domino effect of this situation was heavy and the consequences of it were severe. He would have to be more careful around her; the world depended on it.

Zoe broke the silence first. "Well, I bet our genealogy is an absolute mess, especially since the Greek Gods were known for their affairs, incest, and taking multiple mortal lovers."

Sefarina cringed. "No, no, no. You misunderstand. *You*, a Purple-Tail, are a descendant of the Greeks. Aquamarine-Tails can trace our lines back to the Norse Gods." She jutted her thumb out toward Farah. "And Yellow-Tails, like her, hail from the Egyptians."

Zoe rubbed her temples. Baxter imagined her head was pounding between the highs and lows of the last several hours and all the new information discovered. His surely was.

"But, yes, the lineage of Tails from all around the world *is* a tangled mess," Sefarina said.

Zoe grabbed a bottle of water, twisted the cap off, and drained half of it in one gulp. "Each color has a specific power, right? I remember Aislinn telling me how White-Tails have healing powers, I think?"

Sefarina shook her head. "No, the Blue-Tails have healing powers. White-Tails control the light and darkness."

Zoe flopped back against the padded backrest. "Ugh, I need a chart or something to keep track of all this information."

Farah's face lit up. "Oh, that's easy. I've got that." She slid the golden cuff from her upper arm down to her wrist, clanging it against her bangles, revealing a tattoo from beneath it. At first glance, it looked like it was a bird-like animal holding a writing quill standing on top of a stack of books with a rolled scroll propped up against it. Baxter shifted to get a better view and realized the bust of the animal creature was of the Egyptian God, Thoth, who had the head of an ibis.

Zoe scooted forward for a closer look as well. "I've been wondering about the tattoos. Murdock has a similar one to an Atlantic-Tail named Lucas."

Farah lifted her arm, giving Zoe and Baxter a closer inspection. "Ah, yes. Lucas. Each pure-colored Tail has one. Since Lucas and Murdock are both Red-Tails, they're marked with the Celtic flames of war."

Farah touched her tattoo with her index finger. A golden light illuminated behind the black ink. "Yellow-Tails are the keepers of mermaid knowledge and history."

No wonder Farah spoke like a professor. "Just as Thoth, I see," Baxter said.

Farah grinned and nodded in agreement. She lifted her hand away, pinching the light between her fingers and thumb. She snapped. A large tome appeared in her hands.

Baxter's eyes widened. Although the magical world intertwined with his, actually *seeing* magic happen was still mind-blowing. Baxter often compared it to watching a fireworks spectacle. All he could do was gawk at it and revel in its glory.

Farah dropped the heavy, tattered book on the bench. With a wave of her hand, the book opened. The aged paper flipped open and stopped on a page with gold embossed lettering in an unfamiliar language.

Farah gently touched the curly font. Baxter sprang backward as the letters animated, transformed to another language, and stood up on the page like a children's pop-up book.

"Look directly at the words," Farah instructed Baxter, and double-tapped the top of the letters. The words glitched and transformed into a boxy-looking language. "Can you read it yet?"

Baxter shook his head.

"Oh, come on," she whined, hitting the letters repeatedly.

"Wait," he called out, putting his hand up to stop her from changing the letters again. "Aquatic Accords?"

"About time," Farah mumbled. She grabbed the inscription from the center and lifted the entire piece up and out of the ancient book.

She handed the scroll to Baxter. The heaviness of holding something so ancient and filled with such a rich history was worth more than any amount of gold, money, or jewels he could ever possess. His hands trembled.

I should not be handling this without gloves...

Zoe rushed over to him, looking over his shoulder. "Open it."

Baxter unrolled the scroll. At the top of the parchment was a brief paragraph, and beneath that, were more than a dozen different styles of signatures, much like the Declaration of Independence. With a quick scan, Baxter caught the names of some very famous deities, including Poseidon himself.

Zoe read the opening line. "The Democracy of Deities present The Aquatic Accords here at Atlantis during the First Point of Aries in the year 1000." She looked up at Farah. "What in the world is this?"

Baxter continued unrolling the scroll. Unlike Zoe, he knew what he was holding. Zoe would soon understand, and have the same inner excitement he experienced, but for the moment, he appreciated Farah for her knowledge. As an educator, he could talk with her about this history all day. Baxter scanned the document. Below the table were notes regarding the different realms. Below that, was a table with each row dedicated to a specific pure-tail color, outlining their magical abilities, tattoos, weapons, and lineage.

"This is a basic structure of how our world is divided and ruled. Study it when you have time. I'm afraid it won't have any answers regarding the locations of the other stones, though," Farah said.

She closed the tome, which transformed into golden light like it did earlier, and then vanished. Her tattoo glowed again, then faded away as she pushed her arm cuff up back in place.

Baxter couldn't tear his eyes from the parchment. He couldn't wait to get home and devour every word of the script.

But then again, how can I continue to teach ancient mythology when I know the truth?

"Farah, perhaps I should not read this. It conflicts with my life as a university professor. One I plan to maintain once Zoe is fully restored."

Farah waved him off. "Oh, don't be, ridiculous. That information is enchanted. You'll only be able to speak of it with other magical beings. And because you're the guardian, you're considered a magical being as well."

Baxter lowered his head. "Thank you." He rolled up the scroll and tucked it safely inside a compartment in the cockpit next to the steering wheel.

"As much as I would like to continue your history lesson," Sefarina said, "the real reason Farah and I came to meet Zoe is that we wanted to see how you were coming along with your search for the other stones. And because I would like to take Zoe on a small journey in the northern part of her realm."

"You were right. The stone *had* writing on it," Zoe said, her eyes lighting up as she recited the riddle.

Baxter noticed Sefarina and Farah eyeing each other, as if something triggered a thought between them.

"Great. Revealing the clue was probably the hard part. Now, you just need to decipher it and find the stone. You know we wish we could directly help you," Sefarina said.

Zoe sighed, "I know."

"Well, I must go." Farah sauntered toward the steps that led down to the swim platform. "I've got a hot date with a vampire."

Zoe looked from Baxter to Sefarina. "Did I just hear her right?"

"Although," Farah sang out as she was halfway down the steps, "one has to wonder which field of science would have the closest relationship to mermaids." She gave a toothy grin, waved, and splashed into the water.

Baxter tilted his head, focused on the wake she left. Something nagged at him. He tried to block out Zoe's rocket-firing questions to Sefarina regarding Farah's love-life.

He thought back to his encounters with other departments and universities. Farah's words about 'a field of science' rang in his mind, repeating themselves like a broken record. He dug through his memories like they were drawers of an old card-catalog cabinet, furiously flipping each index card to find the one with the right keywords.

He closed his eyes, drowning out all distractions. He was so close to pulling out the information he sought. Baxter could feel Zoe's presence next to him, but tried to ignore her so he didn't lose track of his thoughts. His mind slowed. His brows compressed.

Yes, that was it. Oceanography. No, wait. Not just oceanography, but a specific oceanographer. I should have made the connection sooner.

"Baxter? Are you—"

"I have to return home," he interrupted, spinning around, and scrambling to the cockpit. "I have something I need to research." His hands were frantically flipping toggle switches and pushing buttons.

"Zoe and I can meet up with you later," Sefarina said.

"Can you do your magic and transport us to my house?" Zoe asked.

"I can only translocate to places I have been before."

The engine of the boat roared to life. Baxter looked at Sefarina. "Have you ever been to The Greek Theater in Griffith Park?"

Sefarina grinned. "I have."

"Perfect. My house is just a short walk from there," Zoe said. "Baxter, meet me there later. Around midnight?

"Works for me." Baxter held down the button and reeled the anchor in. "Go do what you need to do while I do what I need to do."

Zoe gave him a warm smile, then dove off the swim platform. Sefarina lingered behind, watching over Baxter's safety as Zoe transformed and disappeared below the surface.

"I hope you find what you're searching for." Sefarina gave him the slightest wink just before diving into the water.

Without pause, Baxter sped off, confident he would find it too.

Chapter 17

ZOE

ZOE AND SEFARINA ZIGZAGGED their way through shoals of fish that frolicked through the vibrant colors of the coral reefs. When they reached the sea floor, they hovered over it, following its downward slope into cooler and darker waters.

Sefarina torpedoed across the wide-open terrain with Zoe by her side. Zoe focused on staying in a constant position with Sefarina. At these speeds, she felt like a fighter jet zipping across the sky.

Sefarina slowed and descended until they reached the barren, hilly seabed. As they passed a dirt mound about the size of a classic VW Beetle, a golden light sprang to life, outlining a rectangular shape on the face of the dune. Black script, in the unusual language Zoe saw on her stone pendant, appeared on its glass-like surface.

"What is this?" Zoe asked. As if the peculiar font heard her speak, it faded away into English words. She swam closer to examine it.

The Northern Channel Islands of California, Pacific Ocean

Northeast Pacific Realm

Welcome to Smuggler's Cove: 34° 1 '4.393" N, 119° 32' 12.897" W

"In time, you'll naturally use your internal devices to navigate the sea, but for major landmarks and locations, for those visiting other realms, and to help those who don't have a long history of being a Tail, all kingdoms implemented this modern navigation system. It's quite Avant-Garde, even for Landwalkers. It required collaboration with more than half the Oceanic kingdoms to make a treaty with the Witch's Council to help us enchant them correctly. I'm still not convinced it was worth the cost to get their help, but even mermaids have limited magic."

Zoe circled the sandy mound, wanting to see it from all angles. Each side popped to life as soon as her eyes set on it. "What do you call this thing? How does it work?" She reached out to touch it, hesitated, and pulled away. She looked over her shoulder at Sefarina. "How do you hide these from divers and submarines?"

"Landwalkers see them only as a drift of sediment. We refer to them as See-seas." Sefarina placed her palm on the façade closest to her. "Show me a map of my current location." She released her hand. The location and coordinates dissolved into a bird's-eye view of the Channel Islands. The illustrated design of the map had different points of locations labeled with words or symbols. A glowing aquamarine mermaid tail depicted Sefarina's location on the east side of Santa Cruz Island. In the lower right corner, the map's legend displayed the symbols, which included a tilted bow and mast to represent sunken ships, and a shark fin to represent known clusters of the predators.

Zoe's chest tightened as she remembered the shark attack. She looked back at the map and sighed in relief as she saw the shark fin symbol was north of Santa Miguel Island, two islands west of their location. Right near Smuggler's Cove were three shipwrecks. Enthralled with the map, Zoe scooted closer and touched one of the nearby shipwreck symbols.

The map disappeared. Zoe squealed and ripped her hand away. She bumped into Sefarina, who giggled and nudged Zoe toward the map. "It's interactive. It zooms in on the location when you touch a symbol."

Zoe pressed her hands to her warm cheeks, then swam closer to the See-sea for a better look. The map showed a closer view of the two shipwrecks near Anacapa: The Winfield Scott (1853) and Del Rio (1952). The map also listed more points of interest focused on a smaller area. "This is so clever and advanced. I wonder how long it will take humans to have this type of technology system."

"A while, I'd reason. But honestly, where do you think the Landwalkers learn how to do things like this? A lot of the technology, modern advances, and other genius-level ideas are often either influenced by a magical being, or the inventors have a bit of magic in their own lineage."

Zoe looked over the—*for lack of a better word*—screen of the See-sea. "This system is a GPS, but the ease and design of it reminds me of this new website, Quest-A-Map, or something like that. Only reason I know about it is because my parents recently bought stock in it."

Sefarina placed her palm flat on the map. "Directions to Bodega Bay, California."

The map dissolved as the longitude and latitude coordinates, written directions, and a map of the route appeared.

"Let's stop by here first, before our long trip north. You'll need to eat something for energy, but we can't stay long. Remember, you have a time limit underwater and you'll be pushing it."

Eat something? Zoe's stomach churned.

I'm a picky eater on land—how will I fare in the water? Besides, what do mermaids even eat? Eating fish seems... well, ew.

Zoe motioned to the map. "It's over three hundred miles. How long will it take to get there?"

Sefarina motioned for Zoe to follow along, diving deeper. "About an hour and a half if we swim at our top speed, which is only achieved in the dark zone."

Before she could ask how they would know when they entered the dark zone, an electrical current buzzed through her tail, like tiny pricks of a needle. She twisted around to see her tail lit up in a bluish-purple glow. She gawked over her glowing fingernails and noticed how a beam of white light jetted out from the tips of her fingers like tiny flashlights. A thin layer of translucent liquid surrounded the human aspects of her body, protecting her from the pressures of the deep sea.

She would never get enough of seeing magic.

Sefarina had a similar glow, but her tail emitted more greens and blues. Together, they looked like a mini version of the nighttime parade at Disneyland.

"Keep your arms stretched out in front of you so the beams of light from your fingers illuminate your path, and you can steer around predators and landmasses. Use the tip of your fluke to flutter, not your entire tail. We will swim fast. I believe it's around two hundred miles per hour, if that helps you comprehend the speed."

She imagined, at two hundred miles per hour, her fluke would flap like the wings of a hummingbird. She thought they already swam fast. *Hell,* she thought her speeds in the pool were great. Ha. If only her former teammates could see her now.

At least it would be a genuine complaint.

Sefarina steered them around a massive blue whale, patting her hand on its head as they passed. "After an hour of revving up our energy, a tunnel of light will surround you. A portal opens for you to surge through and transport ahead five hundred miles in seconds; it's how Tails who don't have my ability can travel great distances in a short amount of time."

Zoe's eyes widened. Technology beneath the sea? Portals? The scientific-and futuristic-like concepts juxtaposed with things like old shipwrecks and magic were like a buffet made especially for science-fiction and fantasy fans. She reveled in it. "Is it a complicated process?"

"As long as you're paying attention, you should be fine. But you can bypass your location if you're not careful. Since we don't need to go that far, don't activate the surge. Once the tunnel of light appears, do nothing. Ignore it and it will go away in a few seconds. It will take another hour for the portal to reappear."

"How do you activate the surge into the portal?"

"By swiping your fingers through the portal lights."

Zoe imagined it was much like rapidly passing fingers through the flame of a candle to not get burned. Hard to resist doing, but not impossible. Navigating top speeds and the portal seemed easy enough.

Within seconds, they rocketed across the ocean. The lights from her fingertips penetrated the dark depths, giving them an ample amount of time to navigate around the few sea creatures lurking in the waters. Before Zoe knew it, the tunnel of light sparked to life. White strobes of light flashed around her, reminding her of the DeLorean just before it jumped through time. A current of electricity pulsed beneath her skin. She narrowed her eyes to block the bright lights and reminded herself not to swipe her fingers through it. As fast as it arrived, the portal disappeared.

Soon after, they arrived at Bodega Bay and ascended into the ocean's sunlight zone. A rainbow of colors greeted them as fish, flora, and swarms of mixed-tails mingled together. A Green-Tail with streaks of white swam past them and a Black-Tail with bright yellow hues lightly dusted over his scales waved to Zoe and Sefarina. As if in a garden, small groups of Tails huddled around a large, flat rock sitting on a bed of colorful anemones.

Full of excitement, Zoe followed Sefarina to the group and sat with them. They each smiled at her, but continued with their business. Three light taps patted Zoe's shoulder. She glanced over her shoulder. "Callista!"

The young candy-cane mixed-tail smiled back. She held the same sushi-type roll she tried to give her before. "Wanna' try one? Campbell Cove is just up the way and has the best oysters, which means this roll of yum-yum goodness is fresh!"

Zoe looked around. The buzz of the busy mermaids quieted, each eyeing her, eagerly awaiting the new girl to assimilate. Zoe swallowed the bile that bubbled into her mouth. She couldn't cower away this time. She raised her chin, plucked one from Callista's hands, and shoved it in her mouth. There was a tiny *pop* as she bit into it. The briny juices of the meat oozed around in her mouth and seeped into her taste buds. She moaned, slowly chewing. She moaned, savoring each bite. She'd have to be open to trying to new things more often.

"I knew you'd love 'em," Callista said, elbowing her as she swallowed. She handed Zoe two more and gave Sefarina a handful.

Zoe looked around and noticed the hushed crowd had returned to their own business. "Eat up. You'll need them to reach Alaska," Sefarina said, and took a bite of one.

"Alaska?" Callista asked.

"Prince William Sound," Sefarina stated.

The smile on Callista's face dropped. "Oh."

Zoe looked from Callista to Sefarina. "What's wrong with going there?"

Callista wiggled her brow at Zoe, as if wishing her good luck, and darted off with a giggling group of mixed-tails.

"Ten years ago, Prince William Sound was the site of a horrific oil spill."

Zoe rubbed her hand over her face and tried to recall why Prince William Sound sounded familiar. "The oil tanker that struck a reef?"

Sefarina nodded. "The very one."

Zoe had been eleven, but she clearly remembered the images of people trying to clean the wildlife covered in black oil. "What will we be doing there?"

"You are going to uplift the spirits of the Tails who live there. They are the ones who control polluted waters, and without them, our environment would have been in shambles long ago. The last ten years have been the hardest. Most of them have settled on land. Perhaps, if they meet you, that will give them the will to stay, knowing their magic is about to be restored."

Zoe nodded and stuffed her mouth with her new favorite food. It hurt to know a population of her realm severely suffered, but Sefarina believed her presence would be the ray of light they needed. Zoe could easily do that for them. As captain of her swim team throughout high school and college, she was used to rallying, cheering people on, and hyping them up to believe in their own strengths, but from Sefarina's description, and

Callista's reaction, she wondered if her glimmer of hope might be ten years too late.

CHAPTER 18

ZOE

BEFORE HEADING TO ALASKA, Sefarina made Zoe use the closest See-sea to plot their destination, teaching her how to navigate on her own. Zoe swiped her hand across the surface and asked for directions to Prince William Sound. Zoe blanched. "Are you kidding me? It's over eighteen hundred miles away!"

Sefarina twirled around in the water. "Yes, but this time, you will activate the surges and use the portals to travel further. Remember, in an instant, each surge takes you five hundred miles."

Sefarina traced her finger over the line that directed their route, starting at Campbell Cove. "See, we travel two hundred miles by swimming, which will take us about an hour and put us around Eureka, California. Once the portal opens and we activate the surge, we will then be seven hundred miles from Campbell Cove, which puts us right about the Oregon and Washington border."

Zoe pointed to the uppermost tip of Washington State. "Then we swim for another hour, which is two hundred more miles away, right?"

Sefarina nodded. "Activate the surge again, and we'll be well up into Canada, fourteen hundred miles from Campbell Cove. We will see two more portals, but we can't use them, or we'll go too far."

Zoe bobbed her head. "Surge the first two times the portal opens. Ignore the second two."

"Exactly," Sefarina said, like it wasn't complicated at all.

Four hours later, to Zoe's chagrin, they entered the waters near Alaska with no complications navigating the top speeds and portal jumps. The temperature of the ocean dropped. It no longer felt like a blanket straight from the dryer; it was more like slipping into a bed with cool sheets. As they emerged from the ocean's dark zone, they passed a See-sea signifying they entered Prince William Sound.

Directly behind the See-sea was a blob of goo floating through the water like a wall. Zoe scowled in disgust. She and Sefarina weaved their way around the deposits of oil until they entered a vast valley. Even with the murky waters, Zoe could see the damage done to the area. As they swam farther into the underbelly of the realm, the stench of rot permeated in her nose.

Skeletal remains peppered the coarse sand on the barren seafloor. Oil seeps spurted about and left only mangled coral and blackened ash over the soil. A monstrous pile of litter filled a crater in the center of the valley and had a group of mermaids digging in the sand to bury trash while others picked out trinkets and treasures.

Other curious mermaids swam around, ignoring Zoe and Sefarina's presence. They had jerky movements, not fluid and graceful like the other groups of mermaids Zoe met. Some of them had dark, mangled hair; others had elongated arms and fingers. The ten or so pure-tails were the color of milk chocolate and appeared the healthiest, while the rest were mixed-tails with muted colors and sallow skin.

"The Brown-Tails are probably the most important part of our habitat. They help nourish and protect our flora and fauna, and since the industrial era, they've tried to regulate pollution. They also help control our climate. At one time, they outnumbered every other color by at least four-to-one. Now, we don't have enough Tails, or magic, to take care of our realm. We bring the trash here to help mask the smell using the oil seeps. Plus, it's easier for our small team to control it in one area."

Zoe thought back to the times she and the swim team visited to the beach for a day of community cleanup.

As a human, did I really do my part to take care of the beach?

A few days here and there didn't seem like enough. The mermaids couldn't do it alone, even if they had all their magic. Even if humans didn't know mermaids helped, they needed to do more to keep the environment healthy. Zoe vowed, once she fully returned to power, she would find a better way for their worlds to come together to keep the waters and coasts clean.

A brown-tail paddled over to them. He had a warm smile and dark hair down to his mid-back. Sefarina introduced him as Zale. His twin sister, Sedna, swam behind him, clinging to his lean body. With narrowed eyes and a tight-lipped frown, Sedna peeked out from behind his shoulder. Her fingers pressed into his arm that was covered in a colorful tattoo of the underwater ecosystem.

"Thank you for coming to see us," Zale said. "We are the few who committed to stay here until your return, or until a new leader takes over."

As soon as Zale started talking, Zoe noticed the lurking mermaids encircled them, curious about the newcomers but too timid to come closer.

Will my words really resonate with the Tails who are the pillars of my realm?

"My guardian and I are doing our best to find the remaining stones before we're out of time in less than a month. We're confident. We're working on deciphering the riddle for the second stone's location."

Zale grinned. "Hmm, I heard that old mer-tales claimed there's writing on those stones."

Zoe snickered, remembering how Sefarina mentioned the same thing, which helped in solving the riddle. "That's true."

Zale smacked his hand against his tail and smirked. "I knew it. Hear that?" he said to the Tails swarming around them. "There is progress, more than anything we've had in the past." A humming of chatter erupted around them with some Tails flipping and twisting in excitement. Zoe let out a sigh of relief. It wasn't much, but it sparked some life into the community.

Everyone except Sedna seemed enlivened. She hid behind her brother again, glaring at Zoe with an uneasy intensity.

"As much as I would love Zoe to stay, she needs to return to land before her time expires, and she becomes a Landwalker again," Sefarina explained.

Understanding, he nodded. The other Tails went back to their own business. Zale chauffeured them out of the valley with Sedna, who was never more than an arm's length away. She had two braids, was as thin as her twin, had the same tattoo, and sported a much shorter tail; the right side of her fluke, practically missing.

Was she born that way because of the toxicity of the water? Is that why she's so cautious? She felt a need to win her over. Perhaps, in time, she'd get to know her.

As they passed a mangled ball of seaweed, Zoe eyed a starfish propped against it. Instead of its usual five spines, it only had three. She gently ran her fingertips across the ridge of its abrasive skin, calming its suffering.

A ball of cerulean-blue light glowed from Zoe's fingertips, blanketing the starfish and the surrounding seaweed. Zoe gasped.

"Keep your fingers on her," Sedna shouted as she pushed away from her brother and swam next to Zoe. She wrapped her long fingers around Zoe's wrist to steady her hand over the squirming echinoderm.

Zoe and Sedna stared into the brilliant blue light and watched two spines growing out from the center of the starfish. Its dull pink shade quickly became vibrant once again.

"Carefully pick her up and follow me." Sedna rushed past her brother and Sefarina with Zoe hot on her trail. Zoe clutched the creature against her chest as if holding a newborn baby.

They ascended into shallow waters where there was an abundant amount of sea life. Sedna pointed to some coral that had other colorful starfish on it. "She will flourish here."

Zoe cradled the starfish and placed her on the rocky coral. Sedna hitched onto Zoe's upper arm and cuddled against her. Worried about scaring off the apprehensive mermaid, Zoe froze.

"You healed her. She couldn't do that on her own and was near death. She's happy. I can tell."

Zoe tipped her head and grinned at the bashful mermaid.

"Sorry." Zale tried to peel his sister away from Zoe's arm.

"I want her to heal me!" Sedna cried, pulling her arm out of her brother's grip.

Zoe's heart broke. "I can try." She ran her fingertips over the ridges of Sedna's fluke, the same way she had done to the starfish.

Sefarina placed her hand on Zoe's shoulder. "What if you overdo yourself? You have little time left."

Zoe closed her eyes, not caring about herself. She had to try. If she could heal Sedna and make her happy, it would allow the Tails to further believe their future could change.

If I fail, at least I showed I will help and can try again when I'm stronger.

The bright blue light shone through her closed eyes. She opened them, the side of Sedna's fluke emerged, elongating her tail.

Zoe tried to hold steady, but exerting that much magical energy made her quiver.

Wait, I'm not trembling. The stone pendant is.

It vibrated against her chest. Her time was nearly up. She'd drown if she stayed, but Sedna was close to being healed.

Sensing danger, Sefarina and Zale latched onto Zoe's upper arms, sandwiching her between the two and sped toward the surface. The pendant glowed, encasing the three of them in purple flitters of light.

"We will not make it," Zale shouted.

"As soon as you transform, hold your breath!" Sefarina insisted.

Zoe took one last drag through the slits behind her ears just as her legs broke free of her tail, and her incredible mermaid vision faded away. She squeezed her eyes shut to keep the salinity of the water from burning her eyes.

Seconds later, the three broke through the surface. Water splashed around them as Zoe sucked in the fresh sea air. She wiped her face and tipped her head back, her chest heaving up and down. She shielded the bright moonlight from her eyes, grateful for Sefarina and Zale.

Zale floated next to her. "I should not have allowed my sister to pressure you."

"Wasn't her fault," Zoe said in between labored breaths. "I wanted to." She looked at him from beneath her lashes. "I needed to."

Zale lowered his eyes. "Sedna's fears stop her from coming to the surface, but I know she feels indebted to you, just as I do. Thank you."

"Hopefully, she'll gain the confidence to visit different areas in our realm."

"I agree. And once you return to power, her magic will be just as strong as mine, giving us a reliable pure-tail to help monitor our environment."

Zoe smiled. "That would be wonderful."

Zale lifted Zoe's hand to his lips and gave her a sweet kiss. "Thank you for the gift you gave us. We shall see you again." He slipped below the water and swam off.

Sefarina placed her hand on Zoe's arm. "Come on." She guided her toward the coastline and protected her when a larger wave rolled over them. At the beach, Sefarina transformed from mermaid to her human form, but not before Zoe noticed the graying of her tail. She felt bad, knowing Sefarina had used too much of her magic, which explained why she hadn't immediately transported Zoe to safety the moment she started morphing back into human form.

"Your magical abilities are growing. You *must* be close to finding the second stone, because there is no way you would've been able to use healing magic a few days ago."

"Maybe I should try it on you?"

Sefarina shook her head. "I recover with rest and time, but thank you. Hita will care for me upon my return. I'm going to drop you off in front of The Greek Theatre, but I won't stay to see you off. I'll barely have enough energy to return to the sea, but it was worth having you visit that part of the realm."

"Thanks for taking me and saving Baxter earlier." Zoe stood and helped Sefarina to her feet.

Sefarina gave her a warm, dimpled smile. "Ready?"

Zoe nodded, even though she really wasn't ready. Teleporting was horrible, like trying to breathe through a plastic bag wrapped tightly around your head. She supposed it was the price of magically transporting to any location without the wait time and annoyances of commercial travel. She inhaled the fresh air. Sefarina clutched her hand and whisked her away into a whirlwind of aqua-colored lights.

She landed with a *thud* and toppled onto a grassy area directly in front of the main gates of The Greek Theatre. Sefarina chuckled at Zoe's blunder, released her hand, and disappeared into the quiet night.

Zoe pushed herself to her feet, brushed the dirt off her shorts, and adjusted her bikini top. Having lost her flip-flops in the undersea transformation, she took a few barefoot steps forward and stopped. Even though the night was warm, and the air was still, a tingling chill swept across the base of her neck.

She took a few more steps. The hairs on her neck prickled again. She looked all around, trying to find the source of the disturbance, but saw nothing unusual. As she circled around, she glanced westward toward the outdoor amphitheater, and felt the tingling chill once again. She stared into the dark, knowing something tried to signal her.

The stone pendant softly pulsated against her chest like a faint heartbeat. She twisted her torso; stone changed its intensity depending on the direction she faced. The second stone called to her. It wasn't in this vicinity, though. She gripped her necklace and closed her eyes.

Project your energy outward. Pinpoint the location.

She smiled.

She could feel the stone's energy coming from somewhere to the west.

It was hidden somewhere on land.

CHAPTER 19

BAXTER

SEVERAL HOURS AFTER LEAVING Zoe in the middle of the Pacific, Baxter found the answer to the riddle. Excited to share the news with Zoe, he packed an overnight bag that held his findings and other essentials. He headed to Zoe's house and made himself at home.

He prepped a dinner of salad, buttery garlic chicken and pasta tossed with olive oil and red pepper flakes, knowing Zoe would be famished upon her return. He ate alone. Determined to stay awake through the night, he brewed himself a pot of coffee using his favorite imported Jamaican coffee beans.

As he sipped the first cup, he laid out his findings across the heavy oak table in the formal dining room. He stacked several worn leather journals at the end of the table, spread out some manila folders filled with notes next to them, opened the map of the realms, and placed The Aquatic Accords scroll at the other end.

He perused the scroll for a few minutes but decided it was only fair to wait for Zoe to learn about the different realms and abilities mermaids possessed. It was her history more than his, even though he wanted nothing more than to open it and devour every word. To remove himself from the temptation, he poured the remaining coffee into an insulated thermos and drove to The Greek Theater to wait for her arrival.

As he turned onto the major thoroughfare, he noticed her walking down the street barefoot. He pulled up to her, and she piled into the passenger seat. "I have so much to tell you."

All the way back to her house, her mouth ran non-stop about her adventure to Alaska. She even continued talking while devouring two plates of food, with Baxter only interrupting for minimal questions or clarification. Although her growing magical abilities impressed him, he couldn't help feeling a twinge of loneliness since he couldn't experience those moments with her.

Not wanting to waste a moment, she coaxed him into staying in the bathroom while she showered, firing off questions about what he did from behind the glass door.

Baxter sat on the tiled step leading into the large garden tub, careful to keep his eyes focused on anything but her. "Farah's departing comment about which field of science would contain the study of mermaids kept running through my mind."

"Why?" Zoe asked.

"The myths, legends, and folklore I teach all reside under the umbrella of the humanities curriculum. In the world of science, however, mermaids would coincide with oceanography."

Zoe wiped the water from the glass door and peered at him. "And? What did you find?"

"Well, first, it turns out that you were correct in believing there was something off about the first line of the riddle."

Zoe snickered. "I *knew* there was something weird about it saying 'Clock is science.'"

"Indeed, but it wasn't readily noticeable because 'Clock' is at the beginning of the sentence, and the first word is always capitalized. 'Clock' is also singular, which to me, meant something specific—perhaps a proper noun."

"So, it always would be capitalized, no matter where it was in the sentence." Zoe shut off the water.

"Correct." Baxter leapt to his feet and plucked the towel off the hook next to the shower. He held it out for her to grab and averted his eyes once again. "And if you rearrange the line to "Science is Clock," the word Clock is now a proper noun.

Zoe, wrapped in the towel, bent forward, flipped her hair over her head, and scrunched her hair dry with another towel. "Are you saying clock is the name of something?" She flicked her head up, water flung off the tips of her hair and pelted Baxter in the face.

"No, not the name of some*thing*." He wiped the water away from his cheek.

Zoe's eyes widened. "Clock is the name of some*one*."

Baxter gave her a coy smile. "Exactly. And when Farah brought up where science about mermaids might be found, I deduced that would be oceanography, if they were scientifically studied."

Zoe padded into her bedroom and tossed her towel away. She had an air of confidence in her Baxter never saw before. He stood outside the bathroom door. He fanned his face, trying to convince himself he was warm because of the steam from her shower and not his attraction to her.

"After I realized oceanography was the clue she hinted about, it triggered a vague memory."

"Which was?" She dressed in a lightweight tank top and lounge pants.

"A few months ago, I read an article about the upcoming opening of California's newest state university."

She hummed as she stepped past him, grabbed a wide-tooth comb from the bathroom vanity, and raked it through her hair.

"The location of the university was more interesting than the school itself."

She dropped the comb on the countertop. "What do ya mean?"

Baxter motioned her to follow him downstairs. He retrieved a piece of paper from a manila file folder on the dining room table. "Here, I printed it out for you to read. The article is over two years old, but has the connection we needed to solve the riddle."

Zoe plucked the single page of paper from his fingers, settled into the cushioned leather chair at the head of the table, and read the article out loud.

"It's finally official: The seventeen hundred acres known as Camarillo State Hospital are now abandoned. The last employees said their final goodbyes to a clinic that helped advance the treatment of modern psychiatric care. Camarillo State Hospital had been in use since 1936 and treated schizophrenia and autism. At one time, the hospital had well over five thousand patients, but by the mid-nineties, those numbers were less than one thousand. Due to rising costs, Governor Pete Wilson announced the closing of the hospital set for July of this year. Even though the Chief of Research and the Director of Clinical Research developed innovative methods of treatment for the mentally disabled, it wasn't enough to save the hospital. The campus is now closed, and most employees have been transferred to local hospitals, but the buildings will not remain empty.

Ventura County is in the works to transform the structures into its first public university through the California State University system. Renovation and construction will begin in the spring of 1999. Until then, Camarillo officials would like to remind the public that it is illegal to trespass on the campus, and doing so could result in fines and jail time. Many of the structures are dilapidated and unsafe, while others are under construction. For individuals interested in the hospital's history, the public library will have a permanent display of old blueprints, photographs, and land surveys. There will be a showcase of the motion pictures and videos filmed at the old hospital, including N'Sync's most recent hit, *Thinking of You*. Artifacts will also be displayed, including those from its most infamous patients, like the singer Charlie Parker, and the hospital's very own mad professor, Dr. Abraham Clock."

Zoe's eyes pitched toward Baxter. "Dr. Clock?"
"Keep reading," Baxter pressed. "It gets better."
Zoe leaned forward and held the paper closer to her face.

"Charlie Parker was a respected jazz saxophone player, who spent six months at the facility in the forties. While there, he played his saxophone with the hospital band and wrote the song Relaxin' at Camarillo. Dr. Abraham Clock was admitted to the hospital in 1939, weeks after being forced to resign from his post as a distinguished professor at Scripps Institution of Oceanography. Allegedly, during the summer of 1938, rather than using the schools' schooner, the E. W. Scripps, for academic purposes, Dr. Clock used it to complete deep-sea dives in search of evidence of the mythological creatures, mermaids. Shortly after he arrived at the hospital, he was found brutally murdered, which to this day is an unsolved case."

Zoe waved the article about. "Dr. Clock and Oceanography! Mermaids and another murder? Remember what the riddle said: 'Clock is science, mermaids are not myth.' Get it? Dr. Clock, a man of science, knew mermaids weren't a myth. He wasn't psychotic. He knew the truth. But how?"

Baxter steepled his fingers, wondering what connection Dr. Clock had to the mystical world, and why he would stake his professional reputation on proving it.

Zoe slid the manila folders closer to her and rummaged through their contents. She reached for The Aquatic Accords, unrolled it, and glanced over the words. "Anything in here useful?"

"Only that it reads like a history book and genealogy chart. Remember, Farah said it wouldn't help us in our search."

"That's right. Did you find anything else about Dr. Clock, then?" She rolled up the scroll and placed it on the table.

"He's been dead a long time. The only information I found was about his time at the university and how he used the schooner. I also looked up other oceanographers and professors, but none of them seemed to have subscribed to his belief in mythical sea creatures."

Zoe looked at the article again. "Poor guy. He was only trying to prove the existence of mermaids. Nobody believed him, so they threw him into an asylum, only to be murdered. It's tragic."

"Indeed. At least we know the first part of the clue refers to him. Perhaps we should travel to San Diego and see if he has any descendants, or visit Scripps and inquire about him, stating research purposes."

Zoe tucked the article back inside the manila folder and nibbled on her lower lip.

"What are you thinking?" he asked.

"Like I told you, I could feel the energy of the second stone calling to me as soon as Sefarina dropped me off. It's on land, but west of here, not south. What if instead of going to where Dr. Clock lived and worked, what if we go to the place he died? I betcha' there's a clue around the old hospital grounds, which is west of here."

Baxter considered this. If they found nothing at the abandoned hospital, they would have to make the three-hour drive to San Diego and search for answers there, wasting even more time. But he knew they needed to listen to Zoe's instincts. "You may be right. Hopefully, the stone will call to you again, so we are not wasting our time searching multiple abandoned buildings."

Zoe yawned. "I dunno, maybe. I can feel it fading the longer I'm in human form. But we can easily remedy that. The beach isn't far from Camarillo."

Baxter paced. "The bigger issue is that the university will open soon, and I am sure it is still a construction zone. We can't simply waltz in there."

"We don't have time to waste by trying to get permission."

Baxter studied her. A look of defiance passed over her features. She arched a sly brow at him. The urgency to restore her magic and save her realm overshadowed her ethics of abiding by the law and doing what was right.

Have my own twisted ways rubbed off on her?

"Very well then," he said. "After we rest, though. We will wait until this evening, when the crews are gone and there is still enough light to sneak around the site."

She smiled, but her eyes were heavy. Content with their decision to sneak around the private property, they headed off upstairs to their respective rooms.

As Baxter fell onto the plushy queen bed in the guest room, the early morning sun pierced the sky, casting creepy shadows through the slatted blinds. He was sure they'd find the second pendant at the old hospital. He wasn't too worried about trespassing; that was nothing new to him. His concern was what else they would find at the semi-abandoned location. In all his years, there were only a few things that gave him anxiety. Snakes were one of them.

Ghosts were another.

CHAPTER 20

ZOE

BAXTER EXITED THE 101 Freeway and drove nearly two miles through farmlands and orange groves before reaching the entrance site of the old Camarillo State Hospital. As he took a left on University Drive, Zoe lowered her window, letting the warm evening breeze carry the scent of oranges into the vehicle. Massive trees lined either side of the two-lane road and canopied over it. As they drove over a small wooden bridge, the trees petered out and revealed the sprawling campus tucked up against the base of a rocky hill, secluded from the outside world.

The buildings were in a mission revival-style with white stucco and red-tiled roofs. Huge shade trees, tall palm trees, and expansive fields of grass peppered the campus, and as the pièce de résistance, a bell tower sat in the middle of the grounds, rising high above the other structures.

Baxter made a right turn onto a one-way street with a grassy median separating it from the opposite side of the road. The tranquility of the campus changed the closer they came to it. The structures became increasingly dilapidated as he followed the quaint road. Many buildings had broken or missing windows, chipped stucco and tiles, lopsided doors, and grunge caked to their facade.

Zoe rubbed away the goosebumps that rose on her arm, not truly sure if it was from the haunting serenity of the location, or from the energy of the second stone calling to her. She was confident they were in the right place. She pointed to an entrance between two stucco walls with overgrown ivy. "Park inside there."

Baxter steered the SUV past a fenced-off area that housed construction supplies and maneuvered the vehicle through the opening. The small alcove had newly laid black asphalt and was hidden behind a row of trash bins. Baxter parked the SUV between a pile of broken construction materials and a bin overflowing with landscape waste.

They clambered out of the SUV and exited the alcove. Zoe scanned the campus, trying to decide which direction to head. Baxter walked left, toward the main section of the campus, but to the right, just down the road and along the stucco wall, Zoe noticed another entrance with a turquoise double door securing the alcove.

"We need to go there," she said. Not waiting for Baxter, she jogged over to the wooden doors. Beyond the stucco walls, a lush canopy of treetops poked over the top. They loomed above her, rising to at least twelve feet in height. The turquoise paint was peeling, and the wood was splintering. She gripped the iron handle and pulled. The door was heavy and hardly moved.

"Together," Baxter directed as he clutched the handle with her and pulled. An ear-splitting creek echoed through the air. Zoe guessed the door hadn't been opened in decades. They wrenched it open just enough to enter.

"Be careful," Baxter warned as she stepped through the threshold onto a terracotta pathway.

Baxter followed her inside, dipping his head away from the branches of the overgrown trees. As they sauntered down a pathway that snaked through the secret garden, Baxter tripped and fell forward, catching himself on Zoe.

"You okay?" She helped him stand.

"Fine," he mumbled as he fought at the vines and wispy branches tangled around his shoes and ankles. "These plants are out of control."

Zoe canvassed the hidden outdoor nursery. To her, this place was a gem. The light from the setting sun cast a soft glow throughout. A gust of wind rustled the trees and bushes. She inhaled, relishing the sweet fragrance of the blooming flowers.

Baxter pushed past her and marched down a twisted dirt path that veered away from the main one. It weaved through a rose-garden and ended in a small open area. A wooden stall with a striped canopy was torn and draped to one side. There were a few broken bistro tables and chairs scattered about, and some gardening tables perched against the stucco walls.

Baxter circled around and pulled out a pocket flashlight. He illuminated the dark corners of the lush garden. "I don't see anything of use in here."

Zoe agreed that the café area was not helpful, but something drew her toward the rose garden. She stepped off the pathway and weaved through the thorny plants, smelling a few of the larger flowers as she went. "It feels like something is here, all around me, but I can't pinpoint the source of the energy."

From behind her, Baxter grumbled a slur of curse words. He plucked thick thorns from his arm. She narrowed her eyes at him. "You've been in a sour mood ever since we stepped foot in this garden. Why?"

"I know." Baxter rubbed his forehead. "I, too, feel an energy here, but one I do not like."

The breeze rustled the plants.

A misty cloud of their own breath puffed out of their mouths.

"Damn it. We need to go." Baxter tugged Zoe's wrist, wanting her to follow him.

"What is with you?" Zoe asked.

Baxter increased their pace, getting them back on the terracotta pathway.

Just before they reached the turquoise doors, Baxter skidded to a stop. Zoe clipped his right side, stumbled past him, and caught herself against the trunk of a tree. She whirled around; ready to lash out at him, but quickly understood why he stopped so abruptly.

A billowy white fog hovered and swirled over the pathway, blocking the exit. Baxter's eyes were wide open. He took a step back. "Ghosts," he muttered.

Mesmerized, Zoe's lips parted, her breath visible in the chilly atmosphere. "Are... are they dangerous?"

"The angry ones can be."

The white fog coiled around until it formed a mini twister. Zoe shielded her face from the debris of sticks, pebbles, and dirt. Once the tornado stopped, she brushed her hair away from her eyes to see the white mist form into a figure of a man.

At first glance, he appeared solid, like Zoe and Baxter, but upon closer inspection, Zoe could see the turquoise doors through his body. A faint halo of golden light shimmered around his outline. He appeared to be in his late twenties and had light brown hair and dark eyes. He sported a black fedora, a three-piece wool suit, and wing-tipped shoes; garb that looked like something from the thirties. He pursed his lips into a tight line and glared at an open pocket watch in his hand. He snapped it closed, startling Zoe and Baxter both.

His eyes bore into Baxter's. "It's about damn time."

Zoe's body trembled. The ghost sounded plenty angry, and she wasn't keen on finding out what dangers it could inflict. Her mind kept telling her to run, but her body refused to move, rooting her feet to the ground, as if the overgrown garden had forbidden her from leaving.

CHAPTER 21

BAXTER

ALTHOUGH BAXTER FULLY EXPECTED to encounter some ghosts, he still couldn't avoid the jitters that came during any confrontation with them. While some ghosts roamed the earth to help others and would find peace once they fulfilled their duty, others were merely tricksters and nuisances who wanted attention. The angry ones, those who either had their life taken from them or had refused to accept death by avoiding the peace found in the light, were the ones who caused the most pain to Baxter.

Their hate stemmed from their envious desire to live, and their jealous rage came from knowing Baxter would never have to experience death. And they made him suffer for it. Angry ghosts would siphon out his energy, like a grape drying out in the sun, forcing him to shrivel up and teeter on the brink of death. In this state, they could control his emotions and mental state, akin to an episode of paranoid schizophrenia. It took him the better part of two decades to ward off ghosts, and only through his practice of yoga and suspended breathing could he fend off most attacks.

He drew in a slow, controlled breath then paused. It was during this retention that he could confuse the ghosts into believing he was not alive, frustrating them enough to leave him alone.

"Did you hear me, guardian?" the ghost demanded.

As Baxter exhaled, he felt the familiar drain of his energy leaving his body. At the bottom of the breath, he paused his breathing again, and focused on Zoe. She did not know what he was doing, but she seemed worried.

The ghost ignored Baxter and drank in Zoe's appearance. "You were so worth the wait, m'dear. Just look at you; radiant as ever."

Zoe blushed. Her demeanor shifted. She batted her long lashes at her charmer. "Hello, Dr. Clock," she replied in one of the sweetest tones Baxter ever heard from her.

Baxter inhaled through a snarled lip.

Are they flirting with each other? Or did he place her under some spell?

The ghost covered his heart with his hand and sighed. "My dear friend, it has been way too long." He stepped forward and took her hands into his. "I only wish we had more time together, Melantha—"

"Her name is Zoe," Baxter bit out, forgoing his breathing technique.

"Zoe," the ghost whispered before placing a gentle kiss on the top of each hand.

"Pardon me," Baxter said, upset over the ghost's promiscuous behavior. Baxter attempted to storm over to the pair, but his foot caught in the overgrown shrubbery, detaining him once again. He grunted and tugged at the thin vines raveled around his ankle. He suspected the ghost of the man fawning after Zoe had something to do with his sudden misfortunes in the garden's flora.

Zoe giggled and fanned herself like a giddy schoolgirl.

Feeling like a green-eyed cad, Baxter cleared his throat. "Sir, we are in quite a hurry. How did you know Melantha?"

Without taking his eyes off of Zoe, Dr. Clock replied, "Well, of course you are in a hurry. You squandered many years trying to find this beautiful gem."

That cut deep. He was used to his own guilty conscience, but to be chided by a ghost seemed to hurt him even more.

Zoe arched her brow and stifled her smile. "Well, Baxter did the best he could, Dr. Clock. We're here now."

Dr. Clock dipped his head. "That you are. Please call me Abraham, Zoe."

Zoe nodded. "Can you tell us how you knew Melantha, Abraham?"

Dr. Clock reached forward and swept away the long strand of Zoe's hair draped over her shoulder. "She had intentions of murdering me after I spotted a group of mermaids off the coast of Baja back in 1897."

Zoe groaned. "I should've known; it's what mermaids do, I suppose. Especially when you have murderous eyes like mine."

Dr. Clock laughed. "Your cursed eyes had nothing to do with your reasons to kill me."

"You know about Medusa's curse?" Baxter asked.

Dr. Clock scoffed. "Of course." He cut his eyes to the side and looked over his shoulder at Baxter. "Who *doesn't* know that?"

Baxter clenched his jaw.

Dr. Clock broke the stem of a nearby pink rose and handed the bloom to Zoe. She blushed as she buried her nose in its petals.

How is she so blind to Dr. Clock's unabashed annoyance with my presence?

Baxter stole the flower away from Zoe and tossed it over his shoulder.

"Hey!" Zoe said.

"Care to explain what you meant by saying she had *intentions* of murdering you?" Baxter demanded.

Without hesitation, Dr. Clock picked another bud and handed it to Zoe.

Zoe grinned. "Why would she want to kill you, Abraham?"

"It's what your kind does when a human makes waves about mermaids being real."

Confused at his statement, Zoe narrowed her eyes.

Baxter rolled his.

He wanted more information, but there was no use in asking. The ghost only wanted to respond to Zoe. Baxter nudged her elbow, prompting her to keep him talking.

"Care to tell us that story?" Zoe gave Baxter a subtle but dismissive wave of her hand.

Dr. Clock held his palms face up. A cloud of thin smoke conjured in his hands then formed into a ghostly image of four mermaids diving and circling around a sailboat. Zoe and Baxter stepped closer, hypnotized by the animated image.

"I had been distraught from my first wife's death and was thinking about ending my life when I saw the four creatures leaping in and out of the water. They sang the most haunting, but beautiful, song I had ever heard. Before I could go overboard and welcome death by their hands, the wind shifted, and I hit my head and knocked myself out cold. When I awoke, my boat was drifting aimlessly, and the creatures were nowhere to be found. It took hours to find my way back to land where I foolishly spread the word that mermaids were real."

Dr. Clock wiggled his fingers, and the cloud shifted into a new scene. This time, it featured a California bungalow with a woman on the front porch, speaking to Dr. Clock, who stood on the threshold. Another woman stood near the porch, beneath the shade tree.

"No one believed me, of course. Tales of my madness circled through the town, and I even believed I had imagined it. That was until Melantha paid me a visit several months later."

Dr. Clock flicked his fingers and the misty white images disappeared. "Join hands with me. I can use my energy and project my memories and feelings into your mind and show you exactly what happened."

Without hesitation, Zoe jutted her hands out, took hold of Dr. Clock's hand and clutched Baxter's.

"You are no ordinary ghost," Baxter mumbled as he shuffled next to the man.

"And you are no ordinary human," Dr. Clock quipped as Baxter took hold of his icy hand and closed their circle.

A warm energy circled the trio. A powerful force hit Baxter in the chest, knocking the wind out of him. Emotions flooded him, drowning him with in a turbulent wave of anxiety. The affection Dr. Clock had for Melantha, and the curious appetite he had about mermaids, overtook him. A vision appeared in his mind's eye, and he was transported into a memory not of his own.

Orange and purple colors streaked across the warm evening sky. Dr. Clock stood on the threshold, arms crossed and scowling at Melantha. Behind her stood a woman with long hair. The shadows from the shade tree shrouded her face.

"How can I help you?" Dr. Clock asked Zoe's former self.

"Hello, Abraham. My name is Melantha, and I am the mermaid queen of the Lively North to East realm in the Pacific."

"Well, I'll be damned. You are real."

The corner of Melantha's full lips twitched. "Yes. Well, that's why I'm here." Melantha motioned to the woman behind her. "That's Neala. She, and the others who tried to capture you once before, want you to stop spreading tales of our existence as they are concerned you are scaring people away from the waters. I was brought here to assess the situation and stop you if need be."

"Are you such a coward you must face me while I am alone, whereas you need to have assistance? Madam, I assure you, I no longer welcome death. I have a purpose in this life and will not be murdered in the threshold of my own home." Dr. Clock's hand grazed the butt of his Winchester that was propped against the interior wall next to his front door.

She gave him a warm smile. "I was hoping you would say that." She looked over her shoulder to address the woman behind her. "I am no longer in need of your assistance, Neala."

Neala stomped her foot and marched away from the house, hissing something foreign under her breath.

Melantha faced Dr. Clock. "Please accept my apologies. I don't agree with her, or the others, and they're having a fit about it. To keep peace in my realm, I had to entertain their demands since, by my rule, I am the only one who is allowed to dispose of a human outside of the water."

Dr. Clock nodded, and Melantha continued. "Stories actually help keep the lore of mermaids alive, so you haven't done any harm. My friends are merely being greedy since you escaped them once and have made a name for yourself by boasting about it."

"Then I shall stop speaking about my encounter."

Melantha shook her head. "No. I see you have no ill intentions against us, and I think you should continue to tell your tales. The truth is, we need humans like you, and we need your beliefs about otherworldly beings, magic, and all that is mysterious. It helps power the magic in our world."

Dr. Clock cocked a brow and removed his hand from his rifle. "Are you certain? What about Neala and the others?"

Melantha nodded. "You will not suffer any harm from those in my realm, that I can assure you. I would stay out of the waters near South America, anything past Hawaii, and every other ocean, though. I don't have authority in those realms."

"Understandable."

The memory faded as a new one replaced it.

Melantha and Dr. Clock sat on the edge of a wooden dock, their bare feet tickling the top of the water. Dr. Clock placed his palm on Melantha's back, comforting her.

"I know the decision is difficult but follow your heart. If he loves you, he'll respect any decision you make regarding your magic and realm."

"Thanks, Abraham. You have been such a good friend over the last few years." Melantha conjured a palm-sized tiger nautilus seashell in her hand. "I want you to have this. This may be the last time I am able to use magic," she said, handing the shell to Dr. Clock. "It's a small token of our friendship."

A swirl of white vapor interrupted the memory. The warmth that surrounded Baxter vanished. He opened his eyes. Zoe wiped away the beads of sweat from across her brow and doubled over, catching her breath.

"Sorry," she heaved. She stood up. "I had to break the chain."

Baxter hovered over her, offering her a steady arm. She pushed the strands of hair behind her ears. "Seeing my past self was too much."

Dr. Clock dipped his chin. "I didn't think about that. I'm sorry, Zoe."

"It's okay, really. I didn't think I'd have such an odd reaction. Can you tell us what happened next, instead of showing us?"

"Of course." Dr. Clock paced through the rose bushes and traced his fingers over the roses. "About a year after Melantha gave me the seashell, Neala came to my door to announce the queen had been murdered. She forbade me from speaking about the existence of mermaids, threatening to kill me if I continued. It was then I dedicated myself to the world of Oceanography, in memory of my dear friend.

"Many years, a second wife, and a couple of children later, I was hired at Scripps. All went well until they gave me access to the university's schooner to head my own deep-sea exploration. After all those years obsessing about mermaids, I couldn't resist having the best equipment at my fingertips. I broke. I abused my power to search for Neala or other mermaids."

Dr. Clock stopped pacing and stuffed his hands in his trouser pockets.

"Over the course of our friendship, Melantha explained everything about her world. I wanted answers about her death because I knew without a proper leader, the climate would be affected. Sure enough, it was, and I had the data to prove it. I wanted to create a bridge between the mermaids and humans, to help keep the climate and habitat of her realm safe, but all I ended up with was a forced resignation and a lifetime sentence in an asylum."

Zoe cast her eyes downward and shook her head. "I'm so sorry. Melantha would have been proud that you tried to help. I haven't heard of or met Neala. I wonder where she is?"

"Good question. One I would like answered myself. The last time I saw her, she was right here in this garden." Dr. Clock curled his lip and his nostrils flared.

Zoe's brows rose.

"Why?" Baxter asked.

"About a year after I was admitted here, she showed up. I demanded answers from her. She demanded my gift from Melantha. I refused. Next thing I knew, she'd thrust a dagger deep into my stomach and left me to die right back there, in the middle of the roses."

Zoe gasped and raked her hands through her hair. "What a—"

"Zoe," Baxter stated, trying to keep her focused before she wasted time ranting. "We need to find out who Neala is and where she's at. The Aquatic Accords might have that information. We should return to your house."

Zoe shook her head. "No. The stone's here. It's in the shell. That's why Neala wanted it."

Baxter nodded in agreement. They had to find the stone first, and then they could focus on Neala.

Zoe took Dr. Clock's hand. "Abraham, please tell me you have the nautilus."

The ghost kissed the top of her hand again. "I haven't had it since I arrived here."

Zoe dropped his hand and let out a guttural cry, throwing her arms up in the air. "But I feel it."

Zoe may have felt at a loss, but Baxter noticed the coy smile that flashed across Dr. Clock's face; the cheeky charmer had a flare for the dramatic. Baxter was sure although Dr. Clock didn't physically have the shell, he sure as hell knew where it was hidden.

Chapter 22

Zoe

It took Zoe a few moments to realize Dr. Clock confessed to knowing the nautilus's location. Slightly miffed Baxter came to the realization before her, and let her carry on in such a manner, she sulked behind the two men as they slipped between the narrow crevice of the opened turquoise door and exited the garden.

At least she hadn't displayed any old-fashioned jealousy like Baxter. She especially liked that a ghost could so easily fluster him. Dr. Clock's flirtatious appeal flattered her as she was rarely accustomed to that kind of attention. She quite enjoyed it and knew his intentions were harmless. The dashing man needed to feel alive again, and Zoe couldn't fault him for that. His confidence and charisma emitted from him like rays from the sun, making her want to bask in his ambiance. She easily understood why Melantha befriended him *and* why the stone hid inside his treasured seashell.

Is Baxter's jealousy truly the root of his strange behavior?

She wasn't so sure and was curious about what was going through his mind, but knew it wasn't the time to find out.

"Where are we headed?" Zoe caught up with the two men.

Dr. Clock, who glimmered in the moonlight, pointed toward the rocky hill. "Shortly after they admitted me, I had an inherent need to hide the shell for safekeeping. I always had it on me, and when my therapy group hiked up the rocky terrain for exercise and fresh air, I buried it."

"Let us hope you remember exactly where it is hidden," Baxter muttered and continued to walk down the street.

"My body may be dead, but my memory is not," Dr. Clock said.

"Is that so? Well, by all means, can you tell us more about Neala? Where is she? What did she look like?"

The moment Baxter brought up Neala, Zoe felt a tight knot cramp in her shoulder. She massaged herself, uncertain if her instincts were telling her she was right to believe Neala was involved with Melantha's murder, or if something else blanketed a sense of dread over her.

The night was oddly still and warm. Zoe chalked up her feelings to an internal warning about Neala; Dr. Clock's theories about this mermaid would be important.

"She was blonde and stunning; reminded me of the actress Veronica Lake. Melantha didn't speak about her, so I don't know much. But because Neala was able to murder me while she was on land in human form, I assume Melantha's powers transferred to her, since only the realm's ruler can carry out that kind of deed."

"Nobody has said anything about her. It *was* a long time ago. Besides, Aislinn is my second, not someone named Neala, so something must have happened. The next time I meet with anyone, I will be sure to ask about her."

The sidewalk narrowed, and the three walked single file. As they passed the old hospital buildings, Zoe used a mini flashlight and peeked through the windows. Different murals of varying sizes lined the walls. Some were full landscapes. Others were images from their era, like the famous silhouette of Alfred Hitchcock. Sadly, though, she noticed neutral color paint covering the art, preparing for the new school opening.

They continued to trek across the campus and came upon one of the larger main buildings amid restoration. One side of the structure had peeling paint and stucco, while the other half gleamed with fresh white paint. Zoe admired the red and yellow Spanish-style tiles that adorned the risers of the external stairs leading to the second story. Ornate, black iron rails lined the arched openings along the promenade.

She smacked into Baxter's back, once again, and dropped her flashlight, turning it off. "What the heck? Can you stop suddenly stopping?" She picked up her flashlight and stuffed it into her pocket.

"Shh," Baxter growled. He ducked behind a bush and pulled Zoe along with him.

"What's wrong?"

He gestured for her to look and not speak.

She leaned over Baxter and peered between the branches. A patrol car, with the windows lowered, crept down the road.

"Did they see us?" Zoe breathed, flinching as Dr. Clock appeared.

"They're getting out of the vehicle," he said.

"We should turn around and make a run for the SUV." Baxter took a step away.

Zoe seized his arm. "No," she said. She was too close to the second stone and wouldn't give up. "I can divert their attention if you and Abraham will sneak around the long way and get the seashell."

Baxter vigorously shook his head. "I don't think—"

"Then don't think. Trust me," she ordered. "Get the shell and meet me back at the SUV."

Baxter stepped close to her, swept her hair away from her face, placed a gentle kiss on her forehead. Before she could relish in his sweet touch, he sprinted away, with Dr. Clock by his side.

Zoe volunteered to be the distraction because she knew the police would see her as less threatening than Baxter, an unfortunate reality.

She peered through the branches as the two cops clicked on their flashlights and headed toward the direction of Baxter and Dr. Clock.

Thinking fast, Zoe scanned the area, looking for anything to get them off Baxter's trail. She made her way through the bushes and saw a stack of lumber near the building undergoing renovations. Like a linebacker, she rushed at the long beams, toppling them across the concrete, causing a startling echo across the quiet campus.

"Over there," she heard one of them shout.

She dipped into an alcove and pressed her back against the stucco. Her beating heart matched their hammering feet as they ran across the pavement.

"How did that happen?" one of them asked as they skidded to a halt near the pile of studs.

Zoe sprinted out of her hiding spot, careful to run on the tips of her toes for minimal sound, and slipped into the bushes to hide. Behind her, she heard one man calling into their radio, asking for backup at the campus, claiming that there were "punk kids" hanging around again.

"Great, more cops. Just what we need," she grumbled, wanting to draw the policemen further south from the main drag that led to the rocky hills. She plucked a sizeable rock from the planter, crept through the bushes, and sprinted into the dark shadows of the building next door. Next to her, leaned against the stucco, was an old window with thick glass and lead trim. Not really wanting to be a vandal, but with no other choice, Zoe whimpered as she squeezed her eyes shut, shielded her face, and pitched the rock through the glass.

She sprinted across the small lawn, with shouts from the officers behind her. She crouched behind a dusty, yellow bulldozer which gave her both coverage and perfect view. The two cops dashed across the lawn, the beam of lights from their flashlights bounced through the dark. One officer examined the broken glass, the evening shadows cloaking him. The other scanned the area. His head tipped back, like a bloodhound sniffing the air for the culprit. He took a few steps forward and entered the light from a nearby streetlamp. His head cocked to the side. He glared right at the bulldozer. Zoe bobbed away.

Did he see me?

"Go check behind that unit."

Zoe shifted and peered through the mechanics of the tractor. The officer searching the broken glass marched away from her and back across the lawn. The other officer, though, hadn't moved from beneath the streetlight. He sighed and cuffed the shirtsleeves of his uniform up to his elbows. He sauntered toward her hiding spot, as if he knew she was there.

Zoe surveyed her surroundings. Behind her was a long building with broken windows and stairs leading to a top floor. She could run inside it and lose him there. She swore.

Am I really thinking of trying to outrun a police officer?

She balled her fists, knowing she had to make a choice. She looked at the approaching officer again, about five yards from her.

A tiny gasp escaped. She gripped the rubber tire with shaky hands, eyeing the tattoo upon his forearm; a sword stabbing into flames with a raven perched on its hilt.

Her eyes traveled up to the officer's face.

That shit-eating grin was the same one she remembered him having the night he attacked her in Baxter's office. She should have expected him. Baxter *had* mentioned the man was always a thorn in his side. A pebble in his shoe.

Making an appearance right when Zoe would get her hands on the second stone was Lucas, the wickedly clever Atlantic-Tail, posing as a cop. If *he* was here, then his goons weren't far behind.

Chapter 23
BAXTER

BAXTER FOLLOWED DR. CLOCK across the sprawling campus, but hated every minute of being anchored to a ghost. His bones ached from the fever that invaded his body. His visible breath became a nuisance for his vision. But what annoyed Baxter the most was Dr. Clock's blatant arrogance of knowing he led the charge for their little side quest.

It was easy for a ghost to sneak around and evade the police. Easy for a ghost to disappear one moment, only to reappear the next, and end up several feet ahead.

And even easier for a ghost to traverse up the face of a hill.

"If you plant your toes into the dirt crevice near that large weedy bush, you can leverage yourself up better," Dr. Clock said.

Baxter cut his eyes over to Dr. Clock who sat on a rock, crossed legged and bored.

"It's difficult climbing such a treacherous hill without equipment. I told you we should have taken the path to reach the ridge." Baxter rammed his toes into the crevice and pushed himself up the incline, doing as suggested.

"And I told you, it would have taken much longer than going straight up the incline. Now, stop complaining and use that rock near your right hip as your next leverage point."

Baxter growled. He adjusted his weight to his left leg and planted his right foot on the rock.

It slipped out from beneath him.

He clawed at the earth and the thick stalks from the bush next to him. He caught himself before sliding down any further. Thorns pricked his hands. He winced, not wanting to show weakness.

"Oh, sorry, dear boy. I meant the rock near your left hip."

Baxter glared at his unwanted companion.

Dr. Clock smirked at him.

Baxter let a slew of curse words fly as he readjusted his weight and tried the rock near his *left* hip. He lifted himself up and climbed over to the rock Dr. Clock rested on. He sat down on it, not caring if the ghost was there or not, and drew in a ragged breath.

Dr. Clock appeared next to him, hovering over the hillside.

Baxter wiped the sweat beading on his brow with the back of his hand. He narrowed his eyes on the police car in the distance and searched the grounds for Zoe.

"She'll be fine," Dr. Clock said. "Melantha's strength and cleverness runs through her."

Baxter nodded. Zoe was fierce, for sure. It was one of things he adored about her.

He thought back to the kiss he placed on her forehead. Did it convey his message? He wanted her to be safe and that he cared for her. Immensely.

Perhaps more than I should...

Baxter could feel Dr. Clock's gaze boring into him and refused to acknowledge him.

"Loving a woman like her will wreck your soul, but for all the best reasons possible," Dr. Clock said, floating over to him, like he was sitting on the rock next to Baxter.

A rush of heat radiated from Baxter. The pestering ghost just added another reason to dislike him: he was all too observant.

But is he wrong?

Baxter cleared his throat. "Your commentary was not solicited."

"Be that as it may, it does not make my statement any less true."

Baxter huffed. He rolled his neck, cracking it. Twice.

The ghost pulled out his gold pocket watch. "Well, that's enough of a rest. Let us continue on." Dr. Clock floated off the rock and hovered in front of Baxter.

Baxter bit his tongue from the verbal sparring he wanted to partake in, but knew there was no time for it. He stood up. "How much farther?"

Dr. Clock disappeared in a wisp of white fog. "About thirty feet or so."

Baxter careened his neck back and saw Dr. Clock peaking over the edge of the ridge above him. He waved at him.

The audacity.

Baxter wiped his palms against his shirt and started the climb once more. "You do realize we're using the path on the way down."

"Absolutely," Dr. Clock called from above him. "We probably should have done that to begin with. But here we are."

Baxter stopped. Stared ahead, but seeing nothing. He would give himself to the count of ten to let the backhanded jab roll off his shoulders.

One, two, three—

"Hurry, dear boy. We haven't got all evening."

Baxter clenched his jaw.

If Clock wasn't already dead...

CHAPTER 24

ZOE

"I KNOW YOU'RE HIDING around here, Zoe." Lucas casually strolled closer. "I can feel your energy."

She cringed at the thought of giving herself up. She glanced at the building behind her. It wasn't too far away. She took a breath and jetted off; the coverage of the bulldozer would keep her protected long enough to run inside the structure.

"Oi!" Lucas shouted seconds after she darted away.

Terrified one of his fireballs would pierce her, she made a hard cut to the left. She heard him skid across the pebbly ground, cursing, as he tried to keep up with her sudden change of direction.

She targeted the wide opening of the building where a window used to be. On her approach, she realized the bottom ledge was higher than she originally thought, but there was no other escape. Even though her muscles burned, she powered forward. Like a ninja, she sprang off the stucco wall with her foot and launched herself upward until she could grip enough of the ledge to shimmy herself through the window.

She spilled over the edge and dropped onto the tile floor, right onto shards of broken glass, which stabbed her palms and legs, eliciting a strangled cry. She scrambled to her feet and blinked away the uncontrollable tears swelling in her eyes. She removed her mini flashlight from her pocket, clicked it on, and examined her wounds. Blood trailed down from her knee to her shin, which seemed to be the worst of it. She fanned the beam of light in front of her and hobbled across the dingy room, making her way through the obstacle course of old medical equipment, scattered tools, and loose papers. As she reached the wooden exit door that hung from a single hinge, she heard Lucas struggling with the broken glass at the base of the window.

The man was relentless.

Picking up speed, she pushed the door open and entered a long corridor. She trampled across dried leaves and litter blown in from the broken windows. She pushed on the closed doors and was relieved when she finally found an open one that placed her inside an old waiting room.

At the back of the room was a reception desk with a hallway entrance on either side of the counter. The one on the right had a window with a sliver of moonlight shining into it, highlighting the thin layer of undisturbed dirt on the tile floor.

As much as she wanted to follow the beam of light out of the cluttered maze, her footprints would be a dead giveaway of her location. She had to turn the tables on Lucas. She needed to stop running and take control of the situation. The prey needed to become the hunter.

She bent at the waist and wiped dripping blood off her calf and ankle and hissed as tiny glass splinters stabbed at her hand, but she couldn't afford to have blood trail after her like breadcrumbs.

She stood and peered down the dark hallway to the left. Every inch of her screamed at her for even considering entering the darkness with nothing but her wits and a tiny flashlight. She sucked in a breath.

As long as you don't walk into a nest of snakes, you'll be fine.

She took a few steps forward and stood beneath the hallway entrance. She shined her light down the corridor. No snakes. Just grime. A few spiderwebs glinted in the light, but she could handle that.

She limped through the hall and dipped into the last room; formerly an office with upside down furniture, open filing cabinets, broken bookcases, and scattered papers and litter. They boarded the window up, but had a single plank missing, which let in just enough moonlight for her to see. She clicked off her flashlight, shuffled to the back corner and entered a narrow doorway that led to an ensuite restroom. She closed the door, leaving it open just enough for her to peek into the office.

She lowered the filthy toilet lid and sat upon it, needing to think for a minute. Using her shirt, she dried her sweaty face and fanned herself. The room was stuffy. Suffocating.

Focus.

She could use the lid of the tank as a weapon—

A choir of whispers echoed through the office. Zoe's breath suspended. The hairs on her arm stood. As silently and slowly as she could, she exhaled. Her breath was visible once again.

The first sign of a ghost.

"Abraham?" she whispered and shimmied off the toilet seat. She tiptoed across the tile and peeked into the office. A thick, black mass darted across the small beam of moonlight, then hit the narrow door with a *thud*. Zoe shrieked, slapped a hand over her mouth, and shrank away from the door.

Disembodied voices whispered all around her as the black mass slithered through the door opening and rushed at her.

She stumbled backwards and fell into the corner, losing her flashlight in the process. She tucked herself into a tight ball as a wave of frigid air rolled over her. Even if she could, she didn't dare look. She wanted to scream, but could only will it to go away. This ghost, or whatever it was, was nothing like Dr. Clock. This thing felt—sinister. The unforgiving anxiety that coursed through her was crippling. Her body betrayed her mind's desire to run.

Salty tears streamed down her cheeks and over her trembling lip, as the soul-sucking mass hovered over her. In a whispered stutter, she called out for Dr. Clock. Then, as if someone flicked on a light switch, the chilly darkness around her disappeared, leaving her in the sweltering hot and stuffy room again.

Zoe pulled her head away from her arms and looked around. The room was dead. Not a whisper. Not a rustle. She wiped her tears, then clambered to her feet. She jetted out of the room; her feet pounded on the tile as she made her way back toward the waiting room. She entered the hallway to the right of the reception's desk. To hell with leaving footprints in the dust.

She sprinted to the window at the end of the hall and sat on the glass-free window frame. She swung one leg over the ledge, careful not to lose her balance and plunge down the grave embankment.

"Going somewhere, mate?"

Startled, Zoe yelped, her eyes falling upon a man leaning against the exterior wall of the building. He stepped out of the shadow and into the moonlight that accentuated a neck tattoo and bleached-blond hair. He lunged at her, snatching her dangling foot. He pulled, but Zoe used the window frame for leverage, she slipped from his grip, and fell backwards into the hallway. He reached through the opening, swiping at her legs as she scurried away from the window. She raced down the hall to the waiting room, back into the corridor on the left. She fumbled through the dark as heavy footsteps came after her.

With her shoulder, she pushed on the first door and entered a large room. Blinded by the bright light of the moon, she slipped on a thin layer of dirt and slammed into the wall with a loud *thump*. She shielded her head as bits of old plaster pelted her. She rubbed the specks of dirt from her eyes and slowly pushed herself up.

"Hello, love. We done playing hide-and-go-seek?"

In the middle of the room, Lucas sat in an old dentist's chair with a Cheshire grin and one leg crossed over the other. He expected to see her. No longer wearing the fake police uniform, he rolled up the sleeves of his button-up shirt, showing off the tattoo on his forearm. The other man, with the neck tattoo, shuffled into the room.

Zoe sighed; her shoulders sagged.

Lucas leaned forward, propping his elbows on his knees, and peered down at her. "Bennett should've known we'd follow you here."

Zoe clenched her jaw and glared up at him.

"What do you want?"

Lucas punched upright. Zoe flinched as he squatted in front of her and dragged his pointer finger across her collarbone, hooking it around the silver chain. He slid his finger down the length of it and caressed the stone with his thumb. "We want to stop you." His warm breath tickled across her exposed neck.

Zoe swallowed, then met his gaze. "Go to hell."

"Already there, dearie," Lucas stated. For a half a second, she thought she saw something glint across his eyes. He snatched her wrists and hoisted her to her feet. She struggled to pull away from him.

"Want me to take her?"

"I got her." Lucas squatted low and hoisted her over his shoulder like a sack of potatoes. She could hardly breathe as his broad shoulders pressed into her diaphragm. Zoe struggled, trying to break free, but Lucas marched forward with the other man following them, his eyes trained on her. Zoe balled her hand into a fist, pounded on Lucas' back, and demanded to be let go.

But of course, it was no use.

Ever seen a movie where that actually *worked?*

As they entered the main corridor, a brilliant blaze of white light flooded the room. The man with the neck tattoo shielded his eyes and stumbled to the ground. Lucas cursed and sank to his knees, dropping Zoe.

"Zoe! Run!"

Zoe opened her eyes. Dr. Clock glowed like an angel descending from the heavens, hovering over the men who lay crumpled and squirming at his feet. "I can hold them long enough for you to get away. Meet the guardian at your vehicle but be careful. There are others nearby!"

Adrenaline surged through her. Zoe sprang to her feet and clambered out of the nearby window. She dashed across the abandoned campus, terrified of how many more members of the Atlantic-Tails might be around, and what their plans for her were if they caught her.

CHAPTER 25

BAXTER

BAXTER HAD NEVER BEEN an outdoorsy type of guy. He preferred intellectual activities. Under normal circumstances, he would never dig in the dirt like a dog. There he sat, scraping at the soil with a jagged rock with mud caked beneath his fingernails, flinging dirt this way and that, in search of a seashell that most likely held the second stone to Zoe's pendant.

"Try a little more to your left," Dr. Clock instructed as he coached from the sidelines.

Baxter wiped away the sweat from his brow. He shifted slightly to the left and started digging again. He hit something hard beneath the dirt and paused.

"Careful, there," Dr. Clock stated as he squatted next to him. "Use your hands."

Baxter tossed aside his primitive tool and delicately dug at the soil. After removing a few large scoops of dirt, he unearthed a fully intact nautilus seashell. He gently scraped the dirt from its fragile exterior. "It's beautiful."

"Uh, oh," Dr. Clock said.

Baxter plugged his ears as a high-pitch ringing invaded them. He furrowed his brows at Dr. Clock. "What was that?"

Was it the shell?

Dr. Clock stood, shaking his head. "I sense a disturbance with some of the other ghosts. Zoe might be in trouble. I'll help her. She'll meet you at your vehicle," he said then vanished with a tiny *pop!*

"Shit," Baxter exclaimed as he got to his feet, shoving the shell into his pocket, imagining the worst. If he were arrested, the shell would be confiscated.

He raced down the steep incline, forgoing the path. He skated across loose dirt and pebbles. As he reached the base of the hill, he tripped over the exposed roots of a tree and tumbled down the slope. Spiny thorns stabbed him as he rolled through a bush. He finally came to a stop when the left side of his body slammed into a cluster of medium-sized stones.

Ignoring the throbbing ache in his side and the dizziness, he reached for the shell in his pocket. He sighed. He would not question how it didn't break. Using the rocks that stopped his fall, he pulled himself up and stepped forward. His knee wobbled beneath his body. He clutched his ribs and took another uneasy step forward, limping, zombie-like, down the rest of the hill and across the campus.

As he came to the turquoise doors to the courtyard, he heard the steady pounding of someone running across the pavement toward him. Zoe raced past him.

"Lucas is here! We gotta go!"

"What?" Another surge of adrenaline billowed in his gut. Baxter stepped in pace with her then entered the alcove.

"He was impersonating the cops." Zoe ran around to the passenger side of the SUV.

Baxter dug in his pockets for the fob, unlocked the SUV, and swung open the door. "He must have been in the patrol car that exited the freeway behind me."

Zoe clicked herself into her seat. "Yeah, and then he hung back when we turned into the campus, knowing he had us cornered out here in the middle of nowhere."

Baxter uncomfortably eased into his seat, gritting his teeth as the pain near his ribs stabbed at him. He dropped the seashell into the cup holder of the center console and clicked his seatbelt into place.

"You okay? What happened? I thought—I thought the magic of my stone still protected you?"

Baxter moaned and clutched his side as he fired up the engine. "Well, probably only against death. Everything else must be free game."

"Baxter..."

He maneuvered the steering wheel and the gearshift. "I will be fine. I simply slipped down the face of the hill." He motioned to the blood and dirt on Zoe. "Looks like you had a similar encounter."

"Something like that."

He hit the gas, raced out of the alcove, and maneuvered the SUV down the one-way street. On the opposite side of the grassy median, a patrol car barreled toward them. Baxter narrowed his eyes at the two passengers. "Looks like Sebastian and Dmitry." The patrol car jumped the curb to cross over the median to head them off, but Baxter veered past them, narrowly missing the nose of the patrol car.

"Where's Lucas and the other guy?" Zoe looked out the rear window.

"What other guy?"

"I dunno. Some guy with a tattoo on his neck."

Baxter slammed his palm on the steering wheel. "William. Damn it."

"What's wrong with William?"

"He was there the night we were attacked at USC. He was the lookout, and apparently, he's Lacy's boyfriend."

"Whoa, what?"

Using his peripheral vision, Baxter could see her looking at him. "Later." He focused on their exit across the narrow wooden bridge up ahead.

"Watch out!" Zoe shouted. She threw her arms out, pointing to a red, heavy-duty pickup truck that intersected them at the bridge.

Baxter slammed on the brakes, squealing the tires, and came to a stop. He flipped the gearshift into reverse and rocketed backward. He lifted off the gas and yanked the wheel around. The spin sent Zoe sideways, slamming her against the door frame. Baxter engaged the forward gear and sped up. "Are you okay?" He swerved past the patrol car.

Zoe clutched the handle above the door and gripped at the seatbelt that locked her in place. "Where'd you learn to drive like that?"

"The seventies."

"Just get us the hell out of here." Zoe rubbed her temple.

"Working on it." He glanced in the rearview mirror. The red truck barreled along with Lucas at the wheel and William in the passenger seat. The patrol car tailed right behind it. Baxter took a hard right to lose the cars in the maze of streets at the back end of campus.

"Turn left at the next street," a familiar voice insisted and startled both Zoe and Baxter.

"Abraham!" Zoe faced the ghost in the backseat.

Baxter jerked the steering wheel and made a sharp left onto a bumpy one-way road. Dr. Clock leaned forward and pointed to a grouping of palm trees. "Turn right at those palms and follow the road until it merges with the Pacific Coast Highway. Go left, and it will take you right into the heart of Malibu."

"Thanks." Baxter pushed down the accelerator.

Dr. Clock reached forward and dragged his finger across the nautilus. "The shell is just as I remembered. But I no longer need it."

Baxter glanced over to see Dr. Clock stroking Zoe's cheek. He had a peaceful smile on his face. "You will do great things, my friend. Until we meet again,"

Tears swelled in Zoe's eyes. "Thank you, Abraham."

A light, unexpectedly bright, erupted from Dr. Clock's chest. Baxter shielded his eyes, veering the SUV off the paved road and onto the dirt. He hit the brakes and as the SUV slowed to a stop, the blinding light vanished.

Zoe rubbed her eyes. "His spirit is at peace."

"Unfortunately, we are not." Baxter checked the rearview mirror and hit the gas. "Here they come." He maneuvered the SUV back on the road, hooked a right at the palm trees, and merged onto the main highway.

Zoe watched out the rear window. "Those sneaky jerks. They switched on the patrol lights and had the red truck follow like it's an emergency escort. They're gonna catch up to us if you don't start hauling ass."

Baxter glanced at the speedometer. He was creeping past eighty miles an hour, well above the posted speed limit. "How much faster shall I go? This road is risky as it is; it swerves through the hills and overlooks the ocean."

Zoe hard-set her jaw and slumped into her seat.

Baxter gripped the wheel tighter as he passed a slower moving car. "You know them best. Are they the type to run us off the road?"

Baxter paused. He wanted to say no. With William tagging along, though, he wasn't so sure. William was higher in rank than Lucas, and over the years, he rarely made an appearance to antagonize Baxter. Twice in the past few weeks, William put himself in the trenches trying to get Zoe and the stone. The days of a simple cat-and-mouse game with Lucas were gone. William meant business.

"Regrettably, I think they would try anything to stop us at this point."

Zoe's silence unnerved Baxter. She leaned her head against the window.

A shimmer of light from the cup holder caught his eye.

"Look. The shell is broken."

Zoe shifted in her seat. "It must've happened when Dr. Clock went into the light." She picked through the broken pieces. "Hello, there."

Pinched between her fingers, she held an irregular shaped stone. She moved it closer to Baxter's line of sight. Overall, it had a lustrous white pearl sheen with veins of blue and yellow hues tracing through it.

Baxter carefully took the sweeping turn then peeked over at Zoe, again. She butted it up against the stone from around her neck. Swirls of yellow and white magic crisscrossed around the two pieces, fusing it together.

For the second time, Baxter shielded his eyes away from a blinding light. He released the gas pedal and squinted, trying to keep his eyes on the road. As the light faded, Baxter realized he slowed down too much.

The patrol car was in the lane to the right of them with the red truck driving in the oncoming lane, boxing the SUV between them. The patrol car tried to sideswipe them, but Baxter swerved, nearly hitting the truck next to them. In the oncoming lane, the headlights from a semi-truck careened toward the red pickup, its horn echoing from the canyon.

"Hold on!" Baxter slammed on the brake pedal again, this time with two feet, causing them to grind. Both him and Zoe hurtled forward. The two vehicles rocketed past them. The truck cut into their lane, narrowly escaping a head-on collision with the semi-truck.

Baxter's heart thumped in his chest. He couldn't control the shake of his hands. There was no way to get off the main road until they reached Malibu. Thankfully, there would be little to no traffic at night. He couldn't bear the thought he caused an accident.

Up ahead, the two vehicles pulled over onto the shoulder, waiting for Baxter to continue.

"What do we do?" Zoe asked.

Baxter nudged the SUV forward until they reached the upcoming road sign. Point Mugu Rock was a mile away, and El Matador State Beach was fourteen miles. "If we can get to a tourist location, they might be hesitant to try anything with the public around."

"Might be?"

At a slower speed, Baxter approached the waiting vehicles, with plans on making a U-turn and driving back toward Oxnard if Lucas and his goons refused to let them pass. Once Baxter's SUV past without harm, Baxter's gut wrenched even tighter at the dangerous game the Atlantic-Tails were playing.

Baxter raced past them, but they were quick to follow, ramming them as soon as they were away from Point Mugu Rock. The SUV jerked, but Baxter held it steady on the road. The metal guardrail to their right would do little to protect them from the steep drop into the ocean. "Can you blind them with magic somehow?"

"Yes! Callista said white magic controls light, and the new stone has white in it." She unfastened her seatbelt. She slid the seat as far back as she could and clambered into the backseat then into the trunk of the SUV. "Lower the window!"

From Baxter's side mirror he saw the patrol car passing the truck, trying to box them in again. "Hurry!" she cried.

He pressed the button to roll the rear window down, glad he purchased an SUV with that upgraded feature. In the side mirrors, he could see the silhouettes of the four men. Whatever she did to distract the Atlantic-Tails in the patrol car worked enough for they stopped trying to run them off the road and dropped back.

"Come on, Zoe. You can do it." He wasn't sure if she heard him with the wind whipping through the SUV.

Baxter passed a sign that warned about traffic entering from Sycamore Canyon Road. If he took a hard left, he could follow that through the hills and get away from the edge of the cliffs.

A flash of purple light erupted behind him. He kept his eyes on the road, even though he would rather see what she was doing. Squealing tires and metal smashed together like a choir of clashing thunder. He drove the SUV onto the shoulder, slammed it into 'Park' and scrambled out of the seat to survey what kind of mess Zoe's magic caused.

CHAPTER 26
BAXTER

THE PATROL CAR LOST control and skidded into the cliffs on the opposite side of the highway. Smoke billowed out from under the hood with bits of metal trailing behind the car. The truck spun out and became a tangled mess with the guardrail, its bed teetering dangerously over the edge of the cliff. One wrong move and the truck would slide down the bluff and into the ocean.

"Shit!" Baxter raced toward the truck. No matter what was happening between them right now, Baxter didn't want anyone's life to be in jeopardy. He couldn't live with himself if he didn't help.

"Look! They're fine!" Zoe shouted from the rear-view window.

Baxter stopped. Sebastian and Dmitry staggered out of the patrol car, rubbing their necks and heads. Lucas and William, unharmed, jumped out of the truck and examined its damage and closeness to the edge.

"We can lose them." Baxter scurried back to the SUV. "Get back up front."

"Uh, Baxter. I can't."

Baxter stopped at the rear hatch. "Why?"

Zoe pointed down at her lap. Baxter shuffled forward and peeked inside the window. Her mermaid tail uncomfortably overtook the cargo area. The tips of her fluke fluttered, as if it were innocently waving at him.

"Have you lost your mind? Change back!"

"Don't you think I've been trying?" she countered. "Something's stopping me."

Baxter raked his fingers through his hair and paced in a tight circle. He stopped.

"Perhaps you're prevented from shifting out of your mermaid form because the riddle on the new stone wants to be activated."

Zoe threw her arms up. "And to do that, I gotta get in the water. Great. How will—" Zoe leaned to the side and looked around him. "Baxter! They're coming!"

Baxter pivoted. The red pickup pulled forward, getting loose from the grips of the guard rail. All four men were inside it.

Baxter hurried to the door behind the driver and folded down the back of the seat. "Scoot back and lie down!"

Zoe fell to her side and dragged herself across the fabric backing as Baxter slammed the door and rushed back to the driver's seat. He put the SUV in gear and took off, fishtailing and kicking up a cloud of dirt behind him.

"Roll the window up," Zoe yelled from behind him.

Baxter pushed the automatic window button. "Hang tight. I will get you to the water as soon as I can."

He looked over his shoulder. Zoe sat on her hip, her tail s-curled beneath her, with her fluke splayed out across the trunk. She clutched the seat next to her, hanging on.

For the next few minutes, they rode in silence. Baxter continued to check the mirrors; the pickup truck took too much damage and couldn't keep up with them. As they drove closer to Malibu, more traffic appeared on the highway. It would be risky to take her to a beach in this area, but Baxter didn't want to make her wait any longer than needed.

Just down the road, the wooden signage of Neptune's Net, a seaside restaurant and market, caught Baxter's attention. He slowed the car and made a left into the parking lot.

"What's the plan?" Zoe asked, shifting to get a better view out the front window.

He parked the car so the trees on the embankment blocked the view from the street. He unbuckled his seatbelt and spun around to peer out of the rear window. "Watch for the truck. Once it goes by, we can backtrack to a less populated area and find a turnout where we can get you in the water without being seen by them or the public."

Zoe beamed. "Great idea." She shifted, leaning against the back of the front passenger's chair. "I'm sorry for snapping at you earlier."

"No need to apologize." He stayed slightly behind her and did not look directly into her eyes. He wasn't sure if the curse would have an effect on him since she wasn't in the water, but he wasn't about to risk it.

"In fact, I apologize to you. I didn't prepare you for the unexpected. Always expect Lucas and the others to be around. And when you are in the underwater world, be prepared for anything to happen."

"I know." Zoe sucked in a tight breath as she peeled the dried blood from her palms. Baxter disliked seeing her in pain and wished he had the power to take it from her.

"Care to tell me how you received the cuts on your hands?" he asked.

She took a cleansing breath and retold the story of being chased by Lucas and William and how the strange dark mass that terrified her ended up being the thing that saved her.

Over the next ten minutes, they retold their separate adventures at the hospital. Baxter fumed as he pictured Lucas and William's scummy hands all over her.

Zoe pointed at the highway. "There it is!"

Baxter blinked. Sure enough, the red truck traveled down the road, its rear fender dangling and dragging behind, shooting sparks everywhere.

Baxter followed it until it was out of sight. He started the SUV and pulled out of the parking lot. At the Pacific Coast Highway, he turned right to go back the way they came. A few minutes later, they were out of the populated area, alone on the two-lane highway. Baxter slowed and made an illegal U-turn and pulled onto the shoulder where they had access to the coastline. He switched on his emergency lights and exited the vehicle.

He opened the back hatch, scooted Zoe's fluke to the side, and retrieved the tire-changing equipment from the compartment in the trunk. "For appearances," he explained and closed the hatch door. He set the scene with the tools and jack. He opened Zoe's door. "Come on," he directed.

Zoe wrapped her arms around his neck. He cradled her and pulled her through the door, but as soon as he held her full weight, he wrenched in pain and collapsed against the door of the SUV.

Zoe let go of him and clutched the frame and held herself up. "You can't carry me with your injury. You probably cracked a rib sliding down the hill."

"I will heal," he said through gritted teeth. "I always do."

Zoe shrugged her shoulder. "I dunno, Baxter. Maybe this isn't a great idea."

They both trained their eyes on the oncoming car that came their way. Baxter held his breath.

As it flew by, Baxter exhaled and turned his back to her. "I may not be able to hold you like that, but I can carry you on my back. Hurry, before another car comes."

Zoe scoffed but did as he asked. She wrapped her arms around his neck. He leaned forward and pulled her out of the door. He gripped her arms, so she wouldn't slip; she bent her tail, so her fluke didn't drag.

Trying to hide his pain, Baxter hiked down the small embankment, crossing over pebbles and small rocks. He splashed into the ankle-deep water and treaded through the thick sand until the water reached his knees. He let go of her arms, dropping her into the water behind him.

She slipped below the surface. Baxter watched her cut across the dark water and flipped and flopped around, stretching her tail from being cooped up too long.

When she was out of his sight, Baxter walked out further until he could no longer touch the sandy bottom. He floated for a while, waiting for her return, and when she didn't, he safely dipped below the surface to let the water cool the top of his head. The last few hours had been intense and the waves sloshing above him were calming. He could understand the appeal of living a life in the ocean. When his lungs couldn't take the pressure anymore, he pushed himself to the surface and planned to wait for Zoe in his SUV.

From behind, he heard water dripping off Zoe as she surfaced. She touched the back of his upper arm. "Thanks for getting me here," she said.

Baxter lowered his head and covered her hand with his.

"I'm going to swim for a bit," she continued. "And hopefully get this stone to activate the next riddle. I'll meet you at your car in what? Half an hour?"

Baxter nodded. From the corner of his eye, he saw her majestic tail flapping around. He wanted to tell her to be careful, but not as much as he wanted to drink in her beauty. Unable to control himself, he dropped his hand from hers and slowly faced her. She leapt back in horror, but her violet-blue eyes glowed, beckoning him to her.

The internal pain that surged through his ribs immediately disappeared. Weightless, he floated toward a celestial light filled with an array of violets and silver. He was ready to leave his earthly body, blissfully, in the arms of his sea-creature angel. She only needed to kiss him. He leaned into her, her rosy lips parting. But her face morphed. Her lips blackened. Her eyes grayed, hardening into stone—

A searing pain sliced across his cheek.

"Baxter, breathe!" Zoe shrieked and pleaded in the distance.

The bright moonlight penetrated through his closed eyes. He inhaled the salty sea air as her arms wrapped around him, swimming them back to shore. "Zoe," he muttered, thankful she had slapped him from the urge of her deadly kiss.

"I'm not Zoe," the voice in his ear whispered.

His heart lodged in his ribs. He opened his heavy lids.

"She is staying out there. I'll take you back to shore," said a woman with a heavy Asian accent. She had porcelain skin, ruby red lips, and black hair with a thick highlight of gold. A black tattoo with delicate lines stretched down her upper arm, from her neck to elbow. It was an Asian-style dragon slithering through pink flowers.

"Sorry I had to hit you, but you were millimeters from death," the mermaid stated as Baxter stretched his neck to look behind her. Zoe bobbled in the water behind them, looking defeated and scared.

Baxter sighed. He felt so foolish. "Medusa's curse strikes again. Sefarina warned me not to look at her, but I cannot help myself."

She smiled. "You both have powerful feelings for each other. It makes the curse worse."

"How so?" he asked as his savior stopped holding him once his feet could touch the sea floor. She slowly circled him, her sparkling golden tail surfacing.

"Even when you refuse to look at her, your desire for her will force you to."

Baxter raised his chin. "Desire? I am her guardian, nothing more."

She stopped swimming as a high-pitched laugh squeaked out of her. "Stubborn man. You hypnotize her too, you know."

Baxter's cheeks warmed. "Who are you?"

"Kasumi." She treaded water next to him. "I was in the area and swam over as soon as I felt Zoe's energy in the water. All pure-tails have orders from Aislinn to remain near the California coastline in case she, or you, need us."

Baxter appreciated the gesture. "Thank you for saving me."

"My pleasure." Kasumi lowered her head in a slight bow and paddled forward.

"Wait." Baxter didn't want to waste this moment with the stunning creature. Kasumi twirled in the water, giving him her attention. "Did you ever know a mermaid named Neala?"

Kasumi's brow creased. "I was traded into Melantha's kingdom days before her death, so I am not familiar with past Tails of her realm."

Traded?

"Do you know how Neala would have murdered a human while on land? I thought Melantha had a law against that in her realm."

Kasumi nodded. "She did, but any laws she created specifically in her realm were all voided upon her death. It gives the new leader a chance to make the realm the way they want it."

"I see." If Kasumi had been in the realm for the last hundred years, and Dr. Clock was murdered in 1940 then it was reasonable to assume Neala hadn't been a part of the realm since Melantha's death; although, Dr. Clock assumed she had been.

If Melantha traded for Kasumi, what had she given away? Neala, perhaps?

"I am unfamiliar with mermaid trading. Can you tell me about your experience?"

The gold mermaid grinned, twirled around, and perched herself on a nearby rock. "I'm from the northwestern realm, near Japan. Melantha didn't have any Gold-Tails in her realm, and my king had plenty. He wanted access to the Mexican shorelines, where his Landwalker girlfriend lived. I wanted to be in the waters next to America's booming west coast, so Melantha and my king, Takahiro, struck a deal. She granted him legal and unlimited passage through her waters to visit Puerto Vallarta and put me into her personal service.

"But by the time I transitioned and settled in, she was dead. Her agreement with my king was nulled upon her death, stopping him from using the passageway, but my magic was tied to her stones, so I couldn't go back to his realm. For a long time, I felt alone. Farah was the only one who had the energy to take care of me and teach me the ways of Melantha's kingdom. You should ask her about Neala."

Well, that hadn't been the answer he wanted. He wondered if The Aquatic Accords had any information about Neala and was eager to look at it.

Baxter glanced over Kasumi's shoulder. Zoe paddled closer to listen to her story.

"Will you do me a favor?" Baxter asked Kasumi.

Kasumi nodded. "Hai."

"Take Zoe to your world and let her have some fun. She found the second stone and deserves a break. We believe the second riddle activates once she is in the water, but I want her to relax as well. I can meet her at the Santa Monica Pier around ten o'clock tonight."

Kasumi's eyes lit up, and she clasped her hands together. "I would be so happy to do that." Kasumi gave him a slight bow and dove away to meet up with Zoe.

From afar, Zoe waved at him before diving below with her newfound friend. Baxter trudged through the water toward the rocky beach. Before hiking up the embankment, he perched himself on some driftwood, finally able to take a relaxed breath. He peeled his wet shirt up and examined his side. His skin burned from a wide scrape. He was swollen near his ribs and expected a dark bruise to appear soon.

He hadn't had a bruise since he was a child.

It unnerved him to see his body not healing as it did when he wore the necklace. In fact, he never saw his body so damaged before. If the magic of the stone still protected him, as the vision of his mother said, it sure had a strange way of showing it. He wasn't even sure he would completely heal from this injury. In fact, well below the truth of how he felt about Zoe, Baxter sensed his end nearing. After a hundred years of eagerly awaiting his demise, he wanted nothing more than to live.

CHAPTER 27

ZOE

As Zoe swam behind Kasumi across the shallow waters, an all too familiar feeling crept up. The wall she strategically built around her emotions after the swim team betrayed her was calling to her once again and she desperately wanted to heed its call. It would be easy to hide behind it once more and block out any confusing feelings she had for Baxter. Twice, she nearly killed him because of her cursed eyes. The loneliness she felt when Kasumi saved him, while she watched from a distance, was the cherry on top. She felt like she didn't belong in his world anymore, yet she didn't quite feel at home in the underwater realm either.

Will I ever feel like I belong to anything? How do I balance between my two lives?

Kasumi must have sensed Zoe wallowing in her self-pity because a moment later the golden mermaid somersaulted, flipping her swimming direction, and headed straight at her.

Kasumi's brows furrowed. Panic washed over her face and gasped in horror.

As she reached out for Zoe's outstretched hand, a powerful swell struck them, hurling Zoe upside down and backwards through the water. She slammed into the rough edges of a reef, unable to contain a ragged cry of agony as the sandpaper-like peaks scraped along her bare back. She sank down, finally coming to a stop in a tangled mess of sea grass and anemones. Sediment floated all around her, encasing her in a fog-like cloud. Not wanting to move and kick up more sand, she reached out and weaved her fingers through the pink tentacles of the anemones and was surprised to find they felt velvet and were not at all harmful. To ignore the stinging pain of the salty water against her raw skin, she continuously rubbed the anemone tentacles between her fingers, soothing her enough to stop the infernal spinning inside her head and the high-pitched ringing in her ears.

Once the silt settled, she saw Kasumi face down in the sand. Unmoving. Was she—dead?

Zoe pushed herself up, but it was as if the ocean became a swamp of molasses, slowing her down from getting to her friend.

With arms outstretched, Zoe finally reached Kasumi and rolled her over, ready to perform the blue healing magic she had used once before. She leaned over her and brushed the sand from her face. Then she saw them—tiny air bubbles. She sighed in relief.

"Kasumi?" Zoe said in a shaky voice.

She didn't respond. Zoe gently nudged her shoulder. "Kasumi?"

Kasumi moaned, and her eyes fluttered. Zoe nudged her once more.

"Are you okay?" Zoe asked as she helped Kasumi sit up.

Kasumi rolled her neck and nodded.

Zoe freed Kasumi's fluke from a knot of kelp. "What the hell was that?"

"Something I have only heard about," Kasumi said as she massaged her temples. "I tried to warn you, but it happened so fast. Tails must not enter another realm without prior permission. If there *is* an illegal entrance, we feel a ripple of the trespassers' energy, which is stronger the closer you are to the intruder. But that sonic-like boom? Not only are we very close to the point of entry, it means it wasn't just one or two illegal entrances. It's—"

"An invasion," Zoe said, as the shadow from a boat stopped above them.

Zoe gripped Kasumi's wrist and guided her off the sandy ground. "We've got to go," she said. "Would we be safer on land?"

"Not necessarily. Our magic is strongest when we are together in the water. Everyone in our realm would have felt this. Protocol is to reach our hideout location at Smuggler's Cove."

Zoe remembered her first encounter with the See-seas navigation system. "Smuggler's Cove is near the Channel Islands, right? There are a few shipwrecks near it."

"Hai. Follow me and stick close to the ground until we clear the boats above us." Without another word, they dashed forward into the clouds of settling silt, blinding them from a fishing net lowering over them.

Zoe screamed as she pulled at the netting. The heated energy inside her was raring to explode out of her hands and free them from this hellhole. Kasumi flayed, trying to find the exit, but it was too late. The net scooped them up and plucked them out of the ocean like a horrible arcade game of Claw.

Kasumi clutched at Zoe, protecting her like a mama bear. Zoe strained her neck to take in the situation. There was one fishing boat with a swarm of red and Green-Tails circling it like sharks hunting for food. Four human men paced around on the deck, waiting for the net to be reeled in.

Zoe wasn't surprised to see that the men on the boat were Lucas and his goons. Lucas, donning swim shorts and a tank top, winked at Zoe. Disgusted, she rolled her eyes. Lucas looked at Dmitry who took a long drag on his cigarette and pushed a button at the rig's controls, lowering Kasumi and Zoe onto the deck.

"It must be our lucky day, mates," William teased, "Coz' we caught ourselves not one, but two, little mermaids." The men chuckled.

Kasumi leaned close to Zoe. "Transform back into a human." Zoe closed her eyes and concentrated.

A familiar tickle surged through her legs. Zoe's eyes shot open, ready to fight for her life.

Kasumi, standing, located the opening.

"Stop them!"

Kasumi and Zoe darted out of the net. Dmitry and Sebastian stalked toward them, catching them before they could get away.

Sebastian twisted Kasumi's arms behind her back and held her at bay. Dmitry's grimy hands gripped Zoe's upper arms and held her close to his body, blowing smoke in her face. She coughed and tried to turn from him, but she couldn't escape his stench.

William closed in on Zoe. Doing the thing girls are taught from an early age, she kicked him as soon as he was close enough. He doubled over and fell limp into her and Dmitry. The three of them stumbled backward and fell on the deck. Dmitry's cigarette dropped from his mouth, landing on Zoe's chest. She quickly brushed it away and tried to scramble out of their tangled limbs.

"That was my last smoke!" Dmitry shouted as William crawled over him to reach Zoe.

William grabbed Zoe's ankle and stopped her from getting away. "Playin' dirty, are we?" He pulled, easily sliding her across the deck closer to him.

Lucas squatted next to her. He reached out and snatched the pendant away from Zoe's chest and pulled the silver chain taunt, bringing them face to face. "We'll be taking that." His breath was warm against her face and smelled slightly of spearmint.

"Screw you."

"That's not in the plans, dearie," Lucas teased.

"Mind your tongue, yes? We have no orders to keep you physically safe," Dmitry growled as he got to his feet.

"I am going to take the necklace. If you're good, I might free you and your friend. If not, you can hand it to my king yourself, and I can assure you, he will keep you for his—collection." Lucas pulled her closer to him.

Zoe wasn't sure what kind of collection the Atlantic king had, but being a part of it wasn't an option. She would have to succumb. Her apologetic eyes flicked over to Kasumi. Sebastian swept Kasumi's long hair to the side and peppered her neck with kisses. "Tell your queen to follow our directions, for both your sakes," he warned.

"Okay," Zoe cried out, her eyes never leaving Kasumi's. "Okay. Just leave Kasumi alone."

Then, in a quick flash, a low-emitting ringing strangely buzzed through the back of her mind. She heard Baxter's voice. Far away and muffled, but clearly it was him.

Stall. Stall them.

How Baxter knew she was in trouble was beyond her, but she gave Lucas all her attention. She had to stall. "The necklace won't come off unless I take it off. You need to let go."

Lucas narrowed his eyes, pausing briefly before he released the stone from his grip. "Don't try anything," he said.

A strange warmth passed over Zoe, but it wasn't the breeze from the warm night. Instinctively, she knew her warriors were nearby, and their presence comforted her.

"Just so you know, there's a possibility of me experiencing a weird convulsing-looking fit as I remove the necklace. I saw it happen to Baxter when he gave it to me, and I don't want you to think I am trying to fight back or anything. It will pass. Just let me be if that happens."

Lucas glanced over at William, who gave him a curt nod. They both shifted back from her a smidgeon more.

"Very well," Lucas said. "Hand it over."

Zoe reached up to the silver chain, ready to slip it over her head when a blaze of fire and green beams of electric magical energy erupted all around them. The boat teetered, knocking everyone aboard off balance. Zoe slid across the deck as the roar of a battle raged in the ocean.

Steadying herself on the hull, she pulled herself up and looked overboard. Sea-warriors from both the Pacific and Atlantic kingdoms cast their specialty magic against one another, lighting up the water like Christmas lights. Weapons of coral and sharp sword-like gear clashed against one another as the Tails fought for control while climbing aboard the ship in their human forms.

"Start the boat!" someone demanded.

"Get us out of here!" Lucas shouted to Dmitry as he pitched his famous fireballs across the deck at some of her warriors.

Dmitry scrambled to the helm, balancing himself as the boat continued to rock back and forth from the wakes the Tails created as they fought.

A memory of some USC defensive linemen flashed through Zoe's mind. There had been a time the football players worked out in the weight room with the swim team, flirting with her and her teammates. They even went as far as showing off correct tackling stances and moves.

Zoe focused in on Dmitry and lowered her body to a three-point stance. The boat swayed left, then right. On the crest of returning to the left, Zoe pushed off, exploding from her stance and ran straight at Dmitry, who had no clue she barreled toward him. She hit him hard, wrapping her arms around his thick legs, and drove him backward. She let go of him, just as the boat shifted again, causing him to stagger and tumble overboard to a grim fate.

Proud of herself, and adding a mental point to her score for human football players vs Tails, Zoe ignored the surrounding carnage. Lucas was about fifteen feet away, stabilizing himself against the rig that controlled the net. By the dumbfounded look on his face, he had seen her excellent maneuver, but his eyes were wild with fire and his rage focused directly on her.

Several scenarios raced through her mind as she tried to analyze a way to escape the blaze of fire that he was surely going to hurl straight at her. Unless she could dive overboard faster than he could conjure his magic, she couldn't escape. Without thinking twice, Zoe pirouetted, ready to fling herself over the hull.

She stopped short. Standing behind her, and oozing with smoldering badassness, were Murdock and Ewalt.

"Stand down, Lucas," Murdock demanded, his baritone voice boomed across the boat and brought the fighting to a halt.

Zoe twisted around to face Lucas again. If looks of loathing could kill, she would have died.

"Get out of our kingdom," Murdock continued. "We've had causalities on both sides today and neither realm can afford any more losses."

"And if we don't?" Lucas challenged.

"Are you forgetting we're stronger than you, mates?" William asked as he stalked closer, paring off against Murdock and Ewalt. "You can't escape us."

"Perhaps *you're* forgetting one thing, *mate*," Murdock mocked.

Kasumi stepped out from behind him, showing off threads of gold glittering lights strung between her fingers. "You don't have me," she announced as she threw her hands up, dispersing the magic like tiny flecks of confetti over Zoe and her friends.

"No!" Lucas and William shouted and lunged at them.

Just as Zoe flinched back, a frigid chill swept through her, making her feel weightless and airy, almost like an ethereal spirit hovering—wait.

Am I dead? Was I struck with something before Kasumi's magic protected me?

"We need to go," Murdock instructed to Zoe as he gently tugged at her arm.

"What just happened? Are we ghosts?"

Ewalt, ever so stoic, smirked then chuckled as he lifted Kasumi's hand and placed a chaste kiss upon it.

"In a sense, yes," Kasumi answered, her cheeks reddening as she looked at Ewalt with loved-filled eyes. "The magic of Gold-Tails stems from ancient dragons that reigned over our waters and could disappear and reappear at will. When I use it, not only does it make the subject invisible, but it makes it untouchable, like a ghost."

"The Atlantic-Tails can't touch or see us. They'll go back to land," Murdock explained as he helped Zoe climb onto to the ledge of the boat. "But it won't last long. We need to meet up with the others and plan from there."

Well, she wasn't dead. That was comforting, at least. But nothing that happened in the last few hours was comforting. She assumed from here on out, nothing would be.

CHAPTER 28

ZOE

LESS THAN THIRTY MINUTES later, Zoe and the other Tails who aided in the ambush of the fishing boat arrived at an underwater grotto off the coast of Santa Cruz Island, near Smuggler's Cove. The cave was somber as most of the mixed-tails grieved over losing their friends. Ewalt held Kasumi's hand as she lay curled up on a large rock, drained from the amount of magic she expelled to save them.

Zoe leaned against a rocky mound near Murdock, who stayed near the entrance, always on alert.

"You held your own today, Zoe. I am eager to see how powerful you will become once you gain, and know how to wield, the magic available to royalty," Murdock said.

Zoe appreciated the compliment even though she wished she could have done more. "Thanks."

Murdock straightened when he caught sight of something in the distance. "Here she comes."

Aislinn's bright pink tail illuminated the grotto like a neon light, demanding attention from all. "Atlantic-Tails, I assume. Give me an estimate on how many there were," she said to Murdock.

"The normal three. Plus, William. And perhaps another twenty to thirty pure and mixed-tails." Murdock avoided Aislinn's intense gaze.

"No need for your accusations, Murdock. I was near Central Mexico and couldn't get here in time to help."

Murdock anchored his eyes with hers. "Stay out of my thoughts."

Zoe dove across the water, placing herself between them. She held a hand at Murdock's chest, stopping him from advancing on Aislinn. "This situation has us all stressed, but we can't be fighting with each other. There are bigger issues that need our energy. Worry about personal squabbles later."

Murdock instantly backed away, lowering his chin. "My apologies, my queen."

Ewalt swam up to them. "We need to form a plan, Aislinn," he looked from a sleeping Kasumi to Murdock, "and allow all of us to rest and gather our thoughts."

"I can agree with that," Aislinn said. "The safest place will be Hawaii. It's the location hardest for Atlantic-Tails to reach and the closest to the other realms if we should need any assistance from them."

Murdock cocked his head at Aislinn. "Hawaii? I thought you didn't enjoy being near there *because* it's too close to the other realms."

Aislinn gave him a hard smile. "You're right, I don't enjoy being that close, but I'm more concerned about safety."

Zoe made a mental note to ask why Aislinn didn't enjoy being near another realm. She wondered if those Tails weren't as friendly as the ones in her realm. She sighed. There was so much she needed to get caught up on.

Ewalt fluttered his fluke. "Very well. I will escort Kasumi and the others then return here once they feel safely settled. I'm sure some, including Kasumi, will want to retreat to land and hide among the tourists."

"And I'll gather our strongest Tails from across our realm and meet you back here," Murdock said to Ewalt.

Zoe blew out a line of bubbles. She felt horrible for leading Lucas and his goons into the water and putting her kingdom at more of a risk than it already was. She kneaded at her temple, something tickled below the surface of her skull, making her want to slam down her mental walls and shut out the alien force.

Murdock placed his hand on her upper back. "Zoe?"

She opened her eyes, not remembering she closed them. "Yeah, sorry. Felt strange for a second. I may be tired. I think I'm ready to return to land. The Santa Monica Pier is where I'm supposed to meet Baxter."

"I'll escort you, lass. I have the strongest powers," Aislinn offered.

"For the moment," Murdock mumbled, just loud enough for Zoe to hear him.

She leaned into Murdock. "Why is that? Is she stronger than everyone else because she's the interim queen?"

Murdock's jaw tightened. "Supposedly."

Zoe took a breath. The hostility between the two was strong. Her curiosity was getting to her. She would ask Aislinn on the way back to shore. Perhaps she could get a few more words out of her than she got from Murdock.

"Shall we?" Zoe said to Aislinn after she said her goodbyes to the others.

Aislinn nodded and led Zoe out of the grotto, swimming close to her.

"I know you don't like it when I enter your mind, but I want you to understand that what happened with the Atlantic-Tails wasn't your fault. You didn't lead them to us. They were going to enter the waters illegally and cause havoc, no matter what."

Zoe touched her temple. "I felt you. Inside my mind. That strange tickling sensation. It was like when I sensed Murdock and the others surrounding the boat."

"Yes. Sensing the magic of other beings. The second stone must have some yellow in it."

"And blue, from what I saw. But I was already exhibiting the healing powers of Blue-Tails well before I found the second stone."

"Seems fitting. The stone calls to you, allowing you to siphon off its energy in times of need, but just briefly until you actually locate it, I'm sure. But being able to sense another creature's magic is essential. It gives you an advantage of knowing what the person opposite you is capable of. It takes practice, though. Be wary that not everyone you encounter will be your friend."

Zoe let that warning settle in her mind. Reading thoughts and sensing the magic of other beings could be incredibly dangerous, especially in the hands of the wrong type of people—magical or not.

They swam the rest of the way in silence and didn't take long to reach shallow waters. As they surfaced, the ambience of Pacific Park, an amusement park on the Santa Monica Pier, engulfed their senses.

"Before I go, can you tell me what's up with you and Murdock?"

Aislinn rolled her eyes and chortled. "Well, that goes back to our ancestry. Red and Pink-Tails both stem from The Morrigan, a trinity goddess in Irish mythology. She was a shapeshifter, hence our mermaid and human form. She was an influencer of war which is why all Red-Tails like Murdock are sea warriors. She was also known to predict the future, but really, she could read minds and stay steps ahead of everyone else."

"Which is why Pink-Tails can read minds, right?"

Aislinn nodded. "The color red stimulates physical and mental energies. Since Red and Pink-Tails were formed under the umbrella of The Morrigan, we each can wield power over one another and read minds, which makes us both dangerous creatures. He can't read them as well as I do, nor do I have the physical strengths like him, but let's just say there have been many times where we have invaded each other's thoughts and things got... messy."

Zoe wondered what exactly messy might be. "Hmm." She swam forward then stopped. "Oh, one more thing."

Aislinn cocked her head, curious.

"Baxter and I met an old friend of Melantha's. He claimed a mermaid murdered him back in 1940. Her name was Neala. What do you know of her?

Aislinn exhaled her pent-up breath. "Well, that's a name I haven't heard in ages." She raked her fingers through her blonde-and-pink hair. "It's been, well, decades since I've seen her. I'm embarrassed to say I can't even remember exactly when she disappeared or what happened to her. As far as I know, she permanently chose human form as she is not in your kingdom and never got permission to make allegiances with another realm. Or she could be dead. Why do you ask?"

"I'm convinced she's the one who murdered Melantha."

Aislinn's brows rose. "That's quite an accusation. The possibility of having some answers is—"

"Overwhelming?"

Aislinn nodded, not quite able to shake the shock off her face. "Yes. Trust your feelings. I'll do some research on my end and try to locate her last known whereabouts. But don't get too wrapped up in solving Melantha's murder. We need you to find the other stones first. After the amount of magical energy used earlier, we are severely compromised and nearly depleted."

"I know. I'll stay focused." Zoe said. She gave her a warm smile and Aislinn gave her one in return. Aislinn dove below the water. Zoe's smile faded.

Trusting her gut, just as Aislinn advised, Zoe whole-heartedly believed Aislinn kept something about Neala from her. Not only did the warmth of her smile not reach her eyes, the window to the soul, but Zoe briefly sensed a cloudy fog surrounding Aislinn's words.

Zoe paddled forward, deep in thought.

What is Aislinn trying to protect me from? Is Neala truly a threat?

As the interim queen, surely, she would have kept tabs on each Tail, especially one who went rogue. Maybe she knew of Neala's involvement in Melantha's murder but didn't want to admit it. Whatever it was, Zoe was sure Aislinn knew more than she let on. Trouble was, Zoe wasn't sure how to extract that kind of information out of a master who could read and possibly manipulate the mind.

Chapter 29
BAXTER

BAXTER SAT AGAINST A concrete pillar beneath Santa Monica's colossal pier, waiting for Zoe's return. The black waters danced below the moonlight, soothing his impatience. The breeze, carrying the salty sea air and amusement park sounds, whipped around him like a warm hug.

Everything seemed perfectly normal in the world of humans.

Normal.

Baxter bowed his head and sighed. Over the century, he debated with himself if humans were blessed to be cloaked in blindness to the magical realms entwined with reality or pitied for being unable to experience and witness the amazing truths those realms held. More times than not, he wanted to be blissfully oblivious. It was only then that he genuinely appreciated how fortunate it was to have one foot in the magical world and one in the world of humans. For nearly a hundred years, he wasted his gift of time yearning for normalcy.

But what was normal anyway?

For him, sitting in physical pain from a couple of bruised ribs after tracking down a magical stone with a ghost, engaging in dangerous car chase like an action-packed thriller, and falling in love with a mermaid *was* normal.

Baxter lifted his head, the corner of his mouth quirked upward. Falling in love with Zoe.

No.

He wasn't falling. He already fell. Hard. To him, she felt like home. His soul ached whenever he wasn't around her. He knew it wasn't because of her cursed eyes. *That* he was sure about. When he was under the spell of Medusa's curse, a terrible feeling of longing and lust washed over him. The curse was purely physical. Lust, not love. It simply wanted him to follow her into the depths of the sea with the promise of her physical love, which probably would never happen because he would be dead or hardened to stone before he got a single kiss.

Only after the second time of being rescued from her deadly eyes, did he realize he truly longed for her.

And sure, the bruising and agonizing pain were new, and something he wasn't used to, but he could handle that. At least long enough to welcome his demise, which was creeping upon him.

He wouldn't waste any more of his time. If he only had weeks to live, he would live the way he should have—with no regrets. As frightening as it might be, he would profess his love for her. What happened from there was out of his control, even if it meant her feelings weren't mutual.

But first, he needed to channel the magic of the guardian. Ever since Zoe took control of the necklace, he ignored the low-emitting tone humming in his ear. But after her capture by Lucas, he knew exactly what it was.

It was Zoe's life force.

The guardian's spell linked their energy together. He realized the pitch of the frequency changed twice before. The first, when she fell into the cavern in San Francisco and transformed into a mermaid. And then earlier that evening, when he was digging for the seashell with Dr. Clock.

And again, right now.

The frequency of the pitch warned him of her state of being. Baxter closed his eyes, his brows knitted together. He shoved his fingers in his ears, shutting off the world. He focused on the hum, which grew louder every second until a flash blinded his mind's eye, dropping him over a scene, like from a movie.

He had a bird-eye's view of a fishing boat. It was lit up with floodlights and had Green and Red-Tails circling it. About a hundred yards away, a group of Tails raced along the surface toward the boat. His view zoomed in closer to the boat. Lucas had his hand around Zoe's necklace.

Baxter's muscles tightened as restless rage prowled inside, warming his skin.

What can I do?

He pictured himself standing next to Zoe, whispering in her ear. "Stall. Stall them." A repeated chant, begging her to not surrender the stone because help was on the way. Not able to hold on to the scene any longer, he slumped over, falling into the wet sand.

As if someone waved some smelling salts beneath his nose, Baxter woke with a start.

The only sound around him was the low tide rolling in and out. The pier was silent; all operations were closed for the night. He was utterly alone.

He wiped the sweat and sand from his brow, rolled his neck and shoulders to relieve the knots in his muscles. Feeling his true age, he used the piling as support, and stood. Clutching his side, he shuffled down the beach toward the shore.

He had to trust his actions and believe Zoe would be okay. He did everything he could for her and would give her until sunrise to return.

And if she doesn't?

Well, he only had one card left to play. He wanted to hold on to it for as long as possible, but if this was the time—

Purple flittering lights danced over the water.

He threw himself into a sprint, ignoring the pain in his side. He splashed through the waves into thigh-high water as she swam toward him in her human form.

She stood. Their eyes joined in an implacable lock as they rushed at one another. Zoe wound her arms around his neck. His arms twined around her middle, crushing her wet body into his. He deepened their kiss. Baxter buried his fingers into the plump swell of her bottom, lifting her higher and closer to him. The waves pushed them around, but the animalistic need to become one controlled them both. Nothing else in the world mattered. This was their time; their moment.

She pulled away from him, starving for air, groaning as he peppered kisses down her neck and pressed himself into her. She found his lips again, nipping at the bottom one and drawing out a growl. He lifted her again, high enough for her to wrap her legs around his hips.

But his body betrayed his desires.

The pain from his bruised, if not broken, ribs stabbed him. He collapsed, dropping her into the shallow water. He clutched his side. His breathing labored. The waves washed over him, desperate to drown him. He heard Zoe screaming for him, felt her hands on his body, helping him crawl out of the water. He crumpled on the wet sand. She pulled at him, rolling him over. The cool air pricked at his skin.

He blinked his heavy eyes. Fighting to stay coherent.

A blue glow radiated around him. A surge of panic pulsed through him. It was *the* light. The one people saw just as death took them. On a current of breath, he begged to stay, not wanting to leave her yet.

He reached for her; his hand settled on her thigh. He dug his fingernails into her flesh and refused to let go of her as his soul was dragged into the next life.

"Baxter?" Her voice was like an echo reverberating through his ears. "You can open your eyes. And let go of my leg."

Baxter remained still. He... wasn't dead? The rising tide ebbed and flowed around his body. He uncurled his fingers, stiff from clutching onto her so tight. He opened his eyes to see her leaned over him, grinning. He ran the tip of his fingers along her jaw line. "What happened?"

She reached her hand out to help him sit up.

"Your ribs were broken, probably stabbing you in the lungs. As you passed out, I healed you, like I did with that starfish I found in Alaska. You kept mumbling something. I assumed you thought you were dying. I must need some practice if it feels like you are being tortured when I use my healing power."

Baxter chuckled. Slightly embarrassed, he let his imagination get to him. "I feel great. Thank you."

The corner of her mouth twitched. She plopped next to him and before he could stop her, she removed her necklace. Bright purple light flashed. She fell into a full body spasm and collapsed into his arms.

"Zoe?" He traced her cheek with the back of his fingers.

She opened her eyes and blinked.

"Why did you do that?" He helped her sit up.

"You should wear this. I don't like the idea of you not being physically protected. What if magic strikes you and hurts you? Kills you. I—can't lose you." Her voice trembled on that last statement and handed him the necklace.

"Dying is a terrifying thought," he said and swatted her hand away. "But we both need to do as we must. It is my destiny to protect *you*, not the other way around."

Tears filled Zoe's eyes, as she dropped her hands in her lap. With the pad of his thumb, Baxter wiped away a small tear from her cheek. She looked at him through wet lashes. He leaned in and kissed her again. Slowly and deliberately. She pulled him closer as she reclined backward. He nestled between her legs. Zoe withered against him. Finally, the flame between them ignited. Was going strong. Was on... fire?

Zoe screamed for him to roll off her and shoved his chest. Embers of ash fluttered between them as the stone in Zoe's lap cooled from a searing red-hot molten blaze to its normal, colorful kaleidoscope of colors.

Baxter's brows furrowed at the cruel reminder there was no time for romance. The stone burned for their attention, like it had the first time the riddle came to life. He pinched the silver chain between his fingers and lifted it off the wet sand. Logically, he knew it was ridiculous to feel such irritation at an inanimate object, but any man would feel the same.

Zoe swept the stone into her palm and studied it. Baxter leaned close to her, trying to ignore the remnants of her suntan lotion wafting off her skin. Black script appeared across the yellow and white stone, the newest addition to the pendant. Her back stiffened and her face went blank. Then, as once before, in the same haunting minor key tone, she recited the riddle.

"Upon a rock, the bronze mermaid rests.
Love comforts the saddened,
Vanish or stifle unwanted pests."

Baxter quickly repeated the spell in his mind. Zoe slumped forward and awoke from her trance.

"Upon a rock—"

"Quick! Follow me. I have a notepad in the SUV." Baxter urged her to follow him. He noticed she didn't put the necklace back on, but they didn't have time to argue about it. They sprinted across the beach and down the street to where he parked.

Once inside, he dug around in his glove compartment for a notepad and pen and scribbled the riddle before he forgot a single word. Zoe looked over his writing then made some corrections of the punctuation and capitalization.

"There. Now to analyze it." She reclined in the passenger seat and read over the riddle; the necklace still in her hand.

Baxter shut the driver's door and started the engine. "We will tackle the riddle after we have cleaned up and rested." Even though she nodded in agreement, something told him that was the last thing they would do.

CHAPTER 30
BAXTER

ZOE PLEADED AND PRACTICALLY begged to stay up and research the riddle. Baxter assumed she would, but he stood his ground. After a minor debate, they retreated upstairs, showered, and went to their own beds.

Always so responsible.

He should have listened to her for sleep never came. The events of the evening kept running through his mind. First, he obsessively blamed himself for leading Lucas and his goons into the water after Zoe. He assumed they searched the road for his vehicle and, while he and Zoe were in the water, they spotted it and planned accordingly. Perhaps if his pain and the danger of Zoe's eyes didn't distract him, he would have seen or stopped them from attacking Zoe and Kasumi.

Perhaps.

Once he fully convinced himself his foolish actions were the root cause of everything wrong, the thoughts of kissing Zoe, of nearly having her, plagued his mind. They felt the same about each other, but their circumstances would never allow their love to blossom—not until their mission was complete. Or they died because he failed at his duty, which was more likely. In the end, he decided he should put any feelings between them to the side if they planned to stay alive.

Of course, that was easier said than done.

After tossing and turning for the umpteenth time, Baxter growled and punched the pillow next to him. He rolled out of bed, put on some flannel pajama pants, and padded across the hardwood floors down the hallway to Zoe's room.

The door was ajar and a sliver of light from the hallway shined into the room, onto her sleeping form. The top sheet draped across her hips, with her legs outside of it. He stopped and sighed.

What am I doing? I can't just go in there, blinded with desire. Can I?

He pivoted.

"Baxter?"

He stopped. His muscles rigid. He had an excuse for his voyeurism ready on his lips. She sat up, half in shadow and hair swept to the side, with her tank top tight against her chest. The silence between them heavy.

He rushed at her. He wanted to claim her. The ache within him needed her touch. She swept the top sheet to the side, wrapped her arms around his neck and straddled him as he dropped onto the edge of the bed. He slipped his hands beneath the elastic of her cotton panties and dug the tips of his fingers into her plump bottom, moving her hips with his own. He nuzzled her exposed neck; her cucumber and melon scent wafted around him.

Nothing would stand in their way.

Nothing except his damn chivalrous ways. He pulled away from her roaming lips and pressed his forehead against hers. Breathing hard.

"We cannot do this."

"Why?" she whispered; her breath warm.

He pulled away and tucked a strand of hair behind her ear.

"High stake situations make people do maddening things. If this is more than passion, we need to sort out other pressing matters first. We should wait."

"We don't need to wait," she said between her soft kisses as they trailed down his neck.

Baxter ran his fingers underneath her tank top and up her spine. He was such a hypocrite—always on a seesaw between his logical mind and his feelings. For the moment, his body was out of control, ripping away her top. She pressed her voluptuous bare chest into his, and nibbled at his neck. He growled, wanting to ravish her. It was clear they longed for each other, but her stone pendant was cold against his skin. A reminder.

He broke their kiss again. "I shouldn't have come here. We have such little time for this. We cannot let romance come between our duties."

"Which is why we should enjoy the moment and embrace one another. It could be the last time we have to do so."

"I agree with that, but I am an old-fashioned man living in this fast-paced world. I want to court you. Properly."

She slid off his lap, covering herself with the top sheet. His rejection hurt her, and he hated himself for putting them in that situation. Baxter kneeled next to the bed, held her hand, and looked at her flushed face. "I desire you greatly. On many levels. Know that."

She leaned in, her face close to his. She grinned, and his heart warmed. "I know that. I feel the same about you. Have for a while, actually."

Baxter placed a chaste kiss on the top of her hand.

"I hate to admit this," she said, "but I think you're right. We should wait until things are less... life and death."

Baxter nodded. He could live with that. He would have to. As much as he physically wanted her, he wanted her mind *and* body. His heart swelled, knowing she felt the same about him. He leaned in and pressed his lips against hers. Slow enough to commit the feel of her to memory. And long enough that his lungs ached for air. He pulled away and ventured back to his room without another look.

Hours later, after little sleep, Baxter and Zoe sat in his office, trying to avoid being too close to one another, and focused on deciphering the riddle. He stared at the riddle on the paper as Zoe browsed through some of his thick textbooks on the opposite side of the room.

A tedious routine of theirs.

"Baxter!"

Baxter startled. "What?"

"What were you thinking about? I said your name three times."

Baxter shook his head as he shifted in the chair to give her his full attention. "I apologize. What were you saying?"

"I said I'm such an idiot. The mermaid statue by the pool at my house is bronze *and* she sits on a rock."

Baxter sat up. "Of course. And you are not an idiot. Sometimes we overthink things instead of looking at what's right in front of us."

Zoe pushed the books from her lap and clambered out of the overstuffed chair. She walked over to Baxter and plucked the paper from his hand. She folded it and stuffed it in her pocket then bent over him and gave him a gentle peck on the cheek. "We have time for minor victories. Come on, let's go visit my bronze mermaid."

A few hours later, they sat by the pool, staring at the mermaid statue. Defeated was an understatement. They tried everything to find a clue or hidden compartment for the next stone. Zoe not only touched the pendant to the statue but put it on her.

Baxter dipped his bare feet in the cool pool water. He lay back on the warm terra cotta tile and shielded his eyes from the bright summer sun as Zoe read over the riddle once again.

"Upon a rock, a bronze mermaid rests. Upon a rock, a bronze mermaid rests..."

Baxter sat up on his elbows. "The mermaid is not resting."

Zoe cut her eyes at him. "What?"

Baxter fully sat up and pointed to the statue. "The mermaid is not at rest. Look at her. Head back, basking in the sun, flicking water off the tip of her tail. She is clearly in action, not at rest."

Zoe scrambled off the boulder and came around, scanning the statue like it was her first-time setting eyes on it. "You're right. The riddle clearly states the bronze mermaid on a rock should be resting." She growled and threw her arms up. "We've wasted so much time on this. I truly thought this was the answer. Dammit! Now what?"

She plopped down next to him.

"The first riddle led us to Dr. Clock, who had a connection with Melantha. Perhaps there is a statue of a mermaid, or even of Melantha, we need to find."

Zoe chewed on her lower lip. "Maybe. But the first riddle was also connected to you. You found the article that led to the old state hospital, only because of your connections with the university circuit. It had nothing to do with me."

"Perhaps this time, instead of a connection between Melantha and me, it's between you and Melantha. Have you ever seen, or been around, a mermaid statue besides this one?"

Zoe sunk her feet into the water and sloshed them around. "No. My parents bought me this statue because I swam and was their 'little mermaid'." Zoe clutched Baxter's thigh. "Little mermaid! I *have* been around another mermaid statue. In Solvang, that cute Danish town north of Santa Barbara, there is a bronze statue of Hans Christian Anderson's *The Little Mermaid*. The statue doesn't have a tail and fin, typically associated with mermaids, like my statue. It's transforming from mermaid to human, and she is clearly resting on a rock. My parents took me there a few times when I was younger." She stood up, splashing water onto Baxter, ready to bolt out of there.

But Baxter knew something she didn't.

He leapt to his feet and clutched her arm, stopping her in her tracks. "Sounds like a solid idea, but there are some problems with that theory."

Zoe raised a brow. "What problems? Don't you think Melantha would've known about the Hans Christian Anderson story?"

Baxter released her arm. "I am sure of it. Among others of the time. *Undine,* was a popular German novella about a water spirit. There were several adaptations of Melusine, and let's not forget about the sea-women in the *Odyssey*. That statue, and many others like it across the world, are simply replicas of the original. Hans died before the 1880s. The statue wasn't even commissioned for another twenty-plus years. Melantha would not have known about the original because she was murdered before it was unveiled. She never could have sent a stone to the statue because it wasn't there yet."

Zoe's shoulders sagged. Baxter hated he deflated her spirits again. "I suppose you're right." Zoe stared at her mermaid statue, nibbling on her lower lip. "But the second part of the riddle says: 'Love comforts the saddened.' As you said, my statue is in action, not resting. But *The Little Mermaid* statue is designed to look sad because of the tragic tale she endured. I still feel like that's the answer Baxter. I'm not sure how, but that's it."

Baxter ran his fingers through his hair. Clearly, logical reasoning was something he would have to put aside. Zoe's natural mermaid instincts were getting stronger, and he needed to stop discounting them. "Okay. If you truly feel *The Little Mermaid* statue is the correct answer, then I'll believe it is as well. We may not know *how* the stone arrived at the statue, but it shouldn't matter as long as it's there. Making sense of the actions of someone from the past will only hurt our heads."

Zoe beamed. "If it isn't there, then we'll re-analyze the riddle, and I'll profusely apologize for being wrong."

Baxter grinned.

She looped her arm through his and guided them forward. "Come on, if we leave now, we can get to Solvang in less than three hours, grab the stone, have a nice dinner, and be back here before midnight."

Baxter stopped. She looked up at him. "What's wrong?"

"If there is anything that I know, it is that the stone will not be in the replica in Solvang. That is far too easy. Think about it. It will be with the original. In Copenhagen, Denmark. Sitting in the harbor that feeds into the Baltic and North Sea which—"

"Flows right into the Atlantic Ocean." Zoe dropped her arm from his and stared into the pool; her eyes transfixed on the water gleaming under the sun.

"The moment you transform in that harbor, the king and all his followers will know. And let us be honest, Lucas and his goons will probably follow us and already know you are in their territory."

She picked at her fingernails. "I know. But you're right. It's there. Nothing is ever easy, is it? And it's not like I can take anyone from my realm with me. They aren't strong enough for another fight with the Atlantic-Tails. What do we do?"

Baxter fiddled with the thick, silver ring on his right hand which felt heavy on his finger. It was time for some outside help. "As it so happens, I know of someone who *is* strong enough to go against the Atlantic-Tails."

Zoe's eyes widened. Baxter held up a hand, stopping her from her over-giddy excitement. "Mind you, this solution is not ideal, and I was holding onto it until we absolutely needed it. Before we go overseas to Copenhagen, there is someone you need to meet first."

CHAPTER 31

ZOE

THE NEXT AFTERNOON, ZOE stepped out of Baxter's 4Runner onto a driveway lined with lush trees and thorny hedges. She drank in the ominous castle-like mansion in front of her. Overgrown ivy trailed over the red brick and black stone façade. Projecting from the right side of the house was a round turret, complete with a coned roof and weather vane. The mansion reminded Zoe of houses found in old European towns, and for the life of her, she couldn't understand why something like this was built in the middle of the desert.

Las Vegas. Sin City. Home of neon and twinkling lights of glitz, drugs, and other shady dealings.

Behind them, the wrought-iron entrance gates closed, locking them inside. Her hair stood on end. "Okay, enough with the secrecy. Why did you drag me here? Who are we visiting?"

They walked up the windy cobblestone pathway. It was Friday the thirteenth, and the superstition mused around in the back of Zoe's mind like a bad horror flick.

What could go wrong in a place like this?

She scoffed. "Looks like a witch or vampire lives here."

"Neither. Something more sinister, actually. And she's the closest thing to a friend that I ever truly had."

Zoe stopped. She didn't imagine Baxter with anyone else, and a deep-seated jealous feeling burned in her gut. "An old girlfriend?"

Baxter looked at her from the corner of his eye. "Not in the slightest."

Zoe took a breath. "So, who is she? What's makes her so special?"

"Do you remember when we found the antique map of the different mermaid realms?"

"Yeah. You said a woman who had an unhealthy obsession with mermaids gave it to you?"

Baxter nodded.

"But I thought you said she was dead and couldn't help us and *wouldn't* help us even if she was alive, because you had nothing to offer her in exchange."

Baxter shook his head. "I never said she was dead. *You* made that assumption. I simply did not want to talk about her just yet. It was not the right time."

"Baxter," Zoe whined, drawing out the last letter. "Who in the hell is this chick? And what do you have to offer her?"

The massive iron front door swung open. A lanky man dressed head-to-toe in black, including his eyeliner, stepped out onto the steps, hands on his hips. His pale skin practically glowed in the afternoon sunlight. "Are you going to enter, or stand there ogling the house all day?"

Zoe and Baxter's eyes locked on one another. Baxter straightened and climbed the steps. "We're coming," he said. Zoe followed close behind.

They followed the man into the foyer, where Zoe did indeed ogle at the interior. It was just as ornate and spooky as the outside. A grand double staircase with black, wrought-iron rails and dark hardwood flooring greeted them. A massive candelabra dripping in crystals and candles hung high above their heads. Large gothic paintings of eerie landscapes lined the wine-colored stairwell walls. Zoe wiped the sweat beading at the nape of her neck.

They followed the lanky man down a dark hallway and stopped at a black wooden door. He twisted the crystal doorknob and pushed it opened. "The mistress will be with you in a moment. Meanwhile, she asks you to make yourself comfortable in her study."

Zoe rubbed her eyes, trying to adjust to the dimly lit room. Black cabinets and floor-to-ceiling bookshelves lined the walls. Instead of an overhead light or lamp, there were numerous candles placed all around the room; each one cast an eerie yellow glow over the books and unusual artifacts displayed on the shelves.

A feeling of unease washed over her. "We shouldn't be here," Zoe said.

Baxter ran his fingers along the top edge of the velvet chaise. A black, cloudy mass swept through the room, blowing out all but a few candles. Baxter protectively positioned himself between Zoe and the mass which didn't help her sense of dread.

Zoe peered around him to see a boney, pale hand with long, red fingernails emerge from the mass. It dragged its sharp fingernails across Baxter's chest, seized his shirt and yanked him close. The woman's auburn hair matched the flames glowing in her eyes. Clad in a leather corset strung with red satin ribbon, her voluptuous curves spilled out of the tight clothing. A slit in her skirt cut high to the top of her thigh. She eyed Baxter and glided her teeth over her bottom lip.

"Hello, darkness," Baxter mused.

She released his shirt. "Baxter, my old friend." She wrapped him in her embrace.

Zoe raised a brow at the unexpected greeting. The woman looked past Baxter and tipped her head to the side, her eyes tethered to Zoe's. In a flash, she pushed Baxter aside and gripped Zoe's necklace, ready to rip it from her.

"Madam, please!" Baxter shouted. "By the bounds of your word, you know you are not to touch the queen or her belongings." He waved his hands wildly in front of the woman's face, to distract her from Zoe.

Zoe froze in terror. Her heart threatened to hammer out of her chest and the blood flowing through her veins was turbulent and deafening as it tried to pump through her.

Who the hell is this woman?

A thin rope of fire sprouted from the stone and lashed around the vixen's wrists. She dropped the necklace from her hand and backed away; her eyes returned to the dark shade of auburn-brown.

She giggled. A most hauntingly terrifying giggle. "Demons can get a little out of control when we see something we want."

A forceful swallow worked its way through Zoe's throat. She took a step back and wiped her sweaty palms over her jean shorts. "A demon?" She prowled toward Baxter. "A demon?" she said, louder.

The woman sneered at Baxter. "Oh, and here I thought you were more of a gentleman, Bennett. You didn't even properly inform her of me. I deserve better than that."

Baxter sighed and dipped his head. "My apologies." He looked at Zoe with an expressionless face. "This is Lil. A demon."

Lil lifted a sharp brow at him and cleared her throat. "You promised," she sang.

Baxter rolled his eyes and plastered a forced smile on his face. "This is Lil," he said sweetly, "A demon and my friend for the past..." he looked at Lil, "What? Sixty or seventy years?"

Lil flipped her long hair over her shoulder and eyed Baxter. "Seventy-two, to be exact. Although it's been a while since I've seen or heard from you."

Zoe, still rooted to the ground, exhaled. This was the most unusual, beyond wildest dreams, circumstance she found herself in thus far. She wanted nothing to do with demons or things that creepily went bump in the night. The fact Baxter was friends with her... *it?* She had an unwavering feeling that dealing with Lil, a freakin' demon, would turn bad real fast.

How does Baxter not see what a terrible idea this is?

"Why are we even here?"

Baxter stood next to Zoe, brushing his arm against hers. His warmth was most unwelcome.

"Lil, this is not a social call. We are here on business."

Lil stomped her foot like a bratty child. "It never is. Always business with you."

"Play nice and stop with the theatrics," Baxter directed.

"Whatever. Fine." She waved her arms over her head and stepped inside another cloudy black mist. When it dissipated, she, and the room, transformed from her seductive enchantress vibe to a soft chic ambiance.

Zoe blinked at the unexpected change. She took a faltering step, drinking in the changed room. Every dark wooden tone was now covered in white-washed wood, making the room bright and inviting, even if the strange artifacts on the bookcases were still there.

Lil gathered her, now, blonde hair, tying it into a messy ponytail. She wore distressed, flared jeans and a hoodie and plopped down on the light pink chaise.

A demon. With soft, pink feminine crap all around her.

What kind of fresh hell is this place and who are we dealing with?

Zoe, wide-eyed, glanced at Baxter. He shrugged his shoulder, as if it was nothing new to him.

"She is always so dramatic with people she meets for the first time," he explained.

Zoe shuffled over to the cream color chair across from the chaise and sat on its edge. Baxter perched against the edge of a desk in front of the bookcases. His silver ring glinted in the light streaming from the delicate, crystal chandelier above their heads.

"Your ring," Zoe said. "On the day of my final, you told the class you got it from a demon. I thought you said that only to entice people to take the second part of your class. But you weren't lying. You really *did* get it from a demon."

Baxter held out his hand and examined his ring. "Indeed."

Lil giggled her hauntingly sick giggle once again. "Awe, how adorable. Talking about me to your students. I'm flattered. Perhaps I should make a guest appearance next term."

Baxter shook his head at the woman who looked more like a college student than a damn demon. "No. You will not do that." He faced Zoe. "Yes, Lil is the demon I spoke of. She can help us—you."

"Is that right?" Zoe sneered. "Tell me, demon, what do ya' know about *The Little Mermaid* statue in Copenhagen?"

Lil caught Baxter's eye, slithered off the chaise and climbed the wooden ladder against the bookcases. She plucked a small leather-bound book from the shelf and dropped it on the desk Baxter leaned on. She flipped the cover open to the first page, revealing a water-color painting. It was of a bronze statue perched upon a boulder in the water right off a boardwalk. The nude woman had a look of longing on her face as she sat on her hip with her legs mid-transformation from mermaid to human, tucked beneath her. At the bottom right of the page were the words, *Copenhagen, 1913.* "The statue is not from the cutesy fairytale movie you sung along with when you were a child," she said.

"I'm well aware that the statue is the Hans Christian Anderson version," Zoe said. "Do you know of any reason Melantha's stone would be located all the way in Copenhagen? Any thoughts on how I can get the stone from it without causing an all-out war with the Atlantic-Tails?"

Lil smirked. "Ooh, all the questions, feels like an interrogation, I love it."

"Lil," Baxter warned. "Stay on topic."

Lil waved him off. "Well, Melantha had been fond of good ol' Hans, especially when his published story helped popularize mermaids worldwide."

"Makes sense. Sounds similar to her relationship with Dr. Clock." Zoe stepped away from the book.

Baxter nodded. "Indeed. She liked it when people talked about mermaids. It helped keep their lure alive. I am sure that Hans Christian Anderson's contribution was significant."

Lil continued. "Did you know that some of the most famous writers in history have come across at least one magical being in their lifetime and used those experiences to write their stories?"

Zoe pursed her lips. "You don't say."

Lil lit up and nodded, completely unaware, or ignoring, Zoe's deadpan charm. "Oh, yes," Lil said. "Charles Perrault, author of *Sleeping Beauty*, once met some fairies. Lewis Carroll, in his delusional state of mind, somehow had a run-in with some hellhounds and loosely based his Jabberwocky creation off that. The Brothers Grimm based *Rumpelstiltskin* off imps and goblins they came across in the Black Forest—"

"What does that have to do with me?" Zoe asked.

"Lil always had a hobby of meeting the authors of fairy tales because she wanted to hear how they were inspired to come up with their stories," Baxter said. "Her interest in stuff like that is one reason she created the map we have." He dipped his chin at Lil. "Which we both appreciate."

Zoe trawled up a smile. "Yeah. Thanks." She threw a look at Baxter. "If you knew she was that into fairy tales, why didn't you know about Melantha's friendship with Hans Christian Anderson?"

Baxter thought for a moment then faced Lil. "Good question. Lil? Why did you never tell me that crucial piece of information?"

The demon shrugged her shoulders and batted long lashes at him. "If I'd told you everything, you wouldn't have any reason to pay me visits throughout the years, would you?"

Baxter sighed heavily, nearly growling in his frustration with her. "This is not the time for games. I cannot pay you any more visits in the future if I'm dead. You know my life is tied to hers, which is tied to the stone."

Zoe snapped the book closed. "We don't need her bullshit games. She can't help us. Let's go, Baxter." She marched toward the door.

Like a flash of lighting, Lil was in Zoe's path. Her hair went stark white, busting out of her ponytail. Straight and stringy. Her blue eyes hollowed like a skull. The corner of her lips ripped across her cheeks, giving her a Joker-like grin with teeth as sharp as a piranha. Her elongated fingers snatched Zoe's jaw, forcing her to look at her demon form.

A warm rush of adrenaline washed through Zoe. She trembled trying to hold off from the knee-jerk reaction of a fight-or-flight response.

Evil radiated off the demon.

This bitch...

But Zoe refused to be the one to back down.

"I can feel your disdain toward me coursing through your soul," Lil whispered, her voice raspy and breath hot against Zoe's ear. "Truly a benefit. It makes your magic radiate and puts a pep in my step."

"Lil! That is enough!" Baxter shouted, his arm between them.

Without losing eye contact with the demon, Zoe lifted her hand and pushed Baxter away.

"Fuck you," Zoe snarled.

Lil giggled her horrible little giggle. "Maybe one day." She opened her fingers, releasing Zoe's jaw. She didn't drop her hand, though, as if daring Zoe to move or say something.

Zoe, of course, had a ton she wanted to say. Hell, she wanted to run screaming, but there were some things she learned during her swimming PED scandal that she could use here: Keep a cool head and say nothing to cause an uproar and make things much worse. She swallowed, trying very hard to fight the urge to retaliate. "Baxter and I are going. Your so-called friendship with him ends here and any information you would have provided is no longer needed."

Lil took a step back, her natural demon form melting away to the pretty-in-pink Barbie look. "You and Bennett didn't come here for information, love. It was for this—" Lil opened her hand.

Sitting on her palm was a familiar silver ring.

CHAPTER 32
BAXTER

BAXTER LOOKED AT HIS ringless hand. The weight of it gone, but it left him feeling empty and naked, like he lost a piece of his soul. The same feeling from when he took the stone pendant off.

This was not what he planned when he brought Zoe to Lil.

"This ring is from the underworld, forged in the depths of hell," Lil continued. "If the wearer should ever need protection against *anything*, magical or not, it will activate and save you. But it will work only once, you understand?"

"Thanks for the offer, but I can protect myself with my magic. I will have nothing to do with something so wicked."

Lil straightened. "You don't trust your guardian's judgment? He wore this for decades."

"Him, I trust. You? Not at all. You're up to something."

"You think, oh, newly made-mermaid, that your magic will protect you when you dive headfirst into Cavan's territory without the aid of an army?" Lil spat. "Foolish child. Do you forget it was the two of you who came to me asking for help?"

Zoe's jaw tightened. She glared at Baxter, but there was no warmth behind her violet-blue eyes. "*I* didn't ask for your help," she said to Lil.

Baxter took a single step closer to the two women. "Lil, I thought that ring was to protect me. Do you not have another one for Zoe?"

Lil tossed her long locks behind her shoulder. "There is only one, Bennett. Besides, you probably don't need it anymore. Zoe is your protection, and I suspect your own magic has activated now that the guardian found his queen." Her mouth curled into a wicked grin. "But who shall protect the queen when she is underwater, all alone and desperate?"

Zoe's brows furrowed as she tightened her jaw. Lil, however, took Zoe's anger as an invitation. She clutched Zoe's hand and slipped the ring onto her pointer finger.

Zoe shoved Lil. She pulled at the ring. Strained. But it refused to slide off. Baxter could see the panic spread across her face; something he understood because Lil did the same thing to him decades earlier. Zoe did not find Lil amusing and almost instantly hated her upon arrival. Baxter knew Lil wasn't a problem. She had been his friend for so many years, always doing things her way, but in the end, always helping him. She wasn't evil. And now it seemed Zoe was pissed off at him for introducing her to Lil and her strange antics.

This tension certainly would not help their relationship.

Zoe held her hand up to Baxter, showing him the ring. "This? *This* is why you brought me here?"

Yup, definitely pissed off.

"To attach a demon-made ring to me? What if it hinders my magic? How could you have done this without trusting me enough to talk to me about it first?"

Worse than he feared. He broke her trust. He could almost feel the wall rise between them.

What can I say?

"His intentions were good enough, love. And it won't interfere with your magic—think of it as a onetime enhancer. A boost, if you will."

Baxter wished Lil would shut up. He didn't need her antagonizing Zoe further. "I thought Lil had another ring. You need something extra to enter the Atlantic realm. She has never steered me wrong before. I apologize for springing my plans, and her, on you like this. I made the assumption you wouldn't even try to accept her help if I'd explained my plans beforehand."

"You're right! I wouldn't have accepted her help if you had told me beforehand, and I don't want it now." Zoe tried one last time to yank the ring off her finger. She held out her hand to Lil. "Take it off me."

Lil batted her lashes. "Sorry. Can't. It hasn't done its job. Only then will it be removed."

"But you took it off me," Baxter stated.

Lil faced him; her hands shot to her hips. "Because it did its job. It was there to protect you in case you needed it before you found the queen. You found her, and you never needed it, so its job is done. You could have taken it off the moment she transformed into a mermaid."

Tight-lipped, Baxter said, "Would have been nice to have known the rules."

Lil shrugged her shoulder. "Now you know."

Zoe ran her hand through her hair. "When will I be able to take this off? What's its job?"

Lil stepped closer to Zoe, who flinched back, but only slightly. Lil lifted Zoe's hand, closed her eyes, and rubbed her thumb over the ring, channeling its magic. "The only job it has is to help you in the Atlantic-realm, if you should need it. If you don't, and can leave the realm unscathed, you'll be able to take it off. Perhaps you should give it back to Bennett. He looks so good in silver."

"Like hell." Zoe shoved past both Lil and Baxter toward the door.

"You'll thank me, and him, later," Lil called after her.

Baxter straightened. "You look lovely as ever, Lil. I'll be in touch." Baxter gave her a slight bow. "Stay out of trouble," he said over his shoulder and rushed out of the room.

"Oh, Bennett," Lil sang out from behind him.

Baxter knew Zoe was done and didn't care what else Lil could want, but like a trained dog, he stopped and turned around.

Lil held onto the wooden doorjamb and playfully swung out into the hallway. "I highly recommend you to still wear the necklace, even if it is just a small part of the stone, especially since you don't have my ring as backup. I'd be so sad if something happened to you."

Baxter balled his fingers into a fist. Dealing with Lil was maddening, and he often questioned why he put up with her, especially since Zoe couldn't stand her. "You said I did not need the ring or necklace anymore because I had my own magic as I found the queen."

"Well, just in case. And I said probably. You *probably* don't need it. I rather enjoy our visits. I'd hate to see that end even if Zoe thinks she has a say over our friendship."

Baxter shook his head. He felt Zoe walk up next to him, facing Lil. "How can he wear part of the stone pendant if the pieces we found are all fused together?"

Good, Zoe's talking to her. Could they work together without issue?

"Well, I don't have *all* your answers, queen Zoe," Lil quipped. "You'll have to figure that out for yourself."

Well, there went that.

Zoe ripped around and stomped away, mumbling something about bitchy demons.

Baxter flashed Lil with a look of annoyance.

She blew him a kiss.

He snarled at her and clambered after Zoe.

Baxter climbed into the car and started the engine. Zoe glared out of the passenger window. "Lil may seem unhinged, but I trust her completely. There is a reason she wants me to wear a part of the necklace, and I think we need to heed her warning. Any ideas on how to break the stone so I can still wear a piece of it?"

"I dunno," Zoe mumbled.

A short, dismissive response was never good. Their first bad disagreement. Baxter didn't have much experience in this situation, but this was part of a relationship.

The really shitty part of a relationship.

Baxter took a breath. They could only get stronger from this.

"What about what she said about me having guardian magic? I have never come across such information, but I know she wouldn't have mentioned it if it wasn't true. I just wonder how to access it. What can I do to help you?"

"Right now, I don't care," Zoe sassed. "Let's just get on the next flight to Copenhagen as quickly as possible, so we can get this over with, and I can get this damn ring off."

Baxter became unnaturally still. That was more than a bad disagreement. That was more than her being pissed off.

It was a complete fracture.

Nearly forty-eight hours later, that fracture grew into a rift.

Booking a flight from Las Vegas to New York had been simple enough. Both snoozed the entire way which kept her tidal wave of emotions at bay for at least a few hours. Unfortunately, once in New York, they learned there was only one flight a day from New York to Copenhagen, and because of their short notice, the next flight wouldn't be leaving until the following day, causing an awkwardly long delay.

Zoe refused to leave the airport for a nearby hotel, surely not wanting to be alone with him, which caused another argument between them. After taking a breath, Baxter stopped being the fool, gave into her, and stayed in the dirty airport to wait. Because of their impromptu adventure to Copenhagen, the flight had no first-class seats available which severely annoyed Baxter since he was not fond of flying. There was almost nothing worse than being cramped inside a metal shell for hours on end with knees bent up and elbows tightly squeezed into his body.

Strike that. There was something worse: having your partner ignore your existence because they are angry and hurt by something you did. He knew she wanted to stay in public, so they couldn't talk about things like magic and demons. The wait slowly drained Baxter of all his energy. He couldn't stand the mundane pleasantries and the thick air between them. A darkness he hadn't felt since the turn of the century rose within him.

The isolation of being alone in the world took him to some rather dubious places, both mentally and physically. Even though she was right next to him, her silent treatment made him feel completely alone like he had so many years ago. In his darkest moments of trying to find creative ways to numb his new reality, he found Lil. Sure, she preyed upon him at first, but once she learned who he truly was, her front as a demon faded away, and they became friends. It had been Lil who taught him how to navigate an eternal life. It had been Lil who looked out for him over the decades, making sure he stayed on his path. She even helped him along the way by collecting information regarding mermaids.

He hated that Zoe and Lil hadn't found a rapport with one another, but grandiose ideas rarely seemed to work out. Lil would probably have to be cut from his life. This thought brought him to a heart-wrenching understanding that he truly was alone.

That simply would not do. If they were going to survive this disagreement, pettiness could not be a hindrance. He would not survive another moment, nor a sleepless night in a foreign country, without addressing their feelings. Now was as good as any to say what he needed to say.

He glanced around Copenhagen's Langelinie Promenade. Baxter gripped Zoe's upper arm and gathered her into his arms. His eyes, a burning shackle to her wide eyes. "I have had enough of your silent treatment. We've traveled half-way across the world and before you get in those waters, which could change everything in our future, whatever is going on between us needs to stop. I dislike being ignored. Or feeling alone."

Zoe yanked her arm out of his hand and stepped back. "And I don't like the trust between us being broken. You let her put this wicked ring on me, and I can't take it off. I don't understand why you aren't more concerned about what she's up to. And I don't get why you let me think the person who wrote that map of my world was dead? I've been wracking my brain trying to understand your motives, but I can't seem to get my head that far up my ass!"

Baxter sighed. "I have apologized profusely for that. I cannot take back how I introduced you to Lil. Zoe, believe me, I never wanted to involve you with her, which is why I never talked about her until then. I know Lil, and yes, I am sure she has an ulterior motive, but I also know she has a good heart and would never hurt me, or by extension, you."

Zoe eyed a nearby family and stepped closer to him and whispered, "How do you know that? She's a demon, Baxter. Manipulation and getting people's souls are, like, their thing. And also, what did you offer her?"

Baxter knitted his brows and tilted his head to the side.

"You mentioned you had nothing to offer her in exchange for her help. So, what did you offer her?"

Baxter hissed out a breath and ran his hands through his hair. "You. A chance to meet you. To smell you, touch you... I had always told her I would never let her meet you because of her unhealthy obsession with magical creatures, so when I called to arrange our meeting, she was more than willing to help. Especially after making me grovel for half an hour."

Zoe grunted. "Some friend."

Baxter shrugged his shoulder. He knew his friendship with Lil was odd and didn't have the words to explain it anymore. "Again, I am sorry."

Zoe nodded, blinking away some tears. "You of all people know I'm still dealing with last year's betrayal of my teammates." She looked back to Baxter. "I can't take that from you."

Seeing the hurt in her eyes stabbed at Baxter like a knife to the heart. He did that to her. He put that doubt in her mind.

She moved closer to him in a way that made Baxter hopeful the rift was closing between them. "I'm sorry for ignoring you and making you feel alone. That was shitty of me. I can tell that's a trigger for you, just as betrayal and trust issues trigger me. We both have some things that need to be worked on."

Baxter placed Zoe's hand in his own. "Indeed. But, we need to focus on what is about to happen. There is too much at stake. You know if I could go with you, I would, right?"

"I know. Which is why I understand why you wanted Lil to help with this ring. I can accept that, even though I don't like it."

"Fair enough. Whatever happens under the water, trust your instincts and the magic that flows inside you. But if things go wrong, and you do not return, I will do whatever I need to get you back. Even if that means getting help from Lil."

Zoe squeezed his hand. "Understood."

Baxter looped his arm with hers, and they strolled down the pier, stopping in front of the bronze statue perched in the water a few feet off the boardwalk. Just as the riddle stated, upon the boulder, the mermaid rested. Some of the patina oxidized into a greenish-teal color, but she was still beautiful. She had her legs tucked tightly beneath her, sitting more on her hip. Her shoulders were rounded, slouched over, and she stared longingly toward the land.

Zoe surveyed the water at the base of the boulder tower. "Are we *sure* the Oresund strait is part of Cavan's realm? We're pretty far from the Atlantic Ocean."

Baxter guided Zoe to a nearby grassy area beneath a shady tree. "Don't let that fool you. Cavan's territory isn't wide open waters like yours. His is broken up by landmasses and seas. The waters here feed into the North Sea, which eventually ties into the North Atlantic." He wished they brought the map of the realms to be one hundred percent certain, but he was confident enough.

Zoe sighed and looked over her shoulder, toward the busy port. "It was a longshot."

Baxter understood. He, too, wished this hadn't been the case.

"I can feel the pull of the stone, somewhere in the water beyond the statue," she said as she faced him. "It's time."

CHAPTER 33
ZOE

WITH BAXTER'S DISTRACTION, ZOE followed the boardwalk to the end of the pier, took the stairs down to the water, lowered herself in, and glided across the surface. She wasn't quite ready to do what she intended. Her illegal entry would alert the Atlantic-Tails the moment she transformed, the same way they entered hers only days ago. And, yet, here she was, about to do the same. Worse even, she was going to steal something from their realm, even though the item was rightfully hers. Her actions would inevitability cause havoc to the Atlantic realm and fan the flames of war against her own.

This was the point of no return.

She scrubbed her face. The only thing she was sure about was that the line between villains and heroes was thin and extremely blurred. From what she learned, the centuries of hate between the Pacific and Atlantic realms were reminiscent of that of the Montagues and Capulets, and it ached her to her core. What had gone so terribly wrong to cause such animosity? Why couldn't they work together? Did things really have to be this way? Had Melantha done something that helped cause the problem?

Her name did mean dark flower... Maybe she lived in a world of gray...

With nothing but wild imaginings, Zoe paddled farther into the harbor, away from the statue, following the call of her pendant. She eyed the ring from Lil and hated that it represented even more hostility within her world. Perhaps she could get her stone through other, friendlier means. There was still time to convince Lucas and his goons of a peace offering.

Right?

Her lips curled. Time, or the lack of thereof, was her biggest enemy, not the Atlantic-Tails. *If* she had more time, she could find a peaceful way to conduct her business, but unfortunately, she didn't have it.

She drew in a long breath and dipped below the surface to transform. A sonic boom erupted through the water signaling her arrival into the Atlantic realm. The race was on, and an army of Atlantic-Tails would ambush her soon enough. She torpedoed forward, following the pull of the stone to a cluster of rocks and coral near a small, rocky hill. At the base of the boulders vibrant red flower-like plants danced in the current. An electrifying tingle tickled her scales, and Zoe knew the next stone to her pendant was close.

She examined the small forest of flowers and unveiled an opening between two of the boulders. Her tail illuminated in the darkness as she swam through the rocky channel. Zoe popped her head above the water and noticed she was inside a grotto. Stalactites dropped from the rocky ceiling. A musky aroma filled the stale air. She slithered around the stalagmites protruding out of the water and came across the mossy remains of an old wooden ship strewn across the cave.

At the back of the grotto was a large, jagged column with another opening in the wall next to it. She paddled forward, curious why the water bubbled from the opening. But just as she reached it, a tremor rumbled through the grotto. She gripped the closest tapered rock formation to steady herself as water sloshed her face. A billowing cloud of white foam erupted from the large opening. She dove beneath the water and hid behind a cluster of stalagmites. She peeked around the rigid rock.

Red and Green-Tails splashed into the grotto, canvasing the area. The blueish-white tattoos glowed beneath the surface. Green orbs burst out of their hands. Katanas sculpted from coral sliced through the waters. Balls of water-proof fire danced around the cave.

Then a single Orange-Tail with a tribal tattoo on his neck entered. William.

"Come out, come out, little mermaid." He drifted toward her; he knew exactly where she hid.

Zoe rested her head on the rock. The Atlantic-Tails attack may have been expected, but she was still angry with herself for getting trapped. The pull of the stone was so strong she knew it hid in the cavern somewhere. She needed a bit more time. She resurfaced, looking for an exit, but only saw more of the red flowers. But buried within the red was something white.

Without a plan, she jetted forward, exposing herself to the At-lantic-Tails and catching them off guard. She had seconds to herself before they realized where she headed. Tunnel vision blinded her as she outstretched her arms. A force hit her back and sent her off course. A fiery ball screamed past her bare arms, its flames licking at her skin.

Out of options and terrified, she folded into herself, like a person fending off a bear attack. Her magic quivered inside her body as she felt the presence of the Atlantic-Tails' army surrounding her.

What do I do? Something... anything...

An energy within her warmed. She embraced the tingle until violent convulsions controlled her body. A kaleidoscope of colorful magic erupted from her fingertips and fin. The cavern shook, stalagmites crumbled. Atlantic-Tails sailed across the grotto, striking rocks and floundering in the water.

Zoe opened her eyes and rubbed the water away from her face. The grotto looked like the aftermath of a bomb. Mangled red flowers were scattered about like blood. Moans echoed across the cavern. Embers of pebbles and dust clouded the air. She threw a look behind her and blanched as she saw a Green-Tail skewered on one of the broken wooden masts from the remains of the ship. Choking back bile, she pressed her hand to her mouth.

She touched the ring from Lil, wondering if the magic of the underworld or her own powers had protected her. Weak from the rush of magic, Zoe slumped through the water. She had to find the white stone. Careful to look past the carnage, she spotted the white object tangled in some moss. Using the rocks to support her, she glided through the water and passed the debris. She scooped it up, surprised to see it was a white marble statue of a boy. She clutched it to her chest, knowing that her stone must be hidden inside, just like the one in the nautilus.

On the other side of the grotto, she noticed William drooped over Sebastian.

She crept her way toward the passage opening. The carnage would distract the Tails enough to forget about her. She leaned against some driftwood. Her head sunk to the side as she gulped down a steady breath.

From somewhere around her, she heard, "Look at all the blood. Sharks will be coming."

She hadn't even considered *that* threat.

A booming voice echoed across the rock-strewn walls. "Which is why the lot of you will go contain them while Queen Zoe and I have a chat."

The injured Atlantic-Tails squared their shoulders and bowed their heads. Without another word; the Tails hurried out of the cavern, dragged their injured friends with them, and left her alone with the newest person to enter the grotto. Cavan. The king. He skated through the water toward the center of the grotto.

Zoe lifted her chin and drank in his appearance. Her eyes fell on the similar, but complete, stone pendant lying against his bare chest. Cavan ran his fingers through his short salt-and-pepper hair, his thick arms flexing as he moved. He had an aura of arrogance about him—he knew he was stunning and embraced it. His blazing violet-blue eyes meet hers. Royalty against royalty.

"Of all the beautiful seas in my realm, we meet here in a dark grotto. It wouldn't take us long to go somewhere more suitable in the Mediterranean. Somewhere warmer with crystal blue waters, perhaps?"

Zoe shook her head. "I don't think so."

"You are just as stunning as Melantha." He circled her. Zoe caught a glimpse of a tattoo on his right shoulder blade. She careened her neck and stole a glance at the elaborate trident jutting out of a wave

Their tails intertwined. Zoe cringed as he laced his fingers in the strands of her hair, moving it aside to brush his lips on her bare shoulder. "Together, we can be the most powerful creatures in the world, ruling the two largest oceans side-by-side. We could even conquer the Landwalkers."

His fingers traced down her arm. She flinched. Bile churned.

Cavan snarled, but the statue in her hand distracted him. "I see you brought me a gift. A wedding gift, perhaps?"

"First of all, Cavan, why would I ever want to join forces with a cocky pretty-boy like you?"

Cavan's cheeks reddened. His mouth screwed tight.

She probably shouldn't sass him, but she wasn't one to back down in an argument. "There's a reason we rule different waters; it's because we all contribute something special to that region, keeping that climate and habitat safe. There's no telling what damage Pacific-Tails could do to the Atlantic waters and vice versa." She couldn't stop the word vomit spewing out of her, even though her inner voice begged her to stop. "Move aside and let me pass. After whatever ancient magic just came exploding out of me, you don't wanna' trigger me a second time. Besides, this statue is mine."

"Yet, stolen from my realm!" Cavan's baritone voice echoed off the cave rocks. His face contorted, his eyes a horrifying red. His jaw distended, revealing long, jagged teeth. Gills sprouted from his neck. His veins and muscles bulged.

Zoe smirked. He wasn't anywhere near as terrifying as Lil been. Except when he ejected forward, thrusting his three-pronged spear at Zoe's chest.

She dove to the right, but not before the prongs sliced down the side of her tail. The pain was sharp. Warm blood oozed from the wound. She whipped behind a stalagmite as Cavan jabbed the trident into it, shattering it. Zoe zipped around the broken shards and flung herself into the opening of the passageway.

"You're mine!"

Eyes wide, Zoe zoomed out of the opening, through the forest of red flowers, and to the open sea. She propelled forward, kicking her tail as hard and fast as she could, expecting Cavan to use his wicked-looking trident to end her life.

But he didn't.

She glanced behind her. He wore a playful grin. This was a game to him and he was relishing every minute.

The question wasn't how far he'd take things.

It was a question of if Lil's damn ring would be of any help once he finally caught her.

CHAPTER 34

ZOE

WITHIN MINUTES, SHE SURFACED near Langelinie Promenade. Night had fallen. The boardwalk was lit by streetlamps. The lights from the boats in the harbor looked like tiny fireflies flittering about.

Will the cloak of the dark be a blessing, so I won't make a very public scene when I try to escape Cavan's clutches, or a curse giving him easy access to do his worst?

She knew he closed in on her. She could feel his presence like a shadow hovering over her, ready to pounce.

Once the underwater wall of the promenade came into view, she transformed into human form. She planted her hands on the concrete and used all her upper body strength to lift herself out of the water and dropped onto the land. Water rushed off her body as she half-rolled, half-crawled away from the edge. Her leg throbbed where he sliced her thigh, but she scrambled to her feet. The rush of water running down Cavan as he climbed over the edge made her turn. He stood on defined legs. Commanding.

Like a *fucking* god.

Cavan took a step forward. "Melantha tried running from me too. But I knew she liked the chase."

Zoe grimaced, disgusted by his comment. "You lie. You probably murdered her. Why? 'Cause she wouldn't conform to your chauvinistic demands?"

Cavan tilted his head back and laughed as if he had heard the funniest joke in his life. Zoe inched back. "What's so funny?"

"Your ignorance. It's amazing how much of her is within you. Why would I murder Melantha if I wanted her realm? I didn't orchestrate the mess you and your kingdom have found yourselves in. I get nothing with her gone and would never have done that to myself."

There was something manic in his eyes, and she wasn't sure if he was telling the truth or not. He seemed too vain to cause himself any struggle as he stated, but he also seemed too vain to let Melantha have the most powerful kingdom.

If he didn't kill Melantha, who did?

Cavan stepped closer, his arm outstretched and his features soft, masking the threat he truly was. "See, Zoe, I'm only here to help. I went about this all wrong. Let us join forces and become one. I promise your Tails will be well-cared for and have all their magic back. Your realm will even be protected. With you on my arm, our kingdoms will flourish and be revered."

"Leave her alone, Cavan," Baxter snarled, his voice dripping with ice as he stepped next to Zoe.

The tension in her body relaxed. Knowing he was here with her made the confrontation more bearable. She didn't dare turn her back on Cavan.

"Well, well, well. If it isn't the guardian himself," Cavan growled. "If I'd only known what a thorn you would be, I'd have taken care of you myself instead of letting my incompetent guards deal with you. Giving me that stone would have saved a lot of heartache for the Pacific-Tails."

"Doubtful." Baxter's fingers grazed Zoe's.

Cavan glared at him for a split second, then gave a mirthless laugh. "I suppose you're correct. Well, seeing that you're right in front of me." Cavan raised his hands, and as if he were Zeus, purple lightning beamed out of the tips of his fingers hitting Baxter squarely in the chest.

Baxter ricocheted several feet backward.

Zoe screamed.

Cavan lunged.

He gripped her and sent her sprawling across a grassy plot between large trees, skidding her knees. The white marble statue of the boy flew from her hands and bounced away. She scrambled to her feet, but Cavan was on her, wrenching his large hands around her wrists and pinning them down. He reached for the chain of her necklace as she thrashed beneath him.

Something pummeled into Cavan. Zoe looked up. Baxter and Cavan tumbled over one another; Baxter crashing on top of him. He punched him across the jaw repeatedly. Blood spattered across Baxter's face. There was a wild blaze in his eyes. This was the Baxter that Lucas and his goons feared. *The Guardian*. The person who possessed some kind of ancient protective powers because of his role.

A person you did *not* want to fuck with.

Cavan wrestled against Baxter, able to reach his trident tattoo. In an instant, the trident was in his hands and the prongs were at Baxter's throat. Without pause, Baxter laced his fingers around the base of the prongs.

Cavan's jaw tightened and the veins in his neck protruded as he tried to push the trident forward to stab Baxter. But he was unmovable, like stone.

Even though Zoe had minimal magic in her arsenal, she sprung forward and locked her arm around Cavan's throat, ready to squeeze. "Checkmate," she whispered in his ear.

Cavan took a breath then lowered his trident.

Zoe glanced over to Baxter, whose eyes fixed on Cavan.

"I want you to get back in your waters and leave me, Baxter, and my realm alone," Zoe said without loosening her grip. "Just go away and mind your own business."

"Not without my property," Cavan muttered as he inclined his head toward the statue of the boy.

"You should heed her warning, Cavan." Baxter wiped blood from his lip, dragging it across his jaw.

"The stone inside is mine, which makes it my property. I don't give a shit if I stole it from your realm or not. Got it?" Zoe said.

Cavan shifted his head to look at Zoe from the corner of his eye. "One more thing, though."

"What?" she said through gritted teeth.

"It wasn't a checkmate. It's a stalemate." In a flash of aqua lights, he disappeared.

Zoe fell to the grass.

Cavan reappeared behind Baxter, stabbing the trident through his back. Baxter dropped and Zoe screamed.

Slow and deliberate, Cavan pulled the weapon out of Baxter's bloodied body. The shock of being stabbed frozen on his face. Cavan reached his arm out, and like a magnet, the small statue of the boy sailed into his hand.

Blinded with hate and tears, Zoe ran at him, her piercing scream ringing out into the night, straining her voice. But he zapped her with the same purple lightning. She flew backward and landed in the patch of grass again.

For the second time, Cavan was quick to get on top of her.

"Two realms, now one, for treasures and fun—"

Cavan leaned over and captured her lips. His teeth nipping at her. Zoe cried out as soon as he pulled away. Would her screams of horror interrupt his spell?

"Binding and obeying—"

He kissed her again, but this time, she could feel her energy, her very core, being syphoned away. He pulled away and a small trace of flowing purple magic bridged between their lips, connecting them as one magical being.

Zoe squirmed beneath him, panicked. She didn't know any spells. She was a newbie with magic and didn't know what she was doing. And physically? There was no way she could overpower him. This was it. Her last moment. Quivers ran through her body as she drowned her lungs with air. She withered once more and slipped her arm out of his grip. She reached up and buried her fingernails in his cheeks, willing any form of her magic to push him off her.

Then it happened.

Silver beads of magic rained over them, pelting their skin like cold raindrops.

From around her finger, something warmed. She eyed the silver ring and could see the black scroll pattern glowing red-orange. A vicious hate swelled inside her. She palmed his face, connecting the ring to his skin like a hot iron, branding him with the patterned scroll.

The rain of silver magic ceased. Cavan hollered and stumbled off her. He dropped the statue and clutched his face. The purple stream of magic broke and rushed back into her like an overwhelming breath of fresh air. Zoe sat up. She lifted her hand and looked at the ring once again.

The scroll pattern floated off the band and twirled into billowing, black smoke, growing larger and larger with each twisting motion. It rushed at Cavan, encased him in a coil and squeezed. His screech pierced the night like a needle into skin. The smoke plunged into his screaming mouth. His eye vessels burst. Veins bulged. Face reddened. Skin blistered and oozed pus. Muscles stretched away from his skull, melting away like wax.

Zoe could do nothing but watch in horror.

His body jerked and convulsed, finally exploding into flames. Zoe shielded herself as fragmented debris of colorful magic spewed from his remains. Black smoke exited his carcass, swallowing the released magic in its wake and drifted toward Zoe. Frozen in fear, she watched as it twisted and twirled again, this time shrinking in size. It hovered over the silver band, reformed the original scroll pattern then became one with it again. The ring glowed before disappearing with a tiny *pop*.

Shaking, Zoe flipped onto her knees and heaved. She sobbed, a horrid sound coming from her. For the second time this evening, she killed, but worse, she lost her best friend. Her companion.

Dare she say, her love?

She wasn't sure how long she cried, but someone stood over her and touched her back. A bystander trying to console her.

"Are you okay?"

She took a shuddery breath. She flipped around.

"Baxter!"

She scrambled to her feet. "Am I okay? Are *you* okay?" She ran her hand over his torso, looking for the holes the trident left only moments before.

Baxter hissed as she touched him. "Careful, careful. Still healing."

She wrapped her arms around his neck and buried her face in his chest. "I was so scared. You died." He held her tight and any feeling of being upset with him instantly disappeared.

"I thought I was dead, too. I must still be protected, but I'm not sure for how long. But damn, that hurt. That is something I could have done without."

Zoe looked up at him, but refused to let go. "I guess Lil was right. We need to figure out how to break the pendant. You can wear a piece, so it doesn't hurt or stall your healing if something like this should happen again."

Baxter nodded.

Zoe rested her check against his chest and stared at the pile of Cavan's bones. Embers crackled inside it like a small fire. "Did you see what happened to Cavan?"

"Indeed." His voice vibrated in his chest, against her ear. "A gruesome ending. One he did not expect."

"What did you do, dearie?"

Zoe and Baxter spun on their heels. Behind them, in human form, were William, Lucas, and Sebastian.

Lucas stepped forward. "Did you hear me? What did you do?"

CHAPTER 35
BAXTER

IT DID NOT SURPRISE Baxter to see Lucas and his goons, but that didn't mean he would let his guard down. By reaction, his arm jutted out, pushing Zoe protectively behind his frame, even though he knew she could take care of herself.

The three shirtless men, who looked like surfers stepping out of the tide, marched toward them. Baxter was ready for words, or perhaps in this case, an actual fight, especially after they tried to run them off the Pacific Coast Highway. As they got closer, Baxter noticed something different about their demeanor. They looked... defeated. Scared, even. There was something else. Something Baxter couldn't identify. For the first time, he felt at ease around them, like he knew they weren't a threat anymore which in return made him uncomfortable.

Zoe sidestepped Baxter. "There was no other option. He drained me of my magic and was uniting us together. I didn't mean to kill him."

Sebastian held up his hands and twisted his wrists. "Explains these leaving."

Baxter felt like someone punched him in the gut. *That* was what was different about the three men. The matching tattoos around their wrists were gone. The tattoos that contained their weapons were still on them, but the ones on their wrists had disappeared.

Someone had shackled them.

For what reason?

"Guess it doesn't matter," Sebastian said as he squatted to rummage through the smoldering pile of Cavan's remains. "Cavan was a tosser. We wanted him dead."

"Care to explain what that means?" Baxter asked.

William stepped next to Sebastian. "It means that when she killed him, she released his reign over us. We're no longer forced to do his bidding, mate."

"Well good. He was a cocky slimeball," Zoe said.

"That he was," Lucas said. "Besides, we never wanted a hundred-year war with Baxter."

Baxter studied Lucas. "But why would he enslave you and force you to do those things?"

Lucas and William's eyes cut over to Zoe's necklace. "What other reason is there besides power?" Lucas asked. He dropped his gaze to Sebastian. "Speaking of power, did you find his stone pendant or anything?"

Baxter felt there was more to the story than Cavan wanting power, but these men didn't want to relive their experiences. Cavan forced a spell on his own Tails to do his bidding. A tyrant. Guilt simmered in him. If he knew they were under a spell that made them do the awful acts they did to him, things might have been different.

Sebastian picked something up from the pile and dusted black ashes away from the white statue and handed it to William. "This is the only thing here."

William looked at Zoe. "His death must have been too quick to say the spell, right?"

Zoe's brow furrowed. "What spell?"

"The reincarnation spell. The same one Melantha recited when she was dying."

Zoe shook her head. "It happened so fast. He never said a spell. Never had a chance, I guess. That damn ring just took over—"

"What ring?" William asked.

Zoe's eyes widened. "A ring that I got from a demon who said it would help protect me while in your waters. I didn't want to take it, but Baxter insisted, and I trust him."

Baxter pinched the bridge of his nose and sighed. He knew telling them about Lil was going to fracture any newfound relationship with the Atlantic-Tails. Lil liked to ruffle feathers and had made quite a reputation for herself.

Lucas cut his eyes over to Baxter. "Demon? As in Lil?"

Baxter dipped his chin, giving him a knowing affirmation.

Lucas ran his fingers through his hair and exhaled. "Shit."

Zoe drew nearer to Lucas. "Lil said it would protect me. I'm sorry. I never expected this."

Baxter placed his hand on her shoulder. "This is not your fault. Cavan brought it on himself."

"If his pendant wasn't broken up into five pieces, and is completely gone, then this means what, exactly?" Lucas asked.

They all looked at William, who trained his gaze on Baxter. "It means Lil finally collected the magic of a Purple-Tail. Mermaid and demon magic combined."

"Lil? A mermaid queen?" Sebastian cried an octave higher than his normal pitch.

"And we thought Cavan was terrible," William grumbled.

"You're her friend," Lucas said. "For some reason, you have a handle on her, which means *you're* going to have to figure this situation out for us. We don't need a demon to be a mermaid queen, Bennett. She could destroy our realm. It could be catastrophic."

Baxter knew they were right. Lil obtaining mermaid magic couldn't be a good thing. He knew she had an ulterior motive, but this was beyond anything he could have imagined, and he was worried about her long-term plans. "I will talk to her. She is a collector. She might not be interested in ruling, per se."

Zoe smacked Baxter on the arm. "I told you she was up to something. She used me to kill Cavan to get his magic."

"Indeed, but without the ring, Cavan would have…" Baxter cleared his throat, unable to truly say the words. "Yes, she used you. Us. But she also saved you. The ring helped when neither of us were capable."

"There are consequences to using magic like that," William said.

"And now we have a demon parading around with the magic of a mermaid queen," Lucas grumbled.

Zoe shook her head. "Unreal." She looked at the statue William held. "Can I have that? Or are you guys going to keep trying to stop me and disrupt *my* kingdom?"

A manic laugh escaped Sebastian. "Give it to her. We have bigger problems, now. Cavan is dead and your demon friend is now the queen of the Atlantic-Tails. Your kingdom is the least of our worries."

Lucas placed his hand on Sebastian's shoulder, trying to calm him.

"What's with the statue, anyway?" William asked as he handed it to her.

"According to the Hans Christian Anderson's story, it used to belong to the human that *The Little Mermaid* loved. Melantha hid the stones in places that meant something to her. Besides ancient myths of mermaids, *The Little Mermaid* was the first mainstreamed mermaid story that humans knew about, and I think the next stone—"

Baxter and the others waited for Zoe to finish. But all she did was stare down at the little statue with a bewildered look.

"Is something amiss? Zoe?"

Her voice hitched. "It moved." She held the statue up for Baxter and the others to see. "I swear his eyes just blinked. Look at it." Her violet-blue eyes bright and wondering.

"Blimey, it blinked!" William leaned closer to the statue.

"I saw it, too," Sebastian said.

"I knew I wasn't crazy." Zoe re-examined it.

Baxter looked from William to Sebastian to Zoe but didn't look at the statue again. He would never see what Tails could see. "Well, you have established that statues move. What is the meaning of it?"

"I've heard about statues moving, but I've never seen one myself," Lucas said. He faced William. "Have you?"

William nodded. "From what I know, they move only if they want something or want to give you something."

"It's moving because it wants to give Zoe the stone, right?" Sebastian suggested.

"Perhaps," Lucas said."

Zoe's mouth pinched. "But why would Melantha hide the stone in this obscure statue when the famous mermaid is right there?"

Baxter may have been annoyed that he couldn't see the magic of the statue moving like the surrounding Tails, but if he was honest with himself, that wasn't his role. He was the brains. He should probably stay in his lane. "The white statue is a gift." He nodded in the direction of *The Little Mermaid* statue. "To get the stone from her, you need to give her something in return. Something that is meaningful to her."

Zoe powered over to the water's edge, with each of the men hot on her heel. She climbed down over the rocky side and splashed into the water. She lifted the marble statue, as if she were handing it to the sorrowful mermaid. Nothing could be heard but the gentle sloshing of water and the humming from the electric light poles.

Baxter felt ridiculous staring at the statue, knowing he couldn't see what they did, but he waited patiently, for Zoe's sake. He could not say the same for the three men next to him. Sebastian danced around as William swayed from foot-to-foot. Lucas perched himself upon a rock, his knee hammering up and down.

Like sparks from a firecracker, spurts of gold and bronze lights fluttered about the statue. A ripple of air moved over her.

The bronze mermaid looked up.

Baxter's eyes widened. He stepped forward. He missed the small statue blink the first time.

But how can I see this? Is it because I'm a guardian?

Whatever the case, he would relish it and not question the magic.

The mermaid twisted around and faced Zoe. She reached out and took the white marble statue, which immediately dissolved into bronze, and clutched it to her chest. She stretched out her other arm and opened her palm.

Zoe plucked the stone fragment from her hand.

The statue grinned, then settled back into her original, cast form, as if nothing had happened.

"I love magic," Lucas whispered.

For the first time, Baxter found himself in agreement with him.

CHAPTER 36

ZOE

ZOE'S HANDS TREMBLED AS she climbed up the embankment. She had a hard time comprehending that a statue moving like that was a normal occurrence. And not only that, it gave her the next stone. Even though she knew nothing she did in the last few weeks was normal, she couldn't help but be in awe of the magical world she belonged to.

She ran the pad of her thumb over the irregularly shaped piece, unable to tear her eyes from the different shades of green and the way the tiny slivers of gold veins caught the light. She lifted her pendant away from her chest, held the new stone next to it, and watched it easily meld into place. The additional stone made her pendant resembled the colors inside of a kaleidoscope. She couldn't imagine how much more beautiful the pendant could be when she found the remaining two stones. She knew it would be exquisite, especially since her necklace was looking like the petals of a hibiscus flower.

The four men circled her. Silent but curious to see the newly formed stone like it was a priceless piece of art. Baxter brushed his lips against her ear. "Activate it," he whispered.

They were on the same page. Zoe let the pendant settle against her chest. She climbed down the embankment and splashed into the shallow water. Not caring about entering the water without permission, a warm surge of energy tingled within her as she transformed into a mermaid and the newly acquired magic came to life. She was curious what new things she could do and wanted to go play for a while, but she had to be patient. She kept reminding herself that solving the riddle and finding the next stone were more important.

The moment she stepped out of the water, the four men huddled around her again, which she was grateful for, since the night breeze was cool against her wet skin. She lifted the pendant for all of them to see, and, as before, a black script appeared. She felt the haunting song bubbling within her, rising to her lips, unable to stop reciting the enchantment aloud.

> *"Awaits Santarosae's Winfield Scott.*
> *Flotsam, Jetsam reveal.*
> *Master of surroundings with a thought."*

"Who is Winfield Scott?" William asked.

Zoe looked past the surrounding circle, her eyes focusing on the statue of *The Little Mermaid*. She had heard that name before. Like a broken record, she repeated the name in her head. She read the riddle again, unable to trigger a memory.

"Perhaps another statue?" Baxter suggested.

That didn't feel right. She shook her head, released the stone, and scooted past Baxter, her eyes never leaving the dark waters. It had to do with something with the water, that she was sure of. She stomped around. She found it so aggravating when something was right on the edge of her mind, but she couldn't grasp the information.

Behind her, Sebastian spoke up. "Better question: what is Santarosae?"

"Santarosae was an ancient landmass off the coast of California. After the ice sheets melted away, the ocean rose enough to cover most of it. The Channel Islands are remnants of the larger mass," Baxter said in his most professor-like tone.

Zoe gasped. The dots connected. She hadn't heard the name Winfield Scott before; she had *seen* the name.

She danced around. "The Winfield Scott is a sunken ship! It's near Anacapa, which is one of the Channel Islands. I saw it the first time I was using one of those See-seas. I saw the sunken ship icon near the island and was curious to what it was and learned of two sunken ships: The Del Rio and The Winfield Scott."

Baxter beamed. "We should get this pile of remains cleaned up and start our journey back to California. There is much to do."

"We'll take care of Cavan's ashes." Sebastian waved his hands over the blackened pile. Green flittering energy rained from his palms, lifting the bones and ash off the ground. "Give him the proper burial he deserves." He walked a few steps, just underneath a lamppost, flicked his hands over a trash bin, and let Cavan's remains drop inside. He faced them. Brushed his palms together. "There. That's done."

Zoe blinked. She could see the hate, and hurt, in the Atlantic-Tails' eyes. Wounds like that would never fully heal. Going from one horrible leader to Lil, was an absolute gamble. "Is there anything I can do to help your kingdom?" she asked.

"Besides getting Lil to forgo her grasp on our realm?" William asked.

Zoe raised a brow at Baxter. She felt he was to blame for Lil. Slightly, at least. She couldn't imagine what kind of mischief Lil could do as their new queen. She hoped she wouldn't be the oppressor Cavan had been. It could be a 'bird in the hand is worth two in the bush' scenario.

Will Lil behave even worse? After all, she is *a demon.*

A sickening thought plagued her mind. One that hadn't occurred to her before. She shifted on her feet, set her jaw, and looked Lucas dead in the eye. "Do you think, or even know, if Lil killed Melantha?"

"Zoe!" Baxter said, obviously alarmed.

She ignored him.

Lucas snorted. "Are you really still trying to solve her murder? I thought Pacific-Tails were tight-knit? How do you not know Neala is behind everything?"

Zoe threw her arms up in despair. "I knew it. Neala. We were right." She hated doubting herself.

Baxter apparently felt the same. "Dammit," he growled.

"Know where I can find her?" Zoe asked. "Aislinn said she probably retired to the land many decades ago."

Lucas, William, and Sebastian shared significant looks. A strange tension fell over Zoe. Something wasn't right.

"Aislinn—"

"Blimey, wait!" William held his hand up and stopped Sebastian from speaking. "You're about to tell her the vital piece of information she needs, and you're asking for nothing in return?"

Zoe scoffed. "Are you serious? I have nothing you want. Baxter already promised to intercept Lil. What more do you need?"

"A pardon, mate," William stated. "Forgive us of any wrong doings against you and your realm. We were under Cavan's orders, a spell we could not break. We don't wish you or your realm any ill-harm."

Zoe looked to Baxter for guidance. She gripped his arm and dragged him away from the other three. "I can't do that, can I? Should I?"

"We cannot blame them for being enslaved and forced to thwart me and my duties. Truth be told, if not for their encounters, I might have given up early in my quest. They kept me motivated and alert. But you are the queen, and therefore, can pardon them if you see fit."

Zoe felt strange having that kind of power. But Baxter was right. They had every right to ask to be taken care of; they were the victims. She marched back to the trio and held out her hand. "As the northeast Pacific mermaid queen, I forgive the Atlantic-Tails of their wrongdoing to me, Baxter, and to my kingdom. I'll even put a good word in with Lil about the three of you, in exchange for the truth about everything you know regarding Melantha's murder and to offer friendly peace with my kingdom."

One by one, the three place their hands above Zoe's.

"And shall it be," William whispered. White and silver magic shot out of his fingertips and danced around their hands, binding her word to them.

She pulled her hand away. She pushed her shoulders back. Baxter walked up next to her; his arm brushed against hers. "Tell us about Neala."

It was Lucas who responded. "She's your proxy."

Baxter sucked in a hissing breath. He scrubbed his face. "Shit!"

Zoe's brows furrowed.

What did she miss?

"Proxy?"

"Your second in command," stated Sebastian.

"The interim queen," added William.

Zoe shook her head. "No, Aislinn is my second in command, not Neala."

Sebastian cursed and ran his fingers through his hair. Lucas glanced at William. They both looked back at Zoe. In perfect sync they said, "Neala *is* Aislinn!"

Sebastian nodded. "They're one and the same."

An air of numbness cloaked her. The moment she had been accused of taking PEDs flashed into her mind. The betrayal of her teammates. The implosion of her entire life. The nasty and exhausting legal proceedings. Plans of running away from California to start anew.

Betrayal. The theme of her life.

She tried to overlook Baxter's trust in Lil, but she couldn't ignore the fact she felt tricked by him. Then—Aislinn guided her, welcomed her back to their world. She had been Melantha's right-hand woman.

She tried to swallow away the thumping rhythm in her throat.

Why did Aislinn do this?

"I cannot believe I missed that connection," Baxter said.

"Tails tend to change their names when they change realms," Lucas replied. "We've always known Aislinn as Neala. Melantha welcomed Neala to her kingdom from ours about a couple hundred years before she was murdered. She changed her name to Aislinn shortly after Melantha's death."

"She and Cavan must have planned it all along," Zoe gritted out. "Cavan traded Neala to my realm so she could murder Melantha and take the stones, so that her and Cavan could merge the realms since Melantha refused to do it. Right?"

William shrugged. "Perhaps. Or maybe Cavan was telling the truth and had nothing to do with her death, and it was all Neala. Either way, they used each other. And used Melantha."

"Melantha had time for the resurrection spell. Neala—Aislinn, did not grab the broken stones," added Baxter. "That put her in a mess because her magic was tied to it, which could be lost if the resurrected queen was not found. No wonder she tried to help as much as she could."

"Cavan then forced us to watch after you and try to steal the stones so Aislinn would lose her magic," William stated. "Since Neala blundered on retrieving the stones, he would get them himself and double-cross her."

"And Aislinn?" Zoe asked. "What's her end game? To let me come back to power just to murder me again and make sure she gets my necklace before I conjure the resurrection spell?"

There was a non-verbal agreement between them. That was exactly what Aislinn planned.

Zoe curled her hand into her fist. "That sneaky little bitch! She even warned me that 'everyone was not my friend.' No wonder Murdock didn't trust her! He must have had suspicions about her loyalty."

"She's a Pink-Tail," William said. "Your conversations with her were based on what she took from your mind. She's a master at manipulation. Neither of you should blame yourself."

But Zoe did blame herself. For whatever reason, she was a magnet for people who wanted to take advantage of her. To use her.

Am I that naïve?

She trusted too much—a fatal flaw.

A shudder rocked her. Eyes misted over. Her legs propelled her along the promenade, shooing her away from the situation.

Who else in my realm is deceiving me?

Sefarina or the others? Aislinn probably had her grip on them the same way Tanya had her grip on her traitor teammates at USC. The Atlantic-Tails—they wouldn't help her, especially since Lil now owned them. They'd probably end up enslaved again.

Who can I truly trust?

Baxter? Not this time. His loyalty to Lil cut her deep, and she wondered how she could ever forgive him for making her trust a demon.

Zoe stumbled at the thought of her entire world imploding a second time. Like a massive wave cresting, the full force of everything that happened in her life crushed her. She collapsed. And cried. Tears streamed down her cheeks. She desperately wanted to go home, but didn't know where she belonged.

Somewhere between life as a human and life as a Tail?

She felt hands on her shoulders, but she yanked away, unable to stop the screams and irrational blubbering coming out of her mouth. The overwhelming number of truths broke her. She was strong, but living through betrayals like this was beyond what she could handle.

She was done.

She squirmed away from Baxter's grip on her shoulders, scrambled to her feet and ran toward the water. She needed an escape.

From behind her, William shouted at Baxter, who was trying to catch her. "Let her go, mate. We'll keep tabs on her."

Ha. Let them try!

Zoe dove over the edge of the boardwalk and into the dark water. She didn't know where she was going and didn't care whose waters she entered illegally. Rage fueled within. She needed away from here. Away from Baxter. Away from all Tails.

She needed to swim.

To think.

To be alone.

CHAPTER 37
BAXTER

BAXTER WAS AT HIS breaking point. Zoe had been gone a *fucking* week. Seven wasteful days. Seven days of maddening worry. Seven days of wreaking havoc and taking his anger and energy out on whatever, and whoever, came near him.

But even worse, they were seven days closer to a certain death.

Thankfully, her return would be that day. But he was weary about reuniting with her. Mostly because he had mixed feelings.

How dare she take off for so long? How dare she risk our lives and that of her kingdom?

How dare I even blame her?

Lucas slapped Baxter on the shoulder as he opened the front door of Zoe's house. "I'm going to speak with Stig for a moment and give him our appreciation for teleporting Zoe back here. Relax, you have twelve days left. Zoe can take the time she needs."

"I understand." Baxter followed Lucas, but stopped at the doorway and leaned against the frame. He knew he needed to support Zoe, especially in her state of mind. But the worry of their time coming soon rattled his patience.

Lucas walked down the path to the taxi parked in front. He leaned his head in the passenger side, talking with a man who had long flowing blond hair.

William climbed out of the back door, then helped Zoe out. She clutched him, exhausted. Baxter sighed and ran his hands through his hair. He saw this exhaustion once before. Only it was Baxter she clutched onto. Shortly after being removed from her swim team, when the accusations hit the press, she stopped taking care of herself. Not eating. Not sleeping. When she'd been required to attend court, it took everything for her parents to get her out of the house, which included him helping her walk into the courthouse, the way William helped her now.

He stepped off the porch and onto the stone pathway. He would need to tread carefully with her. "Zoe—"

She sneered at him. "Don't wanna hear it."

"I understand, but—"

"No!" Her fists balled, ready to strike. "I can't deal with you right now. I'm so pissed at you. I don't even want you here."

Well, so much for treading carefully. He held his own temper back since she swam away from him, but after leaving him alone for a week, impatience and rage boiled within. He marched forward, jaw clenched and narrowed eyes. "I am just as furious with you as you are with me!"

"Woah, mate." William tugged Zoe away from Baxter.

Zoe glared over her shoulder as William tried to hold her back. She scoffed. "What the hell for? I did nothing wrong."

Baxter's hands trembled. He hated arguing like this, but like a volcano, he couldn't stop spewing. "For leaving me. We are a team!"

Lucas tore over to them, blocking Baxter's view of Zoe. "Turn around and walk away."

From behind Lucas, Zoe said, "Teammates don't screw each other over and lie about their relationship with a demon!"

Baxter tried to sidestep Lucas, who matched his movement. Lucas's eyes bore into Baxter's. "We talked about this."

"I did not lie," Baxter shouted over Lucas' shoulder to Zoe, who stomped off into her house. She raised her arm high, flipping him off.

"Bennett."

Baxter released his tensed shoulders, knowing his anger was with himself, not her. It came from the truth because he *had* lied. Well, hadn't told her the whole truth, but that was still deception. And to her, that was a lie. A lie that hurt her. His eyes pleaded with Lucas.

Lucas placed his arm over Baxter's shoulder, turning him away from the situation. "Let her get settled. I'll talk to her. William said she was reluctant to return but would listen to reason. That's a step in the right direction."

From his pocket, Lucas took out a set of car keys and handed them to Baxter. "Since it's way too early for a drink, take my rental, and go get some coffee. Grab some donuts too."

Needing to step away, Baxter nodded and followed his instructions. But when he returned, his mood had changed little.

Two more days passed. Two more days of her moping and ignoring Baxter's presence. Two more days of her being coddled by Lucas, William, and Sebastian.

Two more days of Baxter stuffing himself with coffee and donuts.

But this time, when he returned to her house and saw her lounging by the pool, staring into the crystal blue water, buried in her own head, he knew they couldn't wait any longer. They had ten days to restore her to power.

Ten.

Unbelievable to think that when his journey first began, he had over thirty-six thousand days to restore the mermaid queen.

And now, he was down to ten.

He sat at the kitchen table, his knee jack hammering up and down. He had to do something. They didn't have time for gentle pleasantries and therapeutic discussions to work out their issues. Enough was enough. He sprung from the kitchen chair and flung open the French doors.

"Demanding that she snap out of her funk may not end well, mate."

Baxter cut his eyes at William who stood at the kitchen island stirring his hot tea. His brow raised, challenging Baxter to prove him right.

Baxter knew telling someone suffering through depression to 'snap out of it' was the least helpful thing to do. Hell, he knew that even before all the science and research came out over the last several decades. His mother suffered through her own mental droughts. Back in the late 1800s, it had been taboo for women to speak of their inner demons which is why he, his father, and Sterling, indulged his mother with her interests in the supernatural; one of the few things that gave her peace.

The bottom line was that they had ten days left. They were cutting it too close for comfort, especially since they needed to find two more stones.

"Waiting around does nothing either. We are idle instead of actively trying to end this. We do not have the luxury to wait for her to work through her issues. Besides, I did not ask for your opinion."

William shrugged and took a sip of his tea. "Suit yourself. At least Lucas is there in case you two need a referee. Again."

Baxter shrugged him off but knew damn well William was right. He stood at the top of the winding staircase that led to Zoe's pool. He buried his hands in his hair, exhaled, and tried to focus on something positive.

He appreciated the change in his relationship with Lucas, William, and Sebastian. They had been vital in getting Zoe back home after she took off through their waters. Lucas had been the voice of reason that Baxter needed to lean on. It had been Lucas who flew back to California with Baxter and helped keep him calm while they waited for William and Sebastian to return with Zoe.

He thought about all the decades wasted on them being enemies because of Cavan and his damn spell. Baxter didn't dare wonder what things might be like if Lucas and his goons, nay, his crew, had been his ally. The thought of that was too much to bear. The countdown that could end their lives was at stake, and dwelling on what could have been was of no use. Focusing on positive thoughts alone wasn't going to help their predicament either.

Baxter bounded down the stairs and marched across the deck toward the two sunbathing beauties. Lucas eyed him, immediately sat up, and held up his hands to stop him from doing the stupid thing he came to do.

"Zoe." Baxter tapped the edge of her rattan lounger with his foot. "Enough is enough."

Zoe peeled off her dark sunglasses and tipped her head up and glared at him from beneath the brim of her sunhat. Her eyes were red and swollen from crying.

Lucas shot to his feet. "Perhaps—"

"No, Lucas. No 'perhaps.'" Baxter nudged Zoe's legs aside and sat on the rim of the lounger. "Time to listen up. I know you are hurting. So am I. Mistakes have been made. Please understand that I am all for you trying to work out your feelings. You can be angry at me all you want. You can keep shutting me out. I can handle that. I deserve that. But unfortunately, that *must* be put on hold. Our lives, and the lives of your kingdom, are in our hands. We have very little time left, and are too close to restoring you as queen, to quit. We need to keep moving forward instead of being at a standstill. Because if not, we die." Baxter took a breath. "We die, Zoe. And this time, there will be no resurrection."

Baxter rocked back. He tried to swallow the dryness in his mouth. He couldn't back down even if she flipped her lid.

She slipped her sunhat off, glanced at Lucas, then looked back to Baxter. "You're right," she said, her voice barely a whisper. "Too many people's lives and well-being depend on us. I've been in a selfish funk, I know. I understand we don't have time for that. You and I can work things out after we make sure we'll survive."

Baxter sighed. A tremendous weight lifted off his shoulders. "I can respect that."

"If I may," Lucas interjected, "it is obvious a trip to the Winfield Scott is needed, but we both agree that the presence of the Atlantic-Tails in her waters would cause a stir she's not ready to handle yet. She doesn't know who she can trust in her own kingdom, but I've taught her how to spot someone under a Pink-Tail's spell and how to better fight off an intrusion in her mind."

Baxter nodded, thankful for whatever Lucas and William did to help her move forward, for he wasn't fool enough to think his speech did that. "I may not want her searching the sunken steamer alone, but at least you were able to offer some tips."

Zoe swung her legs off the lounger. "Well, like you said, we have little time to waste. Let's head out to Anacapa. I'll eat something on the way."

Baxter raced his white speedboat along the north side of the Channel Islands and eyed the lighthouse at the peak of the island formation.

It was all alone, just like Zoe would be the moment she entered the water. Baxter didn't like the idea and really wanted Lucas and his crew to join her, but he understood how that would add another level of disruption to an already splintering kingdom.

How many others are in on the conspiracy with Cavan and Aislinn?

For Zoe's sake, he wished for none, but that was longshot.

Baxter took a glance at the coordinates, circled around something below, and slowed the boat to a stop. "Welcome to the SS Winfield Scott. Are you ready?"

Zoe stood up from the cushioned seat near the bow and kicked off the yellow flip-flops that matched her yellow bikini top. "We've been over this. Every time I get another stone, I can feel my new powers pumping through me. Magically, I'm strong."

"Mentally, though?"

She unbuttoned her jean shorts, revealing the bottom of her swimsuit. "I'll be fine. Trust me, I can do this."

"I do. But allow me to worry. I feel helpless."

Zoe nodded. "I know you do. We each have a part to play. You got me here, and now it's my turn. Aislinn doesn't know I know about her betrayal. I'll use that to my advantage for as long as I can."

Baxter leaned against the side of the boat. He eyed her, for the first time in a while, and saw a confidence he hadn't seen before. Between the gentle sway of the ocean rocking the boat, and accepting that he believed in her, he felt a calming peace blanket him. He gave her a gracious nod. "Meet me at the usual spot near the entrance to Pacific Park on the Santa Monica Pier?"

Zoe pulled her hair back into a high ponytail. "I can do that. Be there around closing time."

"But if you aren't there, I won't shy away from getting help from Lucas and William."

Zoe pulled at her hair, tightening it. "If that makes you feel better. Just do me a favor, don't involve Lil."

Baxter strummed his fingers across his biceps.

Here we go again.

The lie and the lie by omission. If he didn't directly involve Lil, he couldn't help what Lucas and the others would do, right? "Of course." He held his hand out to help her step onto the small deck near the back of the boat. "I shall see you tonight."

Instead of saying goodbye, she squeezed his hand before diving into the water and leaving him alone. He paused. Wanted her to resurface. But after the two near disasters when her eyes enchanted him, he knew she would do no such thing. Besides, he didn't have time to waste. He had a job to do. A plan to make.

And a conversation to be had with a friend.

CHAPTER 38

ZOE

ZOE SWAM AWAY FAST, ignoring the pull for her to turn back and lure Baxter into the sea with her ancient, cursed eyes. The desire irritated her, like an itch she couldn't quite reach. Only when she heard the rumble and felt the vibration of his boat pulling away did her appetite for stealing his life finally disappear.

She threaded her way through some kelp beds and reached the seafloor to see the remaining splinters of the wooden hull of the old steamer. The vibrant purple hydrocoral blooming around a moss-grown mound just beyond the wreckage caught her attention. She inspected it closer and found one of the paddle wheels of the old ship under the mound. Zoe fixated on the glimmering coral and felt compelled to touch it. The coarse edges of the coral grazed across her fingertips and an elaborate archway peppered with an array of seashells and colored corals appeared.

She sloshed backward. She peeked through the arch into a world beyond the mortal one. Across the seafloor, a stone pathway lined with iridescent pebbles and glass shards led to a castle-like structure, far off in the distance. Spires and arched bridges rose from a rocky seabed; a dolphin pulling a carriage riddled with seashells sped past. Slack-jawed, Zoe floated through the archway and followed the curving pathway into her kingdom, wishing Baxter could see her world. She wanted to share this life with him, and felt bad for shutting him out the way she had, but it was out of necessity to protect her own heart. But then again, he was doing his job by protecting her.

Maybe I don't need to know, or control, everything.

She needed to trust him the way he trusted her.

She hung her head. Relationships were complicated, especially when magic was involved.

She passed giant clam-shell cottages and brightly colored structures built from coral and decorated with sea glass and other trinkets. Other paths forked off the main trail, one of which led to an underwater waterfall, and as much as she wanted to spend more time examining all the wonders her kingdom had to offer, she didn't have the luxury of doing so. After threading her way through the mermaid village at the base of the rocky hill, she sped up to reach the grand entrance of the majestic, medieval-looking castle.

Her castle.

The path of pebbles stopped at a sister archway. It had the same décor as the entrance, but this one had long, flowing kelp hanging from the arch like vines. She swam through it and stopped at the drawbridge connecting one part of the rocky terrain to another. Instead of a moat, like in the mortal world, a dark trench surrounded. Spires of sharp coral towers rose high above the stone walls adorned with glistening white pearls in the crenels, the cutout spaces between the merlons that humans used for observation and firing weapons. The pastel colors of purple and teal made the castle feel inviting despite its imposing structure.

She swam across the drawbridge and through the barbican into a court-yard. Bright sea grass and clusters of giant plumose anemones that looked like fluffy cotton pillows covered the ground. Soft coral curved upward like a staircase, leading to a balcony of stone and glass.

A giggle escaped Zoe. Not in her wildest dreams could she imagine as serene a setting. She rocketed up the faux stairs and zoomed in and out of several rooms filled with trinkets and treasures; items salvaged from shipwrecks and old plane wrecks, lost Spanish doubloons, statues of mythology, and ancient books. Everything was preserved and not rotted by water.

She ran her fingers over a fractured statue of a Greek God and examined a string of pearls hanging from its arm. She rifled through an old chest and found a collection of antique pistols. She darted to an old commercial airplane seat and played with some gears and cogs that came from its fuselage.

An octopus uncoiled from beneath the chair and startled Zoe. "Yes, yes, I know I should be looking for something else. But where is it?" she said like he was her pet. It reached out one of its tentacles, wrapped it around Zoe's hand, and pulled her out of the room and down a corridor with overhanging luminescent Sea Pens; they resembled a ceiling of antique quill pens. They reached the end, and two tall, rigid sea fans blocked them from going any further.

"Thank you," she said. The octopus released her hand and scuttled away.

With a soft touch, she pushed on the sea fans, swinging them open like saloon doors. Red and yellow beds of anemones lined the floor and dark green algae peppered the walls like patterned wallpaper. A vanity made from driftwood and a broken mirror sat on one side of the room. Displays of jewelry strewn over the desk and draped on the coral walls; behind the vanity hung oodles of hair accessories and fashionable attire.

Opposite the vanity, swaying in the water, tattered fabrics and tapestries canopied over a bed of bubble coral. The all-too-familiar tingling of magic pulsated around her and called for her attention.

Zoe zoomed around the room; the pulse grew stronger the closer she got to the vanity. Frantically, she combed through the adornments and gobs of jewelry that she never saw Aislinn wearing. In fact, the only jewelry Aislinn wore was the preserved pink water lily pendant. More of a plain Jane, Zoe, too, had jewelry she only wore once or twice a year. She moved a silver and ruby tiara to the side and stopped. A gold bracelet with a heart-shaped locket encrusted in tiny diamonds stared back at her.

Where have I seen this before?

Her eyes narrowed on the dangling charm as she searched her memories.

Did I have this as a child? No...

A shadowy figure of a man crept into her head like a thick fog. She focused on his features as they slowly appeared.

Baxter?

She shook her head. The man resembled him but was slightly taller and had dark, blazing blue eyes instead of green. An image of the man leaned over her, whispered something in her ear as his hands slipped the bracelet over her wrist and peppered kisses along her neck.

Zoe slumped against the vanity as the memory faded. She blinked. The bracelet hadn't been hers, not exactly. Melantha's. Her memories entwined with her current life, something she didn't consider. She always kept Melantha separate, like a different person. They were one and the same, and the closer she came to having a complete necklace, the more the two merged.

And if that is the case, how will that affect my relationship with Baxter? Especially knowing the passion Melantha had for Sterling?

One thing at a time. Follow the list of priorities.

She reached for the bracelet and laced her fingers through it. A piercing shockwave blasted from it. She flew across the room. The fabric from the bed's canopy tangled around her.

She moved the hair from her eyes and looked at her hand. No scorch marks, but it felt like there should be.

Why would my bracelet refuse me?

She untangled the fabric from her tail and sat on the bubbly coral bed, resting her head in her hand.

She needed help.

And had to trust people and not fear everyone would betray her.

Except Aislinn. Her betrayal was inevitable.

She gripped her necklace, channeling all her positive belief into her hand. "I need you, my friends." The tiny bubbles that escaped her mouth swirled above her and raised high above; her call for help disappeared into her kingdom.

For a moment, she sat there, staring across the room at the vanity, unsure how to proceed if help didn't arrive. Perhaps she could use magic and lift the necklace to take it back to shore. Or maybe she could—aquamarine lights flickered in the middle of the room. She sat up. They grew larger until they became one light. Sefarina appeared with Callista and Farah by her side.

Callista squealed and wrapped Zoe in a hug. Ewalt and Kasumi entered the room soon after, followed by Hita and two Tails Zoe never met; a White-Tail mermaid and a Black-Tail merman.

The ball of light disappeared. Her friends smiled at her. Not one of them was anything but a *true* friend, and she knew that to her very core. Each of the Tails in front of her would use their magic and their lives for the betterment of the kingdom.

Zoe's heart swelled with love for her friends—her team. She finally found home, somewhere she could be herself, be accepted. Her journey over the last few weeks had been worth the fast-paced and harrowing situations. They were a family and welcomed Zoe with open arms.

Zoe floated off the bed. "Thank you for coming. I wasn't sure if my call for help would work or not. Where's Murdock?"

"Patrolling the entrance," said the Black-Tail merman. He was long and lean with tanned skin, straight black hair twisted into a bun, and piercings along his earlobes and his nose. "I'm Bembe, by the way. I've been landside with Omnira." He motioned to the mermaid next to him whose tail shined like a pearl and was a stark contrast to her dark skin. She had rows of thin braids that led into a larger mohawk braid.

"We apologize for not meeting you earlier, cher," Omnira said, "but Sefarina filled us in."

Zoe smiled at them both. "It's a pleasure."

Callista paddled past Zoe and reclined on the canopy bed, munching on a clam roll. "So, what's going on?" she asked her cheeks full like a squirrel.

"I need help with a protection spell that is guarding the fourth stone. Well, at least I think that's what it is." Zoe swam next to the vanity and pointed at the gold bracelet. "I tried to take it, and a powerful blast shot me across the room."

"Orange-Tails can move objects with their minds," Farah said. "Have you tried doing that? You're the only one of us here who could."

"She can't." Kasumi pointed to the stone hanging from Zoe's neck. "She doesn't have any orange colors in the pendant, which means she can't do that magic yet."

"We should know what type of spell enchants it first," Ewalt chimed in.

Farah drifted over to the vanity and waved her hand over the bracelet. She touched her tattoo and pulled a small, tattered book from it. She flipped open the pages and scanned until she found an answer. "It's a Lover's Protection spell. It can only be cast on a gift received from someone they are in love with. Only the person to whom the gift was for can touch the object and break the spell. It's mostly used to protect jewelry and highly rare or expensive gifts." Farah snapped the book closed and made it disappear back into her tattoo.

"But that bracelet was a gift to Melantha. I remember Sterling giving it to her," Zoe said.

"Bembe, can you trace the timeline of this bracelet?" Sefarina asked. "Perhaps Melantha gave it away?"

"Objects are difficult, but I might be able to use Zoe as a conduit."

"What does that mean?" Zoe asked.

Bembe floated over to the vanity. "Black-Tails can manipulate time, view past events, foresee the future, and deal with prophecies. That kind of stuff. By using Melantha's memories that are locked away in your mind, I might be able to piece together the history of that bracelet."

Zoe nodded. "Of course, let's do it."

Bembe waved her over, and Zoe glided next to him. He placed his palm on her forehead and reached a finger out to the bracelet. A black ray of light bolted from the tip, connecting the bracelet to him and Zoe.

The bracelet's past events flashed in her mind's eye like a movie. She saw the final touches of diamonds added to it during its making. Displayed on a bed of black velvet.

Her former self lying in a puddle of blood as a bloodied, white-gloved hand slipped the bracelet off her. A brown and orange stone appeared inside the heart locket. A hand waved over it, sealing it with the magic of the lover's protection spell.

Bembe pulled away his hand, cutting off their connection and snapping Zoe out of her trance. Bembe collapsed. Ewalt caught him.

"He needs to get to land. That nearly depleted his magic." Farah glided over to him and looped her arm through his. "I'll take him."

"Be careful," Sefarina said as Farah pulled Bembe through the water.

"What did you see?" Callista asked.

"Melantha's killer took the bracelet off her dying body. The stone appeared, just like I thought, and someone placed the spell upon it." The 'someone' was Aislinn, a.k.a., Neala, which meant she used the spell to protect the stone. The news about Aislinn's betrayal needed to be shared with her fellow Tails and Zoe dreaded doing it.

"That makes no sense," Omnira said. "These are Aislinn's chambers and have been since Melantha's death. How could the killer have placed the bracelet here?"

"Because Aislinn murdered Melantha," a voice snarled from behind them.

Zoe cast her eyes around to see who stole her moment.

Murdock hovered at the entrance; his sword stabbed into the sandy ground as a spark of poison ignited in his eyes. Zoe quirked her lips. He suspected Aislinn all along. If anyone stole her moment, she was glad he did. He deserved to say it more than her.

"She looted your lifeless body and "gifted" it to herself, which is why she could place it under that particular spell. Tell me I'm wrong," Murdock said.

Kasumi clutched her chest. "Murdock, how could you say such things about Aislinn?" The rest of the Tails mumbled in agreement.

Zoe gave him a clipped nod. "Aislinn poisoned their thoughts, but how did you escape her mind tricks? The animosity between the two of you is apparent. She said it was because both of you descendant from The Morrigan."

"Our powers don't work as well on each other and I never trusted her," Murdock growled. "I could slow her toxic manipulations enough to have suspicions, but I couldn't fully piece them together. I was always missing some fragments of the larger truth. Even Callista had a sense of foreboding about Aislinn."

The water rippled as Callista swam next to Zoe. "I never fully trusted her but didn't understand why."

Sefarina wiped her hands across her face. "Aislinn used her magic to manipulate us? Why? What do you know we don't?"

Zoe inhaled and leaned against the edge of the vanity. "It all goes back to Neala."

"Neala? She disappeared long ago. Probably landside," Ewalt said.

Zoe shook her head. "No, she didn't. Aislinn concocted that story and planted it in your minds, so you all didn't remember that Neala *is* her."

There was a collective befuddlement between the Tails. Before they could bombard her with questions, Zoe went right into the tale of how Aislinn and Cavan schemed together then double crossed one another to have ownership over Melantha's realm. She explained how Aislinn murdered Melantha, and used her magic to deceive the Pacific-Tails to be sure Melantha's reincarnation didn't succeed, so she could truly rule it.

"Why were the Atlantic-Tails such a menace to Baxter for protecting the stones then?" Kasumi asked.

"Because Cavan placed the Atlantic-Tails under a spell to force them to retrieve the stones so *he* could control them, which would stop Aislinn from gaining control of the realm. Lucas said that for a long while Cavan thought if he stopped Baxter from finding the queen then the stones would never be found. The realm would become a free-for-all after Melantha's one-hundred-year spell, but he was wrong. Somehow Aislinn knew if the reincarnated queen failed, the realm would cede to the interim queen or king. Once Cavan learned of this, he wanted the Atlantic-Tails to ensure Baxter and I succeeded, but under his watch. Once I came to power, he could force me to join his realm."

Murdock gripped the hilt of his sea-sword, stabbing it further into the seafloor. "I knew Aislinn was up to no good. Should've done more and trusted my gut feelings. But she always evaded me. She was simply more powerful."

Zoe floated over to Murdock and placed her hand on his shoulder. "You did what you could. If you hadn't had suspicions, things might have been worse. We know the truth and we can stop her." She shifted her eyes around the room. "But I need that bracelet."

"The bracelet is yours, cher. Melantha is alive within you. By default, the bracelet should return to your ownership. You must believe in your status," Omnira explained.

Callista grabbed Zoe's hand. "Have your beliefs, yes, but it wouldn't hurt to channel whatever energy we can give to Zoe to boost her magic to help break the spell." She eyed the other Tails. "Right?"

Murdock gripped Zoe's other hand. One by one, her friends connected, forming a circle in the middle of the room. Zoe could feel their energy warming her hands, like an electrical current arching between them.

She closed her eyes, focusing on the moment when Sterling gave her the bracelet. Before she knew it, her lips moved. A chant. A spell. It came to her on the wave of magic pulsating through her.

"I am Melantha. I am Zoe.

Together, we are one.

What once was mine answers and owes me."

Louder and louder, she chanted and believed in her words. Her hands were hot, burning from the energy surging through their connection. She felt the water stir on the outside of their circle. The harp in the room's corner strummed as the water plucked at the strings. Pieces of coral and shells clanked against one another as small trinkets and fabric floated around them. A deep-rooted roar reverberated off the trembling castle walls.

When Zoe couldn't take the force of all their magical energies anymore, a force exploded from her chest, breaking her grip with Callista and Murdock.

She moved her hair from her face. Her friends were sprawled across the room as well, but nobody was injured. Zoe pushed off the rubble of odds and ends covering her tail and paddled to the remains of the vanity. She dug through the pile of doodads and trinkets until she found the gold bracelet. Without hesitation, or worry it would deny her, she reached for it.

She dug her thumbnail between the two sides of the heart locket and pried it open. An orange stone with flecks of different shades of brown rested inside. She grinned, proud of herself, and proud of the teamwork she had been a part of. She pinched the stone between her thumb and pointer finger, lifting it out of the locket, and connected it to her pendant.

She slipped the bracelet over her wrist. "Thank you all. But I have to return to land, activate the riddle, and finish this."

Sefarina nodded. "We all need to go landside to recover from that bit of magic. Let's travel together."

"Baxter's meeting... me..." Zoe reached up and massaged the base of her neck as something tickled the back of her head. No, tickled her mind. She lost her train of thought; a feeling of dread overtook her.

Jealously.

Loathing.

A wave of dizziness hit her, but she whirled around, scanned the room. From her fellow Tails, blank eyes stared back at her, stuck in a daze.

Except Murdock's. His were closed as he pinched the bridge of his nose. He flayed around, looking for something to steady himself with as he fought off the trance.

Something moved just beyond him.

Zoe swam forward even though the room felt as if had been knocked askew. She narrowed her eyes, focused on closing off her mind and taking back control, even if only for a moment, just as Lucas taught her.

Her heart skipped a beat as she realized Aislinn, with her manic eyes and aura of furious rage, blocked the entrance to the room.

CHAPTER 39

ZOE

AISLINN SNAKED INTO THE room, pushing a piece of splintered driftwood aside with the tip of her finger. She eyed the bracelet around Zoe's wrist. Her lip curled in a snarl. "I see you found what you were looking for."

"I did. They know your truth."

The corner of Aislinn's lip curled upward.

"Let them go," Zoe growled. "This is between us, Aislinn. Or should I say, Neala?"

"Whatever. They're useless anyway." She snapped her long fingers, releasing the Tails from her mind control.

From behind Zoe, the Tails cried out in relief, but she didn't dare turn her back on the dangerous creature who stood in front of her.

Aislinn flicked her fluke to float closer to Zoe, but Murdock swept into her path; a muscular barricade.

Tiny bubbles sputtered from Aislinn's lips. "You have always been in my way." She lunged for him, and as she did so, her face transformed into a hideous version of herself. Venomous barbs, much like the spikes of a lionfish, sprouted from her neck. Long razor-sharp teeth grew over her lips.

Her blonde-and-pink hair faded to icy white, and her eyes bulged from her sockets, glowing yellow. Currents of white lightning torpedoed from her bony, elongated fingers, pitching Murdock backwards to avoid being hit. The water sloshed around as the other Tails scuttled away, but Zoe didn't flinch.

Zoe shad seen this act before.

She twirled a tendril of her hair around her finger. "You know," she said, almost bored, "Cavan's wicked side was much more intimidating than yours. The spikes around your neck are a good touch, though."

Aislinn growled, shook her head, and reverted to her normal, stunning self. "You think you are so righteous." From her hair, she removed a star-fish barrette and fiddled with its spiny thorns. "You don't even know half the story. You, and Melantha, are always so quick to assume and judge, without having all the facts. Melantha was poison." She held the starfish chest-height, aiming its thorns at Zoe. "Just like these spines." Aislinn flicked her wrist. The venomous spikes broke off the starfish and rushed at Zoe like a hail of gunfire.

Zoe shielded herself and barrel-rolled away as her tail took the brunt of the thorns stabbing into her like needles.

Get out of here!

A whirlpool of aqua-colored lights engulfed and suffocated her. Using the power of translocating, without the help of Sefarina, Zoe drifted outside the castle, right next to the archway.

She glanced at the stone pendant and saw the aquamarine-colored vein glowing, but dying out.

Red and green lights erupted out of the crevices of the castle. The water rippled with energy. She wanted to get back to her friends and help them fight off Aislinn, but the unexpected teleporting drained her. She felt incredibly useless. She looked around trying to find a way to help.

A loud blast ruptured the castle.

Zoe's head jerked up. A tall spire crumbled as Aislinn swam away from it. Zoe coiled herself in some tall seagrass near the arch, ready to pounce on her as soon as she came close enough.

As Aislinn passed, Zoe sprang out of the seagrass, colliding with her. They tumbled through the water and tangled in greenery. Zoe felt the familiar tickle of Aislinn invading her mind, but concentrated on the magic flowing in her stone. In her hands, green orbs bubbled to life. Like pitching a baseball, she heaved them through the water, hitting Aislinn square in the face and breaking her mind-control. Depleted, they both drifted down to the seabed. Zoe tried to move, but her limbs felt heavy from the venomous spines. Aislinn, though, was stronger, and overcame the Green-Tails magic much faster than Zoe thought.

The tips of Aislinn's fingers glowed red.

Zoe wouldn't be able to get away this time.

A fiery ball collected in Aislinn's palm.

Flaming spears flew through the space between the two mermaids.

Murdock swam toward Zoe with Ewalt following close behind.

Aislinn darted off.

Murdock and Ewalt flanked Zoe, slipped their arms beneath hers, and lifted her up. "Don't do any more magic, Zoe. You could transform back to human and drown," Ewalt warned. "Fight her again another day."

Even though she was relieved, Zoe couldn't rest. She needed to activate her other stone in order to tap into even more magic and fight off Aislinn. The other Tails swam toward them. Kasumi reached Zoe first and pushed

Murdock aside, taking his place to help hold Zoe up. Murdock led their small group through the village and to the archway.

As they crossed beneath it, a cold fluttering trickled over her back, but it wasn't just the signal of her being back in the moral world.

It was the sight of Aislinn sitting on the remains of an old airplane wreckage, waiting for them.

Murdock, Ewalt, and Kasumi came to an abrupt stop.

Zoe eyed Aislinn's arms stretched out at her sides, palms faced upward with black flittering lights spewing out of them.

"She wouldn't dare," Ewalt whispered.

"Dare, what?" Zoe asked.

"Don't do it, Aislinn." Murdock raised his coral sword, ready to strike.

Aislinn's hair fluttered behind her, angelic-like. Her face said something else. Her wild eyes fixed on Zoe's, and the ends of her lips stretched in a smile that held no happiness. She flipped her palms downward, thrusting the black magic into the wreckage she sat on.

"No!" Murdock shouted.

Piles of bones floated up from the seafloor, twisted around one another, and formed an army of skeleton warriors.

"The dead are rising!" Ewalt bellowed.

"Get out of here! Head to land!" Murdock roared.

Zoe couldn't tear her eyes from the reverse decomposition. Rotting flesh and tattered clothes appeared on some of the zombie-like creatures, giving them an even more menacing appearance. They marched toward them; jaws dislocated. A thunderous roar bellowed through the ocean, shaking the ground, and stirring the water. They jumped away from the wreckage, like missiles, and spread out like shotgun shells.

"Leave us alone!" Callista zoomed forward with a tiny fireball in her hands.

"No!" Murdock followed her.

Zoe darted through the water after the siblings. One zombie skeleton gripped Callista's wrist and tossed her through the water into a nearby boulder. She slumped over and floated down to the seafloor. Zoe didn't know if she was dead or alive.

Before she could check, another zombie skeleton appeared in front of Zoe, snatching her tail, and biting through her scales. Zoe screamed as its razor-sharp teeth sank into her flesh. She slammed her fist into its bones and jerked her tail back and forth, trying to wiggle free, but it refused to let go.

She screamed for help. Ewalt charged toward her, blasted the creature apart with an orb of green magic, and released her from its clutches. She reached forward and placed pressure on her open wound, trying to staunch the bleeding.

Ewalt wrapped Zoe's arm around his shoulder and pulled her along. "Get to shore!"

Zoe winced as she tried to propel forward; the intense pain slowed her movements.

"Here, let me." Hita swam next to her and formed a blue light over her bleeding tail. "I might have enough magic to close it up, but I'm not sure if I'll beat the sharks."

"I will keep us hidden as you work," Kasumi said, her voice small and tired. "But my magic will not last long. We will need to swim together to stay beneath my umbrella of invisibility."

Omnira wrapped her arms around Zoe's torso, freeing Ewalt to fight off the dead army with Murdock.

"Callista," Zoe croaked.

"I've got her," Sefarina said from behind Zoe.

Kasumi cast her silver magic above the small huddle of mermaids. Twinkling lights shimmered over them, cocooning them in a safe environment. They worked together to swim in sync with Hita, who worked on healing Zoe. Beyond, a horrific scene unfolded for Murdock and Ewalt, which she could do nothing to help.

On top of the army of the dead, two great white sharks appeared. Their mouths widened as they swam through floating red blood, exposing rows of serrated teeth. One nearly bumped into them beneath their invisible shield.

But the shimmering encasement wasn't enough. It flickered and disappeared. Zoe could feel her blood seeping out of the jagged opening and running down her body, catching the attention of the sharks. But worse, she could see Hita fading from using the last bit of her magic.

Murdock looked at Ewalt. "Take care of my sister. I will hold the sharks off and distract the dead."

Murdock dodged a zombie-skeleton reaching for his neck. He batted his sword against the bones, crumbling the zombie skeleton into a pile.

"Murdock, no," Zoe shrieked.

Omnira held her tight against her chest. "It's his choice, cher."

Murdock looked behind him, slicing the edge of his sword across his chest. Blood pooled around him as two sharks lunged at him. He zigzagged through the giant plumes of kelp, drawing the sharks away as he fought off the skeleton creatures. Tears filled Zoe's eyes, and anger swelled in her heart, fearing her most apt warrior would not make it.

Chapter 40

Zoe

Hita finished healing Zoe's tail just enough, so she could swim again. Breaking through the surface never felt so freeing, especially when she felt the sea air against her face and saw the red-and-orange hues in the dusky sky.

"There's a small beach just beyond that reef," Ewalt said. "I'm going back for Murdock."

"No," Kasumi cried out. "He sacrificed himself to keep us all safe, and we barely escaped with our lives."

Ewalt shook his head. "Aislinn didn't invade his mind like she did ours. He has more strength than we think. I don't have time to argue with you. I'm going after him."

"I'm coming, too." Sefarina shifted Callista's body into Omnira's arms. "If he's still alive, I have just enough energy to transport him to land where I can get him help."

Before anyone else could protest, Sefarina and Ewalt disappeared beneath the water. Tears streamed down Kasumi's cheeks, but she paddled toward a ragged reef that jetted out of the island. Zoe trailed behind, helping an exhausted Hita. Behind her, Omnira held onto Callista, dragging her through the water.

They rounded the corner of the reef and entered a cove. The massive cliffs of the island rose around them, protecting them. They used the waves to help float them onto shore where they transformed into their human forms. Kasumi and Omnira lifted Callista out of the shallow water and carried her to dry sand.

Zoe fell onto her knees next to her. A knot formed on Callista's temple. The red and white candy-cane stripes in her tail faded. "She's dying. What do we do? We're too far away from the mainland to get help."

She felt a hand on her shoulder. "You can do it," Hita whispered in her ear.

Zoe squeezed her eyes shut and reached her hands out, hovering them over Callista's head. The image of the starfish she healed came to her mind. Then Baxter. She did it twice before, but this?

This is so much more.

"Focus on your intent to heal her. Channel your energy," Hita coached, as if she knew Zoe raged in battle with her nerves.

Zoe took a breath and concentrated. She pictured the blue light traveling through her and into her warming hands. Behind her closed eyes, she saw the flickering of a light. She thrust her gaze upon a bright blue energy field that fluttered from her palms and into Callista's head.

After a moment, Callista twitched. Kasumi and Omnira anchored her, holding her shoulders down.

"Keep going, even though it looks like you're hurting her," Kasumi commanded.

"It's working, cher," Omnira said. "The color in her tail's coming back."

Zoe pressed on, but it felt like she was sprinting up a steep hill wearing a backpack full of rocks. The blue field of energy flickered once. Then again. No longer able to heal any longer, she collapsed into Hita's arms.

Callista gasped for air. Her eyes opened, brimmed with tears. Her arms flailed, clutching at Kasumi and Omnira. The red and white in her tail shimmered.

"Where's my brother?" Callista asked once she finally calmed down and transformed into her human form.

Callista's question was like an arrow to Zoe's heart.

How can I deliver such news to someone I just saved?

"One of those creepy zombie-skeleton creatures attacked me," Zoe said. Her mouth ran dry. "Sharks came. Murdock…" Zoe looked at Hita, who nodded at her, encouraging her to get on with it. "Murdock stayed behind so we could escape. Ewalt got us to safety, then he and Sefarina went back to help him."

Callista's face paled. She curled her knees up to her chest and buried her face in the crook of her arm. Her body shuddered as she wept; she came to the same conclusion as Zoe.

For a while, the four mermaids sat on the beach, watching the night sky come alive. Would Ewalt, Sefarina, and Murdock arrive? Aislinn probably would come instead. But once it became apparent neither of those events would happen, Hita curled up and napped, trying to regain her energy. Omnira paced up and down the shore, tossing small rocks and shells into the water. Zoe monitored Callista, who finally ran out of tears and stared into the distance.

Zoe wrapped her arms around her legs, letting her long hair drape over her bare skin. She wrapped a strand around her finger, not sure what to do next, stranded on a desolate and rocky island. She knew they needed to get to the mainland, but that begged the question; did her friends even have the energy to swim? And then not only that, she'd said she would meet Baxter at the Santa Monica Pier, which was even farther away. If she didn't show up, Baxter would get Lil involved, and who knew what kind of mess that would lead to? Zoe rubbed her face and tried to form a plan that didn't involve abandonment or a sitting duck scenario.

The middle of her chest warmed. Excited, she fumbled for the stone pendant and lifted it up, ready for the tiny inscription. From the corner of her eye, she saw Callista watching her. Zoe focused on the words of the next riddle scratch into the stone, but she could sense the others surrounding her, also watching. The need to chant the riddle in the same haunting melody as before, bubbled up from within.

"Love and greed curse a dead man walking.
Betrayal frees your woes,
Mind, body, time will be unblocking."

Her eyes unlocked from the stone. With bated breath, everyone waited for her to speak. She looked at Omnira. "I need to get to the mainland, but I don't want to leave any of you here."

Omnira smiled at Zoe. "With the fourth stone activating its riddle, it means you're only one step away from restoring your powers, and ours." She looked at Hita and Callista. "There's been a surge in our magic, I can feel it, can't you?"

"Yup," Callista said. "I do feel stronger."

"Refreshed, even," Kasumi said.

Zoe scrambled to her feet. "I have no idea what the riddle means, but Baxter and I will figure it out. I have to meet him at the Santa Monica Pier."

"Santa Monica? But Port Hueneme Beach is much closer from here," Hita said. "We may have some of our energy back, but we don't want to use it all, in case you need us to help fight against Aislinn. Besides, it's where Farah and Bembe would have gone and where Sefarina and Ewalt will go. We have Tails who live in Oxnard and have a safe house. We can drive you to Santa Monica from there."

"I appreciate that. But it will be much quicker if I swim directly to the pier. You three go there and save your energy. Sefarina knows where Baxter and I live. She can come find us tomorrow."

Callista grabbed Zoe's hand and squeezed. Her eyes were puffy from crying, but there was a determined look in them. "Be careful. Stick close to the coast in case you need a quick escape."

Omnira ushered Zoe toward the water. "Follow me to the closest part of the mainland, cher. From there, you can make your way to Santa Monica while we go where we need to."

Zoe and the three mermaids dove into the waves and made their way out of the cove. Within minutes, they arrived at their parting location. After a quick group hug, Zoe sped off. It was easy enough to swim in the shallow areas, cruising just beneath the waves that surfers would have been riding if it was daylight. Unfortunately, she knew it was a longer route than cutting through the deeper water, but it gave her time to mull over the riddle.

If Aislinn had the fourth stone, perhaps she had the last one as well. But who was the dead man walking? Did it have something to do with the zombie-skeletons Aislinn had conjured? And what about the part that talked about betrayal freeing her woes?

Before Zoe could think, she heard a choir of strange noises. Her mind raced, expecting Aislinn to attack her, but then, the noises became clear, like barking. Zoe surfaced. The tip of a rocky bluff jutted into the sea, and a herd of sea lions sat barking in the night.

Zoe chuckled at the lazy mammals as she paddled by. As she passed a cluster of boulders, she heard a bark much closer. Harrowing. Zoe raced around to the front of the rock to find a smaller-size sea lion on its back, a web of green plastic netting and other rubbish suffocating it.

She shrieked, horrified at the sight. The pup clawed at the plastic as Zoe slid her fingers beneath it to stop it from slicing through the skin of his neck. If she could break him free, she could heal him with her magic. An orange smoke-like energy billowed from her fingertips, wrapping around the plastic.

Orange—her newest magic.

Whatever it was, the energy felt like an extension of her fingers, giving her a good grip on the plastic. She yanked at it, stretched it to its breaking point, freeing the pup.

The orange smoke disappeared. The sea lion fell into her chest, and she cradled him.

He no longer whimpered. Or moved.

Tears streamed down her cheeks as she conjured the blue magic in her hands to heal him. But the energy just sat in her hands, it didn't go into him like it had done to Callista.

She had been too late.

She peeled away the rest of the netting and put her nose against his, letting his whiskers tickle her cheeks. "I'm so sorry," she cried.

She cried not only for him, an innocent being looking for food, but she cried for her realm. If Melantha had been alive, her Tails would have their magic to do their jobs better and keep the oceans safe from tragedies. They could help regulate the amount of pollution in the water and educate the humans. She cried for her own life and Baxter's, too. The full understanding that they could be dead within days raged within her. If they failed...

Zoe sucked in a ragged breath. She lifted her chin and stroked the top of the sea lion's head. "My fury won't bring you back, little one." She pressed her finger on the tip of his nose then opened her arms and released him into the water. "But I promise to use it and save our kingdom."

CHAPTER 41
BAXTER

BAXTER LEANED AGAINST THE railing near the fishing platform on the Santa Monica Pier. He tapped his foot along with the music from the band playing at the pier's small amusement park. The pier seemed busier than usual, but perhaps the band drew in the crowd, or people wanted to enjoy the last few summer nights before school started again. Whatever the case, Baxter felt uneasy.

All day he worried about Zoe, but that wasn't the issue. There was something different with *this* kind of uneasiness. There was something off in the atmosphere. He was being watched.

But by who?

Aislinn wouldn't waste her time on him. Lucas and the others were still at Zoe's house when he left to go to the pier. Lil had been with them too. They'd been in the pool, relaxing after Baxter made Lil and Lucas spend much of the afternoon purchasing a boat and docking it at the same marina as his own.

The question remained.

Who would watch me?

Paranoia. That's who.

Baxter rolled his shoulders and popped his neck. He really needed to loosen up the tension. The sounds of people screaming on the roller coaster, and the laughter of small groups of people, echoed around him. Not even the sweet smells of waffle cones fluttering past his nose or the sound of the gentle waves breaking could relax Baxter's heightened state. He lifted his chin and let the cool breeze blow across his warm cheeks.

"Get it together."

His chest tightened as he sucked in the crisp air.

He emptied his lungs. Long. Meditative.

Nothing helped.

A frigid chill crawled up his spine like the hand of death itself, tickled the hairs at the base of his neck, and rooted Baxter to the ground. A raspy, familiar voice of a man whispered near his ear.

"Bennett. Irving. Baxter."

Baxter held his breath. He pirouetted—scanned the blurred faces of the crowd on the pier. As if in a slow-moving trance, he teetered forward, nudged someone out of his path, so he could get a better view of the man leaning against the rail on the opposite side of the pier.

Baxter didn't see the crowd anymore. He had tunnel vision. Gutted and shocked, he stared at a man clad in flip-flops, board shorts, and a tank top. This man smirked at him, and his bright blue eyes gleamed in the lamppost's light.

A man who was certainly not missing. Nor dead.

Sterling!

Baxter took a heavy step. Then another. The maddening sounds of chatter and life around him rushed back into his ears as Sterling walked away from him, down the pier. Desperate to reach him, Baxter cut through the crowd and vendors without losing sight of his uncle.

As he passed the entrance to Pacific Park, three teenage boys came running out, pummeling Baxter, and knocking him to the ground. He scrambled to his feet. The boys profusely apologized. He mumbled he was fine and pushed past them. He raced along the pier toward the main entrance, but his uncle vanished. He stopped near the end of the trail marker for Route 66 and weighed his options. To the right, a parking lot behind the buildings; to the left, stairs leading to the beach. His thumping heart reverberated in his ears, but he thought he heard someone call his name.

It came from the left.

He sprinted down the wide concrete staircase and followed the wooden plank path across the sand toward the water. There were pockets of people along the beach; some took photos of the neon lights from the amusement park reflecting in the water while others strolled through the sand.

Only one person walked alone beneath the pier behind the thick concrete columns.

As he lunged forward, a clammy hand gripped his wrist and reeled him around.

"What are you doing? I've been calling your name and chasing you from the top of the stairs," Zoe said. "How could you not hear me shouting for you when you ran past me?"

Baxter stepped back, confused at seeing a woman standing in front of him with jean shorts and a yellow bikini top. He shook his head. Seeing Sterling alive completely wrecked him.

"What's wrong?" Zoe asked.

He snatched her hand and pulled her along. They traipsed through the sand, ran below the dark pier, and weaved through the pilings until they found Sterling standing at the edge of the water on the opposite side of the pier.

Baxter stopped and let go of Zoe's hand. "Explain how and why you are alive?"

Sterling cocked his head to speak over his shoulder. The lights from the pier overhead were just enough to see his face. "The same way you are."

"What does that mean?" Baxter asked.

"Who are you?" Zoe pushed past Baxter.

Sterling eyes fell on Zoe. He longed for her. "It's been a while, my dearest."

"Holy shit." Zoe took a tentative step back nearly falling into Baxter. "Sterling?"

"Melantha—"

"Zoe," Baxter bellowed. "Her name is Zoe now."

His uncle, who was once engaged to Melantha, and thought to be dead, was alive and well one hundred years later. Not only that, he stood before his nephew and the woman he once loved, who was now the woman Baxter loved.

This strange triangle made Baxter's head spin.

Zoe raked her hands through her hair, clearly unnerved, like Baxter. "This isn't happening."

"Oh, but it is." Sterling lifted a gold chain from around his neck. Dangling from it was a stone pendant. Shades of blood red to pink colored the stone. Black veins crept across it like overgrown vines.

Baxter narrowed his eyes. "Unbelievable."

"I intend to get that back," Zoe growled.

Sterling snickered. "I look forward to it."

"You were a part of this," Baxter said, more to himself than his uncle. "Why?"

Zoe hissed, clutched her forehead, and dropped to her knees. Baxter placed his hand on her back. "What happened?" He looked up at Sterling. "What did you do?"

"It's not him," Zoe said through clenched teeth. "Aislinn's nearby." She massaged her temples and took a breath. "I'm fine." She used Baxter's arm to help her stand. She glared at Sterling, and Baxter could feel anger radiating from her. He dared not interrupt.

"I've been getting some of Melantha's memories back, and it's all so clear." She glanced at Baxter. "Aislinn, was the mastermind, as we suspected, with the help of Cavan, of course." She pointed her finger at Sterling and stalked toward him. "But you? You're the one with my blood on your hands."

Sterling set his shoulders and drilled his gaze into her.

Baxter looked from Zoe to Sterling. "What does that mean?"

"I can recall that awful moment like it happened only minutes ago. Just before my final breath, I saw the killer. You. My fiancé, with his bloodied, white-gloved hand, stealing my last stone before it could get to safety."

Baxter furrowed his brows and stared at Sterling. His beloved uncle, who he mourned, was a murderer and the reason Baxter suffered through a hundred years of stress and agony.

How could my best friend do that?

And worse, the 'why' of it all. Baxter had no reasons why Sterling would team up with Aislinn and betray those who loved him.

"That is truth, yes," Sterling stated.

It had been decades since Baxter felt such anger seethe within him. He balled his fists and paced away from Sterling, unable to look at him anymore. The monster inside him wanted out. He needed to release his rage. Whenever his emotions were uncontrollable, or he reached the pit of despair, he heard the echo of his mother's voice. Soothing and calm. He needed her.

Now.

"Be careful of judgement, Habibi."

Baxter scrubbed his face. "Why?" he asked his uncle and mother the same question.

"You are more like him than you realize," his mother said, her voice trailed off as she left him. His eyes narrowed on Sterling, who seemed unaffected by his outburst.

Zoe held her hand to her chest, her face full of concern. "Baxter?" she asked.

Then Baxter saw it. Somehow, through the red lens of hate, he saw the truth about his uncle. His mother had been right.

She's always right.

Baxter sighed. His judgement *was* irrational. Sterling wasn't who he made himself out to be. He murdered Melantha, yes. But not of his own free will.

Baxter pointed at his uncle. At his wrists. "Tattoos."

Zoe's brow lifted. She followed Baxter's gaze. Sterling had the same tattoos around his wrists as Lucas and the other Atlantic-Tails had before Zoe freed them from Cavan's curse.

"Ah, don't be so hard on Sterling," a woman purred as she sauntered out of the dark from behind a piling. "As you can see, it wasn't *entirely* his choice to kill you."

Baxter straightened. He never came face-to-face with Aislinn. Secretly, he never wanted to, but he knew it was her even before Zoe cursed under her breath.

The painted image of Aislinn in the mural in Baxter's childhood bedroom didn't do her justice. She had a specialty in manipulating minds, but he knew it wasn't the only asset she used to control others.

Aislinn stalked over to Sterling, who looked at her like a love-sick puppy. Baxter believed it was because of a curse she placed on him. He'd hate to think his beloved uncle had true feelings for the psychopath.

"Do you still love Melantha?" Baxter asked, wondering if this Sterling had any sort of resemblance to the man he once knew.

Sterling crossed his arms over his chest, and wrinkled his nose, like he smelled something putrid. He scoffed. "Not at all."

Ah, there it was. Baxter felt a wave of relief as he watched his uncle strum his fingers against his biceps as he denied it. The lie and the strum, an old habit Baxter learned from Sterling when he was only a teenager.

He did still love Melantha, well, at least the Sterling trapped inside Aislinn's curse did.

Aislinn laced her arm around Sterling's neck and pulled him in for a kiss. Zoe trembled.

Does the Melantha part of her still love Sterling too?

"This ends now. That stone belongs to me!" Zoe lunged at Aislinn, and an emerald glow of energy sprouted across her hands and crept up her arms.

Aislinn pushed Sterling to the side as Baxter rushed Zoe, bear hugging her and spinning her away from her two targets.

"Lemme at them!" Zoe struggled against Baxter's arms, trying to slip out of his clutches.

"Now's not the time," Baxter demanded. "Too many people around."

"He's right, Zoe," Aislinn shouted from behind them. "Why do you think Sterling and I showed ourselves here?"

Zoe growled.

Baxter squeezed her tighter against his chest. "Ignore her."

Zoe sagged against him. Her breath hitched. "I'm fine." she pushed her hair from her face. The green glow around her limbs faded. "I hear you."

Baxter nodded and released his grip on her. When they turned around, Sterling leaned against a piling and looked down his nose at them. Aislinn stood next to him in a fighter's stance.

"You won't ever get that stone pendant," Aislinn warned.

"Maybe not tonight, but I'm coming after it."

Aislinn lifted her chin and shrugged a shoulder. "Sure thing. With what, ten days left before I'm rid of you for good?" She tossed a strand of hair behind her shoulder.

Baxter always prided himself on being a gentleman, but even he wanted to knock her self-assured ass senseless.

Zoe rolled her eyes, paced in a circle, and stopped. "Fine, then. Since you're so confident we'll be dead soon, at least give me the truth. Why did you place Sterling under a spell? Why did you have him kill Melantha? What's your end game?"

"Truth is, you were a dictator. You never listened to my advice, never listened to my ideas. You never made me feel good enough—"

"So, you resorted to murder because you were disgruntled?" Zoe blinked over to Sterling. "And you? You must have had some reason for betraying Melantha. There is no way in hell you're innocent."

Sterling pushed himself away from the piling. "You do not know how it was to feel so useless around a mermaid queen," Sterling snarled. "Compared to you, I was so ordinary. How could I compete with magic and the underwater world? It was impossible."

"And when you wouldn't turn him into a Tail, I stepped in and gave him the love he deserved. But Melantha was such a controlling tyrant, she imposed a law restricting us from luring Landwalkers to their deaths while at sea, or turning them unless they were in dire need. It was her infuriating relationship with that damn oceanographer that made Melantha soft. She made the ruling right after she met him and spared his life."

Zoe eyed Baxter. Aislinn's story seemed legit. Neala couldn't stand Dr. Clock, and not being able to, well, do what mermaids have always done, was a sound reason for mutiny. But also, perhaps, Melantha wasn't as great as either he or Zoe assumed.

That still didn't account for Melantha's murder or the upheaval of ancient mermaid territory.

Aislinn took a few steps across the sand, dragging her feet through the rising tide. "I was elated when Sterling told me your plans for wanting to give up the magical world to be a mere human. I was ready to forgive you for everything, because as your second, that role should have been passed down to me." She tilted her head toward Zoe. "But that's not what you did, did you? Always wanting to ruin things for me. You had to enact an ancient ritual of naming your predecessor instead of letting the role pass down naturally. When Sterling told me about your plan, and who you wanted to take over, I knew I had to stop you... her. And I did. My only downfall was that I didn't account for the reincarnation spell."

"Why not kill me yourself? Didn't have the guts to pull that off, did you?"

Baxter placed his hand on Zoe's shoulder and looked at Aislinn. "No, I am certain that is not why. Am I correct in assuming there is a mermaid law barring Tails from murdering their own kind?"

Aislinn's doe eyes immediately focused on Baxter, looking at him for the first time. "In Melantha's realm? Of course. Your uncle's anger when she refused to turn him was the key. I needed to control him enough that he would stab that dagger into her."

"Without his anger, your spell probably wouldn't have been strong enough to force him to do such an unthinkable thing, yes?"

Aislinn nodded.

If there was any silver lining to this mess, it was that Aislinn used magic on Sterling to get him to murder Melantha. That meant she didn't taint his soul as badly as Baxter assumed. His uncle could still be redeemed if they could break the spell on him.

"Let me also assume once you had Melantha's realm, you planned to unite with Cavan and kill him as well, so you could rule the two most powerful kingdoms."

The corner of Aislinn's rosy lips curled. She took a step closer to him, sizing him up. "You grew up to be quite brilliant, little Bennett. You were always so inquisitive and smarter than you should have been. I remember watching you and Sterling together. You wanted to be just like him."

A flash of pink light crossed her eyes and Baxter felt a strange tingle travel from his scalp to the base of his neck. His body relaxed—like floating on his back in a pool.

"You understand Sterling's motives, don't you, Bennett? You've been contemplating the same things about your relationship with Zoe as he did with Melantha. What's your place next to a mermaid queen? Beyond your role as a guardian, what worth do you have to her while you're on land and she's in the water? You know she'll never turn you."

Something shoved Baxter. He fell to the side; his body slammed into the coarse sand, waking him from his relaxed state of mind. Water sloshed over his face, and he could hear another voice echoing from afar.

"Stay out of his mind!" Zoe shielded Baxter from Aislinn's view.

Baxter rubbed his forehead, feeling like he smacked his head on a rock. "Zoe," he croaked.

Zoe kicked up sand as she squatted next to him. "She got into your thoughts. You okay?"

Baxter nodded and held out his hand for Zoe to help him up. More than anything, he was embarrassed. Not because Aislinn went into his mind, but because she called him out on his issues, which had been exactly like Sterling's.

And look how that ended up. With a little help from Aislinn, could I betray Zoe the way my uncle betrayed Melantha?

Zoe spat a few strands of hair from her mouth. "So, you had Sterling murder Melantha because she wouldn't turn him into a *fucking* fish, and because she had the smarts to know you should never rule anything? Sounds to me this had nothing to do with Melantha's laws, but selfish greed from both of you!"

Aislinn stepped forward and straightened her shoulders. "Stop belittling the truth to make yourself feel better. You have no idea the problems Melantha caused. She was ancient and stuck in her ways, never wanting to progress into modern times or do things differently, no matter how many realms begged her to."

"Valuing human life seems pretty progressive to me." Zoe clutched Baxter's hand. "Let's go."

She tugged at him to follow, but he had to have one more look at Sterling. The turmoil of his conflicting feelings about his uncle stirred within. He hated him for his role in Melantha's demise, but he was still his uncle. He could save him. His uncle could atone.

Right?

Baxter tilted his head down, and he watched his feet shuffle through the sand as they walked away.

"Don't forget, you have ten days—well, its past midnight, so nine days," Aislinn called from behind. "Enjoy the rest of your life."

Zoe squeezed Baxter's hand, digging her nails into him, and used her other hand to flip Aislinn the bird.

Zoe could always make Baxter crack a smile, even in the direst of circumstances.

When they reached the pavement of the parking lot, Zoe dropped his hand and stopped walking. His mouth went dry. His worries surmounted. One, she would address the similarity of Baxter and Sterling. Two, his chance of redeeming their personal relationship wouldn't happen between their row, her distrust of him and Lil, and Sterling's return. And three, Aislinn could be in Zoe's head, manipulating her desire to get the stone away from Sterling.

"Well, at least the case of, 'Who Murdered the Northeast Pacific Ocean Mermaid Queen?,' is solved," Zoe said. "Gotta admit it, though, Aislinn had a good plan and almost pulled it off. Which means we should assume she'll have a good plan for keeping us away from Sterling and the last stone. Good thing we have the one thing she doesn't have."

Baxter's eyes narrowed. "What might that be?"

Zoe lifted herself on the tips of her toes and wrapped her arms around his neck, pulling him close. "Love. So, we had a little tiff. It happens in good relationships, and we grow from it. We've already talked about how important you are to me and my world, so stop imagining that I think you are exactly like Sterling, 'cause you're not."

Baxter felt the heat rush to his cheeks.

She knew him well.

"And whatever Melantha did, or didn't do, is in the past. We either win together, or we die fighting together. I'm sorry for thinking you would ever make me feel like I couldn't trust you. That's my issue, and I'm going to work on it, okay?"

Baxter sighed; his shoulders relaxed. He should have known not to worry. "I'm with you. All in," he whispered.

"Good. We need a plan, or a few plans. But we're going to need Lil."

Baxter raised a brow at her. "You asked me not to involve her."

"Oh, I know. But I've noticed something about you lately. Something I should have picked up on sooner, but didn't realize until Sterling did it just moments ago. Do you know that when you want to avoid a topic, or flat-out lie, you strum your fingers? You did that earlier, just before agreeing to not involve Lil. And Sterling did it when he said he didn't love Melantha."

Baxter's jaw fell slack.

She caught on to his and Sterling's bad habit. Grinning, she winked at him. "Don't worry. Sterling and Melantha are in the past. It's Zoe and Baxter now."

He liked the sound of that.

"And I know you lied to pacify me because you wanted to help in any way you knew how. Besides, there was no way you spent your day all alone, trying to avoid Lil and the Atlantic-Tails. So, tell me: Are they ready to help us win this war?"

Baxter lifted a brow. "Two steps ahead of you."

"Figures," she stated.

She knew him so very well.

He leaned in and kissed her in the streams of moonlight, enjoying their last quiet moment together before they rained hell on Aislinn.

CHAPTER 42

BAXTER

THEIR SWEET, QUIET MOMENT became heated. Primal. He knew if he died in nine days he'd have a shit-eating grin on his face when it happened. She pulled him along, and he followed her like a dog on a leash. His heart hammered against his chest—he knew what came next. When they reached the SUV, she stood on her tip toes and snaked her arms around his neck. She deepened their kiss and he pushed her up against the passenger door. He was unrelenting, wanting every part of her against his body.

She hesitated. "I'm sorry. I'm sorry for taking off for a few days and acting like a petulant child. I'm—"

"No, I'm sorry. The pressure of all of this." Baxter took a breath. Then another. "I am to blame, not you."

He rested his forehead against hers. They shared breaths. She exhaled, he inhaled. The smell of her strawberry ChapStick wafted across his nose. She threaded her fingers through his wild hair. Her touch ached with need.

"And with," he paused, "Sterling back in the mix..."

Will my uncle be a problem?

She pressed up against *his* body. Not Sterling's.

Of course, the obsessive ego that took up residence within him needed to know for sure. He needed to hear her say it. He grazed his lips over her cheek then whispered into her ear. "He could be problematic—"

"I don't give a shit about Sterling," she stated. "I care about you. Us."

That was it. She unlocked the ravenous beast within him, and he gave a low moan. He grabbed hold of her long hair, tipping her head up, tasting her soft lips once again. He hitched her up on his hips, his hands slid up her smooth thighs, his fingertips pushed beneath the seam of her jean shorts. He pressed into her. She wrapped her legs around him, arching into his body.

She reached between them, tearing at the opening of his trousers. He yanked his tank top over his head, flinging it somewhere behind him. He pulled at the nylon ties of her bikini. She unwrapped her legs, shimming out of her shorts. She gripped his hips. He thrusted. They rocked together.

Against the side of his SUV was not what he imagined or planned. In the raw moment, the setting didn't matter. But still, it was improper to behave like adolescents. He was a homeowner, for goodness' sake. They should tousle in his sheets, not out in the wild like animals.

He pulled away from her. Her lips were red. Swollen. "What's wrong?"

"Not here. Not like this."

She nodded, lowering her legs from his waist. He pulled his trousers back over his hips. She pressed the cups of her swimsuit against her with one hand and grabbed her shorts from the ground. He found his tank top and slipped it back on. They got into the SUV without another word.

The drive back to his house was quiet, save for the mechanics of the vehicle. A pause, to gather their own thoughts. He glanced over at her. She fiddled with the buttons on her jean shorts but kept her eyes forward. He definitely ruined the moment, again.

He pulled the SUV into the garage. She hopped out and entered the house without a look back. He sighed and banged his fists on the steering wheel.

Why did I do that?

She wanted him as much as he wanted her, but had to be a damn gentleman and break up the moment. He dragged himself out of the SUV and walked through the threshold, knowing she'd already be upstairs in her room, angry with him.

As he entered the dark house, she grabbed him, pushed him against the sub-zero refrigerator. He dropped the car keys. Her hands buried in his hair; fumbling with urgency.

He moved them into the living room, onto the sofa. She fell into his lap, straddling him. Pushing into him. In the privacy of his own home, there would be nothing to hold him back. He raked his fingers across her back, ripping the bikini top off her body. He nibbled at her shoulder, then trailed down to her breasts. She groaned.

He lifted her; his fingers gripped her bottom. They stalked up the stairs, their hands, and lips never far from one another. She wrenched his tank top off and scratched her nails down his back, eliciting a groan from him. She fell to the bed on her stomach. His body covered hers. He peppered her neck with kisses and trailed down her spine. His hand wrapped around and under her hips, his fingers plunged into her warmth. She arched back into him as he slid into her.

Oh, immensely better than against the doorframe of his 4Runner.

Days later, Baxter's eyes fluttered open to the summer sun beaming in from the bedroom window. He grinned. Not able to get enough, he rolled over, wanting to wrap himself around Zoe's body and wake her from her slumber.

But she wasn't there.

He sat up. The bathroom was empty.

The doorbell chimed. Muffled chatter. The front door slammed.

Baxter groaned and ran his fingers through his hair. The countless hours exploring one another in his bed, around the house, in and out of the pool, and even once, up against his 4Runner, which was parked safely in the garage, was over. His hands, fingertips, lips, and tongue had claimed every inch of Zoe's curves. He marked her as his. Unaware of time, as it had been nonexistent for them.

Until it wasn't.

Reality was always such a thorn in his side.

Baxter rolled out of the empty bed. He showered, dressed, and padded down the hallway. He stopped at the base of the stairs, surprised to see the amount of people gathered around the island and kitchen table, munching on sandwiches and chips.

Zoe had talked about inviting her friends over for a meeting someday soon, knowing it would take time to bring them all together.

When did she have time to do this? Probably after the many times you exhausted yourself in your overindulgence of her body.

Baxter continued and entered the kitchen. Lil, Lucas, William, and Sebastian mingled with Farah, Kasumi and Sefarina, as if the politics of their two separate realms, and a demon amongst them, hadn't been an issue. Baxter shrugged. Perhaps it wasn't anymore. Things certainly changed between Baxter and the Atlantic-Tails; it wouldn't be much different for them.

Zoe closed the refrigerator and caught his eye. "Baxter! Come have some lunch."

Baxter weaved through some people he didn't know and made his way to Zoe. He wanted to lean in and kiss her and was slightly miffed that there were people around preventing him from his desires. "What is going on?"

She handed him a glass tumbler with iced tea. He tipped some sweetener into it and stirred it with a straw.

Zoe looked at the two women sitting on the barstools at the island. "This is Omnira and Hita."

"Ladies," Baxter greeted them politely. They each smiled at him.

Zoe pointed to a tall, slender man, leaning against the cabinets. "That's Bembe." The man nodded at Baxter and took a bite of a roast beef sub. "He's talking to Ewalt and Murdock." The other two men were large and very well built, except one of them had bandages around both his arms. "Murdock's the one who saved us from the sharks," Zoe said in a lower voice. "He should be dead. His willpower is unimaginable. His sister Callista is over by the French doors, talking with twins, Sedna and Zale. After nearly losing her brother, Callista won't leave Murdock's side. And the twins go where she goes because they are comfortable with her—it's their first time on land." The three teens looked over at Baxter. Callista gave him a big smile and waved.

Baxter dipped his chin at them, glad everyone in her realm was safe. "I'm glad you could arrange the meeting." He sipped the iced tea. Refreshing and coo, just what he needed.

Zoe put her sandwich on a paper plate and tapped her fingertips together, knocking off the crumbs. "Well," she finished swallowing, "I called Farah at her house in Oxnard a few days ago. I asked her to gather any of our Tails who still had a bit of magic in them and to make arrangements to come here. Turns out, it's only the pure-tails who have magic, but all the Tails are living on land, waiting for me to get that last stone and restore our magic."

"Have you told them about Aislinn and Sterling?"

Zoe nodded. "Yep. They're all caught up."

Baxter took another, longer sip of the cold drink. Zoe talked fast, a sign she was anxious, which he could understand. He looked around at the faces before him. They all depended on her, probably none more so than him. He would have to do whatever he could to ease that burden on her. And leading an audience was something he was good at. He placed his glass tumbler down and cleared his throat, stepping into his professor-mode.

"Good afternoon, everyone." Eyes roved over him as voices hushed. "Thank you for coming. I am going to cut to the chase here, as we have little time. We need a plan, or ideas, on how to find Sterling and get the stone away from him, all while battling Aislinn, who will do whatever she can to stop Zoe."

"Well, if we're low on magic, that means Aislinn is as well," Sefarina stated. "She probably isn't in the water because of it. Especially if she is with Sterling."

Hita nodded. "She literally can be anywhere in the world."

"Okay, so we don't have time to play a game of 'Where in the World is Aislinn?' So, is there any way we can track her? Follow her magical trail or something?" Zoe asked. "I thought we could sense one another."

Farah nodded her head. "Normally, yes. But none of us have that kind of power anymore. It's like going nose-blind after a scent. After a while, you don't smell it anymore, except faint hints every once in a while. That's how it is for us with sensing each other right now. And the Atlantic-Tails can't help with that because they don't belong to our realm."

"Hmm." Zoe nibbled her lower lip.

Baxter could see frustration setting into the people in front of him. Except one. Ewalt. Baxter knew the look of someone who wanted to speak up but was apprehensive to do so. He saw it on students' faces a million times. "Ewalt?" Baxter said. He assumed Ewalt wasn't usually the one who had ideas. He was the muscle, but that should never discredit his intelligence. "What are you thinking Ewalt? No idea is bad."

Ewalt stiffened his back. "The riddle on the fourth stone. Zoe said she didn't need it because you quickly found out Sterling had the last one, but have you analyzed it? Maybe it has a clue? Or will help spark an idea."

Baxter looked at Zoe, who glanced up at him with the same dumbfound expression he felt he displayed. She quickly lifted the necklace off her chest. "Come on, appear, dammit," she said as she ran the pad of her thumb across the brown-and-orange section of the pendant. She shook her head and looked up. "It isn't working. It said something about betrayal—"

"I remember it perfectly." Callista jumped off the countertop. "Love and greed curse a dead man walking. Betrayal frees your woes. Mind, body, time will be unblocking."

"Clearly, it refers to my uncle in the first part."

"And the last part probably references the magic you will gain once you get it," Farah said.

"But what does the middle mean?" Ewalt asked. "Whose betrayal does it refer? Aislinn's? Zoe's?"

Baxter cut his eyes to Zoe. They held each other's gaze for a mere moment. Zoe's eyes widened as she concluded the same answer as he did. "Sterling," they said in unison.

"If Sterling betrays Aislinn, the problem of getting the stone and saving our realm, will be over." Zoe danced on her toes. "We just have to get Sterling to betray her. But how? Of course, we have to find him first. And how do we get him to betray her when he's been cursed to love her?"

Baxter lifted his glass to his lips, his head spinning with thoughts. He caught a glimpse of Lucas from across the room. Another man who suffered a curse. "Lucas?"

Lucas shifted his attention to Baxter.

"When you and the others were under Cavan's curse, did you ever feel like there was a possibility of breaking it by sheer will? As if the real you were inside, trying to claw its way out?"

Lucas lifted his brow then looked at William and Sebastian. "We were quite aware we were under a curse."

"There were times, yes, that we despised doing what Cavan demanded of us, but we could do nothing about it, mate," William added.

Lucas shrugged his shoulders. "I don't think any of our desires to fight against the curse were strong enough to overcome it."

Sebastian leaned forward in the dining chair and ran his fingers through his blond locks. "Hell, we couldn't even lie to him about anything. That's how powerful the curse was."

Baxter's stomach fluttered. "Sterling lied when I asked him if he loved Melantha. He lied because Aislinn was right there."

There was an indistinct murmur of whispering. The three Atlantic-Tails shot each other confused looks. Lil stared at Baxter over her steepled fingers and lifted her chin to the top of her fingertips so she could speak. "Stop questioning your theory, Bennett. You're boring me while I wait for you to catch up to the answer I've already figured out."

The whispers stopped as everyone looked from Lil to Baxter.

"Sterling has the power to break the curse. We have to use his love for Melantha to do it," Baxter said. "But—"

"But?" Zoe echoed.

Baxter eyed Lil. "But we need Lil to help."

The corner of Lil's lip lifted. "There you go. Took you long enough." She leaned back in the dining chair. "It would be my pleasure to help, you don't even need to ask."

"Explain," Murdock demanded.

Baxter could feel Zoe staring at him, waiting for the same explanation. He faced her. "Lil can possess Sterling to weaken and confuse him. Zoe will need to coax Sterling to fight against the curse and give her the stone by reminding him of his love for Melantha."

Zoe rolled her eyes. "Are you kidding me? A possession and using his feelings like that?"

"It's the only way, Zoe, dear," Lil sang out. "It'll be fun working with you."

Zoe scoffed. "Fine. Well, at least we have the 'how' of getting the stone away from him. Now we need to find him."

"I have an idea on how to do that," Bembe said. "I'm not sure it will work, but you said the two of you walked away from Aislinn and Sterling, leaving them alone on the beach. What if I used your memories to see if you heard them saying anything behind your backs?"

Before anyone could respond, William stood and scuffed the dining chair across the wooden floor. "The sand. I'm the only Orange-Tail here, which means I can use objects to see the history of it, the way Black-Tails can use memories to view history. Between the both of us, we might be able to piece something together."

By the late afternoon, every person from the meeting followed Zoe and Baxter to the Santa Monica Pier. They circled around the area where Aislinn and Sterling ambushed them. Beachgoers and tourists flocked the area and made it risky to do magic, but they had no other choice. Kasumi blanketed them in an invisibility shield; Murdock, Callista, and the twins stood outside the screen and acted as a deterrent to keep people away from the area.

Bembe and William went to work. William sank to his knees and buried his hands in the sand as an orange light glowed below the grains. Bembe placed his palm on Zoe's forehead. A black wisp of light circled around her head.

Baxter wished he could see what they saw. Zoe twitched under Bembe's spell. His eyes rolled to the back of his head. The whites fluttered beneath his lids. He fell back onto the sand.

Zoe opened her eyes. "The moment we walked away from them, I could hear Aislinn say, 'It's time for you to go back into hiding.' I guess I didn't process it at the time because I was fuming."

Sefarina and Farah helped Bembe stand on his shaky legs. "Sterling responded to that," he panted. "Asked her what another couple of weeks were? That he's been hiding for a hundred years. Zoe was too far away to hear what Aislinn said, but they were arguing."

Baxter felt a pang of sadness for his uncle.

"You did great." Zoe helped Bembe knock the sand from his pants.

"Hey, mates, come over here and let me show you the rest of that conversation," William shouted from over his shoulder.

Baxter and Zoe scrambled over to William and stood behind him. In the sand in front of him, just above his buried hands and about two feet in height, were wispy orange images of Aislinn and Sterling, much like the ones Dr. Clock produced to show his memories of Melantha.

In the image, Aislinn clenched her hands and stood next to Sterling. "Stop your complaining. It's not like you have ever had to rough it. I could have put you somewhere up north where the winters last most of the year and the bitter cold and loneliness would have driven you insane." Her vision planted on him as she stalked toward him. "But no, I've asked you to live in perfect weather, in a mansion where you could be waited on hand and foot. You've traveled around the world with me and gotten whatever you desire. All I have asked is that you keep away from your nephew until the time was right. So, what if you have to stay there a few more days?"

Sterling's shoulders sagged. "You're right. I'm grateful for that, Aislinn. I guess actually seeing Bennett, seeing... her... I lost my mind for a moment. My apologies."

Aislinn sighed. "Come on." She led him down the beach, away from the pier.

"Don't you think I'll be a little too close? What if they find me?"

"How? They don't have the magic to reach you, even if they took a—"

Their images were dissolving, their conversation cutting out the farther away they walked.

"Following," Aislinn continued "—dies… taking the pendant and staking claim…"

William lost the connection to the sand. He collapsed, sitting on his hip. "It's the best I can do."

Baxter placed his hand on his shoulder. "It was fantastic. Thank you."

Kasumi collapsed.

Ewalt and Baxter rushed to her. Ewalt reached her first, fell to his knees, scooped her head into his hands, and cradled her. "Kasumi?"

"I'm fine, just tired," she whispered.

Ewalt ran his hand over her forehead. "She used the last of her magic."

"Like me," Bembe whispered.

Zoe reached Baxter and squatted next to Kasumi, tucking her straight black hair behind her ear. "Get some rest, my friend."

Murdock, Callista and the twins walked over to them. "You four can take Kasumi and Bembe to Zoe's house to rest," Baxter explained. Seeing the life drained out of Zoe's friends hurt. He wanted to take care of them—but there was too much happening around him.

"Get on with it, Bennett," Lil purred from beneath her pink parasol. She slid her oversized polka-dot sunglasses down her nose. "You were lucky Aislinn and Sterling talked about what we needed. But luck won't be on your side too much longer. Think. Where is Sterling?"

Lil liked her word games and toying with him; she found him entertaining as he worked out a puzzle. She was only straight with him—serious even—when things were dire. She knew the stakes and made it clear she didn't want him to lose.

The conversation between Sterling and Aislinn ran through his head, repeatedly. "Somewhere with perfect weather, close by, though. But needs magic to reach him? Even if they take a—take a what?" Baxter ran his fingers through his hair, pacing as he pieced the information together. He stopped. "A boat!"

"He's on an island!" Zoe said. "Hawaii?"

"No," said several Tails at the same time.

"Why not?" Zoe asked.

"It shares the border with King Takahiro's realm," Murdock said. "Aislinn would never be that close to another realm without her full magic. Too much possibility of conflict near borders."

"There're no houses, let alone mansions, on the Channel Islands," Farah said. "So that leaves those out."

"Islands up near Puget Sound?" Zale offered.

Zoe shook her head. "Probably gets too cold up there. Sounds like there is no true winter where he is."

"The islands off Baja?" Callista said.

Farah shrugged. "Sounds plausible."

"Think they're too far, though?" Zoe asked.

Ringing pierced his ears. He knew the answer, but he had to find it within the noise. He needed to focus. His eyes narrowed in on the waves rolling onto the shore. One over the other, the white foam frothing after each crash. Finally, everything around him went still and quiet, except the sound of the waves, that thundered in his ears like an old pipe organ playing the somber lullaby of a broken-hearted pirate.

An island that had permanent residences, but close enough to the mainland, so Aislinn and Sterling could easily monitor Baxter. The excitement from the beachgoers and the crowds on the pier rushed back into his ears. The merfolk still debated locations.

"No!" he demanded. They stopped. He locked eyes with Lil. Her brows folded down.

It felt nice to be one step ahead of her.

"Catalina," he stated.

Lil pushed her sunglasses back up on her nose. "Only one way to find out."

CHAPTER 43

BAXTER

WITH FIVE DAYS LEFT to restore Zoe as the rightful queen, the pressure to succeed weighed heavily on Baxter's mind. There was little time for anything to go awry with their plan. Lil and the Atlantic-Tails were on her new black power cruiser, trailing behind Baxter and the others on his white boat. The odd group of people neared Avalon Harbor at Catalina Island. The jagged green hills of the popular California island peeked out of the dark blue water with its iconic circular building perched on the right side of the half-moon-shaped bay.

Baxter, Zoe, and the Pacific-Tails would search the island for Sterling either by foot or in rentable golf carts. The Atlantic-Tails would take control of the two boats and monitor the waters. Each group would have a walkie talkie since only Baxter owned a cellular phone, which didn't have service that far off the mainland.

But that plan changed in an instant.

Most boats kept their distance from one another as they entered and exited the area, but one circled all the entering vessels. It owned the area like it belonged to the Coast Guard.

Baxter rubbed his forearm as goosebumps spread across it. Without needing confirmation, he knew Aislinn was in the boat searching for them. She knew they headed that way, confirming his suspicions that she followed their movements. It was a good thing he made a call earlier the previous day to his Lycan ally and friend, Detective Dominguez, asking for his help in keeping an inconspicuous security detail around Zoe's house and anywhere they traveled. Dominguez had been delighted to help and immediately assembled his pack and made their way down from San Francisco. Baxter checked in with him before leaving for the marina earlier and knew they would protect them by land. Baxter hated having to call in a favor, and truly couldn't imagine what kind of mess wolves and mermaids might cause, but with their lives on the line, he had no other choice. Thankfully, Zoe didn't object to his plan and welcomed the extra help. They kept that information between them, until it was of absolute need, unsure of the reaction Lycans coming to the aid of Tails might bring about.

Baxter's eyes flashed to Zoe at the front of the boat, who leaned on a cushioned bench, sunbathing next to Sefarina and Hita. She hadn't seen Aislinn's boat yet. He glanced behind him to see Murdock and Ewalt engrossed in a conversation he couldn't hear over the engine noise and the whipping wind. They didn't see Aislinn's boat either, nor did Omnira and Farah, since they were below deck. He glanced over his right shoulder to look at Lil's boat. They made a point to catch up to him.

They saw the boat.

Baxter down-shifted the throttle to slow the boat, so William could pull up next to them. The water sloshed between their two boats, teetering them from side to side.

Zoe and the two others sat up. Murdock and Ewalt ceased talking.

"See what we see?" Lucas shouted from his deck.

"Indeed. She knows our plan," Baxter said.

Zoe sat upright. "What's going on?"

Murdock and Ewalt flanked Baxter as he pointed to the speedboat. "That's Aislinn's boat. She's been circling around each vessel that enters the harbor, looking for us."

"How did she even know where to find us?" Farah muttered as she came up from below deck.

"Wondering that myself," Murdock growled. "She must have people working for her. She has plenty of money, and we all know she's a master of getting what she wants from others."

Zoe shielded her eyes and looked out over the water. "Look at her. She's driving like a madman. I'm surprised the coast guard hasn't stopped her."

"They can't stop something they can't see," Ewalt stated.

Lil slinked out from beneath the hardtop cover of the cockpit on her boat. She whipped her oversized sunglasses off, gripped her stone pendant, and fixed her gaze on the reckless boat. "Ewalt is right. I can see the golden ripple of an invisibility cloak around the boat. It's faint, but it's there."

"Shit." Baxter's skin crawled. They were sitting ducks. Lil and the At-lantic-Tails could use magic, but, technically, Aislinn was still in charge of Zoe's realm which meant they couldn't legally enter the water. They would suffer consequences to their magic if they did.

"Think we're lucky enough that Sterling's with her?" Zoe asked.

"If she's smart, no," Ewalt said.

Baxter turned on his heel and lifted the seat near the captain's chair and dug around in the compartment. He hoisted out some heavy-duty binoculars and scampered to the front of his boat. He held them up to his eyes and made some adjustments until he caught the boat in his sights which disappeared behind another while circling it.

As it came into view, heading straight for Baxter's and Lil's boats, his stomach sank. Standing next to Aislinn, who resembled the crazed Cruella de Vil, was her quartermaster. Her sidekick.

Sterling.

"Consider us lucky." Baxter lowered the binoculars.

"She's keeping him close." Zoe plucked the eyepiece out of his hands and looked through it.

"They're headed straight at us. We need a plan," Murdock stated.

Zoe dropped the binoculars on the captain's chair. "Lil and I need Sterling away from Aislinn in order to break her curse. What if the Atlantic-Tails use magic to fight against her so she retreats into the water, knowing they can't follow her, and we can grab Sterling?"

Baxter's eyes settled on Lucas, who nodded at him. "We can do that. As soon as she comes close enough to identify us, we'll rain fire on her."

"And if she speeds off? What then, mate?" William asked.

"We have two boats. We can sacrifice mine, so you all don't accidentally, and illegally, fall into the water, affecting your magic," Baxter explained. "But be sure you swing by and pick us up from the wreckage." He eyed Lil more than others.

Lil waved a folding fan in front of her face. "As if I would leave my dear friend in his time of need."

Baxter raised a brow. "You have before."

Lil scoffed. "I came back, didn't I."

"Four hours later," Baxter grumbled.

Zoe pinched the bridge of her nose. "Okay, this," Zoe pointed from Baxter to Lil, and back to Baxter, "is a story I'd really love to hear about another time. Aislinn's this close," she said, pressing the tip of her thumb to her pointer finger, "from finding out we're on this boat."

Baxter gave Zoe a curt nod as he refocused his attention.

Lucas and Sebastian scrambled to the front of their boat as William shifted the throttle and drifted away from Baxter's.

Aislinn eased her boat and swung around their boats, kicking up a rough wake behind her. "Thought you were clever," she shouted at them then laughed as her hair danced wildly behind her. "Idiots, all of you!"

Lucas touched the tattoo on his forearm and conjured his sword from it. He sliced the blade in front of him like a zigzag, igniting it in flames.

Sebastian touched his fingertips to the tattoo on his chest and summoned a large metal shield. He looped his arm in the straps at the back of it and held it out in front of him, activating a green glow around the perimeter. "Let's do this," he said.

As soon as Aislinn passed by their boat, Sebastian thrust his arm forward. The green glow shot outward, like a wide beam of light, hitting Aislinn and Sterling dead on. They froze. Immobilized for a split second. Lucas swung the sword in their direction, almost like a bat. The flames rushed off his sword, and like daggers, drove at the boat. Aislinn shrieked, but they both moved slowly as if swimming in a vat of Jell-O. She tried to duck behind the wheel as Sterling shielded his face, but the fiery blades were faster and pierced their arms.

"That's how you get shit done!" Lucas high-fived Sebastian.

But because the Atlantic-Tails were on land, their magic wasn't as strong, allowing Aislinn and Sterling to quickly gain control of their bodies and pat out the flames.

"Dammit!" Sebastian growled.

Murdock slammed his hand on the side of the boat. "Ram her!"

"Hold on," Baxter shouted to his passengers as he circled the wheel around to line the boat up like a 'T' to Aislinn's. He accelerated forward. She revved her engine and sped off. Baxter narrowly missed the stern. He steered the wheel and waved his arm for William to follow her.

The three boats sped across the ocean toward the mainland. Even at top speeds, Baxter and William could not catch Aislinn. Baxter could only guess what her next move would be.

Zoe placed her hand on his shoulder. "Any idea which way we're headed? Do we have enough gas to make it back?"

Baxter glanced at the instruments on the panel. "We should be fine. Looks like we're going toward Marina del Rey."

Zoe ran her fingers through her hair. Fury pinkened her cheeks. "What is she thinking? It's not like we're going to let her get away if she steps foot on land. She's cornered."

"Don't underestimate her," Murdock said from behind them.

Zoe faced him. "You're right. She obviously has a plan."

"Probably to get us near a bunch of Landwalkers, so nobody uses their magic, especially Lil. Can you imagine the panic and outcry?" Murdock said.

"Well, whatever her plan is," Baxter said over his shoulder, "we are about to find out."

Baxter pointed to the landmass peeking over the horizon.

Zoe plopped down on a cushioned bench next to Baxter. "We may have to risk using magic in front of humans. We can't let her get away with Sterling. I have a feeling we'll never get the chance to take him if that happens."

Baxter agreed. He couldn't lose his uncle again. "What are you thinking of doing?"

Zoe nibbled on her lower lip. "How close does Lil need to be to possess Sterling?"

Baxter pressed his lips together, thinking back to what he knew about Lil's powers. He shrugged his shoulder. "Not sure, but I believe she must be fairly close. It's worth her trying, though."

Saying nothing else, Zoe nodded, grabbed the walkie talkie, and moved to the front of the boat. Baxter knew she was right; they probably wouldn't get another chance to nab Sterling. Even if they were at one of the most trafficked marinas, it was a risk they had to take. If Lil could possess Sterling from afar, the others could grab him and hopefully force him to hand over the stone.

Baxter sighed. Of course, like most plans, nothing was a sure thing.

Especially with unhinged magic, a crazed mermaid hell-bent on revenge, and a demon who *sorely* needed to be on a short leash.

CHAPTER 44
ZOE

ZOE SAT ON THE cushioned bench at the front of the boat and kept a steady eye on Aislinn. She ran the plan through her head again. Trusting others, especially a crafty demon, had been a hard pill to swallow, but Zoe knew she wouldn't get anywhere without that connection. Of course, having Lucas and William on her side to help control Lil, made it easier to trust her.

As they approached Marina del Ray's Wave Mound, a permanent breakwater that protects the harbor entrance, Aislinn's boat slowed and carefully maneuvered between the other boats. Zoe stood; Sefarina and Farah followed her.

"I'll go tell the others to be ready." Farah turned on her heel and walked to the stern.

Aislinn passed a similar boat to her own then took a hard left around it, U-turning, and pulled up next to it. Baxter eased up on the throttle, and William stopped his boat next to him.

The four boats faced one another, but they were still too far apart for anyone to do anything. The only thing Zoe could see was a group of people on the second boat helping Sterling transfer to it by climbing over the ledge of his and onto theirs.

Zoe scrambled over to Baxter who stood with Murdock and Ewalt. "What are they doing?"

Baxter shrugged a shoulder and looked at Murdock who used the binoculars.

Zoe lifted the walkie talkie to her mouth. Before she could speak, the static sound of the radio waves sprang to life with Lucas's voice on the other end. "She has a small army! Are you seeing this?"

"Son of a bitch." Murdock handed the binoculars to Ewalt and held his hand out for the walkie talkie. "Copy. We see them. Who are they?"

"Unknown, but they're protecting Sterling." Ewalt lowered the binoculars and handed them to Zoe.

"We don't recognize them," Lucas said over the walkie talkie. "Lil says she needs to be even closer to him now that he is surrounded by more people."

Baxter pinched the bridge of his nose. "Of course."

"Copy," Murdock said into the walkie talkie.

"There's ten to fifteen beautiful women on that other boat. And they all seem to shield Sterling." Zoe peered through the lenses. "Based on her gestures, it looks as though Aislinn is giving those on the other vessel instructions. She probably has them under a spell as well."

"Not likely. I didn't see any tattoos around their wrists," Murdock said.

"May I look?" Farah made her way over to Zoe.

Zoe handed her the binoculars.

Farah made some adjustments to the lenses then whispered something under her breath. She rubbed her eyes and looked through them once again. "How is that possible?"

"What's wrong," Zoe asked. "Who are they?"

Farah moved the binoculars away from her eyes and whirled around to face them. Her face was pale, and goosebumps riddled her tan arms. "Those women are not under any spell. They're Freshwater and Saline-Tails."

A chaotic chorus of disbelief erupted around Zoe, as Murdock conveyed the information to Lucas and the others.

"F.T.," Baxter whispered to himself. "Freshwater-Tails. Of course. I remember seeing F.T. on the ancient map of the mermaid realms, but never followed through with my curiosity."

"Whoa, settle down," Zoe said, raising her voice. "Somebody needs to explain why this is a big deal and what it means to our situation?" Zoe planted her hands on her hips.

Sefarina placed her hand on Zoe's shoulder. "Sorry. This was unexpected."

Zoe was glad to be heard and felt respected as her friends quieted and looked to Farah to explain. Baxter was already on the same page with them, and she was the only one out of the loop.

"They're our counterparts to all the freshwater locations such as rivers and lakes. The saline Tails are those who can survive the extreme saltiness found in the saline lakes across the world, like the Dead Sea."

"How do you know its them?" Zoe asked.

Farah tapped the gold cuff around her upper arm. Zoe remembered the tattoo beneath the cuff; it was of Thoth, the Egyptian bird-like animal, standing on top a stack of books. "It helps that I'm a historian," she said.

Zoe nodded at Farah to continue.

"Ocean-Tails are relatively long, but Freshwater and Saline-Tails are quite small in their mermaid forms and don't have the strength of magic we do. We can't ever enter each other's waters in our mermaid forms since we aren't made to withstand the chemistry makeup of the different types of water."

"Freshwater, Saline, and Oceanic-Tails certainly do not work with one another," Ewalt said.

"Well, that explains why you all freaked out," Zoe said.

"I haven't even told any of you the worst part." Farah's shoulders sagged.

Omnira covered her mouth and mumbled something in French.

Farah took a breath. "I recognized two of them. Lorelei, from Germany's Rhein River, and Great Britain's Lady of the Lake."

Sefarina ran her fingers through her red hair and sighed.

"Lady of the Lake? As in the Arthurian legend?" Baxter asked.

Farah nodded. "Two powerful Freshwater-Tails. Who knows who else is on that boat or waiting on land?"

Zoe rolled her eyes. Nothing would ever be easy for them.

"What in the hell are they doing here, working with Aislinn?" Ewalt growled.

Zoe nibbled on her bottom lip. Something in the back of her mind annoyed her like a buzzing fly. Something she noticed about Aislinn but never questioned. Her eyes widened. She reeled around at Farah. "How long has she been wearing that necklace with the pink water lily?"

Farah's brow furrowed as she looked over at Sefarina. Farah shrugged. "I don't remember. Years? Decades?"

Sefarina rested her hand on Farah's shoulder. "At least since she became the interim queen. I remember asking her about it shortly after Melantha's death. She said it had been a gift from a special friend on land. Why?"

"Well, she didn't lie," Zoe said. "Water lilies only grow in freshwaters, which is why I thought it was odd to see an ocean-based mermaid wearing one. It was a gift from them. She never takes it off. I'd bet everything I have that it's enchanted to give her stronger magic and protect her until I returned, or, until she officially took over. It probably even lets her swim in their waters. Which means she's been working with them since Melantha's murder."

Farah hardened her brow. "What could she have possibly given them in order to side with her?"

"We are about to find out." Baxter pointed at Aislinn's boat speeding toward them.

"Shit. Here, help me over to Lil's boat," Zoe shouted at Murdock and Ewalt. "You guys hold Aislinn off, and we'll try to take Sterling."

"We should meet on Venice Beach, near The Pit," Baxter whispered in her ear.

Zoe nodded, knowing the popular area that was covered in graffiti and was a place skaters liked to frequent.

"If your group, or our group, doesn't show by midnight, activate a search and rescue with Dominguez," Baxter continued.

"Or search and recovery," Zoe mumbled as she climbed up to the ledge and steadied herself using the beam holding up the cover over the captain's area. Baxter creeped the boat closer to William's. Lucas and Sebastian stretched out their arms, helping Zoe cross from boat to boat. She planted her feet on the deck and went to wave at Baxter, but he already pulled away and headed straight for Aislinn.

With a heavy heart, Zoe watched him drive away.

If things went badly...

The knot in her stomach tightened. William shifted their boat forward, teetering her away from that thought.

She and Lil had a job to do and failing was not an option.

"Farah says she recognized two of those Freshwater-Tails as Lorelei and the Lady of the Lake," Zoe warned.

Lil spun around, an evil grin snaking up upon her lips. "Did she? How delightful."

Lucas waved a finger at her. "We don't have time for whatever thoughts are brewing in your pretty little head, Lil."

Lil shrugged and wiggled her brow. "Not yet, anyway."

"Focus," Zoe drew out the last syllable for emphasis. "From what Farah said, you guys, as in Ocean-Tails, have stronger powers than Freshwater-Tails. So how about you use some of that magic and slow their boat before they reach the marina, so we can get Sterling away from them?"

"Do I have to do everything?" Lil shoved her sunglasses into her hair.

"No. William can do it," Lucas said as he moved past Zoe to take over the driving.

William rushed to the front of the boat and held both his arms up, his palms faced the Freshwater-Tails' boat. He inhaled and planted himself in a small squat, as if about to absorb a tackle from a defensive player. A powerful shockwave erupted from his palms and hit the boat from the back. It lurched forward. William grunted and his fingers wrenched tight.

A stream of orange energy pulsated from his hands, connecting him to the boat. He pulled. The boat revved, spitting up water from the outboard engine.

"Get ready, Lil," Lucas shouted from the captain's deck.

Zoe and Lil hurried next to William.

"I'll fight the Freshwater-Tails off for as long as I can," Sebastian said.

Zoe wiped her palms on her shorts then nodded. She knew it was the end. "Once Lil possesses him, she can throw him overboard and get out of his body. I'll get him and swim to safety. With the stone protecting him, he won't succumb to any spells my eyes could do to him."

"When we're safely away from them, come find us and we'll reel you two in and get the stone from him," Lil said. This was the real Lil—the one Baxter knew. Not the sarcastic, dangerous, socialite she displayed, but the one who was loyal and would do anything for her friend, no questions asked.

Zoe finally felt at ease with her.

They were mere yards from the other boat, and Zoe could see William's magic waning as the group of Freshwater-Tails used their powers against it. "Ready?"

"Always." Lil disappeared into a whirl of thick black smoke.

From William's other side, a barrage of green orbs darted out of Sebastian's shield that he pulled from his own tattoo. Screams from the Freshwater-Tails rang out across the ocean. Zoe wondered how many boats behind the Wave Mound heard, and saw, their high seas attack.

And how long it would take for the Coast Guard to arrive.

Lil's smokey form disappeared out of Zoe's view which was her cue to dive overboard. Before she splashed into the water, something punched at her left side. She lost her concentration and fell into the cold ocean in her human form. She surfaced, gasping. The salty sea sloshed into her face. She strained to hear Sebastian's screaming, but his words were just noise among the panic. Whatever hit her spread a frigid energy through her veins.

Zoe slapped her chest, looking for the chain of the necklace to guide her fingers down to her pendant. She gripped it in her fist. Everything would be fine once she transformed.

But no. Everything was not fine. Instead of the comfort she felt upon transforming, the ice in her veins became fire. She screamed, scratching her throat, burning from the inside out. She couldn't breathe. Desperate to reach the boat and get out of the water, she floated onto her back and kicked her tail. Her tail. She lifted it again. The majestic purple shades that ebbed and flowed across her scales were nearly gone as a silvery tone crept across it, consuming her purple hues.

Her tail dropped back into the water, sinking her like a heavy weight. She convulsed, not able to take a breath. The raging fire within her vanished. In its place was a heaviness that made her feel like a rock. A statue.

From somewhere above her, she heard the hollow sound of something falling into the water. The shock wave hit, vibrating through her body so strongly she thought her stone-form would shatter, killing her faster than the slow suffocation.

She felt something tug at her wrist. Instead of sinking, it pulled her back to the surface.

The rush of surfacing to a frenzied chaos filled her ears. Hands were all over her, hoisting her out of the water. A blue energy hovered over her. A quiver ran down her frame. She blinked.

She wiggled her fingers, her feet.

I can move.

She gripped her pendant, transforming back to her human form. She spit the water out of her mouth. "What the hell happened?"

"My fault." Sebastian held out his hand to help her stand. "I missed the enchantment that hit you. It briefly made you into a Freshwater-Tail."

Zoe's brows furrowed, trying to process that bit of information. As much as she wanted to address being a Freshwater-Tail and all that came with that, she couldn't. She had to focus. "Was Lil still able to possess Sterling?"

"No worries, mate." William draped Sterling over his shoulder.

Zoe felt her body relax at the sight of him.

William continued as he sat Sterling down. "We had to enter your waters illegally, and are a little worse for wear, but we got 'em. The Freshwater-Tails, however, got away. Probably landside."

Zoe didn't care about the Freshwater-Tails. If they were lucky, Officer Domínguez and his wolf-pack would sniff them out and take care of them. She was happy their plan worked, even in a roundabout way, which nearly caused her death.

Sterling glared at her; his eyes stabbed into her soul. His lip was curled in a nasty snarl, and tiny pools of spittle gathered at the corners. He fought against the ropes latched around his wrists and secured to a cleat. Zoe briefly wondered if Lil was still in him, or if he was just pissed off that they caught him. Whatever the case, it didn't interest her—the black and red pendant hanging against his bare chest had her full attention.

It was time to collect what was hers.

Chapter 45

Zoe

Zoe raised her hand; her eyes latched onto the glowing stone. It called to her, the way the cursed spindle had to Sleeping Beauty. There was an itch in her hand, and the only way to satisfy it was to snatch the stone. To finally claim it. She reached out, her fingers so close to gripping the pendant she could feel it pulsating like a heartbeat.

Something blinded her.

She stumbled. Clawed at her face. Tore at the fabric covering her eyes. She jerked away as large hands gripped her upper arms and pulled her backward. "Get off me!"

"Settle down there, dearie," Lucas whispered in her ear. "We don't know what would happen if you touched that stone. Aislinn could have a spell on it. Remember the riddle and the plan; Sterling must break Aislinn's curse and betray her by willingly giving the stone to you."

Zoe fell slack in his grip. "Sorry. I must've lost my mind for a moment."

"It's the stone," Sebastian said. "If you look at it, you'll want to take it, and we can't have that."

Zoe nodded her head and let Lucas turn her around. He removed the fabric from her eyes which she realized was Lil's sweater. Zoe could still feel the pull of the stone from behind her, but she had coherent thoughts. "How are we supposed to get him to break the spell if I can't look at him without going into a trance and grabbing the stone?"

"As long as you don't see the stone, we believe you'll be fine." Lucas tossed the sweater to Sebastian. "We'll make him wear this and put a life vest over that, just to help block the stone from your view. Lil's possession has weakened him a great deal, so that should help."

"Is she still in him?"

Lucas shook his head. "Not anymore. It affected her, more than she thought. Seems that mermaid magic lessened her demon powers. She's below deck resting."

"You can turn around," Sebastian called from behind her.

Lil's sweater was as tight as a wet suit, with a life vest strapped around his chest. Sterling no longer looked crazed. Instead, he looked broken, just a shell of a man. His head hung low.

"Sterling?" she whispered. She wanted to take a step closer, but decided against it as she could still feel the pull of the stone.

Sterling lifted his chin. His green eyes were lifeless. His cheeks sunken.

The after effects of possession.

"Do you remember me?"

"Depends whose asking," Sterling's voice cracked from dryness. "Melantha or Zoe."

Sebastian guided Sterling onto a cushioned seat and helped him sip on a bottle of water. Zoe wanted to stay where she was, but Lucas nudged her to sit across from Sterling with Lucas sitting next to her as security.

The boat lurched forward. William focused on getting them away from the marina. If all went right, Zoe would have to get back into the water to activate the magic of her last pendant. She wondered where Baxter and the others went. Wondered whether they staved off Aislinn.

For a moment, they sat in silence and stared at one another as the boat sped off, chasing the horizon. Once they were a good enough distance from land, William slowed to a stop.

Zoe leaned forward and rested her elbows on her knees. She gave him a look layered with affection. If this didn't work...

"Melantha."

A smile crawled up his face. A glint touched his eyes. "My dark flower."

Zoe's breath hitched. During her first conversation with Aislinn, she told Zoe the meaning of Melantha's name. She remembered feeling odd as if it had been a subliminal warning of the true Melantha.

"I suppose I am a dark flower. A selfish ruler known for making dubious decisions. An oppressor of many. My thorns were unkind, I see. Perhaps it was best doing away with me."

Sterling shook his head. "The only one selfish was me. You are the dark flower *because* of your beliefs and rule. Never stuck to old traditions. Always wanting to evolve. Showing love and kindness when others feared it. Perhaps you went about things in the wrong manner, but your intentions were heartfelt."

Perplexed, Zoe sat up. "But I thought you hated me, just like Aislinn."

At the mention of her name, the light in Sterling's eye was snuffed out. His brow furrowed. He looked down at his wrists.

"Always imprisoned," he muttered.

Zoe elbowed Lucas in the side as she motioned at the ropes around Sterling's wrist. Lucas leaned over and untied Sterling.

Sterling lifted his head. "Thank you. But the ropes were not what I was referring to."

Lucas gave him a curt nod. "Of all people, I understand that kind of enslavement. But unlike you, nothing freed me except death."

Sterling sat forward. "Do tell me, ol' boy. What do I have that you did not?"

"Love," Lucas said.

Zoe reached out and covered Sterling's tattoos on his wrist. At her touch, they glowed a faint white. "And forgiveness. Melantha's. Baxter's."

Sterling's face softened. "My nephew, Bennett. For the life of me, I can't figure out why he likes to be called Baxter, though."

Zoe always thought it was because it was his pompous youngest-professor-at-USC attitude, but the truth finally hit her. "Because for one hundred years, it has been his connection to you. The one he thought of as a brother. The Baxter boys. It was his only way to have you as a part of him, even though he had been devastated by your disappearance."

Lucas lifted his chin. "That's the type of love I was talking about. A love like that can break any curse."

Sterling closed his eyes. Zoe could see tears forming beneath his lashes. He looked up at her. "You were supposed to be a Baxter as well, my dearest."

Zoe's stomach bunched into knots, and it wasn't from the swaying of the boat. Even though Melantha's memories were coming back, she wasn't Melantha, and she didn't love Sterling.

"And I think you still should be, Zoe," Sterling continued.

Zoe held her breath. He recognized and referred to her as Zoe.

"Bennett's love for you is pure and much deeper than what I had for Melantha. Seeing how he looks at you. Seeing that love in his eyes. It brings me joy, you see? Much more than the desire for power and magic."

Zoe reached out to him, but yanked her hands away as if they burned from touching dry ice. His tattoos glowed a blinding bright white. There was a small *pop* as the ink around his wrists disappeared.

Zoe pressed her hand to her mouth, stifling her cry of relief as Lucas patted her knee.

Wide-eyed, Sterling examined each of his wrists, making sure the tattoos were gone. He looked up at Zoe and Lucas. "Is it true?"

Zoe nodded. Both she and Lucas sprang to their feet. Lucas opened his arms to Sterling. "Welcome to freedom."

Sterling embraced Lucas. Sebastian and William scrambled over and joined them. Zoe tried to keep her tears at bay as she witnessed the relief and pure elation of the four people who understood what freedom truly felt like.

William was the first to release their bond. "Oi, as much as I want to keep celebrating, we have a mission." The three others stepped away from one another. "Zoe really needs that stone pendant, mate."

The four men looked at Zoe. She wiped away her tears. "May I have the stone, please?"

"It was never mine to begin with." Sterling unlatched the hooks of the life vest. Lucas helped him pull off the tight sweater, ripping the seam of an arm. Sterling lifted the chain from around his neck and fell straight to his knees.

The Atlantic-Tails rushed to his side.

"It's okay!" Zoe shouted over their worried voices. She made her way through them and kneeled in front of Sterling. "That happens when you take the necklace off. It's normal. It's the magic leaving you."

"Leaving him? Meaning he could... die?" Sebastian asked.

Zoe glanced up at the thin blond man and nodded. "He isn't protected by magic anymore."

Sterling waved off their looks of concern and placed the stone in her hand. "It's fine. It's what I deserve. Cursed or not, I murdered my fiancé. It was my hand that took the life of a beautiful mermaid queen."

Zoe stood; the stone finally gripped tightly in her fist. She felt Sterling's sorrow and guilt. The pain everyone dealt with for the last hundred years weighed heavily on her heart, but it could not be her focus. "We can think of some way you can atone for your mistakes later. I've got to save my kingdom first."

"Just remember," a silky voice said from behind Zoe, "as soon as you attach that last stone with the others, she, too, will have her full powers back."

Zoe looked to Lil who stood there with an air of nobility, holding her black parasol like she was the preserved corpse of a dark princess.

"Yes, I realize that," Zoe said.

"Do you also realize that if Bennett and your friends are still chasing her, they could be sitting ducks? She's a master at mind manipulation. It would take only a split second for her to control each one of them."

Zoe cursed beneath her breath. Lil, having a rational thought, irked her. She would never publicly admit Lil was right. She looked at William. "Time to head to Venice Beach. Baxter and I planned for us to meet there by midnight before any of us should worry or do anything rash."

Even though she said the words, Zoe didn't believe them. How could she not be worried about Baxter and her friends? They kept a sadistic mermaid at bay while Zoe and a fickle demon stole away the last piece of that mermaid's elaborate hundred-year puzzle.

Worry was an understatement.

CHAPTER 46
BAXTER

KEEPING AISLINN AWAY FROM her allies proved easier than Baxter expected. About two minutes after chasing her across the open water, with none of her erratic driving or attempts to stop Zoe and Lil on the other boat, Baxter's suspicions of her motives were confirmed. She *wanted* Baxter to chase her.

But why, though?

Why would Aislinn want to give Zoe and Lil the opportunity to capture Sterling? Or had she been so confident that the Freshwater-Tails would protect Sterling and the stone while she...

While she did what, exactly?

He fell for her trap. Baxter's hands coiled into tight balls. She wanted to keep his party split apart. Weaken them. Take them on a wild goose chase until their time literally ran out. He shook his head. He couldn't allow Aislinn to control them like that. He needed to get back to Zoe. They were stronger together.

Time to end this.

Baxter pushed the throttle forward and closed in on Aislinn's boat, passing her. He shouted at the others to take hold, as he bent his knees and jerked the steering wheel counterclockwise while shifting into reverse idle. The stern kicked out to the left. Shifting back and forth from reverse to neutral and tugging the wheel from left to right, Baxter thrust the boat into a pivot turn, in line for a head-on collision with Aislinn's.

Aislinn swerved, but seconds too late. Baxter's fast-moving boat pierced through the hull of hers. Fiberglass crushed. Metal shredded and scraped at Baxter's skin as he ducked. The stench of gasoline flooded his nostrils. Flames licked the sky.

Baxter slapped away the embers on his skin. He pushed the throttle forward, blindly driving. Next to him lay Murdock and Ewalt, using their bodies as shields for Farah and Sefarina as debris rained down.

Ewalt pointed toward the bow. "Get us back to shore! We're taking on water!"

Baxter scrambled to his feet. He looked back at the abandoned wreckage behind them. Fire and black smoke engulfed the other boat, sinking it fast. "What about Aislinn?"

"What about me?"

Baxter whirled around. Marching up the steps, bloodied and bruised, was Aislinn. A look of pure hate blazed in her eyes.

Before Baxter could react, a shrill scream deafened him. He pushed his fingers into his ears. A sharp ache stabbed at him from behind his eyes. He lost his balance and fell. Water sloshed around his knees. He needed to get up. Needed to get them to shore.

He forced his eyes to open. Aislinn stood at the rear of the boat. Her teeth bared as the strange shrieking tone emitted from her distended jaw, piercing their eardrums. But no. It was worse than that. Her song was hurting the Pacific-Tails. They withered, crying, and screaming at her feet. Torturing them. He couldn't let her hurt Zoe's friends.

His friends.

Baxter got to his knees. Planted his foot and stood up. Even though he didn't wear the stone anymore, he somehow could feel its presence as if it hung around his neck and rested on his chest. His nerves stirred within.

"Enough!" A booming voice suppressed Aislinn's song. Baffled, she snapped her head around, searching for the interruption.

Baxter's heart raced. Not because of Aislinn, but because that demanding voice came from him. Somehow, he recognized it as nothing new. It had always been with him.

The Guardian's voice.

A warmth quivered through his muscles, cloaking him in a wall of protection. A wall he needed to extend to his friends. It was his purpose. Aislinn wouldn't harm anyone under his watch, even if she had magic siphoned from the Freshwater-Tails and could display powers that rivaled Lil's. The ancient Guardian magic that ebbed through him for the past one hundred years finally activated.

He squared his posture. His fists balled. He raised his arms, crossed them over his chest like an 'X'.

Aislinn's eyes widened.

He snapped his arms down. Energy erupted out of his chest. A wrinkled vapor of sound waves rippled away from him, striking Aislinn. She buckled over. Her neck cracked as it whipped forward. A terrified cry erupted out of her. Her body flung backward like a bullet racing out of the barrel of a gun.

Then she disappeared.

Baxter cut his eyes down, almost afraid to see the reaction of the Pacific-Tails. But it wasn't fear in their eyes; it was gratitude.

Then worry as he collapsed forward.

His eyes closed, but there wasn't any darkness waiting for him on the other side. He sat on a tropical beach at sunset, watching the gentle waves roll in. He pushed his bare toes into the sand; the warmth of the granules re-energized him.

A hand touched his shoulder. A familiar rose perfume wafted past his nose as a gentle breeze swirled around him.

"Is it finally time to rest?" he asked.

The hand lifted away from him.

"Is that what you want? It's only a choice to wake or not."

He lifted his chin and looked over his shoulder seeing a white cotton gown fluttering in the air current. "Using magic like that must have a price," he said.

His mother sighed as she sat next to him. She reached for his hand. Her hands were warm, like the sand.

"Indeed, it does."

"I fear my physical state would prove useless if I should return. How could I be of any more help to her if I expelled all the energy of the Guardian? Besides, if she failed to secure her last stone, I would be back here with you in several days, anyway."

"You're right, my darling. Your duty as the Guardian is over. She knows the location of the last stone. You used all the magic that had been placed in you, and you're no longer protected by the magic of her stone. But I imagine she still needs your support. Remember what you told her: You both succeed together or die together. You can still offer her that, and your love, which gives her strength."

Baxter shook his head. "Perhaps it once did. But the closer she comes to restoring her rightful ownership as queen, the more Melantha becomes a part of her. And..." Baxter swallowed. He couldn't get the words to form.

"And you're worried about your uncle and the love they used to share."

A tear slid down his cheek. It hurt to think about losing Zoe. "Did you know what truly happened to him?" he whispered, scared of an answer he didn't want to hear.

Baxter's mother squeezed his hand, then pressed her fingertip under his chin, forcing him to face her. "I mostly see what you see. I'm not privy to information like that. Sterling being alive was as much of a shock to me as it was to you. But thinking back on when he went missing, I admit I had my suspicions that his disappearance had something to do with the mermaids. I'm only sorry I never pursued it."

Baxter let out a harsh breath. His shoulders slumped.

"As usual, mother, you are right. She needs my support and love."

His mother placed a chaste kiss on the top of his hand. "I believe in the two of you. As much as it pains me to say this, I don't want to see you anytime soon."

Baxter gave her a half-smile.

"Salam." His mother's faced blurred.

And all went dark.

CHAPTER 47

BAXTER

THE UNCONTROLLABLE SHAKING AND the feel of a frigid blanket wrapped around him jolted him back to his body.

Am I in a morgue waking from a death my friends thought I suffered?

His eyes fluttered. Salt burned his eyes.

He gasped.

"He's awake!"

Baxter looked up and through the water dripping from his lashes, and saw Ewalt, who was tethered to him by a rope. They both wore life jackets. Ewalt had been tugging him through the dark waters of the Pacific Ocean, swimming to shore.

"Oh, thank goodness!" a woman cried from behind him.

Farah's grinning face appeared in front of him. "We surely thought you were going to die, but we couldn't leave you on that sinking boat."

Baxter blinked, trying to process what happened. He looked around. His friends were all with him, each of them in life jackets. None of them were in their mermaid forms. Like him, they no longer had magic. Of all the things flooding his mind like a broken dam, he could only concentrate on one worry.

"You let my boat sink?"

Farah's face screwed up. "Mmm, technically, you sank your boat after you ran into Aislinn's and released that massive amount of magical energy to save us. We were just quick enough to grab the life jackets and flare guns and get away from it before it took us all down. Guess it's a good thing we're skilled swimmers, even as humans. Besides, you did say to save you from the wreckage if you sacrificed your boat..."

Baxter's head throbbed. He tried to paddle, but his body was exhausted. Sore. He needed to rest more.

"We're not far from washing up near Venice Beach," Murdock explained. "It's dark enough that nobody should see us. Just lie back and enjoy the ride."

Baxter nodded and let Ewalt continue to guide them to shore. He wasn't sure how long it took them to reach the tides that washed them ashore, but he knew he had passed out for a bit. The hard sand that dragged against his bare legs woke him. He was able to crawl out of the water with Ewalt. He unbuckled the life jacket and fell onto his back, finally catching his breath. Next to him, the others did the same.

They couldn't rest. There was no time.

Baxter rolled over and pushed himself on his knees. The lights from the boardwalk glistened in the night. Good. It wasn't too late in the night, yet. "I know we've all had a trying few hours, but we need to find Zoe. We have until midnight to meet up at The Pit."

Sefarina sighed and sat up. "You're right. We have to keep going."

This time, on land, Baxter was the lead. He marched their tired bodies across the sand and down the promenade until the graffiti-lined concrete walls came into view. Baxter let out a shaky laughter. A surge of adrenaline pumped through him as he lurched forward and ran to Zoe, sweeping her up in his arms.

She cried out in relief and gripped him around the neck, matching his tight embrace. He hadn't known how much he needed to hold Zoe. To inhale her energy. To feel her warmth once more. He made the right choice in waking from his deathly slumber.

Zoe pulled back from him and held her chin up. A ghost of a smile played on her lips. "We got it." She opened her hand and revealed the last stone. A black onyx with veins of vibrant pink and blood-red channels glistened in her palm.

Baxter swayed on his feet.

His mother had been right. As usual.

But it wasn't over yet. He lifted his chin. He swallowed. "Sterling?"

Zoe smirked and tilted her chin toward Lil, who sat on the top of a round concrete table. Sterling, and the other Atlantic-Tails, were by her side. His uncle gave him a quick nod and wave of the hand. Baxter sighed.

"We were waiting for you all to return before I join it to the other stones because once we do, all our powers will return, making Aislinn incredibly strong. We, especially Lil, didn't want anyone to be a sitting duck for her wrath."

"Good thinking." Baxter raked his hands through his hair. "Because we used everything in us to keep her at bay."

Zoe nodded then narrowed her eyes at him. Puzzled, she looked him over. "What happened? I can feel it. Something's, I dunno, off with you."

Baxter glanced over to Murdock and Ewalt who collapsed on a nearby bench next to Sefarina and Farah.

Zoe rounded on them. "What happened?"

"He saved us from her," Ewalt stated.

"You were right about that water lily necklace. Its enchantment elevates whatever magic she had left," Murdock explained.

"We'd all be dead without Baxter," Sefarina said.

Baxter lowered his head as Zoe reeled around to him. The truth of the situation was something he did not want to burden her with just yet.

She grabbed his hand and held it to her heart. "The Guardian's spell. You used its magic?"

"All of it," Farah said from behind Zoe.

Zoe locked in on his eyes. Searching them for the truth.

"I am but an old man who looks incredibly young," he admitted. "A mere mortal."

She blinked. A tear trailed down her cheek. "I won't accept that."

Baxter pushed a strand of her hair behind her ear. Her passion and determination were commendable. He wanted to let her believe she could save him from an aging life, but that would only hurt her more in the end. "But you must."

Zoe shook her head. "No. I'm the damn mermaid queen of the northeast Pacific Ocean." She lifted her closed hand to her pendant. "I have the power and will protect you once more." She took a breath, opened her hand, and allowed the last stone to fuse itself with the others.

Baxter shielded his eyes from the rainbow of flickering lights swirling around Zoe. The wind kicked up. He stumbled backward, pulled away from her. The magic dancing around her lit up the dark sky like fireworks. A crack of thunder rumbled. The ground trembled.

"Get back," Murdock bellowed as he dove behind one of The Pit's famous concrete walls, tugging Baxter along.

"What's happening?" Sterling shouted as he scrambled over to his nephew.

"She needs energy to restore her magic," Lil yelled over the whipping wind.

Lucas pressed his back against the graffiti-lined wall. "Good to know, but she's causing a scene. We need to cloak this area."

Lil shook her head. "I can't. I'm still drained from possessing this fool." She jerked her thumb toward Sterling, who scoffed and glared at her.

The sky rumbled again; cold drops of rain plopped down on them and fizzled out the magic surrounding Zoe. Baxter stood and peered over the top of the wall. Zoe collapsed to her knees.

Baxter pushed off the wall and darted across the concrete toward her. The others followed his lead.

"I'm okay," she said as he slowed to a stop in front of her. Her necklace pulsated and glowed. The completed pendant resembled a hibiscus flower, each petal with its own set of colors, yet beautifully connected, like a rainbow.

He extended his arm to help her stand.

"Do you feel any different?" he asked.

She shook her head. "No. I still need to get in the water and transform to fully activate the pendant. We should probably get back to the marina and get our boats in the water."

"Just Lil's boat. We lost mine when we were fighting off Aislinn," Baxter explained. "But never mind that. We don't have time to take you to deep waters. Just go now."

Zoe nodded and ran across the sand. Everyone trailed behind. She ran into the water and splashed into the gentle waves as her friends stood at the shoreline and waited. As soon as the water was waist high, she dove. Seconds later, she popped up and waved to them. The fluke of her tail sprouted out of the water behind her.

Farah cupped her hands next to her mouth. "You should be able to conjure fire. Try it," she shouted over the cresting waves.

Zoe nodded and held her hand up, concentrating. But nothing happened. She swam forward, a wave picked her up and pushed her closer to them. She tried again. "It's not working!"

From behind them, Ewalt cursed. "Neither is our magic. We still don't have any."

"Look," Sefarina stated, pointing at Zoe. "The pendant is still pulsating like it hasn't been activated."

Baxter's brows furrowed. Something wasn't right. He waved at Zoe to come to shore. "What did she do wrong? She has all the stones. She transformed. What is different from the last few times?"

Farah tried to summon her historical books through her tattoo, but nothing happened. "I... I don't know. I can't help."

Frantic, Baxter looked to Lucas. "Ideas?"

He shrugged, at a loss as much as Baxter.

Zoe skidded across the sand and transformed back to her human form. Sterling helped her stand up. "Why isn't it working?" she asked him. "Did Aislinn do something to the stone that you haven't told us?"

Sterling held her gaze. "No. Not that I know of. But..."

"But what, Sterling?" Baxter urged.

"Just a theory, but what if Zoe needs to reclaim her title as queen at the location where she lost it? Where, I took it from her..."

"That's a lot riding on a theory," Murdock growled.

"That must be the case," Farah stated.

Zoe nodded. "It makes sense. End it where it started... Close the loop where it was opened... Coming full circle... I think it's a sound theory. Which means, we need to get back up to San Francisco. And fast."

"Oi, we have company, mates," William interrupted.

Baxter looked over his shoulder. The square headlights of several vehicles glowed like monster's eyes appearing in a forest. The rumbles of motors echoed through the crisp air. Stalking them.

"Scatter—"

"Run!"

"Wait!" Baxter recognized the off-road SUVs coming at them.

"They're with us," Zoe added.

Around them, Baxter and Zoe's friends stopped and waited as a Jeep Wrangler slowed to a stop in front of them. Two men, Officer Dominguez and another, just as strapping as he was, jumped out. The other Jeeps circled and enclosed them in a barricade.

"We figured that was you with the pretty lights." Dominguez wiped the rain from his face.

"Who are you?" Murdock asked as he advanced toward Dominguez.

"Wolves, Baxter?" Lil squealed from over his shoulder. Baxter whirled around. Lil scowled at them. "You brought along these filthy animals to help?"

"Well, without us filthy animals, those Freshwater-Tails would have gotten away," said the other man. "And you're one to talk, demon. You're just as filthy as we are with your soul-eating habits."

Lil puffed air through her flared nostrils. She stiffened.

"Werewolves or Lycans?" Farah asked, always inquisitive in any situation.

Dominguez stepped forward. "Lycans," he said to Farah then looked at the others. "We don't have time to debate. That display of magic will have authorities coming to investigate. Get in a Jeep!"

A jumbled mess of people ran to different vehicles.

Everyone but Lil.

She stomped her foot in the sand. "I will not follow a wolf. They smell of dirt and have fleas."

Baxter gripped the rollover bar above him, swung out of the Jeep, and marched over to her. "Damn it, Lil. We do not have time for your prejudices. I'm sorry if wolves remind you of hellhounds, but they are not them. I promise they are not to be feared."

Crimson spread across Lil's cheeks. She stepped close to Baxter and looked up at him. She was so close, in fact, he could feel her icy breath against his throat. "Wolves are descendants of hellhounds, Bennett. You'd be bothered too if they were the ones who chased you from your home."

Baxter felt a pang of heartache for his friend who rarely spoke about her past. He hated asking her to face her trauma, but they were in a precarious situation and time was not their friend. He threaded his fingers through hers. She trembled. "Have I ever led you astray?"

She shook her head.

"I do not plan on starting now. Trust them because I do. Besides, you heard them: they captured the Freshwater-Tails for us. And I know you have an interest in *that*."

Lil grinned.

Baxter sighed. He found her soft spot, for the worry from her face evaporated into her usual mischievous self. He pulled her forward and together, they ran to the last waiting Jeep and clambered inside.

Lil leaned over to Dominguez, who sat in the front passenger seat. "Tell me, darling, how did you and your wolf pack managed to entrap Freshwater-Tails?"

Baxter tipped his head back against the headrest, blocking Lil and Dominguez's conversation from his mind. How many more barricades would they have to break through before Zoe could simply claim what was rightfully hers and save her kingdom?

Baxter rubbed his face, knowing the answer to that question: several. They were at least seven hours away from the Cliff House in San Francisco. The Victorian chateau that once was the Cliff House was no longer there. The wooden observation deck that Melantha cast the spell from, and eventually died on, was gone, replaced with a cold, concrete, square-shaped building. With it missing, they had no guarantee of truly returning to the place Melantha lost her life and realm.

Not to mention, it was past midnight, giving them three days left.

Even if they overcame all those issues, there was still the problem of Aislinn. Baxter knew he hadn't killed her; she had been too protected with magic. But worse, Aislinn would know Zoe needed to return to the site of her death to fully reclaim her kingdom.

She would be there.

Waiting to fight to the death to stop Zoe.

CHAPTER 48

ZOE

EXHAUSTED AND DISHEVELED. EVERY person in their seven-vehicle caravan heading to San Francisco felt the same way. They had no time to gather their thoughts. No time to run back to Zoe's house to clean up and pack for a trip to northern California. No time to rest. Everything had happened so fast, from getting the last stone, to the stone not working, to being rescued by Officer Dominguez and his wolf pack. And now holding fifteen Freshwater-Tails hostages in Jeeps with eight Oceanic-Tails, nine Lycans, two ancient mortals, and a demon.

A demon who almost got herself and Baxter caught by the police. Zoe rolled her eyes. Just when she believed in, and trusted Lil, she would do something out of character and unexpected, making Zoe doubt her again.

Whatever Lil's issues had been, Zoe was glad Baxter was safe. She just wished she was in a vehicle with him. Even though Murdock was with her, Zoe craved Baxter's warmth and attention.

If the Lycan drivers stopped for a quick discussion of a plan, she'd take the opportunity to ride with Baxter. But after racing away from the beach, the line of Wranglers and Cherokees headed straight for 405 Freeway, keeping her alone. She wrapped her arms around herself for any sort of comfort as it became clear they were not going to stop.

The line of Jeeps then merged onto the Five, which took them through the Tejon Pass, and the dangerous six percent downgrade of the Grapevine. As they finally pulled off the freeway at the base of the pass to fill up on gas, Zoe straightened, her muscles eased a fraction.

Finally.

Zoe and Murdock climbed out of their Wrangler while their driver filled up their gas tank, allowing the other passenger, Lorelei, the Freshwater-Tail from Germany's Rhein River, to walk around and stretch her legs. Well, as much as she could. After Zoe's insistent questioning, her driver explained how the Freshwater-Tails stayed tamed while being held captive. Apparently, the Lycans leashed the mermaids to them through their saliva which had magical enzymes that helped them control their prey. Whatever, or however, the Lycans used their magic, was their business. Besides, the thought of these bad-ass young men and women wiping their spit on others grossed her out and their drive had been silent after that.

Zoe circled the Wrangler and eyed Baxter standing outside his vehicle, a few aisles down from hers. He noticed her padding over to him and beamed. His arm curled around her waist and tugged her into his chest. She squeezed him tight; possessive, almost. She didn't want to be away from him anymore.

She looked up at him. "You doing okay? I mean, besides freezing because your Jeep's hardtop wasn't attached."

Baxter gave her a lackluster smile. "Luckily Lil was able to cast a warmth spell around us. Dominguez will put the top on before we pull out of here. But yes, I am much better since I am with you."

"Me too. Put Lil with Murdock and I'll ride with you and Dominguez."

Baxter planted a chaste kiss on the top of her forehead. "Come on. We should check in with everyone and make a plan before we get going again."

Zoe walked arm in arm with Baxter over to the small huddle of people standing near the last aisles of pumps. They chatted as they put the hardtops of the two Wranglers back on.

"No, we should stay away from the Tolls. Let's just go up through San Jose," Dominguez said to a muscular, petite woman. Her blonde hair was shaved at the sides with a braid down the center.

She nodded and placed her hands on her hips. "Good idea, babe. We'll follow you."

Dominguez nodded. "I think the next time we stop; we should get some rest. Mistakes happen with fatigue."

"I agree," Baxter said.

"After that, we'll head to Ocean Beach, where Zoe can do her thing."

"While the rest of us protect her, since Aislinn will be there to stop her," Baxter said.

"Which wouldn't have been a problem if someone," Zoe said, drawing out the last word and cutting her eyes over to the lean, black-hair woman leaning against a Wrangler snacking on a Slim Jim, "didn't give her an amulet to amplify her magic."

The woman looked up and glared back at Zoe. "We would not have needed to if you, Melantha, would have just—"

"We don't have time for this," Sterling shouted, breaking up the verbal fist fight Zoe desperately wanted to get into. He took Zoe's hand and gave her comforting squeeze. "The Lady of the Lake will keep you in conversation if you aren't careful. Ignore her." He looked back at Dominguez. "We need to go."

A wave of heat passed through her cheeks, embarrassed that her anger and fear of everything going wrong fueled her the wrong way. She tightened her grip on his hand and acknowledged him through her eyes.

Something enrapturing sank within her. Would she always have these feelings for the man from her past, putting her in the middle between uncle and nephew? She shook her head as she slipped her hand out of Sterling's. She didn't have time for such intrusive thoughts.

"Agreed. Let us go." Baxter drew Zoe away from the huddle and away from her conflicting feelings.

Over the next five hours, Zoe napped for a bit, but mostly obsessed over the *what ifs*. If Aislinn stopped her. If she and Baxter died. If she claimed her kingdom. If Melantha's memories and feelings took her over. If she lost Baxter because Melantha still loved Sterling. If she fell for Sterling as Zoe. If Aislinn murdered her again before she could cast the guardian spell. If she had to kill again. If, if, if...

"Zoe?"

A whisper. A gentle nudge.

She opened her eyes then quickly shielded them from the bright morning sun. They parked their caravan in front of a motel. The Freshwater-Tails and Lycans climbed out of the vehicles.

"We've arrived. I went ahead and got us all rooms to rest in for today. We'll head to the Cliff House tomorrow morning, before people arrive for the day," Baxter said.

The well-needed rest was like magic in itself. Each of them refreshed and clear-headed. And as planned, by six a.m. the next day, Dominguez and his team parked their Jeeps in front of the Cliff House near the stairs that lead down to the ruins of the Sutro Baths.

Baxter slid his seat forward, and Zoe climbed out of the Wrangler. The salt air was cool on her face. She took a few steps forward to the fencing between the sidewalk and the hilly edge. She eyed the Seal Rocks and the old ruins.

Had it only been a couple weeks ago that I fell into a hole in those very boulders and transformed into a mermaid, changing my life forever?

Between the hunt for the stones, discovering a new world based on magic, battling creatures, and the countless brushes with death, Zoe knew she wouldn't trade those moments for anything in the world. She finally felt complete. Part of a team. And whatever adventures she, Baxter, and her new friends got into in the future, she was sure it was the life she wanted. She would do anything to keep it. To protect it.

The stone pendant warmed against Zoe's chest and reminded her of her task. A task that was three days from becoming a catastrophic nightmare if she and Baxter failed.

But we didn't.

She had only been at it for twenty-eight days but the sense of relief she felt as she watched the waves roll in was massive. She couldn't even imagine how Baxter felt trying to complete this quest for the past hundred years and having it end with only three days left.

Inconceivable.

Leaving the others behind, Zoe took off down the cement stairs toward the beach. She faintly heard the scraping of shoes running after her and the voices of her loved ones begging her to wait. But the call of the sea was too strong to resist.

She splashed through the low tide until the water was thigh-high. She plunged headfirst into the rolling waves. She transformed into her familiar form and immediately, a kaleidoscope of colors erupted out of her stone and swaddled her like a cozy blanket.

Every inch of her, from the tip of her fluke to every strand of long hair, tingled and vibrated with the magical energy reigniting within her soul. From the ancient days as Sirena to the modern times as Melantha, a movie-like montage of her past lives whirled in her mind, fully solidifying Zoe as Melantha, and Melantha as Zoe.

A pain of a thousand needles stabbed through her left shoulder blade. She winced and wrenched her neck to look over her shoulder as a black tattoo of an elaborate trident jutting out of water appeared on her skin. Curious, she ran her fingertips against the ink, and as she lifted her hand away, the weapon became real in her palm.

The head of the golden trident had three sharp prongs with the two on the outside curving outward like the outline of her fluke. At the base of the middle prong was a carved scalloped shell. Engraved on the bottom of each of the side prongs was the scroll-like design of the ancient written language of mermaids. Zoe instinctively knew how to read the writings which proclaimed her the rightful heir of the Triton lineage.

She gripped the golden staff. Diamonds, amethysts, and frosted sea glass peppered the shaft along with finely carved sea waves. She raised the ornate trident above her head. The rainbow-colored energy swirled around her and dissolved into her body. She aimed the trident and shot out a blast through the tips of the three prongs.

Zoe swished her tail and launched herself upward. She surfaced and noticed she was still close to shore, just past the boulders where she first transformed. She looked up at the boxy Cliff House perched on the rocky terrain and remembered when that very spot had been adorned with a grandiose Victorian castle-like building. It had been an exclusive resort that she and Sterling frequented. It had been a reminder of her happiness which was why she chose it as the location where she would end her reign as mermaid queen and begin her mortal life with Sterling.

It was only fitting she end her life as a mortal and begin anew as Zoe, the mermaid queen of the northeast Pacific Ocean.

She smiled, a wide toothy smile, as she looked at the beach lined with all her friends. They danced about despite a sudden downpour.

She realized the jet stream of magic that blasted out of her trident fractured into millions of pieces and showered over the ocean and her entourage like large flakes of falling snow.

As Zoe paddled forward, she heard Farah squealing in delight as Ewalt made his green orbs of magic dance around her. She saw Murdock conjuring fire in his hands; Sefarina transported herself from one location to another, into the water, onto the roof of the Cliff House, and to the top of the Seal Rocks.

Sefarina leaned over and held her red hair back as she shouted, "Welcome back, my queen!" Sefarina dove off the rocks and splashed into the water next to her. She leaned back, flipped her tail up, and showed off its vibrant aqua and teal colors.

Zoe squealed as happiness buzzed within her.

I did it!

Well, she, Baxter, and every other person she met over the last few weeks. They all helped to restore her as the mermaid queen and save the kingdom from certain death. She wanted to leap into Baxter's arms. It was time to start living instead of surviving. Time was finally on their side.

But a cold chill tickled the nape of her neck. She chided herself knowing damn well she never should have let her guard down that far.

Aislinn neared. Her presence briefly penetrated Zoe's mind and hammered against her defensive mental walls.

Zoe placed her hand on Sefarina's tail, steadying her friend. "Aislinn's coming. You need to get everyone to a safe location. Let me handle her."

Sefarina bobbed up and down in the waves. "I will. But you don't have to face her on your own."

Zoe nodded. "She's going to be extremely powerful with her full magic back alongside the magic she's gained from the Freshwater-Tails."

"I know. Which is why there is only one person strong enough to help you defeat her." Sefarina looked over at the beach.

Zoe saw Baxter and Sterling waving at them as the Lycans celebrated along with Farah. The Freshwater-Tails huddled together on the sand, looking bored and surly, while Lil, Lucas, William, and Sebastian sat by themselves on the crumbled ruins of the Sutro Bath Houses.

Zoe knew exactly whom Sefarina referred to. Lil already did so much for Zoe and her kingdom. Surely the demon would want some kind of payment if she came groveling for her help once again.

"Come on." Sefarina looped her arm around Zoe's. "I'm sure she'll help. You just need to ask then grant her permission to enter our waters." In a flash of aqua and teal lights, Zoe and Sefarina disappeared from the water and reappeared next to Lil, both of their tails flapped against the stone ruins next to Lil's dangling legs.

Lil cut her eyes over at Zoe's weapon. "I don't like that. Your trident is prettier than mine."

Zoe glanced back at Sefarina wishing she would intervene with the sulking demon. She simply winked then disappeared again.

Traitor.

Zoe took a breath and concluded there was only one way to deal with Lil: deadpan sarcasm. She rolled the trident between her fingers, admiring its beauty. "Perhaps if you were more powerful, your plain-Jane trident would reflect that." Zoe smirked.

Lil scoffed. Narrowed her eyes. "Wretched Tail." The side of her blood-red lips curled. "You learn quickly."

Zoe grinned. "Yup. Besides, the way you and Baxter interact, it's obvious you enjoy banter. Guess that's why you love him."

Lil looked across the beach at Baxter, who was eyeing them back. "Like an annoying little brother, yes." She arched her brow and glanced back at Zoe. "And if you truly need to know, he isn't my type."

"Is that right?"

Lil leaned back and chuckled. "'Tis true. I prefer to tangle my fingers in long, silky hair and between the soft, plump legs of—"

"I get it, I get it." Zoe held up her hand to stop Lil from continuing the juicy details of her delights even though she was thankful Lil opened up to her. Hopefully it would make her request much easier.

Zoe lifted the trident to her shoulder. It disappeared into the ink of her tattoo. She transformed into human form, hopped off the jagged edge of the rock and planted her hands on her hips. "So, how about adding a few notches to that trident by helping me overthrow Aislinn? Or are you just a demon mermaid queen in name only?"

Chapter 49

Zoe

Like clockwork, the moment Lil accepted Zoe's challenge to help defeat Aislinn, the pink mermaid struck. Every Lycan fell to their knees, covering their ears and hollering as a sound only they could hear flooded their heads.

"Dammit!" Zoe rushed across the pebbly sand. Lil ran right behind her, but William, Sebastian, and Lucas outran them both, reaching their newfound friends first.

"Stop them!" Sterling pointed to something behind Zoe. She came to a hard stop and whirled around just as Lil dodged her, stumbled, and rolled across the wet sand.

There was no time to help her to her feet.

The group of Freshwater-Tails sprinted toward the water and dove into the waves. The obedient spell the Lycans placed on them now lifted, since Aislinn held them at her command.

The now-familiar sonic boom that alerted the kingdom of the illegal entrance of foreign Tails rippled across the ocean like rings.

Their tails were silver. Each of them had a different color threaded across their scales like ribbons dancing across the waves as they leaped in and out of the water, swimming away.

"They'll suffocate in our waters," Farah cried out. "Stop them!"

Whatever tangled mess the Freshwater-Tails got themselves into with Aislinn, Zoe knew in her heart they could be redeemed and didn't need to have such a senseless ending.

Instinctively, she reached for her shoulder blade, activated her trident, and launched it at them like a Hail Mary pass. The trident spun through the air kicking up purple flickering lights around it. The trident stabbed down into the water and disappeared beneath the surface.

The sky darkened; the wind shifted. Thunder cracked through the cool air.

The water stirred, spiraling into several angry purple vortexes.

Mesmerized, Zoe watched multiple funnels drop out of the clouds, and connect to the water's surface. A thunderous rumble echoed across the water as the Freshwater-Tails were lifted out of the sea and captured inside the circular current. A bolt of purple lightning danced across the sky and struck the funnels. Zoe shielded her eyes from the blinding energy.

Still shocked at the strength of her power, she lifted her head from the crook of her arm. She knew how to stop the invasion, but she wasn't sure what she did. Warm sunlight, a blue sky, and the soft rolling waves of the morning tide greeted her, just like it had been moments ago. She looked around, seeing the others doing the same. Everyone appeared fine.

She took a few steps forward, helped Lil to her feet, then padded over to her friends. "Where did the Freshwater-Tails go?" she asked Murdock.

"More importantly, where's your trident?" Lil said.

"Her trident will reappear once it's done transporting the Freshwater-Tails back to their own realms. That's the fastest way to stop them from doing any harm, but it only works if the ruler is in proximity to the epicenter of the invasion," Farah stated.

"It's the rarest, and most exciting, way to rid anyone from your kingdom," Lucas said. "I only saw Cavan do it once."

Zoe sighed. She hadn't wanted the Freshwater-Tails out of her sight just yet. There was so much more to their story. She may have Melantha's memories of important events back, and know how to be a mermaid on instinct, but she still had so much to learn about the magical world. "Eventually, I'll need to confront them about their alliance with Aislinn and hopefully make peace with them."

"One day, yes. But Aislinn is our focus," Baxter reminded her.

Always the student, she wanted to immerse herself with knowledge about the Freshwater realms. Baxter, always the logical one, reminded her she needed to sort out her own kingdom before she could learn about any of the others. As Zoe, she only heard about the stories of the Lady of the Lake from the Arthurian legends and knew nothing of Lorelei and the others. As Melantha, she had a faint recollection of Freshwater-Tails and knew they mostly kept to themselves.

"You're right," she mumbled. She felt something tickle her shoulder blade and knew her trident was back in her tattoo, also reminding her she had more work to do.

She closed her eyes and carefully let the wall around her mind lower just a tad. She reached out, searching for Aislinn's thoughts. It was like flying across the sky, as wisps of clouds floated by, except they weren't clouds, they were the thoughts of others. To find a particular person's thoughts,

Zoe just needed to focus on their physical form or their magical aura, which was probably how Aislinn deafened the Lycans and forced them to break their bonds with the Freshwater-Tails.

Where are you, Aislinn?

Aislinn's blonde-and-pink hair appeared in her mind. Her blue doe-eyes and smiling face. Even with her restored powers as the mermaid queen, Zoe didn't have the magical mental strength of a pure Pink-Tail. No clouds fluttered by her as she flew around her mental image of Aislinn. The Pink-Tail's mind was a vault, and nothing could break through her thick walls.

Except for the power of two mermaid queens.

Zoe's eyes snapped open. She faced Lil and grabbed her hands. "Help me locate Aislinn. We need to unite our minds to break into hers."

Lil gave her a curt nod and gripped Zoe's hands tighter and closed her eyes. This time, Zoe focused on Lil. The wispy clouds appeared, and like a whisper in her ear, she heard her own name summoned as Lil searched for her. Then, they found each other in their mind's eye and held hands once again. They reached out and searched for Aislinn, ramming her mental walls as one.

Where are you, Aislinn?

A crack.

The mist of a cloud seeped out of it.

They flew into it.

A brief image of Aislinn standing over Baxter. He lay in the sand, dead. Blood pooled around him.

They flew around Aislinn. Another misty cloud seeped from her. Another brief image. This time, Aislinn was perched up high, looking down on a beach, watching a group of people who surrounded two women holding hands...

Zoe and Lil's eyes opened at the same time and took in the sight of the Cliff House looming over them.

Had she been there the entire time?

"What is it?" Sterling asked.

"She's there," Zoe stated. "Somewhere up there, watching us."

"And she wants to kill Bennett," Lil added.

Zoe dropped Lil's hands. "Never gonna happen," she muttered as she marched over to Baxter and cupped the hibiscus-shaped stone pendant in the palm of her hands. Tapping into her ancient magic, she felt a song rising in her voice, as if she was reading the spell from a scroll.

"Guardian's magic, life evermore.
Reignite and protect,
'Tis love and friendship will scribe this lore"

As she repeated the incantation, her palms warmed from the magic flowing within the stone. She opened her hands to see a tiny fragment of the colorful stone glowing. She plucked the piece away from the larger stone and noticed a silver thread trailing from it. She narrowed her eyes and realized it was the chain of the new necklace. She gave it one last tug, breaking it completely away from the original, and without any hesitation, slid it over Baxter's head.

A rush of wind engulfed them, and an array of colorful lights jetted around them. Baxter fell to his knees and groaned as the stone's magic pierced his body and protected him once again with the Guardian's magic.

Within seconds, it was over. Zoe squatted down and placed her hand on his shoulder. He wiped away the sweat that beaded on his brow and looked up at her, still trying to catch his breath.

"I know I didn't ask your permission first, but I couldn't risk losing you to her."

"Thank you. I appreciate it."

Zoe smirked. "Besides, I had to do it for myself. I can't live this life without you in it. And I think you feel the same."

Baxter smiled. His green eyes were more vibrant and brilliant now that Zoe's newly resurrected magic flowed through him again. "Indeed. You are my world."

Zoe leaned in, ready to press her lips against his.

Lil's face appeared on the side of theirs. "I hate to break this up, but can we take care of Aislinn first? I have a spa appointment at noon and would hate to go another day without a massage and facial."

Baxter cut his eyes at Lil. She fluttered her eyelashes, then dashed away.

Zoe took a breath and helped Baxter to his feet, but something immediately knocked him backward hitting him square in the chest. "Baxter!"

A raven sporting a pink bowtie around its neck circled over his body, ready to divebomb him again. Before she could react, a ball of fire jetted past the bird, singing its tail feathers. It squawked then disappeared in a flare of pink mist.

"What the hell was that?" Zoe helped Baxter up again.

"That was Aislinn's familiar, since she doesn't have a traditional weapon like your trident or my sword," Murdock said. "The raven represents the Morrigan from Celtic mythology."

"A goddess split into three. One who influences war and can predict futures, a shape- shifter, and one who wields power over others," Baxter added as he patted the sand off his back end. "It's where the powers of pink and red-colored Tails hail from, right?"

Murdock nodded. "We both shape-shift from human to Tail. Red-Tails can wield physical power while the Pink-Tails use their minds."

"Good to know," Zoe mumbled. "Get everyone far away from here to someplace safe."

Murdock dipped his head in acknowledgement.

She gave Baxter one last look then stomped across the beach toward the stairs that led back up to the Cliff House.

Lil jogged up beside her. "So, you protect Baxter once again, but left Sterling a mortal?"

Zoe rolled her eyes and, briefly, imagined pushing Lil down the stairs. "Did you notice the raven attacking? No time for him at the moment. If you're so worried about him, you could have done the same spell to protect him."

Lil shrugged. "Or, I could wait for him to be killed during this fight with Aislinn and just collect his soul."

Zoe stopped. She cut her eyes over at Lil. "I'm going to forget you said that for the moment because we need to refocus. We need a plan before we reach Aislinn."

Lil nodded. She slipped her hand beneath the collar of her blouse, ran her hand over her left shoulder blade, and pulled out her gold, and very plain looking, trident. She struck the end of it on the stone steps. "Let's stab her with these."

Zoe shook her head as she, too, retrieved her trident. "That's the last, most desperate option."

Lil sighed. "You and Bennett always with your righteous ethics. Fine. What do you suggest? If we can keep her out of the water, her powers won't be as strong, but then again, neither will ours."

Zoe nibbled her lower lip as she processed Lil's suggestions. "That's it! We keep her out of the water. Permanently. If she's banned from both our realms, wouldn't her magic be cut off because she doesn't have ties to her current or original home?"

Lil's dark eyes lit up. "The only thing she has is the magic the Freshwater-Tails loaned her, and we both know their magic has nothing on Oceanic-Tails."

"And then we can restrain her and—"

"Torture her," Lil added, her eyes wide and feral.

Zoe blinked. "And work on making her atone for the messes she has created."

Lil's shoulders sagged. "That too."

Zoe raised a brow. "I'm pretty sure the spell to ban a Tail from the realm will naturally come to us."

"Let's find out," Lil said.

They continued running up the stairs, tridents at the ready. They followed the sidewalk down to the veranda and peeked around the corner of the concrete building. Aislinn stood at the railing overlooking the ocean, petting the head of her raven, as it perched on her forearm.

Zoe squeezed the staff of her trident, not wanting it to slip out of her sweating palms. She held up her other hand and signaled a count of three on her fingers; they charged forward.

Aislinn's raven flew at them. Its razor-sharp beak came at Zoe and Lil like a dagger. Zoe and Lil dove to the ground; the bird barely missed them. The raven croaked and circled around. Zoe looked up, pointed her trident at it. Bolts of purple lights shot out from the prongs. Pink magic sparked out of the raven's bowtie; they collided and fizzled out.

Zoe scoffed. "You're kinda' an a-hole," she shouted at the raven who veered toward her.

A scream.

Lil lay on the ground covering her head—her trident lay a couple of feet from her.

Conflicted, Zoe looked up at the raven then back to Lil. She scrambled over to Lil and reached her hand out. An orange beam of light shot out of her palm, summoning Lil's trident to her. With her other hand, she twirled her own trident like a baton. A ray of golden light blanketed over them, protecting them in an invisible and impenetrable cloak.

Zoe dropped Lil's trident and placed her hand on the top of her head. She closed her eyes, found the entrance into Lil's mind. Instead of flying through a blue sky, it was gray. Stormy. There was a large, jagged crack across the sky. Clouds of inner thoughts billowed from it. One of them had pink vapor snaking through them.

Attacking them.

Zoe raged and flew into it. Aislinn's voice echoed in her ear. Singing... no. Chanting and demanding Lil to reveal her true form, whatever that meant. Zoe looked around. Lil, as a young child, was in a dark corner, her arms wrapped around her knees, rocking back and forth; the sound of growling coming from the dark shadows. Zoe ran to Lil, who recognized her. She reached out for Zoe's hand and gave her control of Lil's mind.

Zoe screamed. Her power erupted out of her and forced Aislinn out of the room, out of the inner thought cloud, and out of Lil's mind. Zoe let go of the child's hand then also evacuated. "Put your walls up, Lil. Lock everyone out of your mind."

A beat passed. The crack rumbled and closed. The gray sky dissolved back into blue.

Zoe opened her eyes and lifted her hand off Lil who raised her head. "Thanks. The moment my trident fell, I lost my confidence, and she found a way in."

She handed Lil her trident. The invisibility cloak trembled around them as the raven pecked at it, slowly breaking through the magic. "He's relentless. We need to take him out before we can get to Aislinn."

Lil looked past Zoe. "Shit. She's using the Freshwater's magic."

Zoe twisted around to look behind her. Aislinn stepped away from the railing and stalked toward them. She rolled a ball of fire from one hand to the other.

Waiting for her raven to release her prey.

Between the *rap, rap, rap* of the bird chiseling its way in, the maddening look in Aislinn's eye, and her own trembling hands, Zoe's mind was a dizzying mess.

What to do, what to do?

Baxter was usually the one to calm her. To remind her she wasn't alone anymore. She had a team. She had friends. She had support, even if she failed.

But not Aislinn.

She was all alone. Unprotected. With nobody backing her up.

Literally.

"Watch your six, Aislinn," Zoe said. She gripped Lil's arm. "Be ready to ban her."

In a blink of an eye, Zoe lifted the trident and slammed the base onto the concrete, startling the raven and breaking their protective cloak. She vanished in a cloud of teal and aquamarine lights, only to reappear behind Aislinn.

Like a synchronized swim duo, Zoe and Lil raised their tridents, sparking an electric pulse of green-and-purple magic between the prongs. They hopped into a defensive warrior stance, their tridents pointing at Aislinn's middle. A haunting melody danced from their lips.

Aislinn dropped her ball of fire, which extinguished at her feet. Brows furrowed. Mouth twisted in anguish. She reached out, different colored magic sputtered out of her fingertips. She fell to her knees. An unknown force plucked the source of pink energy from her chest. She screamed in agony as if her soul was being ripped out of her body. Her raven landed on her shoulder and vaporized with a small *pop!*

An eerie silence filled the space between the three women. Aislinn took shallow breaths while Lil stared at her, salivating over what she did to her. But Zoe? She felt empty. She thought defeating Aislinn would be more satisfying, but this feeling was more like a parent having to scold their child. It had to be done, but nobody walked away feeling good.

Except maybe Lil.

Zoe cleared her throat. "Your fight is over. You need to make amends and atone for what you have done."

Aislinn lifted her head and sat back on her knees. She inhaled in through her nose and out, flaring her nostrils, and her eyes never wavered from Zoe's.

But what could she really do with two queens standing over her?

"You can let hate consume you all you want, but you brought this on yourself, Aislinn."

Aislinn stood, drawing herself up to full height, clasped her hands together, and took a calming breath. "And you brought *this* on yourself, Zoe." She twisted a pewter ring on her middle finger.

A ring Zoe hadn't noticed before.

"No!" Lil lunged at Aislinn.

Time stood still.

Bewildered, Zoe glanced from Lil to Aislinn, who pulled off her ring and split it into two pieces, one in each hand. She flicked her fingers at them. Lil reached for the rings, but Zoe knew it was too late. Just recently, she did the same thing to King Cavan with a similar looking ring. Familiar black smoke erupted from the rings and rushed her and Lil.

They were dead.

There was nothing Zoe could do about it.

This was surely karma for what she did to Cavan and whatever wicked deeds she did as Melantha.

Instead of the smoke disappearing into her like it did into Cavan, it coiled around each of them and constricted their arms to their sides. Squeezing. Suffocating. Forcing them to wail in pain and fight for their last breath.

When Zoe thought her ribs were seconds away from cracking, five golden threads, evenly spaced apart, snaked out of her mouth. Looking down her nose, Zoe watched the strange effect and tried to figure out what was happening. She noticed glowing music notes dancing along the lines. A vocal line.

Oh.

It wasn't karma. It was *The Little Mermaid.*

Aislinn was stealing their singing voices. Stealing their ability to cast enchantments and spells.

But for what reason? And where had she acquired a ring like that, especially since Lil's had been smuggled out of the underworld?

Zoe could only watch. Watch as their vocal cords floated over to Aislinn's rings, shrank down, and became the pattern etched upon the metal. Watch as Aislinn pressed the two pieces together, connecting them like a magnet. Watch as Aislinn set her lips in a grim line and shove the ring back on her middle finger.

Watch as Aislinn vanished.

Chapter 50

ZOE

The black smoke dissipated and released Zoe and Lil; they dropped onto the cold concrete. Both groaned and clutched their sides. Zoe drew in a breath, coughed, and tried again until she could finally breathe easily. She pushed herself to her knees and edged closer to Lil, who was curled into a ball.

"I'm really hating that bitch," Lil mumbled through a pained breath.

Zoe grinned and placed her hand on Lil's hip. She didn't *want* to hate Aislinn. Somewhere in the back of Zoe's mind, a quote, perhaps, flickered about. It was something about hate and how it caused problems but never solved those problems. Whatever the exact reference was, Zoe whole-heartedly believed that hate was an all-consuming emotion that wasn't healthy nor was it a path she should travel down.

But, *damn*, Aislinn sure made it hard to not hate her.

Zoe sighed and took stock of the situation.

For now, the battle against Aislinn was over. She had been banned from the two largest oceans and could no longer pull the strings of either of them. The mystery surrounding who, and why, Melantha had been murdered, had been solved. The Pacific Ocean's northeast kingdom had its proper ruler back and could flourish again. And most importantly, Zoe and Baxter would live.

All great things, of course.

Except Zoe knew that this war against Aislinn was only the beginning. Aislinn was the type to plot her revenge. The type who would bury herself in hate, even if it took another hundred years. Because Aislinn had the Freshwater-Tails on her side, she could be anywhere in the world. Trying to locate her was not something Zoe was interested in doing, especially since Aislinn somehow possessed magic that gave her the ability to incapacitate any verbal spells from royalty. Until Zoe knew what she was up against, she was not comfortable chasing her down. One day Aislinn would come for her and Lil, perhaps even others, and Zoe would be ready, powered with knowledge and magic to stop her and, hopefully, help heal the hate flowing through the pink mermaid.

Until then, Zoe had a realm in desperate need of attention. With the help of her friends and a partner who not only made her swoon, but was her best friend, she was confident that all would be well, even after she looped her family in on her new life and situation. Her goal moving forward was to do great things together, as a team.

So why do I still feel like something is off kilter?

Lil stirred, uncurling from her ball. "As much as I have enjoyed traipsing around with you and Bennett on this wild goose chase of an adventure, I'm in desperate need of some R and R. Maybe somewhere tropical with scantily clad women fanning me with giant palm fronds while I sip on a blue drink that has a tiny umbrella stuck in it. Or perhaps up in the Swiss Alps at a resort and spa being spoiled like the royalty I am."

Zoe rose to her feet and offered Lil a hand. "Or how about a few good night's rest in your own bed?"

Lil lifted her chin, stuck her nose up in the air, and arched a sly brow. "That, too."

Zoe smiled as they made their slow march back toward the parking lot in front of the Cliff House. The sound of an urgent hammering of feet rushing at them stopped them in their tracks.

Who would attack them now?

Zoe reached for her shoulder, and her trident appeared in her hand.

From around the corner, Baxter, Sterling, Murdock, and Lucas appeared, skidding to a stop upon seeing Zoe and Lil.

Zoe's let out a pent-up breath as she implanted her trident back in her tattoo. "I told you all to get away from here."

"Everyone else did," Murdock explained.

Baxter nodded. "We were leaving until we saw a black vapor engulf the two of you and after seeing what it did to Cavan, we couldn't bear to leave."

"What exactly happened?" Lucas asked.

Lil shrugged. "Nothing too exciting. We banned her from our realms and the bitch stole our singing voices."

Lucas and Murdock flashed a look at one another.

"And then she vanished," Zoe said.

Lucas ran his fingers through his hair. "Bloody hell."

"That type of magic is rare," Murdock said. "Farah would know more, but I believe that's ancient magic, perhaps even mermaid magic mixed with other types, like from fairies or witches."

"He's right, dearie," Lucas said. "To steal a mermaid's voice is humiliating, but to steal the queen or king's voice is to have ultimate power over them."

Zoe's face muscles tightened. "Fantastic."

Murdock eyed Zoe then cleared his throat. "But that's a problem for the future, I suspect."

Zoe scowled. "Unfortunately."

Lil clasped her hands together, stepped forward, and looped her arm through Lucas's. "Well, then. We can't worry about that. Besides, I've had enough excitement for a bit and am feeling a need for some retail therapy. Milan, Paris, New York." She looked up at Lucas. "Ever been to Argentina? Some of the finest leather to wrap your body in. You'd look good in some chaps."

Zoe chuckled. Lil was probably the craziest sane person she knew. "And you should probably get a few good night's rest in your own bed."

Lil cut her eyes at Zoe and raised her brow once again. "That too."

She stepped in front of Baxter. She squeezed his chin between her fingers. "Bennett, my love," she said as she gave him a quick double-pat on his cheek.

Baxter dipped his head. "Always a pleasure, Lil."

Lil and Lucas took a few more steps and stopped in front of Sterling. "And you," she said, trailing her long red fingernail across his collarbone, "behave yourself until you're ready to hand your soul over to me. Then we can have some real fun."

Sterling's eyes widened.

A smile dangled from the corner of Lil's mouth.

Lucas gave Sterling a subtle wink then sashayed them along, disappearing behind the corner of the Cliff House. Zoe had to admit, Lil had a certain heightened energy around her—the life of the party kind.

"Don't worry, dear uncle." Baxter slapped his hand on Sterling's shoulder. "She is quite harmless. Most of the time."

Baxter and Sterling chuckled, enjoying the moment. Enjoying each other after all those years.

A dull ache pierced Zoe's heart. She finally knew what had been off kilter and bothering her about the future. It was Sterling.

What place does he have in my life? In Baxter's life?

As if Murdock sensed her internal debate, he fiddled with the keys of one of the Jeeps, catching Baxter's attention. "We should probably get headed over to the safe house and check in on the rest of the crew."

Baxter straightened; he understood Murdock's subtle hint. "Yes, of course."

"We have much to catch up on, nephew, but I must pay the price mistakes. I only hope we will have plenty of time with each other in the future." Sterling glanced over to Zoe. "If that seems reasonable?"

Zoe flashed a toothy smile. How could she deny that? It wasn't her place to come between them. He simply wanted his family, the same way Baxter did.

Baxter extended his hand. Sterling gripped it firmly.

"I look forward to it," Baxter said then to Zoe, "I will be at my house, living the quiet life as a professor and historian, whenever you're comfortable being landside again."

He shuffled forward. Zoe closed her eyes as he leaned in and placed a chaste kiss on her forehead. "I won't be away too long," she promised. Her fingertips glided across his forearms down to his hands then gave them a gentle squeeze. She looked up at him from beneath her lashes. He tucked a tendril of her hair behind her ear. She gave him a yearning look, then, he walked away with Murdock at his side.

She swallowed the lump in her throat. Even though she didn't need him to live, she simply didn't want to live without him. No matter what type of business she needed to do in her realm; she would make sure she wasn't at sea for long.

"Shall we go for a stroll on the beach?"

Zoe looked over her shoulder at Sterling, nodded, and followed him down the stone steps to the shore. Even though the sun was higher up in the sky and the day was getting warmer, she ran her hands over her upper arms, feigning off a chill. Sterling made her nervous. Unsure.

"You do know just because I have Melantha's memories, it doesn't mean I'm her, right?"

Sterling grinned.

Zoe wasn't expecting that. "Why do you look so smug?"

"My darling." He slid his hand into hers and threaded her fingers into his. "You may resemble Melantha, but you are not her, by any means."

Zoe cocked a brow. "Is that so?"

"Mmm, yes. Melantha was more formal, whereas you are laid back. She was sultry, but often perceived as cold. You're stunning, that's for sure, but you have warmth that floods your ambiance and people gravitate toward you."

Zoe shrugged her shoulder, thinking back to days of being accused of taking PEDs while on the swim team. "Hmph. Never really felt that way. I've been scorned by people a few times."

"I know all about the scandal at USC. Aislinn followed you closely. In fact, I'm fairly certain she had something to do with them accusing you, but I could never get proof of it."

Zoe rolled her eyes. Of course Aislinn had something to do with that. She could only imagine what Aislinn said to convince her teammates she was a cheater.

"But even then, Zoe, you persevered. Look at how the Tails in your realm flock to you. They didn't even do that with Melantha. She was their queen, their boss. You are their friend. Big difference. And it hasn't taken much time for me to see that."

Zoe smiled, glad to know that the mermaids in her kingdom were the friends she always wanted and weren't obligated to her because she was their queen.

Sterling stopped. People were arriving at Ocean Beach for a morning walk, or run, like the one couple who had a trio of dogs trotting next to them. "I will always treasure what Melantha and I had. I do understand that you aren't her and that my nephew is deeply in love with you, her reincarnation."

Zoe blushed.

Sterling placed his hands on her shoulders. "I've been caged for the past one hundred years, locked under a spell that fortunately gave me a very dashing life. But the moment I wanted to speak to my family, the moment Aislinn identified you as the queen, I was harshly reminded of what I could never have: my family. And now, we are all free, no longer tied to the chains that cursed us so long ago, and all I still want is my family. Bennett. You, as Zoe. Not Melantha. And, one other person. She's a Freshwater-Tail that

I've fallen for. Sadly, she is locked in whatever hold Aislinn has over them and I would like to help free her."

The corner of Zoe's lip curled. She gave Sterling a slight shove on his shoulder. "You sly dog. How did you keep that from Aislinn?"

Sterling lifted his shoulder. "Wasn't easy. There were times I thought she knew. Maybe she does. Who cares, though? The point is, I want the life I never had, just like Bennett does. But I know I need to absolve any wrong doings I had with this nightmare I helped create."

Zoe nibbled her lower lip and looked across the water. He did need to pay his debt to their realm and repair his relationship with the Tails. *But how?*

The tide rolled in and out, washing up seaweed and some plastic six-pack rings and an empty and crushed plastic bottle of water.

Zoe blinked. She faced him.

"Just before you murdered Melantha, you were in a dark place, harboring resentment and feelings of jealously because I had magic and was willing to give it up to become a simple human, right?"

Sterling's brow knitted in a frown. "Yes. It's why Aislinn's spell worked so well and forced me to kill. What's your point?"

"Well, I'm going to give you what you want. You'll have magic, be able to visit both the sea and land—"

"You're going to turn me into a Tail?"

Zoe gave him a curt nod. "Yup. When you're at sea, you'll use magic and work the land that is spoiled with oil and trash. It may take decades to revive my kingdom, but you're going to help. On land, you can visit Baxter and do what you are accustomed to doing. And when it's time to face Aislinn again, you can be on the right side this time, and hopefully, save the one who has your heart. And steal her away from Aislinn's clutches."

Sterling scratched the stubble on his face. "Just another cage I must enter."

Zoe shook her head. "No, it's a choice. It's either that or go free and see what happens without my protection. You'll always be running, and the moment your guard is down, Aislinn will strike. Also, I think Lil was only half joking about taking your soul. She's expressed an interest in it once before."

Sterling rocked back on his heels. "Well, then I suppose it's an easy choice. What's a few more decades in a gilded cage massive enough to let me believe I have some freedoms, right?"

"At least you'll have your family."

Sterling's eyes twinkled. He tossed his arm over her shoulders. "At least I'll have my family," he mused as they trailed toward the water like two old friends having a good time. "You know, this means you'll have to kill me in order to turn me. Fitting, I suppose, given what I did to you."

Zoe took a sharp breath. She thought back to Cavan and the devastating guilt she felt over taking a life and wrestled with the thought of darkening her soul again.

But weren't mermaids known for taking the life of men? I can't help that there is a predator streak running through my veins, right?

It was the only way to keep Sterling safe while having him pay his debt to her realm.

She tugged Sterling through the small waves, careful to not transform yet because people were starting to fill the beach. The last thing she needed was panicked Landwalkers telling stories of a mermaid drowning a man at

Ocean Beach. Behind her, she heard the trio of dogs barking. She peeked over her shoulder. They sensed something. A larger wave crested.

She pulled Sterling beneath it as her tail freed itself from her human legs. She flicked her fluke and rocketed further out, away from the crashing waves and prying eyes of the public. They surfaced, facing one another. She felt a familiar flutter in her eye.

Sterling locked eyes with her, hypnotized. She wrapped her arms around his neck and pulled him into her chest, kissing him. She tethered her tail around his legs, whirling them around a whirlpool as she deepened her fatal kiss, draining his mortal being from his body like a vampire. She could feel her lips stretch to accommodate the forming of her piranha-like teeth, turning her into the mythical monster that sailors always feared. The warmth of his blood traced down the side of their mouths. Stealing his soul was the best tasting dessert she ever had.

His skin paled.

His eyes dulled to gray.

His body stiffened, became hard as stone, sinking them into the depths of the ocean.

Zoe closed her eyes and drew in his last breath as a Landwalker. Her pendant vibrated between their pressed-together skin, revving until energy exploded from it and ejected them away from one another, breaking their connection.

Zoe tumbled through the water and came to a stop, tangled in some kelp and sea urchins. Even though spines of the urchins stabbed at her, she clutched her forehead waiting for the dizziness in her head to stop. Finally able to open her eyes and focus, she clambered out of the plants and paddled forward.

A frothy cloud floated in the water.

Would he be... different? More than just having a tail...

Sterling swam out of the puffy, foam-like substance and zoomed around her. Like the other male Tails, he looked as if he were chiseled out of marble. His muscles were thick and defined, but not overly so. His tail was long, had an angular fluke, and looked like a chocolate-covered strawberry. Peppered around his hips and groin were red scales, which seamlessly blended into the dark-chocolate browns that covered the rest of his tail.

He stopped in front of her and grinned. She sighed, almost giddy-like, glad to see his charming smirk and personality was still there, along with his brilliant blue eyes. "Everything is incredibly clear and vibrant!"

"That was my reaction too. Ready to learn how to be a Tail?"

He gave her a toothy smile and darted around her and hooked his arm through hers.

Just behind her, she pointed to a mound about the size of a classic VW beetle. "I figured we can start with one of those. They're called See-seas and are amazing magical maps that help navigate the entire underwater world."

"Sounds fascinating." He bowed his head to her and held his arm. "After you, my queen."

Zoe giggled and smacked him on his full biceps. "Oh, stop. We aren't doing none of that hoity-toity Nineteenth Century-etiquette crap in my realm."

Sterling tipped his head back and laughed. Tiny bubbles trickled from his lips. It made her heart warm to see him so relaxed, and dare she say, *happy?* It was as if he had always been destined to be a part of her world.

"Like I said," he tugged her hand and pulled her toward the See-sea, "you're definitely not Melantha."

CHAPTER 51
BAXTER

FOR THE PAST CENTURY, loneliness had been something of a normality for Baxter. Sure, he traveled the world in search of the reincarnated queen. He met the most interesting and unusual characters along the way and often found himself in precarious situations. He made a bit of a name for himself at the university, but no matter what acquaintances or adversaries he had around him, he went through his extended life alone.

Not until Farah and Murdock, the last of the group that helped him and Zoe, left his home did he realize the silence that came with his loneliness had been deafening. The rush of scouring the world for the stone pendants, solving Melantha's murder, and restoring the reincarnated queen was over. For fear of getting his hopes up, he never allowed himself to imagine what life would be like if he succeeded in his role as a guardian. Now that he had, he didn't know what to do with himself, or how to handle coming to a complete stop.

He imagined this was what new retirees must feel like.

With his quest complete, he had to take a hard look at who he was or would be. No more unexpected encounters from his rivals; they were allies and friends. No more chasing leads. No more discovering pieces of the magical world.

His only job now was simply to be a professor at USC. Well, a professor who was inundated in the magical world, and was still protected by a mermaid charm that would keep him alive and young for the foreseeable future. Nevertheless, he was still alone. Zoe would be busy ruling her kingdom, coming landside when she had time. As much as he enjoyed being around Murdock and Ewalt, he was sure they'd be busy helping her. Even his own uncle would be busy doing whatever Zoe planned for him in order to redeem himself. Lil and the Atlantic-Tails would be half-way across the world. Dominguez and the others would be back in their hometowns doing whatever Lycan packs did.

They all knew what their jobs were. Everyone else had someone to be with, if they chose.

Baxter plopped down on the barstool at his kitchen island and looked down into his coffee mug and agitated it, watching the creamer swirl into the dark roast.

"Darling, you should admit what is in your heart."

Baxter tensed. His eyes flicked up. He strummed his fingers alongside the mug but dared not move anything else. He feared he would lose contact with his mother after his guardianship ended, and as much as this was a most unexpected, and wonderful surprise, he was in no mood for her motherly advice.

"There is nothing to admit. I have an adjustment to make, one that I do not enjoy but must endure because she has a position of power that must come first."

"Bennett."

He sighed and dropped his head to the counter. "I want her with me. Every night." He swiveled the barstool around and faced her ethereal and glowing presence.

"I ache without her in my company. Pathetic, right? Is that what you want to hear?"

His mother grinned. "I think it's what *you* needed to hear. And no, it isn't pathetic. Whether you knew who she really was or not, she's been in your life for a few years. You're used to seeing her almost every day at the university. Who knows when you'll see her again. It's okay to feel like a piece of you is missing. You could always ask her to turn you, like she did Sterling. Then you'd have the ability to be with her whenever you wanted."

Baxter scoffed and rolled his eyes. "Do not be ridiculous, mother. She is too independent to have me following her around like a lost pup."

His mother laced her arms over her chest and raised a brow. "Well, then. If you're too proud to ask, and want to spend time moping about being alone, perhaps you should make yourself useful and do what you do best: research."

Baxter's brow knitted together. "First off, I am not too proud. It is not my place to ask for something like that. Besides, I am not merman material. Second, research what, mother?"

She shook her head and sighed. "How did Aislinn have access to a ring that has the power to rip the singing voice from not one, but two, royal mermaids? Seems awfully mysterious to me, don't you agree?"

Baxter narrowed his eyes. He hated when she was right.

He straightened. "Always a pleasure speaking with you, mother," he said as he swiveled around and took a sip of his lukewarm coffee. "But you must excuse me as I have a rather busy schedule. I have some libraries to visit and must make a few inquiries to some historian colleagues." He hopped off the bar stool and whirled around.

His mother was gone. Sometimes, he wondered if she truly showed up or if she was a delusion. He paused. Grinned, as the rose floral scent of her wafted past his nose.

He took off, trotting up the stairs to his home office. He booted up his newly acquired grape-colored iMac G3 computer and opened the digital catalogue of his journals. He thought twice about solely using his digital files, though. Lately, society's worries about the newest threat to computers, the Y2K bug, had been becoming more prevalent as time closed in on the new century. Instead, he took every journal he owned out of the closet and stacked them on the floor next to his desk. He dug out a large corkboard from the very back of his closet, which was ready to be filled with information. He carefully removed the large painting of his childhood home that covered his wall safe and hung the corkboard in its place. He laid out his best set of colorful felt-tip pens, some index cards, and tacks. He sat down at his desk, grabbed a pen and a card. He inhaled long and slow.

Exhaled.

He had plenty to do while he waited for Zoe to return to land. He would still be lonely and miss her company, but he knew exactly how to fill the time. More importantly, he had an important role in her life and would stake his claim as the resident researcher. Farah may be the historian of the mermaid world, but by being a human, he had advantages she did not. He had access to mortal tales based on events from the magical world, including those rare editions only found in university or museum systems. He could mingle with different types of magical beings simply because he *wasn't* a Tail. During his previous research, he found the Tails often didn't have the best relationships with other types of mythical creatures, because mermaid magic was so coveted, and jealousy often reared its ugly green head.

Baxter tapped the shaft of the pen against his mouth.

But where to start? Where, and how, could Aislinn have stolen, bargained, or even forged such a powerful ring?

He scoffed at himself. The answer was evident and in plain sight. In large capital letters, he scribbled across the card. He pinned it to the middle of the corkboard, stepped back, and let the word resonate with him. He supposed it didn't matter which mythology's term he used: Greek, Egyptian, Norse. The concept was similar to all the myths around the world.

He sighed, imaging the adventure they would have heading into the depths of the UNDERWORLD.

Chapter 52

EPILOGUE

THE WANING MOON ALWAYS made the night much darker. Spookier. The nefarious often used the dark as a cloak to sneak up on unsuspecting victims or commit treacherous acts. Although one could not do either of those things in Japan's Toyama Bay. Every night in the spring, even during a full moon with a lot of light, the coastline glowed neon blue as tiny firefly squids lit up the waters when they came to the surface to spawn. Fishermen worked hard to capture the small squids as onlookers watched the dazzling light show imitating a galaxy of stars, shifting, and changing as the tides rolled.

Zoe threaded herself between the wide-eyed tourists, but her eyes never left the fisherman who was clearly out of place with a muscular body and spiky black hair tipped with purple.

"I tell you, he will not like this surprise," Kasumi said.

"He doesn't have a choice anymore." Zoe carefully sidestepped the tide rolling in. "I've tried to be polite."

"All right, spread out along the shore, but be sure not to enter his waters," Murdock directed.

"We know," Sefarina said then situated herself around a family wading in the water trying to catch firefly squid with their bare hands.

Zoe made her way directly behind the man she assumed was the king. He was knee high in the water and had a large net in his hands. He was the only person who was not covered from head to toe in thick fishermen's garb and wearing a flashlight on his forehead.

The advantages of being a Tail, even in human form, made him obvious to Zoe.

"Takahiro-sama," she called. Most of the surrounding people glanced at her, and then quickly bounced back to their own business, but there were a few, clearly guards, who froze and became incredibly alert to the situation.

Takahiro straightened. Ever so slightly, he careened his head to look over his shoulder at the closest guard. A petite woman whipped her black-and-silver braid behind her back and stood next to him.

"Retreat to the west bank," he said.

The woman glanced at Zoe, and nudged her head, demanding to be followed.

Takahiro and his guards waded through the water down the shore, while Zoe and her crew walked along on the beach, keeping pace. Once they were away from the crowd, the woman with the black-and-silver braid wiggled her fingers above her head. An arch of silver twinkling lights blazed out of her fingertips and rained down on them, hiding them from the Landwalkers.

Takahiro tossed up his hands. "Why are you here, Zoe?"

With the pad of her thumb, Zoe spun a white gold engagement ring around her finger. A new nervous habit. When she was away from Baxter, the ring comforted her. Besides, it mostly helped her stop nibbling on her lips and allowed the sensitive skin to heal.

"I've told you why," she said.

Takahiro scoffed and waved her off. "I'm not talking about your campaign of saving the flora and fauna of all our beaches. That, I agree with." He pointed to three lean men standing near him. "My personal team, the triplets, will help with full participation in the Pacific northwest realm. I give you my word."

Zoe nodded at the three men, as they walked over to Kasumi and Sefarina to talk about the logistics of Zoe's project.

Takahiro sloshed through the water until his face leveled with Zoe's. He kept his feet in the water of his realm, though. He was taller than her and looked at her through narrowed eyes. "I'm talking about the *real* reason you are here. I do not want anything to do with your problems."

Zoe shoulders sagged. She was getting tired of being the bearer of bad news, especially when giving a double dose of it. "With all due respect, Takahiro, this is your problem as much as mine. Aislinn *will* be coming for your voice. She's already collected the voice of the king from the Pacific's southeast realm."

His dark eyes filled with concern, and not annoyance. "How? Why did she do this?"

Zoe rubbed her forehead. The same questions every Purple-Tail asked her for the past two months. She had no answers.

Yet.

With a few Royal-Tails voices gone, Aislinn's terror on the mermaid kingdoms started to pick up. Recently, some of Baxter's contacts near the Dead Sea spotted Aislinn and described her strange entourage of beautiful people and dark, gothic-types. Clearly, she had been with the Freshwater-Tails, but the gothic-types? Even as horrible a stereotype as it was, Zoe knew the gothic-types could be mistaken for witches, vampires, or dark fairies. Either way, she didn't like the idea of Aislinn mixed up with any of those groups.

"I'm not sure why she is hell-bent on taking our ancestral magic. But my team and I really need to have your permission to access your waters in case she attacks. Think of your family and friends. Together, we are stronger against her, and whoever she has manipulated into helping her."

Takahiro's shoulder blades drew together. He waved his hand in front of him. "Fine, fine. I must say, you have much heart. I can tell. More than Melantha had. In fact, just before her death, she tried to war with my kingdom until I granted her access to it. Even then, she had not been satisfied."

He paced; his hands locked behind his back. "She wanted access to the Marina Trench and Challenger Deep, but never explained why, so I would not allow it. She was always so serious and distant. Too much in her own head. I believe, one must have heart in their decisions, for fear they could be made for the wrong reasons."

Zoe bowed her head. "Thank you." She never enjoyed hearing the negative aspects of her former self, but knew she needed to learn from them. Melantha had been cold, which was something Zoe was not. She agreed with Takahiro's belief, but wondered why Melantha had wanted access to the Mariana Trench. She searched her memories, but it wasn't like rewinding film and easily finding the information needed. There were pieces of Melantha's past missing, especially her innermost thoughts and plans. For now, she would shelve her curiosity.

The king gave her a curt nod then ran his fingers across his shoulder blade, bringing his trident to life. He pointed the prongs up to the dark sky, muttered a spell, and stabbed the water with the three spines. A ripple echoed across the bay. Takahiro placed his trident back in his tattoo and held out his arms, welcoming her to his realm.

Zoe took a step into the water. Then another. She kept going until she could float out into the shallow sea, passing the firefly squids that lit up the waters. Kasumi, Murdock, and Sefarina also entered the water and transformed; each of their tails spottily emitted the same glow as the squids, camouflaging their presence.

Takahiro and his guards joined them. He waved for them to follow him and dove to the seafloor where he perched himself on a boulder. Zoe sat across from him, reveling in the marine life around her. It differed greatly from the varieties in her kingdom because of the warm and cool currents. A school of spadefish and a swarm of green eels weaved their way between them. A massive spider crab crawled along the pebbly seafloor.

The Purple-Tail king popped a firefly squid into his mouth and munched a few times as he stared at her engagement ring.

"Congratulations." He swallowed his catch.

Zoe beamed. The proposal had been a surprise, but one she truly wanted. Baxter proposed on Christmas Eve next to a crackling fire while they drank hot cocoa. The ring had a round center diamond surrounded by tiny pearls and gems, and a twisted, vine-shaped band with scroll engravings and more diamonds. Even though she gave Baxter a piece of her magic to protect him, to keep him in his role of a guardian, it had been a symbol of their friendship and partnership. Like a business deal. The engagement, however, was about their love and commitment to each other. Like the proper, old-fashioned gentleman he was, Baxter even asked Zoe's father for permission. Sterling knew and gave his blessing to them both when he joined them, and her parents, for a family Christmas dinner.

Takahiro stuffed another squid into his mouth. "When's the wedding?"

Zoe's hands briefly clenched, as they always did when asked this question. Mostly because something remained unsettled in her heart. It was hard to remain in a state of happiness and plan a wedding, knowing what kind of trouble headed for them. She tried to ignore it, but like the rumble of a train rolling through town at night, she could still feel the roar of the threat heading toward her. And so, when anybody asked when the big day would be, she couldn't give an answer because she couldn't predict what would happen from one moment to the next.

Zoe shrugged. "Soon enough. There's no rush. Weddings take time to plan."

Takahiro arched a brow at her. He saw right through her words.

Zoe drew a long breath. Meeting with him started off as an ambush, of sorts. She wanted legal access to his realm and never expected it to become a therapeutic session.

He had a way about him and made her feel comfortable enough to want to talk and not be in a rush like she had been for the past several months. Between helping her parents come to terms with her new life, adjusting to living in and out of the water, her campaign to clean up the beaches, getting engaged, and knowing Aislinn planned more mayhem—life was a blur.

"You have a heavy heart. Could your reluctance possibly have something to do with that other thing you came to warn me about?

Zoe exhaled. "In a way, yes. On top of whatever Aislinn has planned with her revenge and stealing our singing voices, it's hard for Baxter and I to selfishly focus on us. Especially knowing the entire Underworld declared war against our friends, which could, by extension, affect your realm."

Takahiro drove out a harsh sigh. "I heard about that. The Atlantic-Tails and their demon mermaid queen are friends of yours?"

Zoe nodded. "Absolutely."

"Very well, then. Count me in as an ally."

She dipped her head to show her respect. Her smile eased wide, glad that he was on her side, because *nobody* would want to get in her way from saving her friends.

And to think, once upon a time, she foolishly mistrusted Lil and the Atlantic-Tails.

SOCIAL MEDIA

WWW.SWEETANDSAUERBOOKS.COM

TIKTOK, INSTAGRAM, THREADS, YOUTUBE, TOMEBOOKS:
@MICHELLESAUERWRITES

PINTEREST, ETSY:
@SWEETANDSAUERBOOKS.COM

PACIFIC TAILS KINGDOM
INTERACTIVE CONTENT

WWW.SWEETANDSAUERBOOKS.COM

Character Aesthetics
Art & Other Visuals
Timeline & Maps
Real Locations Information
Mermaid Magic System & Lore

ACKNOWLEDGEMENTS

READERS—THANK YOU FOR TAKING A chance on me. Your reviews, your word of mouth, and wonderful support are treasured. I could not have followed my dream without you. I look forward to our interactions and supplying you with more adventures.

A huge thank you to my parents who always encouraged creativity and following my dreams. Thank you for reading to me as a kid. And to my mom, who gave me the love of browsing bookstores and smelling freshly printed books, especially the Berenstain Bears. Those are one of the reasons I enjoy the printed book over e-books, even though they are more convenient. I love you both so very much.

To those who had a part in making my dream come true. SI Foote, my editor, who dug me out of a hell-hole of being scammed by a not-so-reputable editor. You have a heart of gold to take on a nearly 113K word novel, for free, just to help me out. You are the epitome of indie authors supporting indie authors. Hidden Gems, especially Ginger, for helping with my blurb, which, if you're an author, you know how blurb writing is the bane of our existence. My stunning cover and inside formatting by Books and Moods. They were the reason I picked up my first contemporary romance novel—the Dreamland Billionaire Series by Lauren Asher. I judged those books by the cover, loved them, and knew that I wanted the team at B&M to create an eye-catching design for my book.

To my supportive older sister Amber and family—I love you all. To my younger sister Samantha, a special thank you for the super late night talking-it-through sessions and the cheerleading—you always have my back and I love you. To my teacher-work-bestie, Sadie, for reading, theorizing, spreading the word, and always being the sounding board for whatever thing I need. Love ya. To my wonderful, book-worm mother-in-law, Lisa, for the beta reading, proofreading, beautiful reviews, and compliments—it truly means the world to me, and I love you very much.

For those who inspired me to become a storyteller and writer. Firstly, my grandparents, who always knew how to tell an engaging story—I wish I were so eloquent and masterful at verbalizing what's in my head. To Becky and Meg, who taught me so much about writing, way back in our heyday of crafting Harry Potter fanfiction. To my screenplay writing partner, Angel, who made me a better writer and supported my decision to focus on novels.

Thank you to my uncle Lloyd for living in San Francisco, which inspired my desire for having some kind of Victorian setting featured within the book. Thank you to all my friends and family for the support—it's been overwhelming and emotional, at times, but I truly appreciate you all with every ounce of my heart.

Finally, and most importantly, to my husband, Mitch. Thank you for all the profound discussions, especially the ones well past midnight, where I had to be up by five-thirty for work, cutting into my beauty rest, and the heated ones that drove me crazy because I have a problem admitting when you're right. But all of them made me into a better writer. Your opinion, your Ravenclaw-like intelligence, and your outlook on life is invaluable to me. Thank you for supporting me in my writing and content-making journey.

This novel took me fifteen years to make. I had no idea how the writing structure worked when I first started. I just had a plot. Over the years, on and off again, this story buzzed around in my head. I wrote it, edited it, re-worked it, made it into a screenplay for my final project of my master's degree, took it out of that format because a novel was better for the story, re-wrote it again, then re-worked it, edited it a few more times, put it down for a while, and finally got serious about publishing it in 2022. Specifically, after watching the Imp and Skizz Podcast on YouTube. My husband introduced me to you through the Minecraft content channel, Hermitcraft, and we both have been watching your podcast since the first airing. Impulse and Skizzleman, if it weren't for the second episode, *What's Stopping You?*, I can one hundred percent guarantee, I wouldn't have a finished book in hand. Your discussions about kind-of wanting it and actually wanting it, how I am the only person stopping me, how to make my want a priority in my life, to maximize my time, and to hold myself accountable, was the rocket boost of energy I absolutely needed to hear and refocus my mindset. I know this episode has resonated with so many people, and I truly believe I am not the only person out there who went from kind-of wanting it to actually wanting it, from going through the motions, to doing the action. You both have affected my life profoundly. From the bottom of my heart, I thank you for the inspiration and the challenge to take the step forward.

It's been a helluva road, and has been inspired by several things, but it all started in 2008 with a spark of an idea after seeing an image of the beautiful bronze sculpture made by Kathy Spalding, which is the statue Zoe has at her house by the pool. Sadly, Kathy Spalding passed away in 2014, but her gorgeous life-like sea-creatures and animal sculptures are featured around the world and one day, I would like to see them in person. Thank you for the inspiration, Kathy.

About the Author

MICHELLE SAUER HAS A Masters of Fine Arts in Creative Writing and a Bachelor of Arts in Art Education with a minor in Art History and Film Photography. By day, she is a Converse-wearing, kindergarten-8th grade Art teacher in Colorado. By night, she loves to spend time with her gamer and sports-loving husband. She dabbles in multiple hobbies such as reading, crafting, fine arts, board games, video games, and driving around in her 1976 Corvette Stingray.

She loves dogs and is mom to Shadow, a black and white Siberian Husky with gorgeous blue eyes. She misses her furbaby Hobbes, a hundred-pound German shepherd and wannabe cop. She often can be found re-watching *Psych*, keeping up on pop-culture, making content, napping, and reading everything from middle grade to dark romantasy. She has co-written screenplays and enjoys the Horror genre. Her debut novel, Pacific Tails, is based off her love of mysteries, adventure, magic, and growing up in southern California.

If you enjoyed Pacific Tails, please consider leaving a review on any/all platforms of your choosing. Word of mouth is the most powerful marketing tool an author has and your recommendations go a long way in helping other readers find Michelle's book and experience the adventure for themselves. Much love and many thanks.